Thompson Carlene
Just a breath away

8

JUST A BREATH AWAY

Further Titles by Carlene Thompson

BLACK FOR REMEMBRANCE
ALL FALL DOWN
THE WAY YOU LOOK TONIGHT
TONIGHT YOU'RE MINE
IN THE EVENT OF MY DEATH
DON'T CLOSE YOUR EYES
SINCE YOU'VE BEEN GONE
IF SHE SHOULD DIE
SHARE NO SECRETS
LAST WHISPER
LAST SEEN ALIVE
IF YOU EVER TELL
YOU CAN RUN . . .
NOWHERE TO HIDE
TO THE GRAVE
CAN'T FIND MY WAY HOME *

* *available from Severn House*

JUST A BREATH AWAY

Carlene Thompson

This first world edition published 2018
in Great Britain and 2018 in the USA by
SEVERN HOUSE PUBLISHERS LTD of
Eardley House, 4 Uxbridge Street, London W8 7SY.
Trade paperback edition first published
in Great Britain and the USA 2018 by
SEVERN HOUSE PUBLISHERS LTD.

British Library Cataloguing in Publication Data
A CIP catalogue record for this title is available from the British Library.

ISBN-13: 978-0-7278-8517-3 (cased)
ISBN-13: 978-1-84751-861-3 (trade paper)
ISBN-13: 978-1-78010-923-7 (e-book)

All Severn House titles are printed on acid-free paper.

Severn House Publishers support the Forest Stewardship Council™ [FSC™],
the leading international forest certification organisation.
All our titles that are printed on FSC certified paper carry the FSC logo.

Typeset by Palimpsest Book Production Ltd.,
Falkirk, Stirlingshire, Scotland.
Printed and bound in Great Britain by
TJ International, Padstow, Cornwall.

PROLOGUE

Twenty years ago

The boy sat forward on the seat of the car, anxiously watching rain batter the windshield. The wipers flew back and forth, but they couldn't keep up with the onslaught of cold, relentless water obscuring the view.

'You're making me nervous,' the woman behind the wheel snapped. 'Sit back and put on your seat belt!'

'I don't like bein' all strapped up.' The boy leaned closer to the windshield, squinting. 'I can't see anything. Can you?'

'Barely.'

'Then let's stop.'

'No. We're almost there. Fifteen minutes tops.'

'But if you can't see—'

'I can see good enough. Be quiet.'

The boy watched his mother frown as she peered through the black-framed glasses she never wore in front of anyone but him. She chewed on her lower lip, and her hands gripped the wheel so hard the knuckles were white. They hit a deep pothole and bounced hard as the car's frame scraped against the crumbling asphalt. Trying to swallow his anxiety, the boy looked around. No other lights shone on the narrow road. They hadn't met another car for at least twenty minutes. He felt as if they were the only two people in the world. And it was almost midnight.

She'd turned on the radio about ten minutes ago. His favorite song began playing and he tried to sing along, very softly. He thought that if he focused on the song, on the words he knew so well—

'So you think you're a singer now? That's a laugh!' She snapped off the radio.

The car slid. She wrestled with the wheel and barely got control again. A tremor of fear forced words from him. 'Can we please stop?'

'Where?' she demanded. 'Have you spotted a nice restaurant? Or a motel? Do you see something I don't?' She glared at him. 'Well, *do* you?'

He lowered his eyes and shook his head, realizing she was getting even madder. He saw the signs – her jutting jaw, her puckered forehead, her voice. He'd always been baffled by how her voice – honey-toned and soft-edged when she spoke to other people – could immediately turn biting and razor-sharp when directed at him. The boy wanted to be quiet, not to make her angrier. But he couldn't help himself.

'It's just that—'

'I said for you to *shut up*, dammit!' she exploded.

The boy shrank in on himself. She was about to have one of the full-blown temper fits that had frightened him for as long as he could remember. Right now, she was concentrating on the narrow road drowning in pounding water, but he knew that when they were safe she'd dish out revenge for arguing with her. The thought of it made him cringe. She was even scarier than the drenching rain, the starless night and the murky fog that seemed like something living as it crept around the car. He hated her, he thought with a red-hot wave of emotion. He hated her for driving on this bleak decaying road in the stormy darkness. He hated her for making him feel so small and weak and terrified.

He looked out the window to see spindly trees lining the side of the road. He'd traveled this way a year ago and remembered that just beyond the trees the land dropped sharply to a creek. While his mother muttered curses, as she drove hunched over the steering wheel, he sighed in misery, closed his eyes and slowly counted to one hundred. When he opened them, ahead he saw orange-yellow lights bouncing dimly off the heavy cloud cover. City lights! He thought he would look at the reflection of the beautiful city lights and try to forget about her. He would pretend she didn't exist.

Lightning sliced wickedly through the darkness, followed by a crash of thunder that made the car vibrate. The boy let out a cry. His mother's arm flew out for a back-handed slap, but he dodged and she barely caught the side of his face, although one of her long acrylic nails nicked his eyelid.

'You deserved that! What's *wrong* with you?'

'I'm sorry,' he mumbled, touching a trickle of blood running from his eyelid.

'You're a coward like your father!'

Again, the boy thought with dull hopelessness. My father, again.

'He isn't even *natural*,' she went on gratingly. 'He's a bastard for turning his back on you. And especially for turning his back on *me*. He doesn't care how hard it's been for me to take care of you. He's never thought I'm good enough for him, but you're his own flesh and blood. His *son*. He knows we're a package deal, though. He can't have *you* without *me* and he'd rather see us both suffer than let *me* be part of his life. But I'm relentless. I haven't given up on him all these years and I never will!' She turned her head, and her eyes seemed to burn at him in the light from the dashboard instruments. 'I could have gotten rid of you, but I didn't. I've held on to you even though you've been the curse of my life. He owes me and he'll pay. He'll *pay!*'

She went on spitting out the wrath she'd fed and nurtured for years until it was taking her past the point of sanity. The boy decided she wasn't even a real woman anymore. She was an evil, fury-wracked creature, like something in one of his comic books.

He also thought that soon she would hurt more than his feelings. She would kill him.

During the last couple of years, though, he'd grown much tougher and much more scheming than he let her know. For months, he'd spent countless hours thinking of how he could escape her. He had no family who would take him in and protect him from her. He'd quickly ruled out reporting her to any government office that would send him to a foster home. He would be miserable, and even if he wasn't she'd find him. And he didn't want to think about what she'd do to him.

When he realized his only hope was to disappear, he'd sought out other boys who'd run away from home and made it alone on the streets. He could be casually friendly and sympathetic. He'd had no trouble befriending them, encouraging their confidences and developing a comradery that showed him the world didn't offer much to stray adolescents. They said his good looks would help him. Some claimed his youth would also be a plus, making him seem innocent and docile, open to anything as long

as it pleased – a prospect that filled him with repulsion. His fear
of his mother grew every day, but he wasn't sure he could go
through with the occasionally degrading or painful acts these lost
boys endured just to survive. Still, when he thought of maybe
dying . . .

Suddenly a form flashed in front of the car – big, brown, with
huge dark eyes. A large buck deer. For a moment it leaped grace-
fully on the road, past the car, as the boy's mother shrieked and
jerked the steering wheel to the right. The tires screamed and
the car spun. The boy's thoughts disappeared as his reflexes took
control. He yanked up the door handle. And as the door flew
open he launched from the car, landing with a thud on his side,
and rolled to a slow stop on the rough asphalt road.

He hardly felt a thing. All of his senses seemed to merge into
one – hearing his mother's shrill screech as the car shot past him
and tore through the line of skinny trees snapping crisply. He
got to his feet and staggered to the edge of the road, watching
the car cut a brutal path down the muddy, vine-covered ravine
until the bumper hit the creek and the car flipped, crashing on
to its roof.

He hunched down and stared at the car. Half of it was
submerged in the storm-swollen creek water which ran toward
the car and split as it reached it, then swirled around the obstacle
and passed it to again become an uninterrupted current. The car's
engine had stopped running. The headlights cast an eerie glow
beneath the water.

The boy didn't know how long he'd crouched in the rain,
looking down at the wreck, listening. No other vehicles had
passed. Even the deer had escaped. Through the half-exposed
windshield, he saw no movement in the car. He heard only the
rain beating on the road and on the leaves of the vines.

The boy looked up and closed his eyes as the rain battered
his face. Then he drew a long breath. He felt as if he hadn't
breathed so deeply and easily for years.

At last, he stood, smiled with slow satisfaction, and began
walking toward the beautiful city lights.

ONE

Two blonde women drifted along the sidewalk, talking and laughing. The taller one tilted back her head and took a deep breath of warm night air. 'I *love* Louisville in the springtime!'

Kelsey March smiled at her younger sister. 'You especially love Louisville during Kentucky Derby week, Lorelei. You have since you were a kid.'

'Who wouldn't? The hot-air balloon races, the steamboat race, the Pegasus Parade, the actual Derby?' Lorelei flashed the smile that had put her on half-a-dozen international magazine covers, then glanced at the neon sign to her right. 'Conway's Tavern. Looks good from the outside.'

'I think you'll like it. I come here two or three times a week.'

'All partying and no work?' Lorelei teased.

'An occasional drink or two at night. Some days I come for lunch. The bar serves great sandwiches.'

'And it's only two blocks away from your store with your big loft apartment above it. It's huge. Do you know how much a loft that size would cost in Manhattan?'

'More than I want to think about, which is why I stayed in Louisville where the cost of living isn't in the stratosphere.'

Lorelei was laughing as they stepped inside, but Kelsey noticed her sister quickly assessing the long, carved mahogany bar with a mirror backdrop, the copper-plated ceiling, the amber light glowing from metal tavern-light chandeliers, the high-backed cushioned wooden booths and the ten tables covered with burgundy cloths. Framed pictures of Kentucky Derby winning horses decorated the walls. Five people stood around a grand piano singing along as a young man played Billy Joel's 'Piano Man.' Three booths and two tables were taken. Nine men and four women sat at the bar. Three of the men smiled at them.

'How quaint! I feel like I've stepped into another world. I *love* it!' Lorelei looked at Kelsey. 'This building was a wreck last year when you bought your store.'

'I couldn't believe how fast they finished such a big remodeling job. Do you want a booth or a table?'

'I like booths. They're cozier.'

They'd just sat down when a petite young woman with pixie-cut ginger hair and hazel eyes appeared at their table. 'Welcome to Conway's Tavern,' she said with a wide smile directed at Lorelei. 'Here are our menus. Nice to see you, Miss March,' she went on in a rush, glancing at Kelsey before her gaze shot back to Lori. 'Excuse me, ma'am, but are you Lorelei March, the model who was on the cover of last month's *Glamour*?'

Lorelei looked up with her striking violet-blue eyes, which the fashion industry had labeled 'indigo.' 'Yes, I'm Lorelei March, Kelsey's sister.'

'I *knew* who you were as soon as you walked in!' she exclaimed. 'I told Rick – he's the owner – "That's Lorelei March!" He didn't know who Lorelei March was, but when I told him he was impressed. He said his mother reads loads of fashion magazines, and she'd for sure be thrilled to know you came to Conway's.' She clutched her hands to her chest. 'You're even more beautiful in person than in your pictures!'

Lorelei smiled warmly. 'Thank you! What's your name?'

'Janet O'Rourke. If it's not a bother, I'd love to have your autograph!'

'Sure, but I don't think I have a notepad in my bag.'

'I'll bring one back with me. Thank you, Miss March.'

'Janet,' a man called from behind the bar. 'Let the ladies decide what to order.'

'Oh, sure.' Janet looked back at a tall, broad-shouldered man with curly chestnut-brown hair and brown eyes – Richard 'Rick' Conway, owner of the tavern. He was handsome in an unassuming way, with even features and a lazy smile. Kelsey smiled at him as Janet hurried to the bar.

'I can't believe she recognized me so fast!' Lorelei said.

Kelsey looked across the table at her beautiful twenty-one-year-old sister with long pale blonde hair, classic bone structure and remarkable eyes. 'You're a celebrity. People have recognized you and asked for selfies all day. Louisville has a population of over six hundred thousand people, Lori. We get fashion magazines and have the Internet here.'

'If we didn't, I wouldn't have grown up wanting to be a model. We've been running around since noon, though. I'm a mess,' Lorelei fretted.

'You're never a mess.'

'Only someone who loves me would think that.' Lori sighed. 'I need a glass of white wine.'

'Wine? No, no. We're having mint juleps. That's why we walked here. It's Derby Week. We're going to have fun and not worry about driving afterward.'

'Think of all the bourbon and powdered sugar in juleps.' Lorelei shook her head. 'I have to watch my weight. The African photoshoot is the week after next.'

'You love juleps and a couple won't spoil your willowy five-foot-ten body. You said you want to have fun tonight, so the matter is settled.'

'Gosh, you're even bossier than usual!' Lorelei giggled.

When Janet returned, Kelsey announced, 'We'll each have a mint julep. I'll also have a double order of chicken fingers. I'm starving.'

'I'll have some crackers,' Lorelei told her.

Janet nodded and headed back to the bar. Kelsey gave her sister a serious look. 'Crackers? All you've had today is a salad. You'll get rickets if you don't start eating more.'

'I've been home with Dad since Wednesday afternoon. He kept pushing food at me and I ate more than I should have. Also, the salad I ordered for lunch was *huge*.'

'It was large, not huge. And you ate less than half of it.'

'I don't want to argue about how much I eat.' Lorelei looked around. 'Janet's cute, Kelsey. So is the owner of the bar. He keeps glancing at you.'

'Only because he knows me. Slightly. He opened this place about three months ago and I've been in a lot since then because the tavern's so pleasant, *and* it's close to my office and the food's good. Rick's friendly to everyone.'

'A *hot* friendly guy. Those eyes are like dark chocolate syrup . . .' Lori pretended to shiver. 'He's really good-looking.

And I bet he'd like to ask you out if you'd give him the least bit of encouragement.' Lorelei looked at him speculatively. 'Is he married?'

'I haven't asked.' Kelsey paused. 'But he doesn't wear a wedding ring.'

'So you noticed?' Lorelei asked archly. 'You're interested.' Then she turned serious. 'You won't go out with anyone because of Brad.'

Kelsey's smile faded. 'It's May now. I broke up with Brad before Christmas.'

'I don't believe *he* knows he's your ex.'

'He's mad. He wouldn't be mad if he didn't realize we're finished.'

'Have you seen him a lot?'

'At a couple of parties. And he came to the store once. I wasn't there. He left a note for me telling me to stop sending his phone calls to voicemail. Also, we both went to the Wiederman wedding. At the reception he acted friendly if people were looking, and if not he could have frozen me with a glance. A couple of times I've thought he was following me, but I can't be certain.'

'Are you afraid of him?'

Kelsey shook her head. 'Brad is a thirty-two-year-old spoiled kid with a bad temper under a smooth facade. We've known him for ages, Lori. He was an annoying teenager when I first met him. But I'd hardly been around him for years when he asked me out and he seemed to have improved since adolescence. Also, I was busy and I thought dating someone I already knew would be easy. The first couple of months were OK, but he was frustrated about not moving up the ladder at the law firm. He started drinking more and he isn't a pleasant drunk. He was also smoking a lot of marijuana in *my* loft. That's when I ended it. I wasn't going to get busted because of his habits. I should have ended it months before I did, but I was getting MG Interiors off the ground and I let things slide with him until he began acting like he owned me.'

'Maybe you should talk to the police.'

Kelsey laughed. 'And tell them what? That Bradley Fairbourne glares at me when no one's looking? That he's possessive and he doesn't take rejection gracefully? He just likes to swagger and act brilliant and indestructible, the way he did when he was young?'

'You're too forgiving when it comes to him.'

'I broke up with him, didn't I? I'm sorry if he's truly hurt, but I couldn't be around him anymore. I don't feel guilty about it. Besides, Brad is an attractive lawyer from a prominent family. He'll meet someone soon and then he'll forget I exist.'

'Well, it's a shame that your breakup didn't make his mother mad enough to stop hanging around our house. Olivia is zeroing in on Dad.'

'You've been saying that since Mom died.'

'Did you know Dad's been riding with Olivia and he lets her ride Yasmine?'

'Well, Yasmine needs exercise.' Kelsey kept her voice neutral as she thought of her mother's beloved gray Arabian horse. She didn't like the image of Olivia Fairbourne on her mother's beautiful horse, either.

'She rides Guinevere, too,' Lori went on indignantly. 'Dad told me Olivia sold their last horse about three months ago. She said close friends really wanted it for their daughter, but I think she needed the money. Everyone knows Milton started making bad investments a couple of years before he died. His fortune wasn't nearly what it was when he married Olivia, and half of what he had when he died went to his daughter from his first marriage. Olivia's probably playing on Dad's sympathy about how she misses her horse, or he'd never let her ride Yasmine regularly. We only have three horses now, and the handlers and grooms don't let them suffer from neglect. Dad said you go home every few weeks and ride Yasmine and Guinevere.'

'Yes, but I can't give them a real workout with my *great* equestrian skills,' Kelsey said dryly. 'Olivia is a much better rider than I am.'

'Guinevere is *mine*,' Lori stated. 'I don't want Olivia to ride her.'

'OK. Tell Dad that Olivia's not allowed to ride Guinevere.'

'And make myself sound like a possessive five-year-old brat? Olivia would love it. She'd go to Dad and act hurt, make her voice quiver, maybe cry. I'd look petty and mean. She's clever enough to take sneaky little steps.' Lori's jaw tightened. 'I despise her.'

'You *despise* her?' Even as a child, Lori had been melodramatic. 'Isn't that a bit strong?'

'No. She came dragging into town with her son and a sad song and managed to meet Milton Fairbourne. He was old, his ogre wife of a hundred and fifty years had just died and he fell for Olivia like a ton of bricks. She just wanted his money and to get him to adopt her kid.'

'I'm not so sure Brad considered his adoption a favor. He and Milton never got along.'

'Did Brad ever tell you about his biological father?'

'Only that he died when Brad was little and he doesn't remember him.'

'That's what I mean – they never give details. Poor Milton was so in love with Olivia that he didn't care. I know a great private investigator in New York. We should hire him to check her out because God knows who she really is!'

'Lori, you were two when she married Milton,' Kelsey said patiently. 'Maybe Milton knew her background. You don't. You've just heard gossip.'

'Not from Mom. Olivia pretended to be Mom's friend, but after Milton died Olivia was after Dad. Even before Milton had his last big heart attack she paid too much attention to Dad, always smiling at him and laughing at his jokes.'

'How did I forget she laughed at his jokes?' Kelsey couldn't help smiling. 'I admit that Olivia likes attention – *male* attention in particular. She's always flirted with any good-looking guy over twenty-one. Mom just ignored it.'

'She shouldn't have. Olivia is a gold-digging opportunist.'

Kelsey took a deep breath and said calmly, 'Lori, Dad adored Mom. No one could have been stupid enough to think he would divorce her for *anyone*.'

'But Mom's dead and Dad's vulnerable,' Lori said bitterly. 'I think Olivia already considers herself part of our family. I *know* she expects to marry Dad, but that will never happen while I'm alive and I haven't made a secret of it!'

Kelsey was shocked by Lorelei's genuine apprehension and softened toward her sister, whose cheeks were burning red with resentment at someone who might take their mother's place. 'Do you want Dad to be alone for the rest of his life?'

After a moment, Lori said reluctantly, 'No, but he doesn't know what he wants right now. He's lonely. She's attractive and charming in that gushy way I can't stand, and she makes him laugh.' Lorelei shuddered. '*And* she knows the time to try to hook him is while he's down.'

Kelsey suddenly wondered if something more than friendship had been developing between her father and Olivia while she'd been too involved in her own life to notice. Still, she didn't want Lorelei to get even more upset.

'You're not giving Dad enough credit, Lori. He's never been impulsive. I know he's still depressed and lonely without Mom, but he hasn't lost his good judgment. I'm sure he's not romantically interested in Olivia.'

Lorelei looked morose before she finally said, 'I want Dad to be happy and find a good woman someday. But Olivia's not a good woman. I can *feel* it.'

After a moment, Kelsey said gently, 'Lori, we spent a long time shopping. I think you're tired. Don't get so wound up over Olivia.'

'OK,' Lori said reluctantly. 'I'll try not to.' Lorelei closed her eyes and smoothed her hair behind her ears. Kelsey could almost feel her trying to calm down. Lori looked up at the framed picture on the wall by their booth. 'That's Charismatic.'

Kelsey glanced at the photo of the beautiful chestnut thoroughbred that had won the Derby in 1999. 'You were always good at remembering the winners!'

'Charismatic's name and the year he won is engraved on the brass plate on the frame.' Lori giggled. 'That helped. Where's our Triple Crown winner, Carmillo?'

'Near the front of the tavern. He's the first thing I talked about with Rick Conway.' Lori raised her eyebrows and Kelsey quickly asked, 'How's Guinevere?'

'Wonderful. I miss riding her so much when I'm in New York.' Lorelei's face almost glowed when she spoke of the Palomino Quarter Horse given to her by her parents on her sixteenth birthday. 'Dad and I have gone riding twice since I came home.' She sighed. 'I'm never happier than when I'm riding Guinevere on a beautiful day.'

'You're an excellent horsewoman. I, however . . .'

'Never really tried.'

'I realized long ago that I don't have the magic touch of you and Dad and Mom when it comes to horses. But I have a cat.'

'A *fine* cat, but it's not the same.'

'You're right. He fits into my loft better than a horse would.'

Lori laughed. 'That's true. But really, Kelsey, you need someone besides a cat to share that beautiful loft with you.' Suddenly she smiled radiantly. 'How about Stuart Girard?'

'Stuart? For me?'

'Well, not for Dad!'

'Stuart is my business partner.'

'He'd be too serious and quiet for me, but he's good-looking and smart and has the same interests as you. He's in his mid-thirties and sophisticated. Dad likes him and he's—'

'Involved with Eve.'

Lorelei blinked in surprise. 'Eve Daley?'

Kelsey nodded. 'They're trying to keep it private. But I know both of them. I can tell . . .'

'*Really* involved? You've known Eve for what . . . three years? Why wouldn't she tell you?'

'You know Eve isn't very open about her private life.' Kelsey shrugged. 'But at the store I notice that they talk to each other a lot, and he always smiles around her. Once I saw him stroke her arm.'

'Kelsey, *no!*'

'It's fine. I'm delighted.' Kelsey laughed. 'When I went to work with Stuart at Durand Designs, I was a beginner and he was so patient with me. I admire him and I'm grateful to him. He's taught me so much, Lori. I'm only twenty-seven. In spite of Dad's financial help there wouldn't be an MG Interiors if it weren't for Stuart, because I didn't know how to start a successful interior design business. But my feelings for Stuart have never been the least bit romantic. He's a dear friend and my mentor.'

Lori groaned. 'Your dear friend and mentor! That sounds pathetic. The fact that a girl like you is twenty-seven and not in a relationship is also pathetic. You act like you don't even care about romance.'

'Sure I do, but I'm not desperate.'

Lorelei said nothing. She glanced at the bar and back at Kelsey. 'The subject of romance brings us back to the handsome Rick Conway. He might be *the one*. He looks like he's in his early thirties. He owns his own business. And have you noticed his arms? He definitely works out.' Her eyes widened as she said excitedly, 'Can't you just see him dancing on the bar like Channing Tatum in *Magic Mike*?'

'Settle down, Lori!' Kelsey laughed.

Janet returned carrying a tray holding sizzling chicken wings along with a basket of crackers and a crock of cheddar cheese. 'I'm sorry this took so long. A waitress called in sick and we're busier than usual because of Derby Week. But maybe this will make up for the wait.' She set down the mint juleps with a flourish.

'Silver Derby cups!' Kelsey exclaimed in delight.

'Rick said honored patrons get our best Kentucky bourbon, the largest spearmint sprigs and silver cups.'

Kelsey turned toward the bar. Rick was looking at her, smiling. She lifted her cup, mouthed *Thank you!*, took a sip and closed her eyes in ecstasy. Rick laughed.

Janet slipped a piece of notepaper in front of Lorelei. 'Your autograph, please?'

Lori smiled and then signed and handed the paper back to Janet, who stared down at it. 'Lorelei . . .' She sighed. 'That's such a beautiful name.'

'My mother named me after the poem *Die Lorelei* by Heinrich Heine.'

'Oh, a poem.' Janet looked unsure of herself. 'I don't know much about poetry.'

'I don't either. My mother was the poetry-lover. Anyway, it's a German poem about a beautiful girl with long blonde hair.'

'Your mother sure chose the right name for you! I've never seen such lovely pale blonde hair. Oh, yours is beautiful, too, Miss March,' Janet dutifully told Kelsey.

'Janet,' Rick called casually. 'I need some help over here.'

'OK!' Janet leaned toward Lorelei. 'I promised Rick I wouldn't bother you.' She glanced at Lorelei's autograph again. 'Thanks so much, Miss March. Can I get you two anything else?'

'We're fine for now,' Kelsey said.

'I'll keep an eye on you,' Janet said, walking backward toward the bar. 'Just nod if you want more drinks or anything.'

Lorelei looked dismally at the crock of cheese. 'Cheddar cheese – my downfall!'

'It comes with a serving of crackers and it's delicious. You need to eat more than a few dry crackers and look at this rich, golden cheese placed right in front of you—'

'You're like a mother hen, tempting me with food all the time.'

'And you're cranky when you're hungry. Take a big gulp of your mint julep and eat at least *two* crackers with plenty of cheese, just to please me,' Kelsey said. Lorelei picked up her cup and sipped. Kelsey frowned. 'I said a gulp.'

This time Lorelei took a sizable drink and shook her head. 'Wow, that's powerful!' She smiled. 'And good.'

'You've forgotten what a real mint julep tastes like. It'll help you relax. You've been working too hard.'

'All we did today was shop for Derby dresses and hats.'

'We shopped for hours. But I meant you've been working too hard at your career.'

'I pose for pictures. My job isn't all that hard, Kelsey.'

'It's hard when you travel for fashion shows, work out five days a week, attend about twenty parties a month and maintain a public profile like you do.'

'I have to strike while the iron is hot. While *I'm* hot,' Lorelei said earnestly. 'The fashion industry is fickle. Maybe in two years I won't even be able to get a booking.'

'That won't happen. You're too popular. Also, modeling is what you've always wanted to do and you're totally dedicated. Not all young models have your work ethic, especially when they've shot to success and people are throwing compliments at them constantly. Thousands of girls dream of modeling, but if they make it into that world they can't handle it.' Kelsey paused thoughtfully. 'I couldn't have. A public presence like yours would scare me to death.'

Lorelei tilted her head whimsically, the way she had since she was a little girl. 'Well, I couldn't have started a design business like MG Interiors. But then I didn't have what it takes to finish college in three years while doing internships and winning design awards. Mom and Dad were prouder of you than me.'

'You're so wrong. Dad is and Mom was *tremendously* proud of you. You're a *star*. I basically make spaces into rooms.'

'Sounds easy but I know it isn't.' Lori looked embarrassed. 'Still . . . Well, what exactly is it you do?'

Kelsey looked at her in disbelief. 'Oh, Lori, you're *not* serious?'

'Yeah, I am,' Lorelei said meekly. 'I tell people my sister has a successful interior design business. Then I hope they don't ask me for details.'

Kelsey grinned. 'No wonder. It sounds so boring compared to what you do.'

'So tell me what you do and make it sound glamorous.'

'Glamorous?' Lori stared at her as if mesmerized. 'All right.' Kelsey took a sip of her julep and cleared her throat. 'I specialize in designing the interiors of houses, offices, stores and restaurants. When I take on a job, I have to think about the function of the rooms and their proportions while keeping the designs within the building codes. I try to create a unique mood within the area specifications and I don't do it alone. I have a brilliant partner and four talented associates.' Kelsey paused and rolled her eyes. 'See? Boring!'

'That's because you're reciting a memorized description. You sound like a robot.'

'How I sound doesn't matter. People would rather hear about being a supermodel like you. Lacking your beauty and height, though, I work with what I have.'

'You have brains. You're way smarter than I am. You're more creative than any of the people you call your associates. You've never thought you were beautiful but you are. And you're only four inches shorter than I am, so you're not always towering over other women.' Lori giggled. 'Also, you don't wear size ten shoes like me. Mom wore size seven. I hate having such big feet!' She finished her drink, held up her silver cup to Janet, who was watching them and mouthed, *Two more, please.*

Janet delivered the drinks almost immediately, and for the next forty-five minutes, as the sisters each drank two more mint juleps and the bar grew crowded, they talked about everything from fashion and movies to how their father was doing after the death of their mother eighteen months earlier. He was as well as could be expected, they said – then shrugged off the cliché.

'Dad will never get over losing Mom,' Kelsey said. 'He's doing better, though. He's even put on some of the weight he lost.'

'He looks good compared with this time last year.' Lorelei squeezed her eyes shut. 'When I think of Mom just closing her eyes and going limp against him while they were slow dancing to their favorite song, I can hardly bear it, even though Dad said she didn't feel anything.'

Truman March had told this story to both of his daughters. Kelsey didn't believe her mother's death from an aneurysm had been so immediate and peaceful, but she never pressed for the truth, especially as the less skeptical Lorelei seemed to find comfort in his version.

'Dad and Mom had a love that most people dream of and never get,' Lori said in a slightly bourbon-fuzzed voice. Her eyes brimmed with tears before she finished her drink then said huskily, 'The guy has stopped playing the piano. Does that beautiful vintage jukebox at the back of the room work?'

'Sure. It has some oldies as well as new songs. By oldies I mean the eighties.'

'Wunnerful!' Lorelei dug fruitlessly in her purse for change. Finally she took all the coins that Kelsey held out to her, then motioned to Janet for more drinks.

Lorelei scooted out of the booth and headed toward the jukebox. Kelsey had no idea how her sister could walk so grace-fully in shoes with four-inch heels after a day of shopping and then ingesting mint juleps on a nearly empty stomach. Lorelei studied the selections on the Wurlitzer Peacock jukebox. Its yellow, green and red neon lights bathed her perfect features and gleamed on the shining baby-blonde hair, which she'd inherited from their Swedish mother, waving almost halfway down her back. Even if Lorelei hadn't been her sister, Kelsey would have thought she was the most beautiful girl she'd ever seen.

Kelsey slowly realized that at least a third of the people in the bar were watching Lorelei. Four held up camera phones and took her picture. Kelsey wasn't surprised. Beauty always drew atten-tion. A wave of misgiving washed through her, though, as she looked around the bar. In more than a few of the female faces she saw jealousy, spite and resentment. A couple of men looked Lorelei up and down with open lust that wasn't pretty. Another man followed her to the jukebox, stood beside her and gazed, his face only a foot from hers.

'Miss March?' Janet had arrived with two fresh mint juleps. 'Are you all right? You look worried.'

Kelsey pulled herself back to Janet's questioning gaze. 'I'm fine. Could you bring some more crackers?'

Suddenly the drums, congas, shakers and marimba of Toto's song 'Africa' soared through the bar. Some people began swaying to the beat and smiled at Lorelei as she walked unsteadily back to the booth.

'Whew, I think these mint juleps are getting to me,' Lorelei said as she thumped down on the padded booth seat. 'It feels good to unwind.'

'Did that guy beside you at the jukebox say anything to you?'

'What guy?'

'The one who stood right beside you staring for all he was worth.'

'Oh, sometimes men do that, sometimes women do. I didn't notice him,' Lori said absently. 'I *love* this song.'

'Getting yourself into the mood for the African shoot?'

Lorelei took a hearty swallow of her fresh mint julep and beamed with slightly bleary eyes. 'I'm *so* excited! I know it'll be hard – the heat and the insects and *four* kinds of cobras!'

'Are you a little bit scared?'

'Well, normally I would be, but now I can hardly think about all that stuff.'

Janet arrived with more crackers and cheese on a tray and, just as she was setting down the crackers, Lori swept her arms through the air and burst out, 'I'm in love with the photographer Cole Harrington!' One of her hands hit the basket of crackers and Janet spilled about a third of them on the table.

'I'm so sorry!' Janet cried, although the fault was Lori's. Lori seemed unaware as she rushed on. 'Cole's father was Grant Harrington, the famous wildlife photographer. You must have heard of him.'

'I don't think so,' Kelsey said distractedly as she helped Janet catch runaway crackers.

Lorelei looked at Janet. 'I want another julep. I don't care if I gain five pounds tonight!'

Janet smiled. 'I'll bring fresh crackers. I'm glad you're having a good time.'

'I'm having a *helluva* good time!' Lori retrieved two crackers from the basket, emptied her julep cup, stuffed the crackers in her mouth and looked at Kelsey. 'Anyway, Cole's a genius,' she sputtered. 'He was a prodigy. He started in the business when he was sixteen and had a great career as a fashion photographer by the time he was twenty-two. No help from his father, Grant, who had five – maybe six – children but only gave his last name to Cole. He also gave him Grant as a middle name. Grant was terrible when it came to women, but he was brilliant and *really* respected. He was interviewed on public broadcasting a bunch of times and they made a documentary about his work. Last year Cole decided to do exotic animal life photography like his father, but he's agreed to do one final fashion layout – my *Vogue* shoot!'

Still astonished by her sister's gleeful announcement of love, Kelsey asked vaguely, 'Well, who could pass up Lorelei March and *Vogue*?'

Lorelei waved her hand again and went on, her speech loud and fast. 'You're prejudiced. There are so many girls prettier than I am. Bigger names. Anyway, Cole signed on for the shoot before he knew it would feature me. It was just luck on my part. We met and I couldn't believe how nice he was – oh, *nice* is such a blah word for him. He's intelligent and captivating and not the least bit pretentious, and he's just so *nice*! And unbelievably handsome. I don't have a picture of him – he hates having his picture taken even though he's a photographer! Isn't that *funny*? He has dark blonde hair and some people say his eyes are almost the same shade of blue as mine. He's a couple of inches taller than me. And he has the cutest little scar on his jaw. He fell off his tricycle when he was small. He's thirty-six. He's so smart and talented and *fabulous*!'

'I'm glad you've met such a great guy.' Lorelei's noisy enthusiasm made Kelsey slightly dizzy. 'Does Cole feel the same way about you?'

Lorelei's smile faded as she seemed to retreat behind her eyes. 'Sure.' She looked relieved when Janet returned with a fresh basket of crackers and two juleps. 'Thanks, Janet! Everything is *so* good.'

Janet beamed. 'It's a special occasion.'

'How long have you been dating Cole?' Kelsey asked as Janet turned away.

'Dating?' Lorelei took a sip of her drink. 'Well, we're not really dating. You see . . . he's . . . well . . . married.'

'You're having an affair?' Kelsey blurted.

'*No!* Well, not really.'

'You either are or aren't.'

'Mostly we just go places and . . . talk.'

'Talk? Does his wife know about all this talking?'

'Don't look at me that way. What he has with her is legal. What we have is . . .' Lori's eyes were too bright with alcohol and her voice rose. 'Magic!'

'Please lower your voice, Lori. People are looking.'

'People are *always* looking! I don't care!'

Kelsey's mood plunged as she looked at her boisterous, beaming sister. 'You've had too much bourbon and not enough food. That's my fault. Why don't we leave—'

'I don't want to leave! I'm having a *wunnerful* time!'

Kelsey was stunned. She'd never seen this loud, glassy-eyed Lorelei before. 'I don't want to hurt your feelings,' Kelsey said carefully, 'but you sound like a twelve-year-old with a crush. You're too smart to have an affair with a married man.'

Immediately she knew she'd made a mistake. Lorelei's expression went from disappointed to insulted. She said coldly, 'He's getting a divorce.'

'When?'

'Soon. People have told me Cole and his wife aren't happy together but she likes being married to him because he's handsome and talented and a celebrity. She's older than him and she has a lot of money. She's spoiled and mean, and she's making things hard for Cole.'

'Do they have children?'

'No.'

'Then she can't be holding custody over his head,' Kelsey said. 'What does her money have to do with anything?'

Besides him not wanting to give up a rich wife, Kelsey thought.

'She can interfere with his career. That's what people have told me. They say she doesn't want him to be a wildlife photographer – she wants him to stay in fashion photography. And someone told me that at a party she was drunk and they got into an argument, and she said if he tries to divorce her she'll cause trouble.'

Kelsey knew asking a barrage of questions would make her

sister mad, but she couldn't help herself. 'You keep telling me what other people say. What does Cole say?'

'Not much. He's a gentleman. But I saw them at a charity event a month ago. Her professional name is just Delphina. No last name.' Lori made a face. 'She's forty-three and there's something wrong with her complexion – that's why she doesn't model anymore – but she still looks good. She kept sending Cole for glasses of champagne like he was a waiter. Then she stood beside him, smirking. I'm surprised she could even manage a smirk with all the Botox in her face. She glanced at me a couple of times and saw me staring at Cole, and started clutching his arm like she was shouting at me "He's mine!"'

'God, Lori, does she know about you and Cole?'

'Oh, chill out, Kelsey. He didn't talk to me that night – he barely looked at me. He knows how to be careful.'

'Because he's had so much experience with other women?'

Lori looked at her angrily. Kelsey knew her sister was on the verge of shutting down the subject of Cole Harrington, but she felt she had to know more about this man her sister thought she loved.

Kelsey changed her tone. 'OK, I'm sorry. Tell me about him.'

'Well, his parents traveled a lot when he was a kid but they split up. Cole doesn't talk about his mother, but I know a long time ago she was a news photographer. Her sister was a fashion photographer. His aunt got Cole into fashion. Delphina was a model. They got married here.'

'Here?'

Lori nodded.

'You mean in Louisville?'

'Yeah. Can you believe it? Her family's from here. They own Arienne.'

'Arienne? The big bourbon distillery?'

'Yeah. That's where Delphina gets all her money.'

'Ah. Her money.'

'Cole didn't marry her for money!' Lori took a deep breath and Kelsey knew she was gathering herself for a fight. 'I'm sorry I told you about him. I thought you'd be happy for me.'

Lorelei looked at Kelsey with blazing, determined eyes. Suddenly, Kelsey remembered Lorelei as a child. Their parents had been married for four years when fertility specialists told their mother her chances of getting pregnant were slim to none. Within a year, the Marches adopted Kelsey when she was three months old. Six years later, Sofie March defied the doctors and gave birth to Lorelei.

Kelsey had been delighted to have a little sister. Like her parents, she doted on Lorelei, who most of the time was angelic. Occasionally, though, Lorelei had turned obstinate to the point of bull-headed. When she was five, their father had brought them a kitten, hoping to teach the girls how to take care of something totally dependent on them. He'd said they'd have to decide on a name. Kelsey had dutifully made a list of names and read them aloud. Lorelei, holding the kitten and standing with her legs planted firmly apart, had announced, 'Her name is Taffy.'

'Daddy said we have to agree,' Kelsey had pointed out. Lorelei had sent her a burning glare. 'Her name is Taffy. I'm her *mother* and I get to pick her name. It's *Taffy*.'

Right now, Lorelei was giving her the same burning glare as she had the day she'd clutched the cat. Kelsey could see that Lorelei had decided Cole Harrington was in love with her and would leave his wife and marry her. Soon. Lorelei had not been a patient child. Lorelei was not a patient woman.

Lori had been an adored, pampered and overindulged miracle child, Kelsey thought without resentment. If a child other than Lori had been treated as she had, she would probably be unbearable. Her goodness, generosity and artlessness, though, outweighed her occasional flares of spoiled entitlement. But her Achilles heel was her sincerity, which often led her close to gullibility. Kelsey knew Lori was heading for trouble with this man named Cole Harrington.

Instead of lecturing Lorelei and making her angrier, though, Kelsey smiled into her sister's famous, now slightly bloodshot eyes. 'I hope everything works out for you, Lori.'

Lorelei smiled with surprised gratitude. 'Really? That means so much to me, Kelsey. Guess what? Cole's coming to the Derby this year!'

Kelsey paused. 'You'll be seeing each other?'

'Sure. We haven't made arrangements yet because he'll be staying with *her* family.'

'I see.' He had to sneak away from his wife and her family to see Lori, Kelsey thought dismally. 'Well, maybe I can meet him.'

'Maybe.'

'Lori, please don't be mad. I'm your big sister. I love you. I want what's best for you and what makes you happy.' As Lorelei gave her a slow, lopsided smile, Kelsey knew it was time for the evening to end while they were on an upbeat note. 'Listen, sweetie, I think we've done ourselves proud tonight. It's ten-fifty. Let's go back to my place and find something good to watch on TV.'

Kelsey motioned for Janet to bring the check and left the money on the tabletop along with a generous tip. Then she and Lorelei started through the now-crowded bar. Three women and two men stopped them, requesting selfies. Lorelei obliged, although she had to hold on to Kelsey for balance. They had almost reached the door when Rick Conway appeared.

'Are you ladies leaving us so soon?' he asked.

Kelsey laughed. 'We've been here for nearly three hours. We need to go home.'

'Then let me call a taxi for you.'

'Thanks, but we'll walk. It's a lovely night and we could use some fresh air.' She smiled. 'We had a great time, didn't we, Lori?'

'A great time,' Lorelei repeated like a child. She beamed. 'Thanks, Rick. And Janet.' She turned to face the bar, raised her voice and waved. 'Thanks *everybody*! Good night! Sleep tight!'

Kelsey blushed as people called out, 'Good night, Lorelei!'

'I should walk you home,' Rick said almost anxiously.

'Oh, Rick, we'll be fine,' Kelsey replied.

'But it's late and you're . . . well . . .'

'Drunk?' Kelsey was slightly offended. '*I'm* not.'

'Kelsey, *please* . . .'

'Don't worry about us.'

Rick's forehead creased. He looked tense, then turned abruptly and headed back to the bar as Kelsey pulled Lori toward the tavern door.

'He didn't want you to go,' Lorelei hissed outside as if her voice might carry through the heavy wooden door. 'He *really* likes you.'

'He's always been nice but not pushy,' Kelsey said, looping

her right arm through Lorelei's left. 'I don't know what's gotten into him tonight.'

'Maybe he's just overcome by love.'

Kelsey laughed. 'Sure.'

'I wish I hadn't told you about Cole,' Lorelei said glumly as they rounded the corner of the bar and began walking down the block. She halted, her face alarmed. 'Don't tell Dad about him!'

Suddenly a surprising flutter of uneasiness stirred in Kelsey's chest. Shaken, she looked behind her but saw no one in the pools of light cast by the streetlights. Still, she tightened her arm around Lorelei's and started moving forward.

Lorelei tried to shake her loose. 'You don't have to hold me up, Kelsey.'

'You're veering toward the curb. I don't want you to trip in those sky-high heels.'

'You're mad at me about Cole. You're dragging me home like I'm a little girl!'

Kelsey didn't answer. Someone was walking softly behind them. Too close behind them. The air felt charged. And they were all alone on the street, not a person or a car in sight. Something bad is coming closer, Kelsey thought, dread rising in her like cold, foul water. Something bad is closing in . . .

'Quit *pulling* on me!' Lori went rigid like a furious child on the verge of a tantrum.

'Excuse me?' A soft voice – high-pitched but male.

Their arms still entangled, Lorelei spun around with angry force, swinging Kelsey with her. Now Kelsey was nearest the curb. 'What?' Lori snapped.

'Nice night, isn't it?' the guy asked pleasantly.

'Yeah, I guess,' Lori said.

Kelsey looked at a thin, slouching figure wearing baggy jeans and a dark long-sleeved shirt. In the glow cast by a streetlight, she could see that he had a wrinkled face and a thin layer of top hair lifting in the breeze. His left arm hung limply at his side but his fingers twitched. He smiled, his dark eyes wide and fixed on Lori. 'I like this weather. I always look forward to spring, don't you?'

Kelsey suddenly realized this was the man who'd followed Lori to the jukebox and stood staring at her. 'The weather's nice but we have to go now,' she said quickly. 'Good night.'

His dark gaze slid from Lori to Kelsey. 'Won't you wait just a second?'

'We can't. Sorry.'

'Oh . . . OK.' The man's head tilted slightly. Then, almost in slow motion, Kelsey saw his right hand rise. He was holding a gun and as Kelsey watched, frozen in horror, his arm stiffened then wavered before a shot ripped apart the quiet darkness. Lorelei uttered a short, small animal-like squeak as she clutched her chest. Her feet twisted and her body tilted in front of Kelsey, who grabbed her. Another shot. Lorelei slammed against Kelsey, knocking her down. She hit the concrete hard, pain searing the back of her head, but she still clutched Lorelei. Wrapped in a dizzying haze, Kelsey vaguely heard the piercing crack of another nearby shot before a man shouted and a woman screamed.

Kelsey managed to lift her head and shoulders and looked at Lorelei, who lay across her chest, her eyes wide and surprised. Kelsey spread her arms around her sister, trying to shield her, mumbling encouragements, pleading for her to live, her gaze locked on Lori's. For a few moments, she was certain Lori looked at her with recognition. Then Lorelei's breath grew slow and shallow.

Kelsey sobbed as Lori's lids slowly lowered over her beautiful indigo eyes.

TWO

Kelsey didn't make a sound. Her world slowed and silenced along with Lorelei's breath. Finally she felt someone touching her neck, placing a hand under her nose, then yelling at her, 'Breathe, Kelsey. *Breathe!*'

She opened her mouth, convulsed slightly and sucked in night air so hard and fast she felt as if her lungs would burst. She let it out, drew another breath and, as she exhaled, looked into a man's face. Terrified, still holding Lorelei, she tried to sit up until a large hand clamped on her shoulder, holding her down, and she was aware of a voice saying gently, 'It's Rick, Kelsey. Rick Conway from the bar. You're safe but you need to lie still.'

She went rigid with fear and stared up at the black sky as the world whirled. Everything seemed unreal. Was it really Rick Conway talking to her? Or was it the other man? The man with the soft voice and a gun? She didn't know.

'Kelsey, it's important that you don't move. You might have hurt your neck. But you have to look at me and let me know if you understand me.' She wouldn't look at him. 'Kelsey, it's Rick, *please* . . .' After a moment, he clapped his hands close to her ear, startling her. She blinked several times as her mind cleared. She looked into a face – a face without wrinkles, a face with kindness and concern in the warm brown eyes, a face smiling at her reassuringly. He leaned close to her and said softly, 'Kelsey, are you in pain?' She didn't answer. 'Kelsey, you need to pull yourself together . . . for Lorelei.'

'For Lori?' Kelsey's gaze moved downward to her sister's eerily still face resting on her chest. 'I want our dad.' She looked at Rick and raised her voice. 'I want Dad!'

'*Shhhhh*, Kelsey. We'll get your father, I promise, but you're safe now. Do you understand? You're safe.'

'Lori's hurt.' She closed her eyes. 'I couldn't do anything . . .'

Someone stooped beside Kelsey. 'My name is Carol. I'm a nurse.'

'Thank God,' Rick muttered. 'Please stay with us.'

The woman had a warm, velvety voice. 'I'll take good care of her. I won't leave you, dear.'

'Carol?' Kelsey felt as if her thoughts were slipping away from her. 'Is that your name?'

The woman nodded.

'Please help my sister,' Kelsey begged.

'It's best to wait for the ambulance. We shouldn't move her. Are *you* hurt?'

'I don't know, but Lori's hurt . . .' Kelsey's voice broke. 'Can't you do something?'

'Help is on the way, honey. For now, you need to relax.'

The woman rubbed her hands over Kelsey's shoulders, as if to comfort her. Kelsey wanted to push her away, to make this kind person leave her and Lorelei alone, but she felt too tired and muddled to do anything. She lay still, clutching her sister, murmuring the poem *Die Lorelei*. Then slowly darkness descended, shutting out everything with a warm, loving embrace. Kelsey felt as if she was floating, floating . . .

She flinched at the sudden shriek of sirens. Glaring alarm lights seemed to pierce into her brain. She squeezed her eyes shut. The police and an ambulance, she thought clearly. The first response team.

The revolving lights were unbearably bright, and her eyelids couldn't entirely shut out their glare. She began trembling. Carol held her shoulders firmly. 'Are you doing OK?' she asked gently.

'I'm so cold. Lori's so cold. Can you get us blankets?'

'I don't want to leave you. I'll take off my sweater and put it over you.'

'No. Lori's bleeding. You'll get blood on your sweater.'

After a moment, the woman said sadly, 'It doesn't matter, dear. A little blood doesn't matter now.'

'Kelsey, I know you're awake. Open your eyes.' Kelsey felt a strong, warm hand holding hers. 'Honey, open your eyes.'

'Daddy?' she asked groggily, keeping her eyes shut.

'Yes, sweetheart.'

'Where am I?'

'The hospital. You're not badly hurt. You just bumped your head.'

'Then why am I here?'

'Do you remember what happened outside the bar?'

She squeezed her eyes tighter. 'I had a dream. A nightmare.'

'No, Kelsey, you didn't have a nightmare. You do remember, don't you?' She said nothing. 'Kelsey?' Nothing. Her father snapped, 'Kelsey March, let "the Bad" in. What do you remember?'

'There was a man! He said he liked the weather!'

'That's better,' he said gently, stroking her arm. 'When you were little, you called whatever scared you "the Bad." You always closed your eyes when you wanted to keep "the Bad" away. But you're an adult now and you must open your eyes and let the bad in. *Please.*' Kelsey let her eyelids drift up and she saw her father's haggard slender, handsome face. Love and relief washed through her.

'I'm so glad you're here.' She felt a tear run down her cheek and he brushed it away with his thumb, smiling at her tenderly. 'I was so afraid, Daddy.'

'I know, honey, but you're safe now.'

'The police came. I remember the sirens. Did they get that man?'

A pause. 'Yes.'

'You're sure?'

Another pause. 'I'm sure.'

Kelsey suddenly felt panicked. 'You don't sound sure, Daddy! You're not telling the truth!' She tried to sit up. She wanted to run. 'They didn't get him! He's coming for *me.*'

Her father grabbed her shoulders and pulled her to him. 'He can't hurt you, Kelsey.'

It's useless, Kelsey thought. I can't get away. Even Daddy won't let me get away.

'Listen to me, honey. You have to stop crying.'

'I c-can't.'

'Kelsey, stop crying like a baby,' her father said sternly. 'You're not a baby. You're a grown woman.'

Kelsey shuddered and swallowed hard. Someone wiped her face with a moist, cool cloth. She began shivering then felt another blanket placed over her. Tears flowed. Then they stopped, as if someone had flipped a switch. She ran the back of her hand over her face. At last she said, 'I'm all right, Daddy. I'm sorry.'

'That's all right, sweetie. I know you don't want to remember what happened tonight, but you have to try. It's important. Pretend you're telling me about a movie. Movies haven't scared you since you were a little girl.'

'Yeah.' Her head pounded. 'OK.'

'The man who said he liked the weather – did you know him?'

'No.'

'Did Lori know him?'

'No.'

'Did you say anything to him?'

'I said I liked the weather, too, but that we had to go . . .'

'And then?'

Kelsey's gaze shifted to the ceiling as she tried to remember. 'And . . . he said, "OK." He sounded like he didn't care.' An image seared through her mind. 'Then he raised his arm. He was holding a gun. I couldn't move. He shot Lori. It happened so *fast*.' Her voice broke. 'Lori fell sideways in front of me. I grabbed her. There was another shot. She crashed against me and I fell. I was still holding her when I fell. I hit my head and everything seemed like it was far away, unreal. But I heard another shot. I think he missed . . .' Her voice lifted hopefully. 'I'm sure he missed! I thought Lori was dead, but maybe . . . Dad, where is she? Where's Lori?'

Her father's gaze dropped. 'She's . . . gone.'

'Gone?' Kelsey heard her father swallow hard, struggling not to cry. 'Dead? *No!*'

'You've shut your eyes again, Kelsey. Open them.' Her father stroked her face. 'If you don't open your eyes, honey, you'll make me feel like I've lost you too.'

She drew a breath and a desolate calm washed over her. 'I knew Lori was dead,' she said flatly. 'I knew out on the street.'

Her father's face was only inches away. She looked into his light gray eyes. The swollen eyelids tipped with the long, intensely black lashes so many women envied, were wet. She felt his warm breath on her face and saw the deepened wrinkles around his mouth. To Kelsey, her vital father looked old and tired and hopeless. 'Dad, it's my fault.'

'No, it isn't.' Her father lifted her up, holding her against the warmth of his chest. She caught the scent of soap on his cool, tanned skin. A long sob tore through her as she clutched him tighter. 'It is not your fault, Kelsey. Never say that again.' She reached up and touched a sore bump on the back of her head. 'You have a concussion, but they tell me it's not too bad. You'll be fine in a couple of days.'

'*I'll* be fine, but not Lori!'

'Don't think about that now. Tell me about the day. What did you and Lori do today?'

Kelsey replayed the day in her mind. 'We shopped all afternoon. Then we took our stuff back to my loft and walked to the tavern. It was only two blocks, and I thought walking would be safer than driving home.' Kelsey burst into laughter with an edge of hysteria. 'I didn't want to drive after we'd been drinking because we might have had a fender-bender. So we walked and . . .'

Her father still held her against him and rocked her gently. '*Shhhh*, baby. *Shhhh*. You couldn't have known a man was stalking you.'

'What? Stalking *me*?'

'Or your sister.'

'Lori didn't say anything about a stalker.'

'You don't remember everything. Maybe she said something important that you've forgotten.' Her father drew back and smiled. 'You just need some prodding. The police want to talk to you.'

'But I don't want to talk to the police now, Dad. Please . . .'

No one answered her. The doctor opened the door and murmured something. In a moment, an unfamiliar deep, smooth voice said, 'Thank you, Doctor. Mr March? I've been hearing voices. I'm Detective Pike and I'd like to speak to your daughter.'

'She's injured and so upset . . .'

'I'm sorry, but I have a job to do.' The man's rich voice conveyed sympathy, regret and determination at the same time. 'The sooner we get this over with the better.'

The doctor sighed. 'Mr March, we should let the detective interview your daughter. Nurse Hiller will stay here in case Miss March needs anything.'

Kelsey's gaze met her father's. 'I'll tell him what I remember. Then I want to go home with you, not to my loft.'

Truman March's eyes filled with tears. 'You can come home for as long as you want. Forever—'

'Mr March, I hate to seem unfeeling—'

Her father looked up at the man standing just inside the door, some of the fire returning to his eyes. 'All right. Just don't drag this out longer than necessary. She's been through a lot.'

'Dad, please—'

Please stay! Kelsey wanted to beg. Then she looked at her father's devastated face. She couldn't make him listen to the hurtful details he'd already heard. 'I'll be all right. I'll see you in a few minutes.'

'Sure.' He managed a wink. 'Love you, sweetheart.'

After her father left the chilly room, Kelsey looked up at the tall, lanky man with piercing dark eyes beneath straight black eyebrows, a slightly arched nose, high cheekbones and narrow lips. His shiny black hair was combed straight back and he had a prominent widow's peak. To Kelsey, he looked like a genteel figure who'd stepped from a nineteenth-century photograph. 'How are you, Miss March? I'm so sorry for what happened tonight. So sorry.'

'Thank you,' Kelsey murmured.

'I'm Detective Pike, ma'am. Detective Enzo Pike. That's an unusual first name around here. My parents came from Florence, Italy, to New York when I was a baby. I was named for my paternal grandfather, who pronounced his first name "Ent-zo."'

'Like Enzo Ferrari.'

Detective Pike raised his eyebrows and smiled. 'That's right. If only my grandfather had started a car company like the famous Enzo!' He'd put her slightly more at ease with the casual tone of his opening conversation. 'I know it's hard for you to answer questions, Miss March, but I need to hear what you remember *now*. Time has a way of altering the facts.'

'Or making them clearer.' Kelsey was still cold, but she'd stopped shivering. I have to be strong, she thought. I have to be strong for Lori. 'The man who killed my sister – is he dead? Did the police kill him?'

'He was shot and brought to the hospital. He wasn't dead on arrival. He wasn't declared dead until ten minutes ago.'

So that's why Dad sounded like he was dodging my questions earlier, Kelsey thought. The man was here and probably still breathing when I regained consciousness. 'Who was he?'

'You don't know?'

'Me? No.'

'I didn't mean to offend you, Miss March. Please relax. This is not an interrogation.' Their gazes held for a moment. Pike's was benign, even sympathetic. But not quite sincere. 'Here's what we know right now.' He looked down at his notebook. 'His name was Vernon Nott,' he said. 'N-O-T-T. Is the name familiar?'

'No.'

'He was thirty-three.'

'He looked older.'

Pike raised his eyebrows.

'I just remembered. I saw him in the bar. He followed Lori to the jukebox and stood beside her, looking right at her. I didn't see him very well then.' She frowned, thinking. 'I didn't see him well out on the dark street either, but I noticed that his skin was wrinkled, so the wrinkles must have been fairly deep.' She paused, trying to conjure a picture of him in her mind. 'His hair was thin. He had a comb-over. It lifted when the breeze blew.'

Pike smiled slightly.

'And he had a high voice. When he first spoke, I thought he was young – a teenager. That probably doesn't matter.'

'Everything matters.' Detective Pike wrote in his notebook before looking at Kelsey with his sharp, dark eyes. 'Vernon Nott lived in a mobile home park on Davy Crockett Trail. That's about eight miles from Conway's Tavern with a lot of bars closer to him, but he was a regular at Conway's.' He paused. 'I believe you go there often, Miss March.'

'I go there a couple of times a week at lunchtime. I've been there maybe seven or eight times in the evening.'

'The tavern has been open only eleven weeks and you've been there eight times at night?'

His tone was bland but Kelsey felt defensive. 'When I stop in during the evening, Detective, it's usually with my friend and assistant, Eve Daley. We work at MG Interiors, just two blocks away from Conway's. Sometimes we work late.'

'I see. Only you don't just work at MG Interiors, Miss March. You own it, isn't that right?'

'I *co*-own it with Stuart Girard.'

'You own fifty-five percent. He only owns forty-five.'

'What does that have to do with anything?'

'That gives you the controlling interest. Is Mr Girard happy with that arrangement?'

'What are you talking about, Detective Pike?'

Pike remained silent.

'Yes, Stuart is happy with that arrangement.'

'To the best of your knowledge.'

'Well, yes . . . But what—'

'Your business is very close to the bar. Also, you live in a loft above MG Interiors. That makes it convenient for you to visit Conway's Tavern during the evening. What nights do you usually go to the tavern?'

'I don't go on any particular nights.'

'Not on Tuesdays or Thursdays, for instance?'

'Yes, I've been there on a Tuesday and maybe a couple of Thursdays.'

'Yet you don't remember this man who frequents the bar on those nights every week?'

Kelsey's eyes narrowed. 'No, I don't remember him. Maybe you should ask Eve Daley. Or Stuart Girard. He's gone with us a couple of times. They might have sharper vision or better memories than I do.'

'Who are your other employees and their duties?'

'Nina Evans and Giles Miller are designers. Our business manager is Isaac Baum.'

'Do they accompany you and Miss Daley and Mr Girard to Conway's?'

'Nina and Giles have come with either Eve or me for lunch. I know Nina has gone for lunch several times by herself. Isaac usually brings a sandwich from home.'

'Does Isaac have money problems?'

'He has four children.'

'Oh, four. Well. Do Isaac, Nina and Giles come with you at night?'

'No.'

'You don't invite them to come along?'

'I've invited them to come with us in the evenings but Isaac wants to get home to his wife and kids. Nina is pregnant and usually tired by evening, and Giles has an invalid mother. Her home healthcare worker leaves at six o'clock.'

Pike stared at her, and Kelsey was suddenly irritated.

'They've never come with Eve, Stuart and me, but I can't say none of them has ever gone to Conway's at night without the rest of the MG Interiors workforce. I don't cross-examine them about their activities away from the store, Detective. Why don't you ask them?'

Pike smiled regretfully. 'I've annoyed you. I'm sorry, Miss March. These are just standard questions.'

'They don't sound "just standard." Maybe it's your tone of voice.'

'Maybe,' he said pleasantly. 'Or maybe you're being too sensitive.'

'Sensitive?' Kelsey's voice rose. 'Yes, I'm *very* sensitive after my sister was just shot dead in front of me!'

The nurse stepped forward. 'I think that's enough for now.'

'I just have another question or two for her and then we'll be finished,' Pike said softly. 'Is that all right, Miss March? It's important to find out how this happened to your sister.'

Kelsey gave him a hard look. The words he didn't say were *If you don't answer, you're not helping the police learn the truth about Lorelei's murder.*

'I can go on for a few minutes,' she told the nurse.

'Thank you, Miss March.' The detective frowned, two deep vertical lines appearing between his thick eyebrows. 'Did your sister ever mention having a stalker?'

'No. Do *you* know she had a stalker?'

'Once again, it's a standard question, especially when the crime involves a young female celebrity. Was there anyone special in her life? A boyfriend?'

Kelsey hesitated. 'She didn't have a boyfriend.'

'A beautiful girl like Lorelei March didn't have even one romantic interest?'

'Maybe she had casual dates, but no one she mentioned to me.'

Pike cocked his head. 'But there was someone special to her?'

Either he knows I'm lying or he's guessing, Kelsey thought. I'm not saying anything about . . . What was his name? She couldn't remember anything about him except that he was married.

'Lorelei was busy. Devoted to her career. She didn't talk about dating anyone. Right now I can't even remember the names of her close friends in New York. I wish I could say more, but—'

But my sister's been murdered and I hardly knew anything about her life and now it's over. She was only twenty-one and her life is over. She's dead.

Kelsey drew in a ragged, painful breath. To her surprise, wrenching sobs suddenly overwhelmed her.

The hospital-room door opened and the doctor, along with Truman March, stepped inside. 'Detective, Miss March has had enough for now,' the doctor said.

'I didn't intend to upset her – I mean, to make things worse for her than they are,' the detective said humbly.

The doctor's voice softened. 'I understand. But as you can see, she's had enough. She has to rest.'

'Yes . . . of course . . . But before I go, I'm afraid I must tell Miss March one thing.'

'Not now—'

'Yes, Doctor, please.' Kelsey squeezed her hands together and looked Pike in the eyes. 'Tell me.'

'Vernon Nott had a picture of your sister in his pocket. It's possible he followed Lorelei to the bar for a reason.'

After a surprised beat, Kelsey blurted, 'For a reason? You think he deliberately came to Conway's to *kill* her?'

'He had her picture. It was an odd picture. Also, he had a gun, so it's probable that he meant to hurt her. You may feel that I'm pushing you too hard with my questions, but I want to find out for certain why this sonofabitch murdered an innocent young woman. Sorry for the language. I'll go now and you can rest.'

How deft he is at interrogation, Kelsey thought in spite of her headache, her swirling thoughts, her torn emotions. He's smart and he can help. That's more important than fretting over hiding Lorelei's possible affair. Pike turned to leave but Kelsey said, 'Wait, please.'

He looked at her.

'I want you to tell my father and me what was odd about the picture of Lori.'

'I really don't want to tire you too much, and the doctor thinks you've had enough.'

Yeah, sure, Kelsey thought with a mixture of cynicism and admiration. You know I won't let the doctor throw you out *now*. Truman March walked to her side and took her hand. 'All right, Detective. What about this picture Vernon Nott had of my daughter? Was it a picture from a magazine?'

'No. In his pocket, he had a photograph of Lorelei. The film indicates that it had been taken very recently. It's in Evidence – I can't show it to you, but it was taken with an old instant film camera.' He paused. 'Are either of you aware of someone taking a picture of Lorelei with one of these cameras?'

'No,' Kelsey said faintly. Her father shook his head.

'I didn't think so.' Pike made another note. 'I'd like to give you some details about Nott, if you're up to it, Miss March.'

'Yes, I am.'

Pike stepped closer to Kelsey and she noticed how slim he was – slim bordering on skinny in his slightly rumpled pants and suit jacket. 'Nott was in the bar all evening. As soon as you and your sister left, he came after you. We don't know how long he'd been following your sister. Last week I saw a piece on a local newscast about Lorelei March coming home for the Kentucky Derby. Maybe he saw it too, or else he followed her on social media. Did she post messages on Instagram about her visit home?'

'I don't know much about social media.' Kelsey felt embarrassingly uninformed. 'She must have had an Instagram or Twitter account. She was a celebrity – they all do. Stuart Girard handles the social media for MG Interiors. I'm sorry I can't give you more information about that.'

'That's all right,' Pike said kindly. 'We do need to find out how Nott knew Lorelei would be at Conway's this evening, though.'

'It must have been a coincidence,' Truman March asserted. 'You said Nott was a regular.'

'Tuesdays and Thursdays were his regular nights, according to Rick Conway. Tonight's Monday.' Pike looked at Kelsey. 'Where were you before you went to Conway's, Miss March?'

'Lori and I spent the afternoon shopping at the Oxmoor Mall. Then we stopped at my loft for about an hour before we walked to the bar.'

Pike looked at his notebook, then frowned. 'Nott arrived at

Conway's almost thirty minutes *before* you did, so he didn't follow you to the bar. Is it possible he knew you'd be there tonight?'

'Only my father and people at MG Interiors knew I was spending the afternoon with my sister, but I didn't say anything to anyone about taking her to Conway's Tavern afterward.'

'You're certain?'

'Yes, I'm certain. I thought we'd be worn out after shopping and would just stay in and watch TV, but Lori wanted to go.'

Maddeningly, Pike took his time writing this down. 'Could your sister have been using anything – Snapchat, for instance – that could have let someone know her location when you were shopping or going to Conway's?'

'She left all of her electronic equipment at my apartment before we went to the Oxmoor Mall. She didn't even take her cell phone. She said she got sick of always being on call and wanted yesterday to be strictly a sister day with no interruption. She didn't make calls, text, Snapchat, anything.'

'I see. But people recognized her. Maybe someone else posted the information that she was in Conway's. Or,' he said with a quirk of his eyebrow, 'perhaps someone tracked her movements the old-fashioned way – by physically following her.'

'Several people at the mall recognized her and six took selfies with her. All were women and I didn't see any of them following us around the mall, but then I wasn't really on the lookout for anyone.'

'No, you wouldn't have been,' Pike murmured vaguely, still writing. Then he raised his head and said abruptly, 'Richard Conway remembers a lot of details about the evening, even though he's very shaken by what happened. Who wouldn't be?'

He didn't give Kelsey or Truman a chance to answer.

'He says that he noticed that as soon as Nott got to the bar, he was acting different than usual. He drank more, looked fidgety and smoked several cigarettes. Conway had never seen him smoke. Nott made some calls on a cell phone. That was new, too. After you and your sister came, Miss March, he rarely took his gaze off you. He even followed your sister to the jukebox.'

Kelsey nodded. 'I told you he did. When Lori came back to the booth, I asked her about the guy who stood beside her at the jukebox and stared at her. She said it wasn't unusual and she hadn't noticed him.'

'If Nott was staring at Lorelei all evening, why didn't Conway call the police?' Truman demanded.

'Because Nott hadn't done anything warranting a call to the police.' Pike gave Truman and Kelsey another one of his kind smiles before frowning over his notes again. 'Conway says that from the day he opened the tavern Nott came to the bar twice a week. About three weeks after Nott started coming in, Conway tried to strike up a conversation with him one night. He told Conway he'd grown up in Louisville, left for a few years, got married, then returned alone six months ago after a divorce. Conway claims getting even that little bit of information was difficult. Nott seemed extremely shy and self-conscious about four circular burn scars on his face, one about half an inch from his eye. They looked like cigarette burns. He was soft-spoken, never caused any trouble and didn't even flirt with the waitresses.'

'So after Conway had this conversation with him, he stopped paying any attention to Nott?' Truman said.

Pike shook his head. 'No. Conway said that even though Nott seemed harmless he had a feeling something was *off* – Conway's word – about Nott. Maybe it was because of the regular schedule he kept. Maybe he'd dodged a few too many of Conway's casual questions. Maybe it was because Conway said he seemed tense if anyone tried to talk to him, even a waitress just being friendly, so he always kept an eye on Nott.' Pike glanced at Kelsey. 'As I mentioned earlier, Miss March, Conway says that when you and your sister came to the tavern Nott never looked away from you. You didn't notice?'

'Lorelei is – was – extraordinarily beautiful, Detective,' Kelsey said. 'A lot of people looked at her – some more than others. It was only the guy who stood beside her at the jukebox that bothered me. I now know that was Nott.'

Pike cleared his throat. 'You must not have been aware of it, Miss March, but Conway says Nott stared at *both* of you. He paid almost as much attention to you as he did to your sister. That caught Conway's attention because most nights Nott seemed detached or sat with his eyes closed, nodding along to the music.

Tonight, he was watchful. He drank four beers quickly then switched to bourbon.'

'Why does what he drank matter?' Truman asked.

'As far as Conway could recall, Nott never usually drank anything except two or three beers. Tonight he had five beers and ordered three bourbons neat. He seemed nervous. *Amped up*, Conway said.' Pike looked at Kelsey. 'When you and your sister started to leave, Nott gulped his bourbon, got up and quickly came toward you. Conway said he tried to stop you leaving and offered to call a taxi, but you were determined to walk and then refused his offer to walk you home. When you got to the door, Conway told a waitress to call nine-one-one, but he knew that if Nott was trouble there wouldn't be time for the police to be dispatched, so he went to the bar and got his gun. He said that when he managed a bar two years ago, a man pulled a gun and aimed it at everyone before shooting a guy, so he decided then that he'd always keep a weapon in his own bar. We checked – the incident in the other bar did happen. Conway's gun is licensed. Anyway, he grabbed it and ran after you.'

'If only he could have got his gun faster,' Kelsey said. 'Nott still had time to shoot three times.'

'Nott shot two times, Miss March.'

'Two?' Kelsey echoed. 'My eyes were closed, but I'm sure I heard a third shot. Didn't Nott try to shoot Lorelei again and missed?'

'The third shot came from Conway's gun.' Pike looked into Kelsey's eyes. 'Nott had his gun aimed at *you*, Miss March. Conway didn't get there soon enough to save your sister, but he shot Vernon Nott in the head only seconds before he tried to kill you too.'

THREE

'Thank you for bringing all these things to the hospital, Eve,' Kelsey said. 'You didn't forget Gatsby, did you?'

Eve Daley pushed her shoulder-length, ash-brown hair behind her ears and rolled her dark amber eyes at Kelsey. 'Forget Jay Gatsby?' she asked, referring to Kelsey's tabby cat. 'How is it possible for anyone to forget Gatsby? Mr Personality greeted me at the door, meowing his head off like he hadn't eaten for a week.'

'He missed me last night.' Kelsey pulled a long-sleeved T-shirt over her head. 'He's not used to being alone.'

'He's used to being treated like a king. Anyway, he's in his carrier in your car, furious,' Eve said. 'I'll ride with you to your father's house.'

'That's not necessary. I can drive home.'

'I'd feel better if I drive you home. Besides, that's what your father wants.'

'When did you talk to him?'

'He called and woke up Stuart and me at about two in the morning—' Eve stopped. Kelsey knew that Eve and Stuart Girard were trying to keep their romance a secret but Eve, off guard, had just blurted out that they'd spent the night together. Her cheeks reddened but she carried on talking. 'Stuart answered. We didn't get many details. Stuart wanted to come to the hospital right away – your father told him there was nothing anyone could do last night but you'd need us today.' She hesitated. 'He asked Stuart to tell me what happened. He knew I had a key to your loft and asked that I bring clothes to the hospital this morning and come with you to his house from the hospital. Your car is in the parking lot. Stuart will pick me up at your dad's house around three, if that's what you want, but I'd be happy to stay with you for as long as you like. I could leave tomorrow or the next day . . .'

'I'd love you to stay,' Kelsey said instantly. 'I know I'm being selfish to ask but the mood at the house will be morbid, though I'm keeping you away from Stuart and leaving him with all the work to do at the store—'

'You didn't ask me to stay. I offered. And Stuart decided to close the store for the rest of the week. We're only finishing up three jobs right now. Nina and Giles have them handled. All Stuart has to do is contact the people we'll be working with, starting next week, and assure them we'll have everything covered. You know how good Stuart is at making every client feel special.'

Kelsey crossed the room and hugged Eve. 'Thank you. I hate to be so weak.'

Eve patted Kelsey's back. 'You're the strongest person I've ever known, but even strong people have feelings. There's nothing shameful in needing someone to lean on occasionally.'

'Thank you.'

Eve immediately began chatting, trying to take their minds off last night. 'Kelsey, you told me someone suggested you get a watchdog because you live alone, but you don't need one when you have a cat as big and territorial as Gatsby. He stayed hot on my heels and looked at me like I was a thief while I was gathering your stuff. He positively glared at me when I was going through your dresser drawers getting lingerie. He kept weaving around my legs and trying to knock me off balance when I took things from your closet. As I was going through the apartment, I saw all the shopping bags you left before you went to the bar. You must have bought half of Louisville yesterday! I loved that Victorian lavender and blue dream of a hat with the peach silk flowers—'

'It was Lori's.' Eve looked stricken, and Kelsey gave her a quick smile to let her know that the memory of the hat didn't hurt. 'She had it made especially for her from a picture of Dad's great-grandmother on Derby Day.'

'Your dad would have loved it. And now she'll never wear it . . .' Eve broke off again, her beautiful amber eyes filling with tears. 'I'm sorry, Kelsey. You're so composed. I wasn't going to talk about what happened but I can't seem to talk about anything else.'

Eve's trembling hands covered her face and she began crying. Kelsey hugged her. 'It's OK, Eve. Earlier, I couldn't stop sobbing. I was a wreck. But I'm composed now because they gave me a tranquilizer. It's the miracle of chemistry, not my fortitude.' Kelsey gave Eve a tissue. 'Wipe away your tears and tell me what else you and Gatsby quarreled about this morning.'

Eve sniffled and tried to smile. 'When it was time to go, he didn't want to get into his carrier. You'd told me he'd only get in willingly for you, so I was prepared. Before I tried wrestling him inside, I found some really bizarre green alligator-shaped oven mitts. We had quite a battle. I actually worked up a sweat, but he didn't manage to scratch me.'

'Good.'

'Gatsby doesn't think so. He's fuming, plotting revenge as we speak. I can feel it.'

'Olivia gave me those ugly oven mitts as a Christmas gift.'

'I guess that's why the mitts were in a kitchen drawer all stiff and unused. What an awful present!' Eve rustled through Kelsey's clothing. 'As for what I said earlier about Stuart—'

'And you being together at two in the morning? I already knew you're involved.'

Eve's eyes widened. 'You did? It only started three months ago. For ages, I thought he was in love with you.'

'He's never been close to it, Eve, and I'm not attracted to him except as a friend. If I had been, I wouldn't have gone into business with him.' She smiled at Eve. 'He's a brilliant, attractive man and you two make a wonderful couple.'

'We've barely acknowledged that we're serious, although it's probably too early to think about getting *serious*—'

'Relax, Eve. I'm happy for you. I really am.'

Eve looked troubled. 'I've worried lately. When you broke things off with Brad—'

'Brad? You thought I was trading in Bradley Fairbourne for Stuart?'

'I've been worried because Brad thought you were trading him in for Stuart.'

Kelsey looked at Eve in surprise. 'What? Did Brad say anything to you or Stuart to make you think so?'

'Not directly, but a couple of months ago Stuart told me Brad kept turning up wherever he was – odd places like the dry cleaner's. Then he saw Stuart and me together at a little restaurant.'

Eve hesitated. 'Kelsey, he walked over and said hello to us, then leaned close to Stuart and said, "They both wanted you but you picked the good, gentle one. If you value her, you'd better take her away from Louisville."'

'*What?* Did he mean I was a threat to you? Or to *both* you and Stuart?'

'I don't know. Maybe I shouldn't have told you, but he gives me the creeps.'

'When did this happen?'

'About a week ago.'

Kelsey felt breathless with anger at Brad. 'Why didn't you tell me?'

'Stuart said we shouldn't alarm you over what was probably just Brad being a jerk. Stuart's concerned about you, though. We both are.' Eve paused. 'I never liked Brad, Kelsey.'

'Neither did Lori.' Kelsey sighed. 'I didn't break Brad's heart when I left him. He might have talked himself into believing he loved me, but he didn't. I guess that's why I haven't spent any time feeling guilty about him, but I had no idea he'd react like this.' Kelsey sighed. 'Well, that's not quite true. In one way, I'm not shocked. He'd been getting more possessive for a couple of months before I broke off with him. It's one of the reasons I ended things.' She looked at Eve. 'If he takes this further, though, I'm going to the police.'

Eve managed a smile. 'I'm glad you're not going to ignore his behavior. Considering what's just happened . . .'

A chill washed over Kelsey. 'Brad didn't shoot Lori, Eve.'

'I know! I didn't mean to imply . . . I didn't mean to start making crazy accusations, I just—'

'It's all right, Eve. We know who shot Lori and he's dead, thanks to Rick Conway. Brad is a different matter. I'm sure he's not dangerous,' Kelsey said with a certainty she didn't quite feel. 'Bradley Fairbourne is just an annoying . . . mosquito. That's all. No, he's *less* than a mosquito. Brad is a gnat.'

'He wouldn't like that description!'

'What a shame!' Kelsey said dryly. She looked at her almost unrecognizably pale face in the mirror beneath the harsh light. 'I hope you brought all of my makeup. I don't want Dad to see me looking like this.'

Eve set a black patent-leather makeup case on the counter beside Kelsey. 'You taught me this – don't go anywhere without your makeup. Always put on your best face for the world.'

'And that's what I intend to do. Dad's lost Mom and now Lorelei. I'm all he has left. It's important to put on my best possible face for him.'

'I love this car,' Eve said half an hour later as they loaded a suitcase and two large shopping bags on to the oyster-colored leather upholstery in the back of Kelsey's metallic midnight-blue BMW convertible. 'It's such a beautiful day I couldn't resist putting down the top. Your father picked a wonderful birthday present for you last month.'

'Dad always gives me extravagant birthday presents. He thinks it makes me feel I'm no less special to him than his biological daughter. I never felt like I was competing with Lorelei, though, and this car was just over the top. I felt guilty for accepting it.' Kelsey smiled. 'But not guilty enough to refuse it.'

Kelsey took Gatsby out of his carrier and hugged all nineteen pounds of him. The veterinarian had labeled him a Red Mackerel Tabby, but to Kelsey the cat was definitely golden, with eyes an unusually vivid green. His thick, soft fur smelled of the almond-scented shampoo Kelsey used on him, and he purred so loudly he seemed on the verge of roaring as he rubbed his face against hers. She didn't want to let go of him, but the sooner she reached her father's house the sooner he could be free of confinement.

Gatsby allowed Kelsey to put him back in his carrier without a struggle. She placed the carrier on the back seat and put on her sunglasses. 'Would you mind driving to Dad's? I still have a headache and that tranquilizer has me feeling sort of dim and floaty, like nothing's quite real. Not even Lorelei's—'

'Don't say it,' Eve broke in firmly. 'Don't think about it. Not right now. Just enjoy the ride.' She got behind the steering wheel, then tilted her head to the left the way she did when she was happy. 'Let's listen to music. Something upbeat.'

In a moment P!nk was belting out 'Get the Party Started' and Eve was smiling, her lovely fine-boned face looking fresh and much younger than her twenty-eight years. Kelsey leaned back her head and closed her eyes. As Eve rocketed out of the parking lot Kelsey let herself relax, feeling nothing but the heat of the morning sun and the rush of clean air blowing through her hair.

For fifteen minutes they drove north on River Road without conversation. The only sound in the car was the music. Kelsey finally opened her eyes and looked at the Ohio River, smooth enough to be a mirror reflecting the nearly cloudless sky.

'You're smiling. What are you thinking?' Eve asked.

'How the river reflects the sky. And the sky is so beautiful today. It's sapphire.' She smiled. 'When I was young, my mother told me the word in Swedish is *safir.* Today we have a *safir himmel.*'

'I'll try to remember the phrase, though I'll never get the accent.'

'Oh, the accent!' Kelsey groaned. 'From the time I was little, Mom tried to teach me Swedish but I was a lost cause. Remembering the vocabulary was bad enough. Getting the accent was impossible. Lori was just the opposite. She took to the language like she'd always lived in Sweden. Maybe it had something to do with our genes.'

'I'm sure you weren't as bad as you thought.'

'Yes, I was. Believe me.'

'Where was your mother born?'

'In Falun. It's about a hundred and forty miles north of Stockholm. It used to have a big copper mine, and a river called the Faluån runs through it.' Kelsey knew Eve was trying to keep their minds off Lori's murder, so she went on talking. 'Mom was an only child. Her parents moved to New York when she was ten. Grandfather Vaden knew Dad's father, but they didn't start March Vaden Industries until they were in their early forties. Dad had the same passion for the company as both of my grandfathers. Grandfather Vaden thought of Dad as a son. Mom was in school in Europe when my Vaden grandparents moved to Kentucky, and Dad didn't meet her until she was twenty-two. They dated for five months and then Dad married—'

'The beautiful Sofie Vaden.'

Kelsey smiled. 'I must have told you this story at least six times, Eve!'

'It sounds like a fairy tale, and I've always loved fairy tales,' Eve mused.

'You might have your own fairy-tale ending with Stuart,' Kelsey said. 'I know you and Stuart are in love.'

'You're being a romantic, Kelsey. I'm more serious about Stuart than I have been about anyone in a long time, but *love*?' Eve shook her head. 'I'm not sure that's on the cards for me.'

'Why? Because of a bad experience?' Eve shrugged. 'OK. I won't press for details. I know you don't like talking about your past.'

Eve gave her a quick glance. 'Why do you say that?'

'Because you never talk about it.'

'That makes sense.' Eve smiled slightly. 'Well . . . there's not much to tell. I've led a very boring life.'

'It can't have been all that boring, but all I know about your early life is that you grew up in a small town in Pennsylvania.'

'Actually, it was *outside* a small town in western Pennsylvania. We had a farm. A very little farm. I have one brother two years older than I am.' She smiled wistfully. 'He was really serious, but occasionally he'd joke that I'm part wolf because I have dark amber eyes. I loved it.' Her smile faded. 'He stayed on the farm. But after I graduated from high school, I left home and came to Louisville.' She sighed and her voice caught as she said, 'I miss him.'

'I'm sorry.' Eve shrugged, but Kelsey saw her face tighten as she fought back emotion. 'Why did you come to Louisville?' Kelsey asked lightly.

'I had a great-aunt who lived here. She was my mother's aunt, although she was only twelve years older than Mama. When I was growing up, she'd visit us and talk about the city. She made it sound as if every week was like Derby Week. She died less than a year before I came here. She left me some money, which I used to get established here.'

'So that's why you moved to Louisville!'

'Yes. I held on to the money she gave me like I'd never see another dollar. I did anything to make ends meet – waitressing, clerking at a department store, even cleaning houses while I was going to Sullivan College. After I graduated, I found more part-time work then finally got the job as a receptionist at Durand Designs and met you and Stuart.' Eve smiled, looking straight ahead. 'You were both nice to me, especially you. You took a serious look at my sketches of designs. And you were kind enough to take me with you when you started MG Interiors. The end.'

'I wasn't being kind. Your designs were great, and your presentations of them so . . . sophisticated.' Kelsey paused before saying something that she'd thought for years. 'You didn't seem like a beginner, Eve.'

'But I *was* a beginner,' Eve said shortly. 'I spent so much time on those presentations. As for my designs . . . well, my soul was in my work. Sorry, but that's it. The story of my life.'

'There must be more. What were your parents like? Did your brother get married? Do you have nieces and nephews?'

'You should have been a reporter!' Eve exclaimed before she seemed to disappear within herself for a moment. Then she tilted her head, smiled, and said brightly, 'For now, that's all. Someday I'll tell you about my exciting family.'

Kelsey felt slightly stung. 'I'm sorry for being so nosy.'

Eve glanced at her and her face dropped. 'I'm awful! You're my closest friend and I reacted like you're—'

'Your life is none of my business.' Kelsey knew she sounded abrupt.

Eve hesitated. 'I don't talk about my family because they aren't really my family any more. They live simple lives devoted to hard work and God. They were appalled that I left home instead of marrying a local guy and living a life like theirs. They sort of excommunicated me from the family.'

'Even your brother?'

'Yes, to please our parents and his wife.' Eve looked sadly at Kelsey. 'Now you know why I don't talk about my family. Can you understand?'

'Eve, you've kept this from me for over three years!'

'I'm sorry—'

'No, don't apologize. I'm just surprised, and so sorry that I had no idea. This must be so painful for you, and here I am asking questions like I deserve to know the answers. I'm the one who should apologize.'

'No need. I've always wondered why you weren't more curious.'

'I thought I was minding my own business, but maybe you wanted – needed – someone to talk to about your family.'

'No. I didn't want to talk about them. I don't know why I'm talking about them now. Maybe it's just the shock of the last two days. It's made me realize that you and your family have become my family. That's presumptuous . . .'

'Not at all, Eve. Honestly, we think of you as family. My mother and Lori . . . we've all loved you. Love you.' She swallowed hard and ended lamely, 'Does Stuart know about your family?'

'He knows a little about my background. He says we're leaving the past behind.'

'Both of you?'

Eve nodded.

'Well, so much for me wanting to hear wildly romantic stories of the prince and princess overcoming huge obstacles until they met each other.'

'Now who's the little girl who loves fairy tales?'

Maybe I do, Kelsey thought. *But not as much as Lorelei. Lori and her Prince Charming – Cole Grant Harrington. She thought they were in love. I think only she was in love, with a handsome man she barely knew. A secret love affair. Even though she was twenty-one, she still wanted the matter kept hidden from her father. Lori's sophistication was just a veneer. Underneath she was still a little girl who loved secrets.*

'Suddenly you look very serious,' Eve said.

'I was thinking about secrets.'

'Secrets?'

'Yes. We all have them.'

'Some people have more than others. For years, I've known so much about your life. You didn't learn much about mine until today.' Eve reached forward and turned up the CD player until it was almost too loud for Kelsey, impossible as that seemed. 'I *love* this song!' Eve burst out, smiling as she began stumbling through lyrics she clearly didn't know.

Kelsey smiled back at her friend, wondering if her smile looked as insincere as Eve's. Then she peered ahead, turned off the CD, and said, 'We're home, and so are the press.'

Two news vans sat at the entrance to the March property. As soon as Eve pulled into the long driveway, a van door whipped open and a man jumped out, snapping pictures. Kelsey turned her head away from him. 'Dammit! Here we are in a convertible! Speed up!'

Without a word Eve pushed on the accelerator, and didn't slow down until half of the driveway lay behind them.

Ahead sat a two-story brick Greek Revival style brick house. Kelsey's stomach clenched as she looked at the porch roof where she and Lorelei – thrilled that they'd escaped out a window without being caught – had sat on warm nights reading 'scary' books that made Lori squeal with fear before begging to hear more. Kelsey jerked at the painful memory.

'Are you all right?' Eve asked.

'Yes. Coming home is harder than I thought.' She gave Eve a weak smile, then looked back at the house. The windows gleamed, the black shutters looked freshly painted and the columns surrounding the entrance were bright white. The hedges were trimmed, the lawn mown.

Eve came to a slow stop in front of the house and they climbed out of the car, Kelsey picking up Gatsby's carrier as she told Eve not to bother taking anything else inside now. They walked in silence toward the house and climbed the three steps up to the wide porch. Eve stood by, and as Kelsey reached for the door it suddenly opened and Bradley Fairbourne stood in front of them, tall, handsome and impeccably groomed.

'Kelsey, you're here at last,' he said warmly, stepping forward and wrapping his arms around her. Then he gently rubbed his face in the blonde hair beside her ear and whispered, 'I always love seeing you, no matter what the circumstances.'

FOUR

For an instant, Kelsey stood frozen in Brad's arms. Then she pulled away and looked into his green eyes. Behind them she saw only calmness. Or was it emptiness? Whichever, there certainly wasn't a trace of sadness for Lorelei. But he and Lori had never liked each other. Never.

'What are you doing here?' she asked coldly.

His voice was smooth. 'I've known Lori most of her life. Our families are so close. Where did you think I'd be?'

Kelsey's father appeared and swept her away from Brad. Neither said a word. They simply clung to each other, Kelsey feeling her father's pain and knowing he felt hers. They didn't part until Gatsby let out a loud meow.

'Well, hello fellow!' Truman said with forced cheer, bending down to look in the carrier. 'Have you come to spend a few days with me?'

'You should have put him in a boarding kennel,' Brad said sharply. 'Mother's allergic to cats.'

'Then she shouldn't pet him.' Kelsey set the carrier on the floor. So 'Mother' – Olivia – intended to be here as much as possible, Kelsey thought. What would Lorelei have said?

Looking fatigued and somewhat vacant, Truman either was unaware of the tension between Kelsey and Brad or had decided to ignore it. He unfastened the door of Gatsby's carrier and ran his hands along the cat's sides. Then he stood up and smiled at Eve. 'Hello, dear. I haven't seen you for ages.' They hugged tightly. Eve and Truman had always been fond of each other.

Eve smiled self-consciously and looked into Truman's eyes. 'I'm not going to say what I feel about Lori. You know without platitudes and tears and . . .' Eve wiped impatiently at her right eye, where a tear trembled and streamed downward. 'Damn!'

Truman almost grinned. 'That's my girl – my third daughter.'

'Except that she *isn't* your daughter,' Brad said sharply.

Truman gave him a surprised, angry look.

Brad softened. 'God, I'm sorry! I'm upset . . .'

'Yes, he is.' Olivia Fairbourne inserted herself between Brad and Truman, giving Truman's arm a quick, gentle stroke. Sunlight gleamed on her thick shoulder-length hair, which had turned completely silver when she was in her early forties. Kelsey remembered hearing women say she should color it, but Olivia had refused, clinging to the shade Kelsey's mother Sofie had called 'moonlight.' Now Olivia's green eyes looked opaque, unreadable. Her unlined porcelain skin seemed almost translucent. Kelsey detected a light sweep of pale pink blush on her cheeks, mascara on her curled lashes and sheer pink lipstick, barely enough to give her color. She'd brushed her hair behind her ears, and she wore tailored black silk slacks and a long-sleeved white crêpe-de-chine blouse. She looked elegant and closer to forty-five than to her fifty-five years.

'Kelsey, I have no words to tell you how sorry I am. I've known Lori since she was a toddler. I just can't imagine . . .' Olivia's voice caught, '. . . life without her.' She laid her hand on Truman's arm again and looked tragically at Kelsey. 'Dear, I'm so glad you're home with us.'

Kelsey couldn't believe what she'd just heard: *home with us*. Olivia sounded as if this house belonged to her and Truman. The *nerve* of her, Kelsey thought. Olivia is welcoming me to my own home. Then Lori's words echoed in her mind: '*I think Olivia already considers herself part of our family.*'

Kelsey realized she was staring and forced herself to speak. 'I would have come home last night if they hadn't made me stay in hospital.' She realized her words sounded hollow. She hadn't seen Olivia since she'd broken off her relationship with Brad. Had her tone been so wooden before then? Would it sound as insincere now if Lori hadn't vented her suspicion of Olivia's determination to marry Truman? The thoughts ran through Kelsey's mind while Olivia reached out to hug her. Kelsey stiffened. Olivia gave her a slightly wounded look, then let out a tiny squeal as Gatsby rubbed against the leg of her black silk pants.

'That *cat*!'

Gatsby turned and brushed in the opposite direction. Kelsey knew he didn't like Olivia. Usually he never went near her. Kelsey could almost hear Lori laughing in the background as

Olivia began gently pushing Gatsby away from her. Every time she moved him two inches, he returned. Olivia's smile froze. Finally, Truman picked up Gatsby, looked into the cat's green eyes and asked, 'Have you gained ten pounds?'

'Four.' Kelsey took Gatsby from her father and walked past Olivia without a glance. 'He weighs nineteen pounds when he should weigh fifteen. Right now, he's in a bad mood because he's hungry. I'll put out some food for him in the kitchen.'

Everyone followed Kelsey into the kitchen, where the house-keeper, Helen Norris, stood holding a dishtowel as she gazed absently out a window over the sink. Her sturdy five-foot-two body had always contrasted sharply with Sofie's tall, slender frame. She turned when Kelsey said her name. Her brown eyes were surrounded by puffy, reddened skin, and her wavy, silver-streaked brown hair had been pulled back carelessly in a French twist. Kelsey lowered Gatsby to the floor, and Helen walked to her, hands outstretched. They hugged, Helen's body trembling slightly. 'Our girl,' she quavered. 'Oh, Kelsey, our girl.'

Helen, fifty and never married, had been with the family since Lori's birth. Although her formal title was housekeeper, the Marches thought of Helen as a member of the family. She lived in a small suite off the kitchen, took part in all March family celebrations and was welcome to have family and friends visit as if this were her own house.

'I know, Helen. There's nothing to say,' Kelsey murmured.

'There should be. Lori always had something to say.'

'Lori always had something to say all right. Not always the right thing to say, but something!'

'She was honest. She said exactly what she thought.' Helen glanced at the others standing behind Kelsey. 'I'll fix coffee.'

'I think we need some pastries, too,' Olivia said with authority. 'I don't believe Truman has eaten all morning.'

He probably wasn't even awake yet when you arrived, Brad in tow, Kelsey thought sourly. She couldn't come up with one pleasant thing to say. She busied herself finding the cat food she kept here and then fixing Gatsby an extra-large portion and a small bowl of milk, which the vet said he shouldn't have, especially on his diet. But Gatsby needed comfort food, Kelsey decided. Next to Kelsey, he'd loved Lorelei the most.

A few minutes later, everyone ambled from the kitchen into the adjoining room, which her mother had called the sun room. Olivia hovered around Truman, obviously planning on sitting next to him, and Kelsey was glad to see him settle into the rattan rocking chair. Defeated, Olivia perched at the end of the couch, as close to Truman's chair as she could get, and Brad sat next to her. Kelsey and Eve sat down on the love seat. Sunlight streaming through the arched windows brought out the rich cream, butter yellow and paprika colors of the decor. Even the plants looked fuller and greener than Kelsey had ever seen them. It seemed as if death could not touch this vibrant room. Yet while Olivia tried to brush Gatsby's fur from her black pants, making a weak joke that didn't cover her annoyance, Kelsey's gaze fell on an eight-by-ten framed picture of her mother, smiling, her arms wrapped around a grinning eight-year-old Kelsey and two-year-old Lorelei. They all looked so happy, so young, so invincible. And two of them were already gone.

Truman glanced out the window to his left. 'It's a beautiful day, isn't it?'

'Yes, beautiful,' the women agreed. Kelsey caught a glimpse of tears in Eve's eyes.

Olivia smiled. 'I think it's supposed to be around seventy-four degrees today. Or maybe seventy-six. I'm so bad at keeping track of the weather. Brad is much better.' She glanced brightly at her son. 'Bradley?'

Brad was running a hand over his short light brown hair. His perfect features were blank. 'What?'

'The temperature today.'

'What about it?'

'He's too distressed to notice the weather,' Olivia explained to all of them, as if he was a bashful child. Brad's cheeks turned dull red. He opened his mouth to say something, but stopped when Helen arrived carrying a tray laden with a white ceramic coffee set and a plate of pastries. Her hands shook slightly as she placed the tray on the glass-topped coffee table.

'I'll pour,' Olivia announced, leaning forward then frowning. 'Helen, you brought mugs instead of cups.'

'I like mugs,' Truman said.

'So do I,' Kelsey and Eve chimed in at once. Olivia sighed

impatiently, poured coffee into a mug, added sugar, and gave it
to Truman, silently telling everyone she knew how he took his
coffee. She filled two mugs and handed them to Kelsey and Eve,
not asking how they took theirs. She gave Brad and Truman
pastries without offering any to Kelsey and Eve.

The grandfather clock in the hall chimed twelve times. Kelsey's
tranquilizer was beginning to wane – her heartbeat was speeding
up, she wanted to cry, her head hurt, her hands had turned icy,
and Olivia was acting as if she was the hostess at a tea party.

Olivia took two dainty sips of her coffee before she began.
'We have to get down to unpleasant details, Truman. I know your
family has always used the Ferris Funeral Home. It's all right,
but I think the Vaughan Home is nicer. I used them when Milton
died.' She finally looked at Eve. 'Milton was my husband.'

'I know,' Eve said politely.

'Of course you would. I'm sure Kelsey told you. Hundreds of
people came to my husband's funeral. The Fairbournes are a very
prominent family.' Olivia turned her attention back to Truman.
'I hate to be indelicate, but are they going to release dear Lorelei's
body immediately or hold it a couple of days to do, well . . . all
those *things* they do to the bodies of murdered people?' She
closed her eyes and shuddered.

The remains of the pleasant haze created by the tranquilizer
vanished, and Kelsey felt as if a firecracker had gone off behind
her eyes. Anger rushed through her. Without having the least
intention of speaking, she burst out, 'Before we talk about funeral
homes, Olivia, I'd like to have some questions answered. Brad,
when did you find out what happened to Lori? *How* did you find
out? Why are you and your mother at our house so early? For
God's sake, you made it here before I did!'

Brad had been silent as he stared blindly out a window, but
Kelsey had startled him back to life. She'd startled everyone,
although Brad was the only one whose eyes focused on her with
steely defiance as the muscles in his handsome face went rigid.
She saw his right hand clench into a fist. Then he slowly exhaled,
relaxed his hand and began talking softly and carefully through
nearly clenched teeth. 'At the hospital last night Truman called
his lawyer. John Reid's out of town, but his wife Elaine was
home. I wasn't feeling great yesterday and I stayed in all evening

and watched TV. *Jimmy Kimmel* was on when Elaine called.' Brad's voice was so tight Kelsey pictured his vocal cords fraying. 'She knows how close our families are and she had my home number. She said Truman needed me.'

'Why would he need *you*?'

'Kelsey, dear, we'll excuse your tone because you're so upset, but certainly you understand that there had been a crime—'

'I can speak for myself,' Brad snarled at Olivia, who flinched and turned her attention to her coffee. Brad shot Kelsey a withering look. 'You don't understand these things, Kelsey. Your father does. That's why he called his lawyer.'

'I called John because he's my closest friend, *and* because I wanted my lawyer—'

'Of course you did, Truman,' Olivia stated. 'Brad was an excellent substitute for John on both counts.'

Truman drew himself up in his chair and seemed to shake off his lethargy. 'Olivia, please stop interrupting.' He looked at the others. 'I wanted John to find out all he could about the case. I wasn't in any condition to do so myself.'

Olivia's pale skin flamed and her chin trembled.

Truman took a deep breath. 'Our emotions are getting out of control because we're all in a state of shock and hurt and tired. There's plenty of time for Kelsey and me to decide on the funeral arrangements, Olivia. *We* are Lorelei's family.' He stood up, looking strong and capable of handling any catastrophe. Kelsey had never loved her father more than at that moment. 'Olivia, Brad, thank you so much for all you've done. I truly appreciate it. I'm afraid I'll be asking even more of you in the next few days, which is why I think it's best if you both go home and relax. I have Kelsey and Helen and Eve here to watch over me now, and Stuart is coming soon. We'll be fine.'

'Stuart Girard! You're counting on *him*?' Olivia looked shocked. 'Milton told me Stuart's father was strange – maybe violent – and his business wasn't aboveboard. He had Mafia connections!'

'Olivia, you're slandering the man,' Truman said firmly.

'I don't think so! *Milton* didn't think so. I don't know why you won't let Brad help you.' Olivia swallowed hard. 'Stuart is polite but he's not friendly. In fact, I think he acts guarded – even a little sly. You've known Brad since he was a boy. You don't know anything about that Stuart person.'

'I've known Stuart all his life, Olivia.' Truman motioned toward the doorway. 'Now, please . . .'

'Well!' Olivia huffed and stood up. 'We're only trying to help, Truman.'

'I know – and I thank you, Olivia, Brad.'

As Truman herded a protesting Olivia and a silent Bradley toward the entrance, Brad flung a look over his shoulder at Kelsey. There was no sympathy and no sorrow in his gaze – only anger and calculation. *Calculation*, Kelsey thought. Is he wondering what effect Lori's death is going to have on our relationship? Or more likely on his mother's potential relationship with Dad. Lori was Olivia's staunchest enemy. And now she doesn't stand in Olivia's way. Will that make a difference? Kelsey listened to Olivia's suddenly syrupy and sympathetic voice coming from the entrance hall. It didn't sound at all like her. She's always been an actress, Kelsey thought. I got so used to her that I never paid any attention. But who knows how she feels? What she wants and how far she'll go to get it? Suddenly Kelsey realized she was as opposed to a marriage between her father and Olivia as Lori had been on the last night of her life. She'd always known Olivia wasn't entirely sincere, but had never realized how deceitful she was until this moment when she was using Lorelei's death to worm even farther into Truman March's life.

Nearly an hour later in her airy bedroom, Kelsey began to unpack. She straightened a pair of jeans and said to Eve, 'I'm sorry Olivia said Stuart seems sly.'

Eve laughed. 'I thought it was hilarious. If any one of us seems sly, it's Brad.'

'That's true. I'm glad that even though Stuart won't be taking you home, he'll be staying here with Dad for a while. Dad needs a distraction other than me.'

'You know Stuart thinks the world of your father.'

Kelsey grinned. '*And* of you. In three months, you'll be engaged. Maybe sooner.'

'Not unless he gives me a four-carat engagement ring.'

Kelsey tried to look appalled. 'Hold on there, girl! MG Interiors isn't making millions.'

'It will be soon.' Eve sat down on the bed and took out a light blue sleep shirt from Kelsey's suitcase. She absently shook it, folded it, shook it again, and began refolding it.

'Eve, what's wrong?'

'Well, I need to ask you something about last night . . .'

Kelsey went still. 'Just ask.'

'What time was the shooting?'

The memory shot a spear of pain through Kelsey, making her gasp.

'I'm sorry,' Eve said anxiously. 'I shouldn't have said anything.'

'I know you'll have a good reason.' Kelsey closed her eyes for a moment. 'I've thought about this all morning so I could give the police an accurate timeline. I glanced at my watch when Rick came up to Lori and me close to the door and asked if he could call us a taxi. It was 10:55. I remember because I was surprised it was so late. I talked to Rick for a couple of minutes before we left. We'd walked part of a block when . . .'

Kelsey swallowed. 'Lori was shot slightly before or after eleven. Why?'

'Last night Stuart and I saw a movie and then went to The Silver Dollar on Frankfort Avenue. We like the food and the music there. What I'm trying to tell you is that we left the bar around ten. Today Brad said he'd felt bad last night and stayed in all evening.' Eve looked troubled. 'On our way out, Stuart and I saw Brad in The Silver Dollar. He was with a young woman. She was tall and very slender with thick black hair that nearly reached her waist. She looked about eighteen or nineteen. They were both drinking. The last I heard, the legal drinking age in Kentucky is twenty-one. She must have had fake ID. She'd obviously passed her limit – she was loud and laughing a lot. Brad was trying to get her to leave, so we hurried up to avoid another scene with him.'

Kelsey blinked in surprise. 'You're sure you saw Brad with a teenager?'

'She looked like a teenager. Maybe she was older, but I really don't think so. I don't want to stir up trouble, but Brad lied to all of us today. He claimed he'd stayed in his apartment all

evening. He didn't.' Eve paused. 'Kelsey, even if she's a teenager, why would Brad want so desperately to cover up being
with this girl that he'd lie about his whereabouts at the time of
a murder?'

Later in the afternoon, after Stuart had arrived, while he and Eve
were in the barn visiting the three horses Eve loved, Kelsey sat
on the terrace, watching the bluebirds dart through the clear,
warm air, the sun shining on the brilliant blue backs of the males
and the grayer backs of the females. Two of the birds flew to
one of the many cypress birdhouses with blue shingled roofs
sitting on poles surrounded by the rich green lawn. Kelsey's
mother, Sofie, had loved bluebirds and Truman had promised to
give her a backyard full of them. Now twenty birdhouses on
straight white poles towered over colorful flowerbeds that Sofie
had tended herself.

Kelsey watched the birds absently, feeling empty of anything
except a deep, ceaseless regret. 'I miss you,' she murmured,
sipping iced tea and thinking that her mother and sister would
never again sit on this terrace with her and her father. The only
other thing she could think about was Brad's lie.

He'd made a point of saying he hadn't felt well yesterday and
had spent the evening at home. But Eve said she and Stuart had
seen him in The Silver Dollar with a very young woman. Was
he seeing someone he wanted to keep hidden from his mother
and his few friends, and from the partners of Reid, Alpern &
Patel law firm? Was that worth the lie?

'Kelsey?' She turned to see Helen hovering just outside the
door. 'There's a policeman named Detective Pike here. He says
he needs to talk to you and your father.'

'Oh, hell!' Kelsey mumbled. Then, 'Send him out, Helen.'

'I'm already here, Miss March. I followed her.'

'Were you afraid I'd make a run for it, Detective Pike?'

'Why, no, Miss March, but the world is full of surprises,' he
said in his beautiful voice. 'Better safe than sorry.'

'Then you might as well come out and ask your questions.
Helen, Dad's taking a nap. Will you wake him?' Helen gave
Pike a look that said Truman March should not be awakened
from a nap for the likes of *him*. 'Dad will want to talk to Detective

Pike, Helen.' Kelsey tried to sound pleasant. 'Detective, would you care for some iced tea?'

'Uh, that would be very nice.' Pike sounded surprised as he stood thin and rumpled behind Helen.

'Come out and sit down, Detective.' Kelsey motioned to one of the cushioned lawn chairs. 'Helen, will you bring out some more glasses with the pitcher of tea? I'm sure Dad will want some, too.'

Detective Pike approached slowly, almost as if he was wary of her courteous reception. He sat down and wiped sweat from his upper lip.

'I lived in Bangor, Maine, all of my life until I moved here in November. I've been told it's unusually warm and humid for this time of year, and the car air conditioner has stopped working.' He glanced with contempt at his wilted white shirt. 'I look like I've been in a sauna.'

Kelsey giggled and he cocked his head at her, his black eyes startled. 'I'm sorry,' she said. 'You're so formal, I didn't expect you to make a joke.'

'Am I formal?' He sounded surprised but she knew he wasn't. He gazed at the lawn spreading in front of them. 'Excellent grass. It looks like a green carpet. And splendid flowerbeds.' He paused then said softly, 'My wife loved flowers. She had a gift for growing them.'

Loved. Had. Kelsey wondered if he was divorced or widowed. He wore a wedding ring. Widowed, she thought, and probably not for long.

Helen returned with a tray, on it a pitcher of iced tea and tall glasses along with sugar and some slices of lemon and sprigs of mint. Kelsey thanked her and poured a glass. 'Sugar, lemon, mint, Detective?'

'Everything, please.'

While Kelsey poured tea over ice cubes in a frosted glass, Pike said, 'The press is already descending on this house. Of course news about the incident is all over the television and the internet.'

'Dad's hired private security. They should be here soon.'

'Hello. Got a tall glass of tea for an old man?' Truman asked. Neither Kelsey nor Detective Pike had seen her father come out. He wore khaki pants and a pale green polo shirt. He sat down heavily, running a hand through his brown hair laced with silver.

'We have lots of tea and you're not an old man,' Kelsey said.

'I feel at least a century old.' Truman tried and failed to smile jauntily at Kelsey. He looked at Pike. 'Well, Detective, I hear you have more questions for us.'

'Some. I hate to be a nuisance but there's no avoiding it.' Pike opened a notebook and clicked a ballpoint pen. 'I need to ask you again about Vernon Nott. You meet a lot of people. Are you sure you've never heard the name Vernon Nott?'

Truman shook his head. 'I wracked my brain last night. If I've heard the name, I don't remember it. It's a fairly ordinary name, though.'

'About your business . . .' Pike said. 'What exactly does March Vaden Industries do?'

'I'm sure the police know that already, but I'll play along,' Truman said dryly. 'We design and manufacture parts for aerospace companies.'

'Was Vernon Nott ever an employee?'

'Possibly. We have three subsidiary companies and thousands of employees.'

'I meant here in Louisville, sir.'

Truman took a sip of iced tea and gave Pike a hard look. 'I'm having our computer records checked as we speak, and you'll have the information by five o'clock. But you didn't come here to ask me if Nott was an employee—'

'Thank you.' Pike turned to Kelsey. 'Miss March . . .'

Kelsey lifted her shoulders. 'I don't remember a Vernon Nott as an employee or customer of Durand Designs, where I used to work. I know he's never been a customer of MG Interiors. I don't have access to Durand Designs' records, but I can give you the records of MG Interiors.'

'Excellent. I hope Durand Designs will be cooperative.'

'I'm sure they will be. I left there on good terms, Detective Pike, even though I took Stuart Girard with me.'

He smiled slightly, never looking up from his notes. A drop of sweat rolled down his narrow, high-bridged nose and plopped loudly on his notebook. Kelsey noticed his high cheekbones redden and handed him a napkin. 'I'm sorry we can't help you more.'

'I'm tired of you asking endless questions about his name.' Truman's voice suddenly sounded old and strained. Kelsey could tell he had one of his migraine headaches. 'Let's get on with what you really want to know. You didn't drive all the way out here to keep asking us if we knew this bastard. Tell us about him.'

'He worked at Boward Construction for six months and never missed a day of work until Monday, when he called in sick.'

'Lorelei came home last Tuesday,' Kelsey said. 'If he knew by Wednesday she was here but didn't miss work during the week, could he have been following her over the weekend?' She turned to Truman. 'Dad, where did you and Lori go on Saturday?'

'Nowhere. She wanted to go riding with me, but some of her friends decided to stop by and then stayed for dinner.' Truman sounded annoyed. 'She was exhausted Saturday night. Sunday you came to lunch. You remember – she said she didn't have an appetite because she was getting a cold. It was an excuse not to eat. She didn't want to gain a pound.'

'Did she act frightened?' Pike asked quickly. 'Maybe she had no appetite because she was afraid.'

'Of a stalker?' Truman frowned. Then he shook his head. 'She acted nervous, restless, but not frightened. At least she didn't hang on to her smartphone constantly like she did during her last visit.' He looked at Kelsey. 'She went home with you Sunday evening. Did she act scared?'

'No . . .' Kelsey said slowly. 'Distracted, maybe.' Because Lori's mind was on Cole Harrington, Kelsey thought, now remembering the name of Lori's married love interest. Kelsey realized her father and Pike were looking at her expectantly. 'I think she was concerned about looking good for the African shoot. She wasn't eating. She had some popcorn Sunday evening and a salad for lunch on Monday.'

'African shoot?' Pike asked.

Kelsey nodded. 'A fashion layout for *Vogue*. She was really excited about it. She was going back to New York on Monday and leaving for Kenya on Tuesday.' She paused and gazed at Pike despondently. 'So because she wasn't using her electronic equipment here and this place is somewhat isolated, Lori was safe with Dad. It wasn't until she came to the city with me on Sunday evening that she was in jeopardy.'

'It's not your fault, Miss March,' Pike said. 'Unless she stayed inside this house for her entire visit and didn't use her phone or social media, she wasn't safe from Nott anywhere.' He paused. 'When we searched Nott's home, we found a picture of him.' Pike pulled a three-by-five photo from the back of his notebook and handed it to Kelsey.

Vernon Nott stared back at her with mournful dark eyes set in a bleak narrow face with high, sharp cheekbones, hollow cheeks and a long chin. He had deep creases in his forehead and thin, dark hair streaked with gray. A round scar obliterated the end of his right eyebrow, and three more trailed down his cheek. Kelsey closed her eyes for a moment then said, 'He was alone in Conway's.' She sighed and opened her eyes. 'I remember thinking he looked so lonely that I . . .' Her throat tightened. 'I felt sorry for him. He murdered my sister and I'd felt *sorry* for him!'

'At the time, you didn't know anything about him, Miss March,' Pike said quickly. 'Don't berate yourself.'

Kelsey turned over the photo. Someone had written on the back:

Here's my favorite guy. J. J. N.

'Do you have any idea who J. J. N. is?' Kelsey asked as she handed the photo to Truman.

'No. It might be someone whose last name is Nott. We've checked for Nott's brothers and sisters, of course, and it seems that he only had one brother, named Boyd Earl Nott, who was three years older than Vernon. But Boyd is dead, as are Nott's parents, so we can't question them.'

Truman's jaw tightened as he stared at the picture. 'Nothing about him is familiar to me.' He glared at Pike. 'Detective, you have a point but you're damned well taking your time getting to it.'

'I'm sorry, Mr March. I have more information about Nott. There's a Kentucky arrest record of second-degree assault on a woman. He and his girlfriend had an argument, it turned physical, and he shot her in the leg. He was sentenced to five years in prison. He was released after three years for good behavior and has been free for almost a year. He hasn't been in any trouble since then and has been seeing his parole officer regularly.'

'He shot his girlfriend?'

'He claimed it was an accident, Miss March, but she said it was deliberate. Most people believed her because it wasn't his first brush with violence. When he was twenty-three, he was charged with assault for hitting a girl in the face. The blow broke her nose and knocked out a tooth. There was a witness. Nott spent one year in prison and was fined.'

'So he had a history of violence toward women,' Truman said grimly.

'Yes. When he was a sixteen, he supposedly slashed a girl's arm with a knife.'

Truman raised an eyebrow. 'Supposedly?'

'She didn't have a reputation for telling the truth and the alleged slashing left a cut that took only three stitches to close. She filed charges but later dropped them.'

Kelsey shook her head. 'A fine citizen just walking around free with the rest of us.' She paused. 'You'd think some of that violence would have shown, but Rick said Nott seemed quiet, shy.'

Pike nodded. 'Quiet. Shy,' he repeated. 'Sometimes people like Nott can fool you. Clearly he fooled Conway because he continued to let Nott come to the bar.'

'Are you sure Conway was fooled?' Truman asked acidly. 'After all, unless I'm wrong, you didn't meet Conway until last night. You don't know anything about him. Maybe he was more interested in the man's continued business than his background.'

Kelsey winced. She knew her father was not only suffering physically but even more emotionally, or he would never have been so scornful of someone he'd never met. Someone who had saved her life. Pike accepted it calmly. 'You're right, Mr March, I don't know Richard Conway personally but we've done a preliminary background check. He has no arrest record and excellent references from former employers. Also, I believe anyone who has just started a new bar is especially careful about his clientele. It seems to me he wouldn't want the business to suffer because of one customer and he'd want to maintain the good reputation of Conway's.' Pike paused, then delivered a verbal slap. 'And because he was keeping an eye on your daughters, he saved Kelsey's life.'

Truman went pale. He lowered his eyes and Kelsey could feel him searching for something to say, something near to an apology, but remembering that Rick Conway had tried to save both her and Lorelei overwhelmed him. She saw a tear run down his face.

'I don't understand why Nott came to Conway's twice a week,' Kelsey said, drawing Pike's attention away from Truman. 'Why Conway's Tavern when there are other bars closer to where he lives? He had Lorelei's picture with him. If he was obsessed with her, did he know that I was her sister, lived two blocks away, and came to Conway's fairly often? Was he expecting me to show up with Lori at any time?'

Pike took a drink of his iced tea and leaned forward, his sleek black brows drawing together. 'That's an excellent question, Miss March. It's one that's been bothering me. I don't know why he was drawn to Conway's. As for him tracking your sister . . . well, he had no computer equipment in his mobile home. We found no family pictures, either framed or in an album. We did find the picture of Nott I just showed you. That's all. Stalkers usually have at least a few photos of their prey even if, as in Lorelei's case, the photos are from magazines. He didn't have even one magazine shot of her. There was nothing to indicate that he was fixated on Lorelei or following her.'

'But he was in Conway's,' Kelsey said faintly. 'You said it wasn't one of his usual nights. He *was* following us.'

'So it would seem.' Pike frowned. 'You said you didn't tell anyone you were taking Lorelei to Conway's last night.'

'I didn't. I knew we were going shopping and I thought we'd be too tired, but Lorelei wanted to go out again.'

'Did you tell anyone you planned to take Lorelei to Conway's at some time during her visit to you?'

'I told Eve and Stuart. I thought they might like to come with us. But I didn't say we were going last night. I didn't know myself until about half an hour before Lori and I left my apartment.'

'Do you remember if you told anyone at Conway's you'd be bringing in your sister this week?'

'No. I'm sure I didn't.'

'So Nott needed to know *your* habits, for instance that you frequent Conway's.' Pike leaned forward. 'Are you certain you've never see him someplace aside from the bar?'

'If I have, I don't remember.' Kelsey paused, puzzled. 'Why do you keep asking me the same question? I've told you I've only seen him in Conway's.'

'And you may be right.'

'*May* be?' Kelsey drew a deep breath. 'Detective Pike, could you please stop circling around the subject and tell me what the hell you are getting at?'

'Your sister is the most obvious target for Nott's attention, but we don't want to jump to conclusions.' Pike put away Nott's photo. 'I came here today because I wanted to show you something, but first I should tell you what we've found out about Nott's finances. He made four hundred and twenty dollars a week, less than twenty-two thousand a year at Boward Construction.

'This is what's interesting,' Pike went on, consulting his notebook. 'On Thursday, he had a little over twelve hundred dollars in his checking account. He didn't have a savings account. On Friday, he deposited two thousand dollars in cash in the checking account. Saturday evening, he spent five hundred and eighty dollars in cash at Walmart, three hundred and nineteen dollars of which was for an HD television on sale.' Pike glanced up and smiled slightly. 'A retired couple live in the mobile home next to Nott, and the husband helped him carry in the television and set it up. The man said Nott was unusually talkative, almost jubilant about his television.' He cleared his throat and looked back at his notes. 'In Nott's pocket we found a receipt for forty-one dollars in cash from a local Stop & Shop. After the shooting, police found ninety-four dollars in his wallet. We searched his mobile home today and found twenty-two hundred dollars tucked into an empty coffee can. His boss said he wouldn't have been paid until the end of this week.'

Pike looked at them. 'Nott seems to have had a cash windfall. We're tracing the bills to see if they came from a robbery. I don't think we'll have any luck.'

'Was he making money doing part-time jobs?' Truman asked.

'That's doubtful. Nosy neighbors, God bless them, are often better than a professional surveillance team. The couple who live next to him said that in the six months since he moved in his hours didn't change. On weekdays he left at seven thirty in the morning and returned at six in the evening, except for two nights a week when he got in around ten o'clock. We know those were the nights he went to Conway's.' Pike allowed himself a slight grin. 'The wife says that sometimes he went out around eight o'clock on Saturday nights wearing khaki pants instead of jeans. She thinks he had a girlfriend, although he never spent the night away.'

'How would she know Nott never stayed out all night?' Truman asked. 'Did she sit up and wait for him to come home?'

'I wouldn't be surprised. She seems to have kept close tabs on him. Nott's boss says that yesterday he called in sick for the first time in the six months he'd been employed at Boward Construction. The neighbors said Nott left around ten in the morning and didn't return all day. We're trying to track his movements, but so far we haven't turned up one person who remembers seeing him until he walked into Conway's yesterday evening.'

'Where do you think he got the money?' Truman asked.

Pike paused then said slowly, 'I told you he had a photo of Lorelei. I wasn't completely forthcoming. It was a photograph of Lorelei *and* Kelsey walking by the storefront next to MG Interiors. As I've said before, it's in Evidence so I couldn't bring it to show you. I can only describe it. The photo was taken from about forty feet behind them and most likely by someone who'd been waiting in the alley separating MG Interiors and the florist shop. Lorelei and Kelsey were just past the boutique. Even though their backs are toward the camera, their faces are turned toward each other and the wind is blowing back their hair. Lorelei is leaning down, her head close to Kelsey's. We can see the right side of her face and the left side of Kelsey's.'

Pike diverted his gaze to a bluebird swooping unusually near Kelsey then said slowly, 'There is an X drawn in black ink above the top of their heads.'

'An X?' Truman repeated blankly. 'On the photograph?'

'Yes, sir. The X is a *bit* closer to Lorelei's head but only slightly. Since the shooting, we assumed that Nott was stalking Lorelei. The X made us look at things differently. If he was stalking her, why would he put an X above her head? He'd certainly know what Lorelei looked like.'

'What the hell difference does an X make?' Truman demanded loudly, the way he did when he was alarmed. 'My daughter is dead and you're concentrating on the placement of an X! I don't think you know what the hell you're doing! You're wasting time—'

'If you'll just be patient, sir, I'll explain our theory—'

Truman leaned forward aggressively. 'Then let's hear about this theory!'

'Dad, just relax. *Please*, for *me*,' Kelsey said softly, like her mother used to do when Truman was getting upset.

Truman looked at her for a moment, then settled back in his chair and said grudgingly, 'Go ahead, Detective Pike.'

'We now wonder if the X was supposed to be above Kelsey's head.'

Kelsey and Truman stared at Pike. Finally, Kelsey asked, 'Why would the X be above *my* head?'

'Possibly Vernon Nott wasn't stalking Lorelei. Maybe he was stalking *you*, Miss March, and he wasn't as familiar with your appearance as your sister's. After all, she was quite a bit taller than you and her hair was much longer. First, why would Vernon Nott need a photograph of Lorelei when she's on the cover of so many magazines? Second, the photo was taken with an instant film camera but we didn't find a camera of any kind in Nott's mobile home. And last, Nott had the photo in his pocket as if he might need quick verification that he was seeing the right woman.'

'The right woman?' Truman asked. 'I still don't get it—'

'Maybe there was nothing *personal* about Lorelei's murder, Mr March. Maybe Vernon Nott had no interest in Lorelei as a woman. She could simply have been a target, and Nott's new wealth was payment for doing a job.'

'Payment for a job?' Kelsey asked faintly. 'What job?'

Pike looked at her solemnly. 'Killing your sister, Miss March. Or killing *you*.'

FIVE

'Grandfather!' Kelsey jumped up from the couch and ran toward the tall, brawny, silver-haired man who'd silently entered the living room. She flung herself into his arms as they closed around her. 'Oh, Grandfather, I'm so glad you're here.' She pressed her head against his wide chest and heard his heart beating hard and fast and a slight crackling sound in his lungs. 'Are you sick?'

'Sick?' He drew away from Kelsey, his thick white eyebrows drawing together in his strong-featured face. 'Do I look sick?'

'You sound sick. Your lungs—'

'It's just a chest cold, *vacker ängel*.' Beautiful angel. Pieter had always called both of his granddaughters beautiful angel. 'Maybe you shouldn't kiss me.'

'I couldn't stand not kissing you.' Tears filled Kelsey's eyes as she pressed her lips to his cheek and caught a whiff of the fruity-smelling Swedish Fish candy he'd substituted for cigarettes twenty years ago. Kelsey had always told him the candy smelled like strawberries. Lorelei had insisted it was cherries. 'I've missed you.'

'I've only been gone two weeks.' Pieter held her tight, his Swedish accent stronger as always when he was upset. 'I should have come back as soon as Lorelei came home but, fool that I am, I put work first. Just like I did with my daughter, just like I did with my wife.'

Truman draped his arm around Pieter's broad shoulders. 'You thought you'd have time with Lori most of this week. So did we—' Truman's voice broke.

Pieter hugged his son-in-law and closest friend. 'If you break down, Truman, we all will. Don't be selfish.'

Truman pulled back and smiled weakly at Pieter. 'Yes, sir.'

'Ah!' Pieter suddenly jumped, then looked down as Gatsby flung himself ecstatically against Pieter's leg. 'My friend! I almost forgot about you!' Pieter bent and picked up the large

strawberry-blonde cat. Something long and gold glittered from
the cat's mouth. Pieter gently pulled it out and held up a heart
pendant on a chain. 'What's this?'

'A necklace,' Kelsey said, taking it from him.

'Yours?' Truman asked.

'No.'

Helen had slipped into the room and stood by, frowning. 'He
was in Lorelei's room a few minutes ago. I left him alone because
he was just sniffing around.'

Pieter looked at Gatsby. 'Where did you find that pretty
necklace, boy?'

'Lorelei never left jewelry lying on the dressers,' Helen said.
'She packed to go to Kelsey's in a hurry and didn't get one of
her suitcases completely closed. When she picked it up, everything
spilled right beside the bed. Maybe the necklace fell out and she
didn't see it.'

Kelsey straightened the fine twisted rope chain and opened
the floral-patterned gold heart locket. A set of initials was
engraved on the left side: CGH. Cole Grant Harrington, she
thought immediately. The other side was empty, clearly awaiting
a small picture of the man Lorelei loved.

'Does it say anything?' Truman asked.

'No.' Kelsey closed her hand around the locket. 'But she loved
hearts, and it's pretty.'

She and Helen exchanged a look. Helen knows I'm lying,
Kelsey thought. She always knew when Lorelei and I weren't
telling the truth. But Helen wouldn't press for an answer. Among
her many admirable character traits was discretion.

Gatsby began purring and rubbing his chin against Pieter's
jaw. Pieter put his finger under the cat's jaw, raised its head, and
looked into its eyes. 'You're here with your sweet mistress but
unfortunately not all of your family. Not all of our beautiful lost
loves are with us tonight and that makes us sad, doesn't it, boy?
I can see the sadness deep in your eyes.'

'Come and sit down, Pieter.' Truman was trying to sound
normal, but Kelsey heard the wariness in her father's voice.
Pieter hadn't been well for several months and at times the
people around him seemed to be fading away. Now he stared
fixedly into Gatsby's green eyes, as if by searching their depths

he could find his wife, his daughter, and now his youngest granddaughter.

Gatsby remained admirably still as Pieter held him high and gazed into his eyes, but finally the cat's hind legs began to twitch. 'He's gotten heavy, Grandfather,' Kelsey said, reaching for the cat. 'His vet has put him on a diet.'

'Oh, phooey on vets.' Pieter dismissed them all with a toss of his head. 'I've never credited one of them with any sense at all. That's why I don't waste my time with them.'

Kelsey raised her arms and closed her hands around Gatsby's body. 'Well, cats and dogs have to get shots once a year to guard against rabies and a lot of other illnesses. He has an appointment week after next to get his shots, and he hasn't lost his four pounds as ordered.'

'And where would he get rabies? He doesn't stalk through the wilderness. They always predict the worst, these vets.'

Kelsey was beginning to think Pieter wasn't going to put Gatsby down when suddenly his hands fell to his sides. If she hadn't been clasping the cat tightly, he would have dropped to the floor. Pieter looked at her warmly. 'He's your cat, dear heart. You must do what you think is best for him.'

Kelsey smiled at her grandfather and stroked Gatsby a few times before turning him loose. He headed straight for the kitchen. Looking for privacy and food, Kelsey thought. Meanwhile, Pieter seemed to slowly focus on all of them again.

'You look tired, Pieter. Bad flight?' Truman asked.

'They're all bad. I hate flying. And I *am* tired.' Pieter always complained, although he stubbornly refused to fly first class where the accommodation was more pleasant. He sat down on the couch with a groan. 'The flight was delayed by an hour. Then I was seated next to a woman who sounded like she was coughing up her lungs, and the child across the aisle stared at me the entire flight. I don't think he ever blinked. Not once. He didn't seem human,' Pieter said querulously and glanced at his watch. 'It's almost nine-thirty. I feel like I've been on that plane all day.' He gave Helen a forced smile. 'Hello, Helen, dear. I didn't even greet you.'

'Hello, Mr Vaden. I'm glad you're here in spite of the alien child.'

Pieter burst out with a ragged laugh: 'I'll tell you what would do me a world of good. I smell the delicious coffee only you can make. Could you spare me a cup with a healthy splash of bourbon?'

'Certainly, Mr Vaden.' Helen smiled.

As she left the room, Pieter said, 'She's known me for over twenty years and she still calls me Mr Vaden, although I've said over and over "It's Pieter."' He shook his head. 'Maybe I remind her of her grandfather. I feel old enough to be her great-great-grandfather.'

'Well, you don't look it.' Kelsey had dropped the necklace into her pocket. She sat down beside Pieter on the couch and hugged him again, hearing his rapid, shallow breath. 'You must be exhausted.'

'I shouldn't be. I'm used to travel.'

'I wish you would have let us pick you up at the airport,' Truman said.

'When my car was in the airport parking lot? That would have been foolish.' Pieter suddenly seemed to see Eve lingering near the doorway. 'Hello, Eve. I'm sorry I overlooked you. I must be more tired than I think.' He cocked his large head with its thick silver hair. 'You look quite lovely, dear.'

Kelsey smiled. Although Pieter was clearly devastated by the murder of his granddaughter, he still had something positive to say. 'Looking at the bright side is part of my husband's charm,' Kelsey's grandmother Ingrid had told her four years ago when she was frail and sick. 'It's one of the many things that made me fall in love with him.' She'd clasped Kelsey's hand. 'I hope you and Lorelei find men like him. I know *you* will.'

'Just me? Not Lorelei?'

'I don't know, darling. Sometimes I feel that your sister's life will be very different from yours.'

'Different how?'

Her grandmother's delicate body had tensed, then slowly relaxed. 'Oh, don't pay attention to me. I'm so often dreary these days.' She'd smiled. 'But I have Pieter. He makes me feel safe when I get lost in the dark.'

But he hadn't been able to save her from the dark three years ago, when she died of the cancer that had ravaged her. He hadn't been able to save his daughter from the aneurysm that killed her within minutes, less than two years ago. And he hadn't been able to save Lorelei. Would he be strong enough to save himself after this latest devastating loss? Would he ever again be able to make anyone feel safe when they were lost in the dark?

Kelsey didn't think so.

The morning of Lorelei's funeral the sun hung like a giant lemon ball in a cornflower blue sky. Any other time, Kelsey would have thought the day was unusually beautiful. Today, all she could think about was the helicopter flying in endless circles above the gravesite, its monotonous hum making her feel like screaming. Inside the copter's glass globe, photographers pointed their cameras downward, hoping to get 'money shots' for the tabloids. Kelsey held her father's right hand tightly, trying not to think about how only a year and a half had passed since she'd clasped that hand while Lorelei clutched his left and wept during their mother's funeral. Two days ago, Kelsey and her father had picked out a casket and arranged for a small, private ceremony in the funeral home chapel. When they'd gone to the cemetery after choosing the rose-granite marker that would be set at the foot of Lorelei's grave, beside her mother's, Truman had finally broken down and cried. Kelsey had held him while she looked at the large monument with the name MARCH carved beneath a beautifully sculpted bough of roses. She'd concentrated on the roses until her father stopped shuddering, although tears still rolled down his face. Five minutes later, they'd slowly walked to the car and driven home without a single word.

Now the young minister was delivering an earnest graveside speech about a woman he'd barely known. Kelsey shut out his words, concentrating on people who'd come to the cemetery after a short memorial service at the funeral home.

To her left, Pieter stood tall and motionless, his face like stone. He hadn't been to his own house since he returned from California. Last night, he'd asked Truman to invite Stuart to spend the night at the March home before the funeral. 'The damned press has converged. They're nearly blocking the front drive,' Pieter had fumed to his son-in-law. 'It'll be worse in the morning when we go to the chapel and on to the cemetery. Stuart and

Eve are both going to the funeral. If Stuart comes this evening, he'll miss tangling with all those loathsome photographers in the morning. He and Eve can ride to the cemetery with us in a limo.'

Kelsey had lingered, listening, when shortly after Pieter had gone upstairs Truman said to Stuart, 'Pieter's not well physically, and he's shattered emotionally.'

'I know,' Stuart had said quietly.

'He's spending the night here and he wants the people he cares about around him. I know staying with us the night after Lori's wake and being with us all morning before the funeral is an imposition, Stuart, but—'

'It's not an imposition. Pieter has been very good to me for years and I'd be happy to stay if wants me,' Stuart had said. Kelsey thought Stuart would probably have been more comfortable in his own apartment, but she'd known he would do as Pieter wished. Also, she was glad he'd be in the same house with Eve during the hectic, mournful hours surrounding the funeral.

But the hours before the funeral had been even more hectic than Kelsey could have imagined. The day after he'd returned to Kentucky, Pieter had risen in high spirits, come into the sun room where they were all gathered, and hugged Eve. 'Lorelei, you look so beautiful this morning!'

Everyone went still. Helen dropped a piece of silverware in the kitchen.

'It's Eve, Grandfather,' Kelsey had said softly.

He'd frowned at her. 'Eh? What about Eve?'

'You have your arm around Eve, Grandfather.'

Pieter had looked closely at Eve as if he wasn't certain Kelsey was telling the truth. Then he'd shaken his head and smiled at Eve. 'I'm sorry, my dear. I'm not my best before my morning coffee.'

Eve had returned his smile. 'It's all right. There's been so much fuss we're all mixed up.'

'I got a very good night's sleep,' Pieter announced. 'The plane ride from California nearly "wiped me out" as the young people say, or is that out of style now?' He'd glanced around. 'Where's Lorelei? Sleeping late on this beautiful morning?'

Kelsey and Eve had smiled weakly as Truman motioned for

them to leave the room. Kelsey knew her father wanted to remind Pieter that Lorelei was dead. Ten minutes later, Pieter walked through the living room looking weary and defeated. He went outside without speaking and they saw him plodding to the barn. He often visited the horses, feeding them carrots and reminding them of times they'd spent with members of the family. She wondered if he were telling stories now, or crying with only the beloved horses to hear. As much as she cared about the horses, Kelsey hadn't been able to bear seeing Guinevere, the adored horse Lori had ridden just last week.

After he left, Helen asked Truman and Kelsey if she could speak to them in her suite at the back of the house. 'Mr Vaden said he'd slept well last night but that's not true,' she said reluctantly. 'The night before last I was closing the drapes in my bedroom and I saw him wandering behind the house in his robe and a pair of rubber boots. I opened the window and called down to him. He came in almost immediately and went upstairs to his room. And last night I recognized Mr Vaden's voice outside. He was asking, "Ingrid, do you know what they're saying happened to Lorelei? I don't believe it. But they wouldn't say such a thing to hurt me. I must have dreamed it. Did I have a nightmare, Ingrid?"'

Helen twisted her hands. 'I went outside. Mr Vaden had passed the house and was heading toward the barn. I called "Mr Vaden" twice. He didn't seem to hear me. Then I called 'Pieter!' He turned around and frowned and squinted and then . . .' Her voice broke as she fought tears. 'He had on those same rubber boots – they're too big for him and I don't know where he found them. Anyway, he suddenly came to me in a stumbling run. He kept saying, "Ingrid! Ingrid!" When he reached me, he hugged me tightly and said, "Oh, darling, I was afraid you were dead." He pulled back and looked at me, beaming. He said, "Let's go ride the horses in the moonlight like we did when we were young. Oh, Ingrid, I don't know where you've been but I've missed you so much. Please don't ever leave me alone again."'

By then, tears were rolling slowly down Helen's face. 'I convinced him that we needed to drink some hot chocolate before we went riding. He came in and I fixed hot chocolate for both of us, only I put bourbon in his. I thought it would calm him and make him sleepy. While we sat at the table together drinking our chocolate, he still talked to me as if I was his wife. Suddenly he said, "The chocolate was *underbar*." I know that means wonderful. He stood up, kissed me on the cheek, and said something that sounded like "*Jag ālskar dig.*"'

Kelsey said, 'That's "I love you."'

Helen nodded. 'He left the kitchen. I followed him. He went to his room but didn't close his door like he usually does. He got into bed and murmured something else to Ingrid that I couldn't quite hear. I stayed outside his room until he fell asleep.' Helen looked at them in misery. 'I feel like I'm betraying him telling you all this and also making things worse for you at this terrible time, but I thought you should know.'

The morning of the funeral, Pieter seemed even more confused as he sat in the sun room, dressed in a plaid robe and one house slipper. Suddenly he stood and began a spectacular stream of cursing when he realized he was missing a shoe. 'I'll find it!' Eve started to dash from the room when Pieter boomed, 'Never mind, Eve.' He rubbed his hand across his forehead. '*Oh himmel!* I'm not behaving well. Look at me – I'm wearing my pajamas and robe in front of guests! And my language! Oh, well, I knew I wouldn't be much help to Truman and Kelsey. That's why I'm so glad you're here, Eve.'

She smiled and bobbed her head slightly.

Then Pieter looked at Stuart and frowned as if thinking. 'I'm sure I know you.'

'Of course you do,' Truman said. 'He's Stuart Girard.'

Pieter shook his head. 'His name isn't Stuart.'

'Maybe you're thinking of my grandfather, Charles,' Stuart said. 'People tell me I look like him.'

'I don't know your grandfather!' Pieter snapped indignantly before his eyes narrowed. 'Blakemore! That's your name. Mafia business. We exposed you. Truman and his father and I got you thrown in prison! What are you doing here?'

Kelsey saw the distress in her father's eyes. She knew that Stuart Girard's father had been involved in Teddy Blakemore's criminal activities and had barely escaped imprisonment himself. Still, Truman managed to say patiently, 'Pieter, Teddy Blakemore is in prison. This is Stuart Girard. You know him and you know he had nothing whatsoever to do with the Blakemore business. He was barely out of his teens when that happened.'

'I know what I know!' Pieter glared at Stuart. 'You're Blakemore!'

Stuart had gone rigid, his smile tight. Kelsey could tell he was deeply embarrassed. His voice sounded so taut it could snap. 'I'm afraid you have me mixed up with someone else, sir.'

'No, I don't! There's nothing wrong with my memory!'

Helen swooped in, set a mug of steaming coffee on the table in front of Pieter and handed him a plate of pastries. 'Look what I made just for you! They're so warm and fresh. Please eat one right now!'

'Pecan-pie bars!' Pieter beamed, Teddy Blakemore and Stuart Girard suddenly forgotten. He looked at Helen with love. 'You spoil me, Ingrid, even though I don't deserve it.'

Pieter's suspicion of Stuart seemed to vanish as he ate. And now, at the cemetery, Kelsey squeezed her grandfather's hand, wondering how much longer he'd be by her side in times of trouble. She could hear his wheezing, although she knew he was making an effort to suppress it. He looked down at her, his gaze sharp and clear with memory. At least he wasn't confused now, she thought. He didn't think she was his daughter Sofie or his wife, Ingrid, or his granddaughter Lorelei. He knew she was his first grandchild. They'd always winked at each other, saying it was their secret sign. He never winked at Lorelei – they had a different sign. Now Pieter winked at her in reassurance, silently telling her that she would always be his darling Kelsey.

Across from her stood Stuart, his short dark brown hair ruffling slightly in the breeze. He was going gray at the temples, Kelsey thought in surprise. He was only thirty-five. She'd looked at him as a partner in her business, not as a man, and she hadn't noticed the gray hair or the new lines around his eyes and the deepening ones across his forehead. His elegant features were sharper, too. He'd lost weight in the last six months. He and Kelsey had labored long hours establishing MG Interiors and the work was taking its toll on Stuart's handsome face. Eve gazed up at him and her hand crept into his.

Kelsey looked past them to see that no one was smiling in the Fairbourne camp. Brad looked detached and impatient. The fingers of his right hand fidgeted and Kelsey knew he needed a cigarette. Two years ago, he'd smoked occasionally. At the time of their breakup, he was getting through a pack a day. He'd also been drinking more and smoking marijuana. Only a week before she'd ended their relationship, Brad had blamed his dependencies on his increasingly demanding work schedule at the law firm.

His mother stood close to him. Against a sea of black and navy blue, Olivia's pearl gray silk sheath dress and jacket provided a beautifully chic contrast. Clearly she was trying to look solemn, but instead her lovely face was sullen. She didn't make eye contact with either Kelsey or Truman. Kelsey knew Olivia considered Truman leaving her out of Lorelei's funeral arrangements an insult. Yesterday, when Truman rejected her latest suggestion, Olivia had glared at Kelsey then left the house without a word, nearly slamming the front door behind her. 'She thinks you're taking over,' Eve told Kelsey.

'Taking over?' Kelsey had exclaimed. 'It's *my* family!'

'Are you sure Olivia knows that?'

Later, Kelsey thought about what Eve had said. On the last night of her life, Lori had been furious with Olivia. She'd said Olivia had always been attracted to him, even before her husband Milton died, and now that their mother was dead she was taking advantage of every chance to improve her position. *But that will never happen while I'm alive*, Lorelei had vowed. And now Lori was dead. Out of the way. Her voice silenced forever. Is that what her murder meant to Olivia? A chance to weave herself more tightly into the fabric of the March family and of becoming Truman March's wife? Kelsey glanced at Olivia, who stood rigidly still, her dark green gaze aimed emotionlessly at Lori's mahogany casket with its blanket of white and pink roses. Suddenly she raised her eyes and fixed them so sharply on Kelsey that a tremor shot through her.

Her father's grip tightened on her hand and he looked down at her. No doubt he'd felt her twitch. Kelsey gave him a shaky smile and tried to listen to the minister. His voice was rich, smooth, and somehow calming even though it was little more than background noise to her as her gaze wandered.

She hadn't given a thought about whether or not Rick Conway would attend the funeral. Now she spotted his six-foot-plus frame standing behind two rows of people. Kelsey wondered how many hours he'd been questioned by the police after he shot Vernon Nott. She closed her eyes, as if that could shut out the sound of the guns firing into the night, but she knew the sound would haunt her for the rest of her life.

When a woman standing in front of Rick moved to the right, Kelsey was startled to see Janet O'Rourke by Rick's side. Her petite body looked several pounds thinner in a simple moss green dress. Her normally glowing complexion was pasty, and she clutched Rick's arm as if she were afraid she'd fall. Rick covered her hand with his. Kelsey had never sensed a romance between the two – only that of a friendly manager and employee. Today, though, Janet was clearly depending on Rick.

Just as the minister finished the last prayer, a breeze swept the gravesite, fluttering the petals of countless funeral wreathes. For the first time, Kelsey noticed a large vase of bright yellow and vivid pink tulips mixed with purple hydrangeas, Lorelei's favorite flowers and colors, near the head of the casket. She lifted her gaze and saw a tall, handsome, slender man with slightly tousled sun-bleached blonde hair sweeping across his forehead and blue eyes fixed intensely on her. Kelsey's heart stopped for a moment as her eyes met his. Then she suddenly felt as if Lori was speaking to her, introducing this man.

This had to be Cole Harrington, Lorelei's lover.

SIX

When the service ended, Kelsey let go of her father's hand and stared at Cole Harrington. He'd begun to move away from the other mourners when someone touched her arm.

'Are you all right, Miss March?'

She turned to see Detective Pike, his quick, dark gaze moving between her and Cole. 'That's Cole Harrington,' she muttered. 'He's the photographer who was going to do a shoot for *Vogue* in Africa with my sister the week after next.' She hesitated, then said in distress, 'I'm sorry. I should have told you this sooner. He's married and I think he and Lori—'

'I know.'

'About their involvement? Their . . . affair?'

'She was talking about him loudly at Conway's Tavern. Several people overheard her, so I checked with two of her friends in New York.' Pike paused and said with a trace of sympathy, 'They'd only heard rumors. It might not have been an affair, Kelsey.'

He'd never called her Kelsey. 'You can be the kindest man,' Kelsey said in a quavering voice.

Pike looked embarrassed and Kelsey cleared her throat.

'I wonder why he's here and if his wife is with him.'

'Cole Harrington and his wife took a commercial flight from New York to Louisville on Monday morning. They went to her family's home here in the city.' Pike looked away from her and frowned at the man edging away from the gravesite. 'Can you keep him here? Isn't there a reception afterward?'

Kelsey nodded.

'See if he'll stay. You might be able to learn something about Harrington's relationship with your sister.'

'Me? He won't talk to me about Lorelei, especially if . . . Well, if . . .'

Pike looked at her with his depthless dark eyes. 'We're fairly certain someone hired Vernon Nott to kill either you or Lorelei. Cole Harrington might be involved in your sister's death. If not him, maybe his wife. They were both in the city on Monday night. I know making small talk with him will be uncomfortable for you, but it's important. *Please*.'

Without wasting another moment, Kelsey turned and headed for Cole Harrington, who was walking slowly, his gaze keen as it skimmed over everyone as if he was scrutinizing them. 'Mr Harrington,' she called as she neared him. He kept walking. Kelsey moved faster. 'Mr Harrington?' He's ignoring me, she thought. I can't just let him leave. I won't get a chance like this again. She reached his side and put her hand on his arm. 'Cole Harrington?'

He finally looked at her. For a moment she thought she saw alarm and furtiveness in his blue eyes. Then he gave her a small smile but said nothing.

'I'm Kelsey, Lori's sister. She told me all about you.' Oh, hell, Kelsey thought. He'll think I'm confronting him about their affair. 'Lori said you're a world-renowned photographer and she was delighted that you'd be doing the shoot in Kenya with her. And other models too, of course. She admired you and was *so* looking forward to the trip and . . .' Suddenly Kelsey felt tears brimming. 'So I . . . I just wanted to say hello.'

He placed a hand over hers. 'I'm so very sorry about Lorelei, Miss March. I know sympathetic words seem hollow at a time like this, but your sister was more than a beautiful face. She'll be missed by a great many people.'

Kelsey smiled, thinking he sounded slightly stiff, just like Detective Pike, but then how was he supposed to sound at a time like this? 'Thank you,' she said. 'I hope you'll come back to the house with us. These post-funeral gatherings can be uncomfortable but I know my father would like to meet you. And Lori . . .' She swallowed. 'Lori would have appreciated you coming to her home, seeing where she grew up.'

She saw doubt in his face. It was a strong face and strikingly handsome, with the straight nose, the smooth tanned skin, the slender lips, and even the lines that ebbed around his intensely blue eyes, as if he'd been looking into the sun too long. No wonder Lori had been attracted to him, Kelsey mused. It had probably been love at first sight. For her, at least.

'If you're sure I won't be intruding, I'd like to pay my respects to your family in a warmer atmosphere. Cemeteries . . .' He looked around and seemed to draw in on himself. 'I don't like them.'

'I don't either. I know a lot of people think they're peaceful, but to me they're just depressing.' He smiled at her. 'So you'll come to our home?'

'Certainly, Miss March.'

'Please call me Kelsey.'

Cole stepped back as three other mourners pushed toward her. Most people were now dispersing, breaking into little groups and complaining about the gall of the press, who were waiting to pounce as soon as they began the migration to the March home, and looking up at the helicopter still circling. Kelsey spoke to a few people whose faces were a blur before she excused herself and began walking toward Pike. His gaze met hers and he barely shook his head. *No.* No? Then she realized he didn't want to be seen talking with her. Of course. The police frequently attended the funerals of people who'd been murdered. She knew that from television. He doesn't want Cole to see me talking to a detective, Kelsey thought. He doesn't want Cole to be on the alert.

And neither did she.

Later, people thronged through the tasteful dove gray, pale sand and cobalt blue living and dining rooms of the March home. At first everyone spoke softly, but soon many forgot the circumstances. The volume rose and occasionally someone would let out a guffaw that made Kelsey wince. After she'd greeted almost everyone and become numb to the phrases that expressed grief, she saw Cole. He gave the impression of carefully controlled intensity as he stood near the big bay window overlooking the side lawn and pushed a piece of apple pie around his dessert plate. Kelsey approached him.

'Something wrong with the pie?' she asked.

He turned and his blue eyes seemed to take in all of her with one glance. 'It's delicious. I was thinking that you have a beautiful home. Your sister must have loved it here.'

'She did.'

Cole looked out the window at the large white barn in the

near distance. Sunlight bounced off the glass of the large cupola set in the middle of the barn's red gabled roof and the two small fanciful cupolas on either side of it. The building looked pristine, graceful and lovely on the sea of dark green Kentucky bluegrass. 'I haven't seen many barns in my life, but the ones I have seen were just simple square buildings. Yours is beautiful,' he said. 'It looks like a mansion.'

'It's a sixteen-stall barn,' Kelsey answered. 'My grandfather March designed it, and that's what he wanted it to look like – a mansion.'

He smiled. 'I like the cupolas.'

'The four small ones mask exhaust fans. The big one lets light into the barn. Horses need light and fresh air to be happy, so the barn has lots of windows and six indoor-outdoor fans. It's beautiful inside as well as outside.' Kelsey realized she sounded like a tour guide. 'My grandfather Vaden goes there often,' she ended lamely. 'He says it's the best place to think.'

'Does your father raise race horses?'

Kelsey paused in surprise. Hadn't Lori ever talked to Cole about the horses? 'My grandfather March did. Four of his horses ran in the Derby. Two won the Race for the Roses. Lori always called the Kentucky Derby the Race for the Roses.'

Cole smiled vaguely, nodding.

'One went on to win the Triple Crown. But when Grandfather March died, Dad said he didn't have his father's talent or expertise when it came to breeding and training horses. Now we have only the three you see in the paddock, and they aren't race horses.'

Cole looked with interest at the horses, so Kelsey stepped nearer the window and pointed. 'The dark brown one is Dad's American Saddlebred, Zane. The gray Arabian Yasmine is – was – my mother's. And Lori's Guinevere is the gold Palomino with the white tail and mane.' She glanced at Cole, whose blue gaze was fixed on Guinevere. 'Oh. Guinevere,' he murmured thought-fully, as if trying to commit the name to memory. Puzzled by his reaction, Kelsey said, 'My sister was crazy about Guinevere. I'm surprised Lori never mentioned her to you.'

He looked up at her. 'Well . . . of course she did. She just never described the horse, at least not in detail. I didn't know

Guinevere's tail and mane look like Lorelei's hair. Oh!' Cole
flushed. 'I meant that as a compliment—'

He broke off and looked almost gratefully at a couple
approaching them. Kelsey turned and smiled at them. 'Hello,
Miss March. We didn't want to intrude but your father insisted
we come to the house after the funeral.'

Tears brimmed in Janet O'Rourke's large hazel eyes, and her
freckled face was pale above her dark green dress. She looked
even smaller than usual standing beside Richard Conway, who
wore a well-tailored navy blue suit and stood very straight. Janet's
hand trembled slightly as Kelsey clasped it firmly.

'Janet, I'm so glad you came. My sister really liked you.'

'*Ohhhh.*' Janet looked like she was going to cry before Rick
stretched his arm across her back and put his large hand on her
slender shoulder. She sniffled and stood a bit straighter, as if
contact with him gave her strength. 'Lorelei was lovely, inside
and out. Not that I really knew her, but I could tell. I'll treasure
the piece of notepaper she signed for me forever.'

More tears rolled down Janet's face, and although Kelsey
knew Janet had most likely told Enzo Pike about Lorelei's noisy
announcement that she was in love with Cole Harrington, she
couldn't be mad at the young woman so genuinely upset about
Lori's death.

Rick put out his hand to shake Kelsey's. 'I wish I had something better to say than I'm sorry.' His voice was deep and grave.
Kelsey realized she'd only heard him speak in the cheerful tones
of a welcoming host at Conway's Tavern. Now he had shadows
around his brown eyes, a furrow between his eyebrows, and his
smile was forced. 'What happened was . . . unspeakable.
Unimaginable. If I'd only been faster . . .'

'You have nothing to blame yourself for,' Kelsey said. 'You
saved my life.'

'And for that, I'm grateful to the depths of my soul.' Truman
had appeared beside Rick, looking alert and composed in a gray
worsted wool suit, but he had hollows beneath his cheekbones.
The wrinkles around his eyes were deeper, and his usually clear
gray gaze was bloodshot from lack of sleep. 'You acted with
incredible calm and bravery. You're a hero.'

Rick gave Truman a long, direct gaze. 'I'm not a hero, sir,' he said quietly. 'I didn't think at all that night. I just reacted when I sensed something was wrong.'

'Many people's reaction would be only to look out for themselves. I'm so thankful that you aren't one of those people.' After a moment of silence, Truman looked away from Rick to Cole.

'Dad, this is Cole Harrington,' Kelsey said quickly.

Cole shook Truman's hand. 'I can't tell you what Lorelei's loss is to everyone who knew her, everyone who worked with her. And to her fans, of course.'

'Mr Harrington was going to be the photographer on Lorelei's African shoot.' Kelsey looked at Cole. 'Has it been canceled?'

For a moment, Cole looked unsure, even cornered, before he finally answered in a careful voice. 'I don't think they can cancel it. So much planning has been done.'

They've already hired another girl, Kelsey thought with pain. Someone else had probably been chosen less than twenty-four hours after Lori's death.

Kelsey's gaze met Cole's and he seemed to read her mind. 'Yes, they'll replace her, although no one can really replace Lorelei March,' he said with feeling. 'She was perfect for the shoot. She was so beautiful. And everyone says Lorelei was a joy to work with – many models aren't. They're demanding divas. I'm sure you know the type. Or maybe not if you haven't been to many of her photo shoots . . .'

'Neither Kelsey nor I ever went to one,' Truman told him, smiling ruefully. 'Lori said we'd make her nervous.'

Cole looked out the window. 'Kelsey showed me Lorelei's horse . . . Guinevere. She's magnificent.'

'Lori loves her horse. She rides Guinevere every day she's home.' Pieter Vaden had appeared next to Janet and seemed unaware of using the present tense. 'She loves grooming her horse. Just look at Guinevere's coat shining in the sun.'

'She's glorious,' Janet said just above a whisper. 'She's like something out of a fairy tale.'

'Or an Arthurian legend,' Pieter said. 'My Ingrid reads them to her.'

'Is Ingrid your wife?' Janet asked softly.

'Yes, my dear. She's a wonderful woman.' Pieter looked around. 'I don't know where she's gone off to right now. You must meet her.' He smiled gently at Janet, clearly taken by her big hazel eyes and delicate, almost child's, voice.

'I only met Lorelei once,' Janet went on. 'She told me she was named after a poem about a girl with long blonde hair. I'm going to read that poem.'

'Lori will be *so* happy to hear that, uh . . .'

'Janet,' she supplied as tears brimmed in her eyes. Pieter reached up to put his hand on her shoulder, only to find Rick's still in place. 'Ah, Janet, you're inspiring so much male affection we're competing over who may place a hand on your shoulder!'

'She's a great girl,' Rick said.

Pieter peered at him. 'I remember you!' *Oh no!* Kelsey thought, her heart sinking as Pieter's forehead wrinkled. 'It's the hair. Brown curls . . . You're Milo! You used to date my Ingrid!'

Kelsey tensed, but Rick smiled at Pieter. 'She married *you*, though,' he said easily. 'She made the right choice.'

'You're not a sore loser, Milo! Very admirable.' Pieter surveyed Rick foot to head. 'You've grown into a fine-looking man.'

'Thanks. I could say the same about you.'

'Ah, I'm not twenty-one anymore. Ingrid liked your hair. Mine is thick but straight and blonde.' Pieter ran a hand over his hair that had been silver almost as long as Kelsey could remember. 'Do you like horses? Have you seen Lori's horse?'

'Yes . . . Pieter.' Kelsey could see that Rick had almost said 'sir' but caught himself. 'She's beautiful.'

Pieter nodded. 'Beautiful. Beautiful.'

Kelsey smiled gratefully at Rick. He smiled back in a way that said she didn't need to thank him.

'I used to have a Palomino like Guinevere,' Brad Fairbourne interrupted. He seemed to have materialized from nowhere and was standing behind Kelsey, his gaze fixed on Lori's horse grazing peacefully. 'My stepfather had it put down.'

'Darling, you make him sound cruel!' Olivia exclaimed. Kelsey hadn't seen her hovering slightly behind Truman. 'You were eighteen and away in college, Brad. The horse was old and ill. Milton didn't want you to watch your horse waste away.'

'He was only sixteen,' Brad persisted bitterly. 'Horses can live to be twenty-five, or older.'

'*Healthy* horses can. Yours was sick.'

'I know he was sick, but Milton didn't waste any money getting the best medical care for him. You can bet *those* horses get top-rate medical care, Olivia,' Brad simmered.

Olivia's gaze turned hard. 'Don't call me Olivia,' she said coldly. 'I'm your *mother*, Bradley.'

Kelsey noticed Cole watching Brad and Olivia closely. Brad looked tired. He was standing so near she could feel his breath on her neck. She glanced at Olivia to see that the woman's fair skin blazed bright pink in the sunlight. Mother and son were having a skirmish at a funeral and Cole was fascinated. Had Lori told him about them, about her fear that Olivia was trying to become the next Mrs March, about her certainty that Olivia had always lied about her and Brad's past? Or had Lori been too mesmerized by this handsome man's vital presence to dwell on stories about people back home?

'Losing the horse was sad but it was a long time ago,' Olivia told her son firmly. Kelsey could tell she was furious with Brad, but managed a brilliant smile for Truman. 'I'm afraid we're ignoring our guests.'

Our guests? Kelsey thought angrily. This wasn't a party, and no one had come to be entertained by Olivia Fairbourne. Apparently her father felt the same way. He looked at Pieter, who was scowling and nodding as his lips moved in a silent conversation. Truman ignored Olivia, and stepped forward and took his father-in-law's arm.

'I think Pieter and I need something stronger than coffee or tea. How does a mint julep sound, Pieter?'

'A mint julep? *Now?*' Olivia exclaimed.

'Yes, now. Pieter?' The older man's eyes were taking on a vague, faraway look. 'A mint julep for both of us.' Truman's voice was strong, almost commanding. 'I'd like nothing better right now. I know you would, too, Pieter.' Truman linked his arm through Pieter's. 'Let's find Helen. She makes great mint juleps.'

'All right.' Slowly, Pieter's faded blue eyes seemed to focus. 'Yes, yes, I'd enjoy a mint julep. That does sound fine. Just fine,' he repeated as he walked away, smiling at his son-in-law.

Several hours later, Pieter sighed and muttered 'I'm exhausted' as he sat down on the side of his bed and tried to struggle out of his right shoe without unlacing it. Kelsey kneeled and began working on his shoelaces. 'I don't understand it. I haven't done anything today except stand around outside and then stand around inside with a lot of people I don't know.' Kelsey bit her lip. Pieter knew almost everyone who had come to Lorelei's funeral. 'Maybe I'm getting sick. I probably have a fever.'

'I'll get the thermometer.'

'Oh, shush!' Pieter waved away any thoughts of a thermometer. 'Your thermometer has glowing numbers.'

'It's digital, Grandfather.'

'I don't like it. I don't trust it,' Pieter said querulously. 'Ingrid can tell just by looking at me if I have a fever. She'll be in shortly. She's trying to make that white-haired woman leave.'

'Olivia?'

'Olivia. Yes. She has her sights set on Truman. Hah! As if Truman would care about any woman except Sofie. He's only being nice to Olivia. I told her so today.'

'You spoke to Olivia?'

'Yes. I warned her that I know she'll do anything to get Truman, so now she knows that *I* know. She hates me for it.' He clenched his fists, looking past Kelsey as if seeing Olivia. 'I will not allow you to cause trouble. Don't even *try* coming between Truman and Sofie. I will *stop* you—'

A burst of ragged coughing tore through his sentence. Kelsey stood up and began helplessly patting his back until he'd coughed himself almost breathless. 'Grandfather, I think you need to go to the hospital.'

He shook his head violently.

'You have a bad cold. *Please*. We don't want it getting worse. You'd only have to make a sudden trip to the emergency room.'

'*No!*' What was left of his voice grated from him. 'No emergency room! It's night.'

'Tomorrow?'

He looked at her and she saw the weakness and confusion in his eyes. But he still had his strength of will. 'Tomorrow, but only to make you and Ingrid happy.'

'It will. I'm sure there's nothing seriously wrong. You probably won't even get a shot.'

Pieter broke into rattling laughter. 'No shot? I won't get a lollipop for not crying?'

'You'll get a lollipop even if you don't get a shot.'

'Good.'

She pulled off his second shoe then stood up. She was about to leave the room and ask her father to help get Pieter undressed and tucked into bed when he suddenly said, 'That tall man who came to the funeral wasn't Milo, the fellow who wanted to marry Ingrid. Milo was my age so the man I saw today is too young to be Milo. It was the brown curly hair that fooled me. I must have sounded very silly.'

'You didn't. It's all right, Grandfather.'

'No, no it isn't. I don't want to embarrass my family.'

Kelsey's throat tightened. 'You never embarrass your family. We're proud of you.'

'Maybe you used to be proud. Now . . .' He shook his head as if trying to clear it, then asked, 'Is that woman gone yet? The one who wants Truman?'

'I'm sure she is.'

'She shouldn't come here . . . No, she shouldn't come . . .'

Kelsey looked at the sagging old man she'd always thought was the strongest person in the world. She put her hands on either side of his face, turned it up toward her, and kissed him on the forehead. 'I love you, Grandfather.'

'I love you, too, *vacker ängel.*' Kelsey smiled at him and he smiled feebly in return. 'Please ask Lorelei to come for a good-night kiss. I haven't seen her all day.'

Kelsey looked around at every corner of the barn. She loved the barn her grandfather March, who'd died when she was nine, had designed for the race horses he'd owned nearly fifty years ago. The barn was always clean and filled with sunlight streaming through its many windows. Now the soft light of a crescent moon shone on the beautiful white and gold horse that belonged to Lorelei. Guinevere nickered softly at her. Kelsey walked to the stall door and reached through the bars of the top half to stroke the horse's face.

'Hello, Guinevere,' she murmured. 'You're usually happier to see me. You can't talk to me, but I know you miss Lorelei. Beautiful Lorelei. She's left us, Guinevere. She didn't want to, but she's gone. Are you sad like me?' The horse nickered again. 'We'll never see Lori again, Guinevere.' Kelsey's throat tightened. *'Never.'*

Suddenly, Guinevere began breathing deeply. Her hooves beat against the floor before she lifted her head and blew through her nose. Kelsey had never been able to translate the language of horses like her sister, but she could see that something upset Guinevere. 'What's wrong, girl?' The horse snorted and shied away from Kelsey's outstretched hand. 'Guinevere?' The horse drew back its upper lip, screamed, reared, and struck her hooves against the lower half of the wooden stall door. Kelsey cried out in shock and fell backward. Lying on the floor while the horse stamped wildly, Kelsey smelled smoke. She looked to her right and saw blinding flames licking the back wall of the barn – flames moving closer, closer . . .

'Fire! Fire! *Fire!'* Kelsey jerked up in bed, sweating, short of breath, terrified. A nightmare, she told herself. You nearly screamed down the house over a nightmare, like you did when you were a child! But now she knew what to do when a nightmare came – assure herself she was in the real world, not her dream world. Kelsey clasped her trembling hands, breathed deeply, and looked around her bedroom. She focused on the familiar yellow and blue butterfly Tiffany floor lamp, the oil portrait of a ballerina her mother had painted for Kelsey's twelfth birthday, the mahogany-framed cheval mirror, the softly glowing amber stained-glass cat night light. Everything was the same as it had been at midnight.

Except that Gatsby wasn't lying asleep on her bed. Except that her bedroom was too bright. Except that she caught a faint smell of smoke. Kelsey knew she wasn't dreaming now. She scrambled from her bed and ran to the bedroom window she always kept half-open in spring, the window where Gatsby stood, his paws on the screen of the window that overlooked the grounds leading to the barn – the flaming barn.

Without thought, Kelsey rushed to her father's bedroom and opened the door. His bed was empty. She called his name in case he was in the adjoining bathroom, but he didn't answer. She went to her grandfather's room. He was gone. She flew down the stairs on bare feet and crossed the black-and-white marble floor to find one of the double front doors open.

Outside, the air felt charged with panic and hysteria. Kelsey closed her eyes and ran through the cool, thick grass toward the barn. When she got close, she saw that the fire had consumed half the building. It wouldn't be long until flames claimed the whole barn. Anguish washed over her as she thought of the horses. Then she heard whinnying in the pasture. Was it two horses whinnying or three? What if one of the horses had been caught in the inferno that was the barn? But how had *any* of them escaped?

Even a hundred yards away from the barn, Kelsey felt the heat from the fire. Beams exploded and shot brilliant flames toward the dark sky. The acrid stench of the fire filled the air, making her eyes water and her throat hurt. Blinking furiously to clear her vision, she finally saw all three horses. They were in the pasture, far enough away from the barn to be safe. They were clearly terrified – screaming, kicking at the wooden fence surrounding the pasture – but they didn't seem injured. The wind was light but blowing the flames away from them. Kelsey squinted at the blazing barn. Someone must have opened the stalls and freed the horses before the fire started. Why? Why would someone who wanted to burn the barn care enough about the horses to protect them from a horrible fiery death?

'Kelsey, what are you doing out here?' She turned and saw her father in his robe and house slippers running toward her. 'You need to go in the house.'

'Why?' She was surprised by how dull and hopeless she sounded. 'I might as well watch the rest of the barn burn down.'

He held up his cell phone. 'I've called the fire department.' His voice was raspy from the smoke. 'They'll be here any minute. At least the horses are in the pasture, although I don't know how they got there. Their stalls and the paddock's gates were closed and bolted.' Truman paused. 'At least I think they were closed. So many people were here for the funeral reception. Maybe someone came down here and messed around with the gates and Charlie didn't check closely enough this evening,' he said, referring to the seventeen-year-old who often helped the full-time groom with the horses. 'He's usually so reliable, though.'

'Where's Grandfather?' Kelsey asked abruptly.

'In the house. Sleeping, I hope. He wasn't in good shape today.'

'He's not sleeping. I checked his bedroom.'

Truman looked alarmed. 'He must be somewhere in the house. I haven't seen him. I don't want him to see *this*. He loved the barn.'

The horses still whinnied, the fire still crackled, but above those noises Kelsey barely heard another noise. Her father started to say something but she held up her hand, shushing him to silence. It came again, splitting the night. A scream. A tortured human scream. A man shrieking in agony. 'Dad, do you hear that? Do you hear *that*?'

Truman went stone still. Then he gasped, 'My God! Someone's in the barn!'

He bolted away from her with the speed and agility of a young man. Kelsey followed, ignoring the pain of stepping on small rocks and broken twigs with her bare feet. As they neared the barn, the screams grew louder and closer together until all Kelsey could hear was a continuous shrill wail of torture that no longer sounded human.

Truman stopped and grabbed Kelsey's hand. Together they stood and stared, horrified, as a mass of flames plunged out of the barn. Burning arms flailed, blazing cloth wrapped around stumbling legs, fire licked at a face. The form staggered in a circle then dropped to its knees and raised flaming arms to the black sky.

The keening sirens of fire trucks tore through the smoky air as Kelsey watched the figure she knew was her grandfather fall face down. Her heart skipped a beat, sending a shudder through her entire body, as the man she'd loved all her life made a futile attempt to rise. He collapsed on to his side, and slowly his burning arms and legs began folding and drawing inward. He twitched twice, then went into a powerful convulsion. *He's fighting to stay alive,* Kelsey thought, *but it's too late.* It's too, too late. Finally, as tears she didn't feel began running down her face, her grandfather's smoldering body went completely still in the sweet darkness of the May night.

SEVEN

Kelsey huddled in the heavily padded ivory-colored rocking chair near the large window in her bedroom. It was afternoon, but she'd closed the draperies against the bright, beautiful day as well as the charred remains of the barn. She wore loose jeans, a heavy blue sweatshirt over a shirt, and on her sore feet an old pair of soft pink slippers shaped like bunnies with stand-up ears. Eve let out a tiny, surprised squeak when she peered into the room and Kelsey said '*Hi!*'

'Kelsey, I didn't see you! It's so dark in here.' Eve squinted. 'Are you holding Gatsby?'

'I'm cuddling him. I'm freezing and he's so warm. Aren't you warm, Jay Gatsby?' The cat meowed loudly. 'See? I think he's too hot, but he knows I need him. Come in, Eve.'

'May I turn on a light?'

Kelsey reached up and pulled the chain on the standing Tiffany light beside her chair. Blue and gold light glowed gently in the room. 'There. It's pretty. And soft. I don't want bright light.'

Eve stared at Kelsey for a moment, then went to the dresser and fumbled until she found a wooden-handled brush. 'You didn't use your curling iron on your hair this morning, did you?'

'How could you tell?' Kelsey asked dryly, lifting a handful of straight, rough hair. 'It was all I could do to manage a shower. I couldn't get the water hot enough, and I washed and washed but I still smell of smoke.'

'That's your imagination,' Eve said as she began running the brush in soft strokes down the right side of Kelsey's hair. 'You smell of honey and vanilla.'

'That's my liquid shower soap. I even used it on my hair. I couldn't find my shampoo and conditioner. I didn't really look for them.'

'Your neighbor took the horses. I met him. He said that, like your father, he has a big barn but only a few tenants. He brought men to help with the move. The horses were still nervous but the men were gentle.'

'I'm glad the horses will be nearby. Dad will probably visit them almost every day.' As Gatsby purred loudly and kneaded Kelsey's thighs with his paws, Eve kept brushing Kelsey's hair slowly, almost tenderly. 'My mother used to brush my hair like that. Lori's, too,' Kelsey murmured dreamily. 'She said it relaxed you. She was right. She was right about almost everything. She was such a kind, smart, loving woman.'

'I didn't know her very long but I felt I knew her well, if that makes sense.' Eve kept running the brush through Kelsey's hair. 'Your mother was always so warm to me. The first time she invited me to dinner, I couldn't believe it. She hardly knew me and you had guests. Important guests. The table setting was so beautiful – the china, the crystal, the flowers and candles, but I didn't feel intimidated. Your family was so informal, so determined to make me feel as comfortable and special as the other guests at the table that I just had fun.' Eve moved and began brushing the other side of Kelsey's hair. 'Then two years ago your mother had you bring me here supposedly to talk to one of her friends about a design job, remember? Instead, she threw me a surprise birthday party! I'd never had a birthday party in my whole life. One Sunday, you and I came here for the afternoon and she tried to get me to ride Yasmine, and Lori wanted me to ride Guinevere. I'm afraid to ride horses on merry-go-rounds, for heaven's sake, so I said no. But both of them wanting me to ride their cherished horses – well, you can't imagine how that made me feel. Knowing what you do about my background, you can understand that to me being treated like family by the Marches was nearly unbelievable.'

Kelsey nodded, remembering that her grandfather had been present at every occasion Eve mentioned. He'd cared deeply about the lovely enigma that was Eve Daley.

'My parents believe that treating children with affection spoils them,' Eve went on, smoothing the ends of Kelsey's hair. 'They don't like visitors. I can't remember anyone having dinner with us aside from my mother's aunt, the one who left me her money when she died. Their method of child rearing – working children hard, being free with punishment and withholding affection – was difficult for me but worse for my brother. He's more sensitive than I am. Once on one of his school papers, a teacher wrote that he had "the soul of a poet." He was thrilled but he tore up the paper before my parents could see it, and made me promise not to tell them about the comment. They would have been horrified. *The soul of a poet.* That phrase definitely would have earned their severe disapproval. Can you imagine? I feel guilty because I left him behind with them.'

'But you told me he's older than you. You said he'd made the decision to stay on the farm with your parents.'

'He did. But I didn't try hard enough to convince him he deserved more of a world than that sorry little farm and the girl on the farm beside ours that my parents wanted him to marry. He told me she'd expected to become his wife for years, and it wouldn't have been fair to abandon her. I left a week before the wedding. I couldn't stand to see my beautiful, intelligent brother make that stupid, sanctimonious, intolerant young woman his bride. I know he would have contacted me during the last few years if it weren't for her. She hated me and she was *so* possessive of David. That's my brother's name. David Joshua . . .' Eve's voice trailed off before she drew a deep, shaky breath. 'Well, I've done a fine job of prattling on and on about myself. I came to help you.'

'And you have helped me. I'm glad to know you have such a wonderful brother. Until this week, I didn't even know you had a brother.' Kelsey looked up at Eve's oval face with its tender mouth and amber eyes. 'You've given me a look into your life. And you've helped take my mind off the atrocities that have happened to us in the last few days. My family is gone. I took it for granted and now everyone is gone except Dad.'

Eve shook her head and smiled. 'You never took your family for granted. You talked about them constantly.'

'I did?' Kelsey asked in surprise. 'That must have been annoying.'

'It was touching.' Eve stopped brushing. 'Kelsey, I can't delay any longer. Detective Pike is downstairs. He wants to ask a few questions.'

'I've already been questioned!' Kelsey burst out. 'All morning I dealt with these people and their damned questions that *had* to be answered even though I couldn't stop crying!' Gatsby stiffened and extended his claws. 'Oh, now I've scared him, too!' Gatsby jumped off her lap, whipped around, and sat down about a foot away, gazing at her. She drew a deep breath and lowered her voice. 'I guess I have to see how many more answers I have left in me. I feel like can't bear it. But I will. Grandfather would have done it for me.' She looked up at Eve and smiled faintly. 'Just stay by me, Eve.'

'Always,' Eve assured her.

Stuart had returned to the city after the funeral. Kelsey had urged Eve to go with him, to get away from this home devastated by Lorelei's murder. Now Kelsey was relieved that Eve had refused, saying she'd go back with Kelsey tomorrow. Kelsey knew Eve had wanted to help put everything in order – as much as it could ever be in order. But now tragedy had struck again and with her father dazed by grief, Kelsey felt she could only count on Eve.

As they entered the living room, Eve held her hand. Gatsby – suspicious or curious as usual – trailed after them. 'Miss March, Miss Daley,' Detective Pike said as he stood.

'Hello. Please sit. And we agreed that you'd call me Kelsey.'

Pike smiled. 'Yes, we did.' He cleared his throat. 'I'm with Louisville Metro Homicide Division, as you know. I'm in charge of your sister's case. The detective in charge of the murder case is required to look into an incident like this one that has resulted in another death. I know you were questioned at length this morning, but I'm afraid I need to ask just a few more things.'

'I understand. Where's my father?'

'He's worn out, Kelsey. We were talking and he got pale and a bit dizzy. I thought we should call a doctor but he wouldn't hear of it. Your housekeeper—'

'Miss Norris.'

'Yes, Miss Norris insisted he go into the kitchen and have coffee and something to eat. But he said if you need him—'

'I don't,' Kelsey lied. She didn't want to answer a barrage of questions without the support of her father's loving strength, but it seemed as if his strength was waning. 'I just wondered why Dad's not here. I'll be as helpful as possible.' Eve, still holding Kelsey's hand, gave it a squeeze as they headed to the couch.

They sat down, the brilliance of the beautiful sunny day shining behind them. Gatsby jumped up, settled on Kelsey's lap, and stared at Pike. 'What do you want to know?' she asked bluntly.

'Your father was the first to see the fire?'

'Yes. At least he saw it before I did. When I realized something was wrong, I looked out my window and—'

'What time was that?'

'I didn't look at my bedside clock, but I heard the grandfather clock downstairs chiming two o'clock.'

Pike made notes. 'So, you looked out your window. Did you see anyone around the barn? Anyone running from it?'

'No. I saw only the fire.'

'What did you do then?'

'I went to my father's room. He wasn't there. And my grandfather's room was empty, too. I ran outside. The barn was half gone but the horses were in the pasture. They're *always* shut in their stalls. They couldn't possibly have kicked the stall doors open.'

'The doors are kept locked?'

'Each stall door has bars at the top for ventilation. The lower half is pine, and the entire door is latched shut from the outside. We've *never* had a horse get a stall door open.'

'I see.' Pike made more notes. 'Go on.'

'When my father saw me, he told me to go back in the house, but I said Grandfather was missing. Then we heard . . . screaming. Human screaming. And someone ran out of the barn . . . someone on fire.'

Pike nodded slowly. 'Does your grandfather go to the barn often?'

'Yes. He loves the horses. He doesn't go in the middle of the night, though.'

'But I understand that he has been wandering at night.'

'Yes, but only recently . . . Since he returned after Lori's murder, he hasn't been himself.'

'That's certainly understandable,' Pike said sympathetically. He looked at Kelsey. 'Investigators have agreed that the fire accelerant was kerosene. Your father says that kerosene for heaters and lamps is kept in a small metal building near the barn, along with equipment such as lawn mowers and the like.'

Kelsey nodded.

'Can you think of any reason why your grandfather would have gotten some kerosene from that building and taken it to the barn? Maybe he wanted to use some of those lamps?'

'The barn has electric lighting and heating. The kerosene lamps are only kept in case we lose electric power. We didn't last night. There wouldn't have been any reason for him to use kerosene.'

'Could he have forgotten that you have electric lighting in the barn?'

'I can't know what he did and didn't remember. But the kerosene is in a locked building. My grandfather didn't have a key.'

'That you know of.'

'Well . . . no.'

'But there is a key around here somewhere.'

'Yes, but even I don't know where it is.'

'Maybe your grandfather found it.'

'I doubt it.'

At last Pike's manner became less formal, his voice warmer. 'I'm asking these questions again because this morning fire investigators thought perhaps Mr Vaden had accidentally set fire to the barn.'

'And they don't think so now?'

'No.'

'No?' Truman walked into the living room looking gray and wounded. To Kelsey, it seemed as if the fire had burned to his soul, leaving it singed and damaged. Still, he stood tall, sending a faint smile to Kelsey, Eve and Detective Pike. 'Do you have any information about the fire?'

'Yes, sir,' Pike answered as Truman sat down on a chair across from him. 'I've spoken with the Fire Chief, and he'll be talking to you later with much more precise details than mine. Kerosene was the accelerant and you keep kerosene here. However, the fire didn't start in one place, as it would have if Mr Vaden had been trying to light a lamp and spilled it. The fire started in *five* places. Which means this was arson.'

Helen appeared with a tray holding four glasses of iced tea. Dear Helen, Kelsey thought. In the summer, iced tea was Helen's panacea for everything, even death. She served everyone and was leaving the room when Truman said, 'Helen, please don't leave. You're part of this family. Sit down and listen to Detective Pike. You deserve to hear the details of the fire first hand.'

Helen, with her long, thick gray-streaked brown hair loose around her ashen face, looked flustered. Kelsey thought she was going to dash from the room anyway, but she never said 'no' to Truman. She hurried to the couch and sat down beside Kelsey, holding the serving tray on her lap.

'Then the Fire Chief doesn't think my father-in-law accidentally set the barn on fire?' Truman asked anxiously.

'He certainly doesn't,' Pike said, 'even though he knows Mr Vaden was wandering at night.'

'Helen told me and I told Detective Pike,' Truman said to Kelsey. 'I was afraid we would have press people creeping in at night and I hired extra security, but I didn't want them to mistake Pieter for an outsider. I also thought it was a good idea to tell Pike.' He shook his head. 'I let them go yesterday. If they'd just been here last night . . .'

'We can drive ourselves crazy with "if's,"' Pike said with feeling. 'It doesn't do you or anyone else any good, sir. We simply must accept what life dishes out to us, no matter how much it hurts.'

You're speaking from experience, Kelsey thought. Recent experience. She remembered him talking about how his wife had loved flowers and had a gift for growing them. Had his wife died recently? Is that why he moved to Louisville, Kentucky, from Maine?

'When I arrived, Mr March had already told the firefighters about Mr Vaden's night wandering,' Pike went on. 'They might have thought he accidentally set fire to the barn – except that wouldn't explain why he should have kerosene and why he should pour some in the tack room, the feed rooms, the foaling stall, and the hay and bedding storage area. All five spots are at the back of the barn. And kerosene burns slower than gasoline. It's as if the arsonist wanted the horses to panic for as long as possible before the fire reached them.'

'But it didn't reach them,' Truman said. 'He set the horses free?'

'The Fire Chief seems certain that the arsonist didn't let the horses out of the barn.' Pike's gaze swept over all of them. 'It seems that Mr Vaden saved the horses. The firefighters found the remains of a watch at the door of a stall,' Pike said. He looked at his notes. 'A stainless-steel Citizen Eco-Drive Satellite Wave watch.'

'I gave Pieter that watch for Christmas,' Truman said. 'He wore it all of the time, even when he slept.'

Pike made a note. 'The Fire Chief's theory is that someone meant to burn the barn and the horses. We know Mr Vaden took walks at night, and the Fire Chief believes Mr Vaden was outside on one of his walks and saw that something was wrong at the barn. He went inside and managed to open the three stall doors to free the horses. He got his watch caught in a steel stall-door hook and it was wrenched off. Then . . .' Pike hesitated. 'The medical examiner hasn't had time to do a thorough investigation, which would include a complete battery of tests, but he's certain kerosene was on the remains of Mr Vaden's clothes. We believe the arsonist threw kerosene over him.'

'Oh my God! Someone deliberately set Grandfather, an old man, on fire?' Kelsey cried in horror. 'Who could do such a thing?'

'Someone who didn't want to be identified by your grandfather.'

Kelsey felt as if someone had kicked her in the stomach. Physical pain nearly doubled her over as she muttered, 'Poor Grandfather. I can't stand it . . . I just can't stand it.'

She felt Eve's arms close around her. 'You can stand it. You can stand anything, Kelsey.'

'I've delivered devastating news. I'm so, so sorry.' Pike's voice held deep regret and sympathy. 'Mr Vaden was a fine man. An extraordinary man.'

'Yes, he was,' Truman said faintly. He swallowed hard, then said 'He and my father were the finest men I've ever known.'

Helen grasped Kelsey's hand and squeezed it. Then she said, 'So there won't be any terrible news stories saying Mr Vaden was an old man suffering from dementia who burned down the barn?'

Pike looked at Helen. 'Not with information from the Fire Chief's office, Miss Norris. The firefighters are absolutely certain Mr Vaden didn't set the fire. The building where your kerosene is stored is locked, the lock is intact and, per Mr March's instructions, the kerosene used here is kept in steel cans rather than plastic.' Pike glanced at Truman, who nodded. 'The firefighters tell me steel melts at 2,500 degrees. Which is why they found remains of your grandfather's steel watch. If Mr Vaden had started the fire by accident, he would have dropped the container in the barn – but there are no remains of a steel kerosene can in the barn. Whoever brought the kerosene either used a plastic can which burned or took a plastic can or empty steel kerosene can away with him.' He paused and looked at each of them. 'So far, we have no idea who the arsonist is. It's important that you try very hard to remember last night and anyone you saw, even if you thought that person was one of the security people Mr March hired.'

'Or someone we know,' Kelsey said emotionlessly. 'Actually, we're *all* suspects.'

Pike looked at her intently. 'Technically, yes – my feelings aside. Until we find the arsonist, the Louisville Metro Homicide Division will consider everyone a suspect.'

'I guess it's to be expected,' Kelsey muttered.

No one else had anything to say. Everyone drank their iced tea and Pike stood up. 'I really must go. I'll check in at the fire site to see if they've found anything new, then I'll be heading back to Louisville.'

They all stood up as if to walk Pike to the door. Kelsey was conscious that no one knew what to do. The detective smiled uncomfortably at them then looked at Kelsey. 'Miss March – I mean Kelsey – may I speak to you for a moment?'

Truman looked surprised and Eve kept her arm around Kelsey as if protecting her from more bad news. Kelsey managed to compose herself and said, 'Fine. I'll walk you outside.'

The afternoon air was mild and a soft breeze blew, ruffling Kelsey's hair. In the bright sunlight, she suddenly realized she was still wearing the goofy rabbit slippers she'd bought when she was fifteen and had found this morning in the back of her closet. Today she didn't care how she looked.

They'd walked away from the house and stopped beside a lush pink flowering dogwood. 'I don't know the extent of your sister's involvement with Cole Harrington,' he said bluntly. 'However, he's married to a rich woman – a woman who has the reputation of being extremely possessive. If Vernon Nott was hired to kill Lorelei, we can't rule out Harrington's wife Delphina as the person who paid Nott.' He paused. 'We also can't rule out Harrington. If Lorelei was threatening a marriage he didn't want to end, that could be a motive for murder.'

'I know,' Kelsey said gloomily. 'I appreciate you not saying that in front of my father. He doesn't know anything about Cole and Lori. He'd be heartbroken. Or, rather, more heartbroken than he is now if that's possible.' She frowned. 'But if Cole wanted to distance himself from Lorelei, why did he come to her funeral? And then come to the reception afterward? He didn't seem nervous. Just watchful. I felt like he was sizing up all of us. I don't understand it. I also don't understand why he didn't know things I'm sure Lori would have told the man she loved.'

'That's because he wasn't the man she loved. Kelsey, the man who passed himself off as Cole Harrington is really Declan Adair, a private investigator from New York.'

'He *wasn't* Cole Harrington? He's a private eye?' Kelsey repeated in shock.

'Yes. I haven't been able to find him – he's done a good job of hiding in Louisville. I've checked him out, but so far I haven't been able to discover much except that he's extremely intelligent and very good at his job.' Pike hesitated. 'He's respected in his field and has a reputation for being ethical.'

'Oh? He's so ethical he let us believe he was Cole Harrington?'

'I think he let us believe that because he wanted a chance to talk to you. Anyway, Cole Harrington and his wife were supposed to attend the Kentucky Derby. Instead, they returned to New York City less than twenty-four hours after Lorelei's murder and Adair arrived the next day.'

He took a step closer to her. 'Kelsey, Declan Adair is Cole Harrington's half-brother. I don't know what scared Harrington enough to make him flee the city and send Adair here to worm his way into Lorelei's home, but the possibilities alarm me. You need to be very careful, because not only was your sister murdered but your grandfather was killed in a fire set the day Declan Adair entered your life and your home.'

EIGHT

For the first time in her twenty-seven years, Kelsey missed the Kentucky Derby. Her proud, doting parents had taken her even when she was a baby. And she'd particularly looked forward to this one because Lorelei, Grandfather and Helen were planning to go with her and Truman.

But she hadn't put on a beautiful hat, or experienced the heady atmosphere at Churchill Downs, or watched what was often described as 'the most exciting two minutes in sports.' Nor watched the winning horse being draped with a glorious garland of more than four hundred roses. Instead, she'd been at her grandfather's funeral while the horses ran the Race for the Roses.

Before the service, her father had taken a tranquilizer that left him detached and foggy. She stood very straight and still beside him, feeling entirely alone.

Pieter's casket, draped with white flowers, lay beside the monument labeled VADEN. Throughout the simple service, Kelsey couldn't take her eyes off her grandmother's name, INGRID, which had been carved into a new rose-granite headstone three years ago. When grief had threatened to overtake her, she'd comforted herself with the thought that tonight her grandfather would once again lie beside his adored wife.

I'll concentrate on that, Kelsey had told herself, her eyes hurting with unshed tears, her chest so tight that breathing was uncomfortable. I *must* stop replaying the horrendous vision of Grandfather burning to death. I can never think about it again. *Never*.

Besides, she needed to think about something else – about the man named Declan Adair who'd come to Lorelei's funeral and pretended to be Cole Harrington. He was a private detective. He was Cole Harrington's half-brother. That explained why he didn't seem to know about the horses, though he had known about the African shoot. How much had Cole told him about Lori? Had he met her? She remembered what Lorelei had said about knowing a great private investigator in New York. Adair? Had he come to the funeral to find out if anyone suspected Cole or Delphina of being responsible for Lorelei's murder? Or had Cole really loved Lorelei and simply dispatched Declan as a replacement for himself? But if he'd loved her, why not come himself? Kelsey had no answers – but, she thought with determination, she would get them. She *would* find out what Declan Adair's purpose had been in attending Lori's funeral, and she knew she could count on Pike's help. Then she remembered his warning to be careful where Adair was concerned.

Kelsey returned to Louisville on Tuesday. MG Interiors was now open. Stuart and Eve had attended Pieter's funeral on Sunday, then Kelsey insisted they return to the city and their normal lives. 'If you don't keep the store going, we'll all be out of a job,' she'd told them lightly, although she hadn't spent a minute stressing about MG Interiors since Lori's death. In light of losing both her sister and her grandfather in less than a week, whether or not her interior design store flourished or failed didn't seem important anymore.

Kelsey turned into the alley beside MG Interiors and stopped in front of her metal one-car garage, then flicked the automatic door opener and watched the door rise. Her father always complained about her garage being separate from her apartment. He seemed certain someone would attack her as she walked the twenty feet from the garage to the steps leading up to her loft. But no one would dare attack her now, she thought with a trace of humor. Gatsby crouched resentfully in his carrier on the passenger's seat. He, with his bad temper, was her protector.

'We're home, fellow,' she said as she pulled into the garage. 'You've been gone so long you probably don't remember your real home. It isn't nearly as grand as Dad's house.'

Kelsey took a deep breath, picked up the heavy carrier, and hurried along the concrete walkway leading to her loft above MG Interiors. The sturdy wooden outside stairway seemed twice as long and steep as it had two weeks ago. She knew that meant she was tired. She was beyond tired. She felt drained, emotionally and physically, and every step she took was an effort.

Kelsey set down the cat carrier on the wide platform at the top of the stairs. She unlocked the black steel security door, pushed it open and stepped into the loft she'd designed with care. Everything looked the same. White oak flooring extended the length of the living room. Floor-to-ceiling corner windows let in a blaze of light at the east end of the loft. A contemporary navy blue suede sectional couch sprinkled with large russet and yellow pillows sat across from the white-painted brick wall bearing a mirror-fronted flat-screen television above a linear gas fireplace. The wall at the far end of the living room was covered by book-shelves, with extra height between the shelves, loaded with books that were well-read and not just for show. Like her mother, Kelsey collected books – as many first editions as possible – and she cherished them just as her mother had done.

She looked at the white leather recliner and flashed back to the day she and Lorelei had returned from hours of shopping. Her sister had kicked off her high-heeled shoes and sunk into the padded chair as she put her slender, graceful feet on the ottoman and wiggled her expensively manicured toes. 'Oh, I could stay right here all night!' She'd sighed. 'Then let's do that,' Kelsey had answered. 'I have some DVDs of great movies I know you haven't seen.' 'No,' Lori had replied. 'We're on a roll. Let's go to that place you like so much. Conway's Tavern? That's it, isn't it?' Suddenly Lorelei had abandoned the chair and reached for her stylish high-heeled shoes. 'I want to go now. I have a feeling that I'm supposed to go to Conway's tonight.' Kelsey had laughed, asking, 'Are you psychic now, Lori? Are you tapping into the cosmic will?' Lorelei had giggled. 'I don't know what you're talking about, Kelsey. I just know what I know. It's Conway's. I'm meant to be there. I feel it. After all, who knows what tonight will bring?'

Death, Kelsey thought. Death for her sister, who was too beautiful and too naive for this world. Death for Lorelei at the hands of an empty-eyed man with a history of hurting women and a recent windfall of money.

Kelsey's stomach tightened. She closed her eyes and shook her head as if she could cast out the memory. Gatsby, who rarely made a sound, meowed loudly in his carrier, his patience at an end.

'I'm sorry, Gats,' she said, setting down the carrier and unlatching its door. 'You're home now, boy.'

The big tabby cat emerged from the carrier and shook himself. He slowly extended his paws and stretched them, separating the toes on each paw. Then he looked around as if assuring himself that he was truly back in the loft where he'd lived for the last five months. Kelsey watched as he eyed the bookcase, then sauntered to the sliding ladder attached to the ceiling-high bookcase. He climbed the steps leading to the place on the fifth shelf where his favorite space lay in the midst of large hardback books. He stepped off the ladder on to his special cushion, nestled between *Moby Dick* and *Anna Karenina*. After circling it twice, sniffing furiously to make certain no other cat had invaded his space, he settled down and began purring loudly as he gave himself a slow, ecstatic wash.

Kelsey went back to her car and retrieved her suitcase. She carried it to her bedroom and dumped the contents on her bed. It contained only the clothes Eve had packed when she brought the suitcase to the hospital after Lori's death. Kelsey tossed most of the clothes into two heaps, some to be washed – and some to be thrown away because she couldn't bear to look at them again, much less wear them.

Finally she went into her open kitchen with its black cabinets, white marble countertops, stainless-steel appliances and white stone-slab backsplash. She opened the gleaming refrigerator. It had been full of fresh food for Lori's visit. Eve had disposed of most of it, which would have spoiled by now. The refrigerator was nearly empty. She gratefully discovered a loaf of wheat bread in the freezer, put two slices in the toaster, found peanut butter and jelly and made a thick sandwich. She'd eaten very little during the past week, and the sandwich tasted unbelievably good.

No one had been aware that she'd returned to her loft, so after she'd finished her food she called downstairs to the store and told Stuart she was back. He asked what he could do to help her, and she said she was fine and ready to return to work tomorrow. He assured her that they could make it through another day without her, but she was determined. She knew the only thing that could save her now was work. She needed to immerse herself in interior design. She was good at that, she thought. Lately she had not been so good at life, but she *had* to keep trying to be strong and stable. She couldn't crumble. As she'd realized this last week, her father would never recover if his second daughter fell apart. For his sake, she wouldn't let that happen, no matter what came her way.

At ten o'clock she curled up on the couch with a bowl of microwave popcorn and tried to watch television, but she couldn't concentrate. She kept thinking about how anxious Olivia had been when she apologized for Brad's absence at Pieter Vaden's funeral. 'He's sick. He says it's the flu, but I think it's exhaustion. I'm worried about him, Truman. That law firm is working him to death.' She'd gazed at Truman with distressed green eyes.

Kelsey's father, cool and distant because of his tranquilizer, had looked at Olivia emptily. 'He's young. He'll be fine,' he'd said tonelessly.

Olivia persisted dramatically. 'Truman, Bradley's not well, I tell you. He's working too hard.'

'Well, what do you want me to do about it?' Truman had snapped. Olivia looked as if he'd hit her.

'I just thought you could speak to one of the partners at the firm,' she'd gone on meekly. 'John Reid is a senior partner. He's *your* lawyer. He's your friend and has influence at the firm.'

'Now isn't the time to talk about this,' Kelsey had said in a hard voice. 'This is my grandfather's funeral, in case you've forgotten. No one except you is thinking about Bradley today.'

But that wasn't quite true. Throughout the service she'd thought of Brad at Lorelei's funeral reception. She remembered him looking at Lori's Palomino before his gaze turned venomous and he announced that his stepfather had had his sick horse put down without getting it adequate medical care. He'd sounded young and wounded, and bitter with a long-nurtured fury. He'd even seemed resentful of the March horses, who received the best medical care possible.

And what about Declan Adair, the man who had passed himself off as Cole Harrington at Lori's funeral? Pike said he was a private detective – a man with a reputation for being an exceptional PI. A man whom even Pike hadn't been able to find in Louisville. A man who'd stood eating apple pie and staring at the barn, admiring it and the horses. A man who'd made her heart skip a beat under his intense gaze. Why had he been so interested? Could he have come back that night with a can of kerosene? She couldn't imagine why he'd do such a thing, but then she didn't know him at all. He could be capable of anything.

Or did the barn burning have something to do with Pieter telling Olivia he knew she was pursuing Truman? He'd said Olivia hated him for it. Could she possibly have set the barn on fire? Could *she* have set Pieter on fire? Now she sat going over it all again while the television rattled on, unwatched. She closed her eyes. 'Don't think about this now,' she said aloud. 'You have to get some sleep. You have to go back to work tomorrow.'

Kelsey shuddered. She hadn't been able to shake off the chill that had gripped her after she watched her grandfather burn to death. Although it was a warm night, she was wearing a long, heavy black velour robe over her satin nightshirt. She'd left the rabbit slippers at her father's house, and now had on the elegant black and gold suede slippers that Lori had given her for Christmas. Lorelei . . .

A tear ran down her face and she looked at Gatsby sleeping peacefully on his cushion. If only she could be so tranquil—

Suddenly, Gatsby raised his head, tensed, and then leaped from his spot on the bookshelf. He hit the floor with a thump and ran to the floor-to-ceiling corner windows, one of which Kelsey had left slightly open. He nosed his way underneath the translucent pleated blind on the window facing the alley and the walkway between the garage and the stairs. He raised himself up on his hind legs and put his front paws on the window, then stood motionless, staring.

Kelsey had never seen Gatsby move so quickly or show much interest in the view from the corner windows. His behavior unnerved her, and she sat frozen on the couch. Finally she glanced at the wall clock and realized Gatsby had stood vigil for three minutes. It was now 11:05. She got up and approached the window. A nearby floor lamp with an opal shade put out muted light. Kelsey pushed aside the semi-transparent blind a couple of inches and peered down. In spite of the light coming from the wall sconce mounted outside her door, all she saw was the outline of a man. He wore a hoodie with the hood raised. His head was turned away from her window – she couldn't see his face – but he stood casually at the edge of the alley, his hands in his pockets. The image of Vernon Nott standing innocently on the sidewalk in dim light before pulling a gun and shooting Lorelei seared through Kelsey's mind. This man looked just as harmless as Nott. At least from this angle he did.

Kelsey's heart pounded and she went cold to her bones, but she couldn't pull away from the window. She longed to slam it shut, but didn't want to make any noise. Besides, it would take at least a twenty-foot ladder to reach the corner windows. The sturdy front door was locked and bolted. No one could get in unless she let them in, and she wasn't going to open the door for *anyone* at this hour – not even Pike.

Suddenly, an idea gripped Kelsey. Wasn't the man's build and stance familiar? Could it be . . .

'Brad,' she called softly. Then loudly, 'Brad? Is that you?'

The man stiffened. She thought he would look up. Instead, he kept his head tilted downward. After a few seconds, he pulled something from his pocket and a small, bright light flared in the darkness. Kelsey flinched, thinking of the barn fire. Then she realized it was a lighter. He was just lighting a cigarette. Mesmerized, for nearly four minutes she watched the glowing cigarette end rise up and down. Finally, the man dropped the cigarette and ground it with his shoe. At last, he turned, still not lifting his head, and began walking slowly down the alley past Kelsey's garage and into the shadows.

She thought he was singing.

NINE

Kelsey leaned back in her pale blue swivel desk chair, looked at the ceiling and thought about brushing up on her handgun skills. Four years ago, her mother had been worried when Kelsey had taken a gun-safety course and upset when she'd proved herself a good marksman, applied for a concealed weapon license, and bought a Glock 26. Her license hadn't expired. Her Glock lay safely in a fingerprint safety box kept in the second drawer of her mirrored bedside table. And if there was ever a time when she felt the need of protection more dangerous than the pepper spray she usually carried . . .

'Kelsey, am I bothering you?'

Kelsey sat up straight and looked at Eve. 'Not at all.'

'You looked lost in thought. Coming up with new inspirations for the Sanderson job?'

'I'd forgotten the Sanderson job exists. I have to get my mind back on business.' Kelsey smiled. 'Come in and sit down. Want some coffee? I just made a pot of hazelnut coffee. I know it's one of your favorites.'

Eve grinned. 'I smelled it as I came down the hall.'

As Eve came in, shut the door and sat down, Kelsey fixed a mug of coffee the way Eve liked it. 'I'm not on a par with Olivia as a hostess, but at least I know you like cream in your coffee.'

Eve laughed. 'She's so proud of what she considers her refined manners, when really she's one of the rudest people I've ever met.'

'She wasn't rude at Grandfather's funeral.' Kelsey handed Eve the coffee mug. 'She just seemed desperate. Did you notice?'

'How could I help but notice?' Eve had attended the funeral with Stuart. 'No one was upset that Brad didn't attend the funeral, but she kept going on about him suffering exhaustion from working too hard.'

'I know.' Kelsey sat down with her own mug of fresh coffee. It was her fifth since she'd awakened feeling heavy and blurry because of the sleeping pill she'd taken when she was still wide awake at 1:00 a.m. 'She's always been so concerned about Brad. Not about his welfare but about *advancing* him. He's very good-looking – she got lucky on that count. But Brad's neither brilliant nor ambitious. Olivia and Milton chose his career. It was their way or else he was on his own, and Brad's attachment to Olivia isn't what I'd call normal. He resents her but he'd crumble without her.' Kelsey took a sip of coffee. 'Milton used his influence to get Brad into John Reid's law firm, but Brad hates practicing law. He's also not very good at it. He isn't going anywhere in the firm. In fact, I think he's on the verge of being fired.'

'Are you sure he hasn't been fired already?'

'No,' Kelsey said thoughtfully. 'I'm not certain, though I wouldn't be surprised. He had a reason for lying about being in The Silver Dollar with a woman the night Lori was murdered. I've thought about it. You said his date looked about eighteen and was tall with almost waist-length black hair. That sounds like John Reid's daughter, Megan.'

'It *was* his daughter,' Eve said quietly. 'I saw her with her parents at Lorelei's funeral. She was dressed and acted much more subdued than at The Silver Dollar, but she was still unmistakable. I noticed that she and Brad made a point of not looking at each other.'

Kelsey slowly shook her head. 'If Brad has gotten involved with her, he's making a huge mistake. John is a senior partner in the law firm. I know he isn't happy with Brad's work. He's also extremely protective of Megan. She's barely eighteen. If he found out Brad was seeing her – taking her places and getting her drunk – he would be furious. It could be why Brad lied, claiming that on the night Lori was killed he was home watching TV all evening. After all, he didn't need an alibi. There was no doubt that Vernon Nott shot Lori, and no real proof that he was hired – at least not yet. Anyway, if Brad is seeing Megan, it could be the end for him at the firm.'

'That makes sense,' Eve said quietly. 'I almost feel sorry for Brad. *Almost*.' Eve looked at Kelsey closely and frowned. 'I know you're devastated about your sister and grandfather, but I get the feeling something else is wrong. You're so pale, Kelsey. Your hands are trembling. Even your right eyelid is twitching.'

'The hands? The eye? Too much caffeine.'

Eve continued frowning.

'Oh, all right. Something odd happened last night.'

Kelsey told Eve about the man who'd stood beside the store last night – the man whose face she never saw. When she finished, Eve burst out, 'You call that *odd*? I'd call it damned scary.'

'It was. And I think it may have been Brad. He smoked a whole cigarette without ever looking up, but he knew I was there, watching him, getting frightened. I could feel it.' Kelsey paused, then said hesitantly, 'I think he was singing as he walked away. It was so odd, and . . . well . . . scary. Something's not right with Brad.'

Eve blinked at her. '*Singing?*'

Kelsey nodded.

'What was he singing?'

'Well, it sounded like "Gimme Shelter." You know, by the Rolling Stones.'

'Oh!' Eve's lips parted. 'Does Brad like that song?'

'He likes the Rolling Stones.'

Eve stared. 'Did you take the sleeping pill before you saw him?'

'Almost two hours afterward.'

'Could you have dreamed it?'

'I don't remember dreaming about Brad or any man, much less one trying to frighten me.'

Eve took a deep breath. 'Kelsey, you should tell Detective Pike about the man and how he stood for so long without looking up.'

Kelsey nodded.

'And . . . well, about the singing, too.'

'Eve, you should have seen your face when I said he was singing "Gimme Shelter." I know it sounds crazy, but Brad has been acting crazy. Think about only a few weeks ago when he told Stuart he'd picked you – the good one, the kind one, and that if he wanted to keep you safe he should take you away from Louisville. He's gone beyond just acting like the hurt, spurned lover. He's acting . . . well . . . creepy. Unpredictable . . . Still, I'd hate to set the police on Brad if it wasn't him last night. And I can't bear to think he might be behind anything more sinister . . .'

'I understand.' Eve looked at her earnestly. 'But two people have been murdered in your family in the last couple of weeks. You need to constantly think about it for your own protection. You also need to tell Pike everything, even if you believe it sounds silly. He's a good man, Kelsey, and he's a *smart* man who respects you. Tell him. Please.'

Kelsey sighed. 'I promise to call him today.'

At two o'clock, Kelsey walked through the doors of Conway's Tavern, trying desperately not to think about the last time she'd come to the bar, with Lorelei. A few people sat at tables eating sandwiches. A couple of them looked at Kelsey and stopped eating in favor of staring. Now *she* was recognized just as Lorelei had been everywhere she went. Self-conscious, Kelsey hurried toward the booths across from the bar, purposely not picking the one where she and Lori had sat that awful night less than two weeks ago.

She was surprised when Janet O'Rourke appeared at the booth holding a menu. 'Hi, Miss March,' she said in her soft voice. 'It's so nice to see you.'

'Nice to see you too, Janet. I didn't know you worked the early shift.'

'We were closed for a few days after . . .' Janet's face colored. 'Well, the incident. Still, I missed some shifts when we reopened. I wanted to make up for them.'

'I see.' Kelsey took the menu Janet offered as her eyes widened. 'Janet, have you just got married?' she asked, staring at the gold band on the third finger of the young woman's left hand.

'I've been married for almost three years. I don't always wear my wedding ring, but when I do I usually wear it on my right hand because I'm left-handed and the ring bothers me.'

Kelsey started to say that she'd never seen the ring on Janet's right hand either, but the argument died in her throat when she looked into Janet's big hazel eyes and saw the plea to believe her. Kelsey wasn't going to press for the truth. It was none of her business.

'Well, it's very pretty, Janet.'

Janet looked relieved, although she said, 'It's just a plain, skinny thing. But it's real gold. At least, I think it is.'

'I'm sure it is.' Kelsey smiled. 'I don't need the menu. I'll have a grilled cheese sandwich.'

'That *all*? Not your usual turkey and bacon with French fries?'

'I'm not in the mood for meat. But I'll have coleslaw too. And a Coke.'

'I'll be back in no time with your lunch.' Janet looked at Kelsey almost shyly. 'It's good to have you here for lunch again, Miss March.'

'It's good to be here. And it's Kelsey.'

Janet smiled at her and rushed away from the booth as if the order was for an impatient, demanding customer. In less than a minute, Rick Conway stood beside the booth. 'Hello, Kelsey,' he said in his deep, slow voice. 'May I sit down for a few minutes?'

'Of course.'

He slid into the booth and smiled at her. 'You look good.'

'No, I don't. I have dark circles under my eyes and I'm too thin.' She paused. 'But thank you anyway.'

'I was very sorry to hear about what happened to your grandfather. So was Janet.'

'We got your flowers. Dad and I were touched.'

'Well, we'd met your grandfather at Lorelei's . . .'

'It's OK to say funeral.'

'All right. Anyway, we'd met him and he was such a kind man. We couldn't come because Sunday was Derby Day and we had to stay open.'

'Really, Rick, it's fine. As for the reception after Lori's funeral . . . Grandfather wasn't himself. A year ago, he was fine. But the last three or four months his physical health started going downhill and he began having a few memory lapses. After Lori's murder – well, you saw how he was. The morning of the funeral, he thought Stuart was someone who's been in prison for years. He thought *you* were a boyfriend of my grandmother's named Milo.'

'So Milo really existed?'

'Yes. He asked my grandmother to marry him. She turned him down, but Grandfather always felt he'd had a close call.' Kelsey paused, smiling. 'I've seen a picture of Milo in my grandmother's old photo album. He was tall and slender and you look a little bit like him, but it was your dark curly hair that caught Grandfather's eye. Milo's hair was just like yours. I think Grandfather had always been jealous of that hair!' Her smile faded. 'Seeing you at the reception was the third time in the last couple of months Grandfather thought he saw Milo. Each time he told us we brushed it off, trying to ignore what was happening to him. Thank you for going along with him at the reception. That night before he went to bed . . .' Kelsey's throat tightened but she swallowed and went on. 'That night he realized he'd made a mistake. He said you were too young to be Milo.'

Rick looked at her solemnly, his brown eyes with their long dark lashes full of compassion. 'I don't know many details of what happened to your grandfather except that there was a fire and he passed away—'

'He didn't *pass away*. He *burned* to death in a raging fire.' Kelsey's hands began to tremble. She put her elbows on the table and clasped her hands tightly. 'Grandfather had begun wandering at night. And that night . . . well, at first we thought he'd accidentally set fire to the barn when he was trying to light a lamp with kerosene. But he hadn't. The fire investigators found evidence of arson by someone who knew what they were doing. Whoever it was must have thrown kerosene over Grandfather when he was freeing the horses. They're fine, but Grandfather—'

'You don't need to go into upsetting details, Kelsey.' Rick reached across the table and grasped one of her trembling hands. His was large and steady. He rubbed his fingers over her cold palms. The gesture was almost intimate but she didn't pull away. His dark brown gaze seemed to wrap her in a warm, sympathetic blanket. 'Would you like a drink, Kelsey?'

'No. I've gone back to work. I don't want to arrive drunk this afternoon.'

'Just a glass of wine?'

She shook her head, smiling. 'I'd like to think I can get through one afternoon without the help of medication or alcohol.'

'OK.' He grinned and winked at her. 'Always the tough girl.'

Kelsey sniffed and, desperate to change the subject, said, 'I didn't know Janet was married.'

Rick suddenly looked unhappy. 'Yeah. His name's Joey and he's bad news. I don't like him to come in here. He starts arguments with Janet and just generally upsets her. He did it a few times when we first opened. Now we seem to have lost his business, thank God.'

'Didn't he object to her coming to Lorelei's funeral with you?'

'He was out of town on – I quote – "important business," though no one except Janet knows what it is he does for a living. He didn't know she came to the funeral.'

'I wonder why she stays with him.'

Rick looked at her steadily. 'He's quick with the slaps and an occasional punch in the abdomen.'

'That's terrible!'

'It sure is, but I've been told battered women often stay with boyfriends or husbands until they're suddenly ready to leave. I suppose Janet isn't ready.'

'That's hard for me to understand.'

'Just try understanding *fear*. It's a great motivator.'

'Oh, I feel so bad for her.' Kelsey hesitated then plunged on. 'Rick, why do you think Vernon Nott came here so often? There were bars closer to where he lived, but it seems he always came here.'

Rick's gaze wandered as he slowly frowned. 'I've thought a lot about that. I believe he liked the tavern atmosphere. He always paid attention when people played the piano and sang. He seemed to enjoy it.' He paused. 'He also seemed to like Janet. He even smiled at her.'

'You mean he had a crush on her?'

Rick smiled. 'Well . . . in a way. I know that's hard to believe considering his assault record. Detective Pike told me he'd actually shot a girlfriend. I didn't know anything about his background before the investigation, and Janet didn't say anything about him being inappropriate with her. She looks younger than she is and she's not the least bit flirtatious – he seemed to treat her like a sweet little kid. Still, I didn't feel comfortable with her being his waitress and moved her to a different section. He didn't follow – he always stayed in the same area of the bar near the piano, so maybe Janet didn't mean a thing to him. I think I made the right decision, though.' He wiped a hand over his face. 'What am I saying? The right decision would have been to ban him from this place.'

'He never caused any trouble, and you didn't know about his past. And you couldn't have imagined what he would do to Lori.'

'That's generous of you, Kelsey, but I feel responsible for what happened to your sister. Nott didn't seem *right* to me. I should have trusted my intuition and checked up on him. I now know he'd done time in prison for assault on a woman – or rather, women. I could have found a record of that if I'd tried hard enough. Why the hell didn't I try?'

'You can drive yourself crazy thinking that way, Rick,' Kelsey said gently. 'You mustn't do it, just as I can't keep beating myself up because I brought Lori here. It won't change anything. It will just destroy us.'

'I guess so,' Rick said reluctantly, then looked troubled. 'A guy has been here a couple of times asking questions about you and about that night. He said his name is Declan Adair. I saw him at the reception after your sister's funeral, but I don't think I heard his name. He has blonde hair and blue eyes—'

'I know who he is,' Kelsey said abruptly. Rick looked at her questioningly, but she didn't want to explain that he was the half-brother of a man with whom her sister was having an affair.

'You know he's a private detective?'

'Yes.'

'Do you know who he's working for?'

'Maybe,' Kelsey said carefully. 'I'm not sure.'

Rick frowned. 'This is none of my business, but you don't seem surprised he came here looking for information.'

'Wouldn't this be the natural place to come if he wanted to know about that night?' Kelsey drew a breath. 'Detective Pike knows about him.'

'I see. Pike checked out Adair and gave his blessing to him nosing into the case? That's why you're so calm?'

'Pike didn't necessarily give his blessing. He just looked into Adair's background and no obvious alarm bells went off.'

'How do you feel about Adair insinuating himself into the investigation?'

'If he was hired to find out what happened to Lori—'

'What happened to her? Vernon Nott killed her!'

'I guess someone wants to know *why* he killed her and they're not confident the police will discover the truth.' Or else someone wants to make sure the police don't discover who hired Vernon, Kelsey thought, and possibly who killed my grandfather.

'They don't think Nott was just nuts?'

'Probably. That's why I'm not upset about Adair.' Which was an absolute lie. Kelsey was furious. Why was Declan Adair sneaking around asking questions? How *dare* he? What did he hope to find out? How much Lori had said about Cole Harrington? Was he making certain his brother was clear of suspicion in Lori's murder? Was he protecting Cole and his wife?

'Well, I didn't answer very many of Adair's questions, especially about you,' Rick said tensely.

'I appreciate that.'

'So you're really not concerned about Adair? You don't care if he comes here asking more questions?'

'Not really,' Kelsey lied again. Then added, 'Maybe you could just say you've told him all you know.'

'That would be the truth.' Rick's brown eyes probed her face. She knew he sensed she wasn't being open and felt slightly ashamed. Still, he said mildly, 'OK. I just wanted you to know about him.'

'Thanks for being concerned.'

Suddenly, their gazes met and held for a moment. Kelsey thought she saw affection in Rick's. She was touched more than she would have guessed possible. Then he glanced to the left. 'Here comes your lunch.' Janet approached the booth carrying a tray and set down the cheese sandwich and coleslaw and a Coke. 'That's not what I'd call a hearty meal.'

'It's what I want.'

'Sure you wouldn't like to have a glass of wine?'

'I'm sure. '

'Good enough. I'll leave you to enjoy your lunch. But Kelsey?'

'Yes?'

'Don't be a stranger here. And if there's anything I can do for you—'

'You've already saved my life, Rick.'

'Which means I'm now responsible for it.' He smiled. 'If there's anything else I can do for you – *anything* – just let me know.'

'I will.' Kelsey looked into his large, sincere eyes. 'Thank you, Rick. For everything.'

Kelsey decided to throw herself into tackling plans for the Sanderson property. Originally built by Jacob Sanderson as a furniture factory in the early 1950s, the property had passed from Jacob to his son and then his grandson, who ten years ago had moved the successful furniture-manufacturing business to a large new building on the outskirts of Louisville and deeded the old factory to his own son, Aaron. Aaron Sanderson and his wife Josie were young, attractive and fun, and two of Kelsey's favorite people. She'd known Aaron for years and was thrilled when the couple had asked her to turn the old factory into a modern industrial-style home for them and their three children, who ranged in age between ten and sixteen.

Peering through her reading glasses, Kelsey studied the three-dimensional design plans on her laptop as well as the architect's blueprints. She frowned over the number and location of the six new rectangular skylights the Sandersons wanted on the building's flat roof. The couple had argued hotly in front of Kelsey over light-filtering versus blackout remote-control blinds for the skylights and then about the size of a seventh dome skylight, which they wanted located on the roof above a three-story floating spiral stairway. Kelsey had worked with dozens of couples who'd nearly come to blows over the most simple design detail. Aaron and Josie were no different. Still, they had to stop bickering and decide soon. The skylight problem had to be solved and the job completed before interior work could begin as scheduled early next month.

Someone tapped on Kelsey's office door and she absently called, 'Come in.' One of her associates, Nina Evans, seven months pregnant and nearing maternity leave, opened the door with a big smile on her long, plain, but always animated face.

Nina nearly tiptoed to Kelsey's desk, leaned over it and whispered gleefully, 'The most gorgeous, sexiest man I've ever seen is waiting to see you. I don't think he's a client.' She paused as if waiting for Kelsey to guess the man's name. Instead, Kelsey merely raised an eyebrow. 'He said he's Declan Adair. *Declan.*' Nina patted her tummy. 'My baby is a boy. I'm going to name him Declan no matter what Harry thinks. He's just the father, after all.' Nina giggled. 'Should I send him in?'

Kelsey forced a patient smile. 'Yes, please.'

'Are you mad at me? You look a little strange.'

'I've been focused on skylights for what seems like hours and I always look mad when I'm wearing my glasses. Please send Mr Adair in.'

'OK. But take off your glasses.'

Without thought, Kelsey removed her tortoiseshell-rimmed glasses as Nina turned abruptly and left, clearly disappointed with Kelsey's reaction to getting a 'gorgeous' male visitor.

What in the name of God is Declan Adair going to say to me? Kelsey wondered as she laid her glasses aside. At least everyone is in the office today, but I still wish an authority figure like Pike was here. Or Rick, with his air of protector. She felt very much on edge, but wasn't sure if that was to do with Pike's warning or the prospect of Declan Adair's intense gaze on her again.

He appeared in the doorway. 'Hello, Miss March.'

'Hello . . . Mr Adair. Is that your real name? Or are you a chameleon, changing your colors to fit in with the environment?'

'I suppose I deserve that. May I come in?'

Kelsey hesitated. 'I don't know why you're here, but yes. And close the door behind you. I don't want my employees overhearing us.'

'Good idea considering what the subject of our conversation will be,' Adair said affably. He shut the door, then walked toward her and sat down on a guest chair across from her desk. He wore slim-fit dark-wash jeans and an off-white shirt, and looked just as handsome as he had at the funeral. For a moment he said nothing, silently appraising her. Kelsey couldn't help feeling momentarily mesmerized by his light hair with blonde sun streaks, his tanned face, his piercing, electric-blue eyes, and his slender but sensuous lips. She had to agree with Nina – he was gorgeous, but in an easy, effortless way. He probably looked almost the same when he rolled out of bed in the morning.

Kelsey narrowed her eyes. 'You're investigating me.'

'Investigating this case, to be precise. I should have told you before I began, but you haven't been available.'

'I have a phone, Mr Adair.'

'And I didn't use it. Sorry. Sometimes I'm impetuous. I'm also sorry I let you believe I was Cole Harrington at your sister's funeral,' he began. 'I never said I was Cole, though. You just assumed I was.'

'And you didn't correct me because you wanted to be invited into our home.'

His expression wasn't the least bit remorseful. 'That's true. But you don't look surprised. I suppose Detective Pike has discovered what I do.'

'You're a private investigator. I've also learned you've been to Conway's Tavern asking questions about me.'

'I was just doing my job – trying to find out what happened that night. And I didn't ask a lot of questions about *you*. Maybe two – three at the most. Who told you? Rick Conway?'

'Yes. He wouldn't know who Cole Harrington is, much less that you're his half-brother.'

'I didn't announce it. It's no one's business, except maybe yours. That's why I've come here to clear the slate with you.' He smiled. 'I'm three years younger than Cole.'

'Congratulations.'

'You're angry with me.'

'I don't like the idea of a private investigator nosing around in my life.'

'Even if he might help you?'

'*Even if.*' She gave him a hard stare. 'If I'd listened to Lori's description of Cole I would have known you weren't him. She said his eyes were almost the same shade of violet-blue as hers. Yours are more sapphire. She said he had a scar on his jaw – you don't – and she said he was six feet tall. You're taller.'

'I'm six-two.'

'Good for you.' If Declan had come here to smooth the waters, she wasn't going to make it easy. 'Lorelei told me that Grant Harrington had several children but only gave his surname to Cole. If you're three years younger than Cole, Grant must have moved on from Cole's mother to yours.'

Declan's striking blue eyes rested on her for a moment, before he looked at the framed poster on the wall behind her. 'Is that Amelia Earhart standing on the nose cone of her plane?'

'What?' Was he resorting to evasion? 'Yes. I've been fascinated by her ever since I was a kid. I wanted to be a pilot.'

'Did you take flying lessons?'

'No. My mother thought they were too dangerous.'

'And you didn't take them after you became an adult?'

'I'm afraid not.'

'It's never too late.'

'I'll give it some thought.'

'What do you think happened to her? Amelia, I mean.'

'I believe her plane crashed in the Pacific Ocean and she died. Why? Do you have a theory?'

Declan grinned. 'Currently no, although I used to believe she survived her crash and lived the rest of her life in happy secrecy on an exotic island. Actually, that is my mother's theory. She's a romantic.' He shifted his gaze to her. 'That smells like fresh coffee in the pot behind you. May I have some?'

Kelsey wanted to tell him to mind his own business and kick him out of her office, but this was not the time for a childish show of temper. She'd already tried to insult him about his father and that hadn't worked. He seemed to take jibes in his stride. Maybe it was best to find out as much about this man and Cole Harrington as possible.

She stood up and lifted a thermal coffee mug. 'How do you take it?'

'Black.'

Kelsey poured the coffee. As she leaned across her desk in order to pass the mug to him, Declan stood and reached out for it. Their hands touched and Kelsey felt absurdly aware of the contact of her skin with his. She nearly jerked her hand away. Declan seemed to ignore it. Before he sat down, he took a sip of the coffee and smiled. 'It's good.'

'It's hazelnut – one of my favorites.'

'I'll remember that.'

'Why? Do you picture us sharing coffee often?'

'I guess *you* don't.' He grinned at her, showing straight white teeth. 'Forgive my assumption, Kelsey.'

How cocky he is, Kelsey thought angrily. He didn't ask if he could call me Kelsey. He's also not one bit sorry that he misrepresented himself so he could invade our home.

Telling him to call her 'Miss March' would sound prissy, so she attacked on another front. 'You mentioned Cole, so I feel

I'm entitled to ask another question about him and I'd appreciate an answer to this one. Don't try to change the subject.'

'Yes, ma'am.' There was a glint in his eye.

'And don't patronize me. I know your father was involved with a lot of women and had several children. Are all of Grant Harrington's children friends, like you and Cole?'

Kelsey had thought she'd at least make Declan Adair uncomfortable, but he only gave her a half-smile and nodded. 'My mother's name is Gemma. She was beautiful – still is – and had a good singing voice. She could act fairly well and wanted to be a Broadway star. Grant "discovered" her when she was twenty. They were together for three years.

'To answer your earlier question,' he went on, 'the only reason Mom allowed me to be friends with Cole was because she came on to the scene *after* Cole's mother, Joan. Grant hadn't even met my mother when he left Joan. Grant wanted Cole and me to be close because we were his sons. Joan allowed it because she thought it would make Grant happy and she desperately wanted him back.' Declan smiled. 'Also, Mom had insisted – very vocally – that my last name be Adair, not Harrington. For some reason, Joan saw that as making me less of a threat to Cole. People still thought of him as Grant's only son.

'When I was about four, Joan got uterine cancer,' Declan went on. 'While she was dying and living with her sister, Mom and I spent time with her and Cole. The end of the story is that my mother never became a star on Broadway – she could sing, but she was no Barbra Streisand and directors said her acting was wooden. Miraculously, though, Joan and my mother became friends and remained friends until Joan's death. Cole and I are still close.'

'I see. Did Grant spend time with Joan after she got sick?'

'No. He said illness depressed him.'

'Why am I not surprised? He was a real prince, wasn't he?'

'He was a jerk, and I've known it since I was about six years old.' Declan flashed his disarming smile. 'He died nine years ago and I've had a lot of time to work on forgiving him. I now realize he was simply incapable of forming a lasting relationship with a woman. And he did provide for his children . . .' Again, the smile. 'All six of them. I have four half-sisters.'

'Gosh!' Kelsey realized she'd sounded like a shocked child and tried to regain her distance by asking coolly, 'Are you close to your sisters?'

'No. One lives in Canada, one in England, one in Spain, and the youngest in Mozambique. Three of them exchange emails with me at Christmas. I've never even seen the one who lives in Spain.'

'Your half-sisters span the globe, but you and Cole grew up in New York City?'

'Yes. When I was eighteen, I went to California. I stayed in Los Angeles until I was twenty-three, then I came back to New York City. Cole never left New York. His aunt was a successful fashion photographer, and Cole had a foot in the door by the time he was seventeen. He was extremely talented – a *wunderkind* – and he's been one of the top fashion photographers for at least twelve years.'

'Which is why his wife doesn't want him to throw over his career in fashion to be a wildlife photographer.'

'Partly. Delphina wants him in New York with her because she has no intention of following him to Africa to take pictures of "filthy animals," as she calls them. Also, she knows Cole is both fickle and refined. No doubt he'd get tired of being a wildlife photographer within a couple of years. He's not like our father, who loved the heat, the dirt, the bugs, setting up camp, and food cooked over the campfire. And Cole is too impatient to wait hours on end for an animal to do something worth a photo. He's not cut out for it, but he wants to follow in our father's footsteps.'

'He wants to be like Grant?'

'He wants to be *better* than Grant. That's the whole point of this planned career change. Competition with his father.'

'And you don't want to compete with Grant?'

'No. I admired him in some ways, but I don't have enough feeling for him to want to emulate him or try to outshine him.'

'How did you become a private investigator?'

Suddenly, Declan's demeanor changed. He hesitated then said tersely, 'I was an officer with the New York Police Department. When I was twenty-six, I decided to quit and become a private investigator.' He looked at her coolly. 'Do you have any other questions for me, Kelsey?'

'Yes. How did you get your tan and your sun-bleached hair?'

Declan looked surprised, then laughed. His laughter was joyous and resonant, and his smile returned. Kelsey felt tension melting away from her slightly.

'I'm back from a three-week vacation in Los Angeles. More specifically, Malibu.'

'Three whole weeks?'

'Yep. I love surfing. Have you ever tried it?'

'I'm a weak swimmer, so no.'

'You're probably a great equestrienne.'

'Not really. None of those horses I pointed out to you the day of Lori's funeral was mine.' Declan had the grace to look slightly abashed. 'About that day. I suppose Cole asked you to come to Lorelei's funeral.'

'Yes.'

'Why?'

Declan's gaze slid away from her and he exhaled. Kelsey could see that he was uncomfortable and hoped that meant she was getting somewhere. 'Do you mind if I smoke?'

'Yes.'

'OK. May I just hold a cigarette?'

'If you must.'

'I *must*. I'm quitting after a ten-year habit.' He produced a cigarette and began twirling it through his fingers. 'I'll start at the beginning,' he said slowly. 'Delphina was at the peak of her career when she met Cole. She was twenty-nine, and he was twenty-two and starstruck when she started coming on to him. Even though she was demanding and possessive and unbelievably insecure, I can honestly say he was in love with her when they got married.' He sighed. 'You probably know where this is going.'

'I'd rather you tell me than to guess,' Kelsey said. 'You witnessed their marriage – I didn't.'

'At first everything was fine. Delphina had to travel a lot for her career, but Cole wasn't a big name yet so was able to go with her. Then, over a course of about two years, Cole's career took off and he was traveling as much as Delphina. They were always going to different places, though. Finally, Delphina's career started lagging. To put it plainly, she didn't age well.'

'Oh?'

A corner of Declan's mouth lifted. 'I know what you're thinking – the PI business is sexist and I'm sexist. Well, the business can be sexist, but I'm not. Let's get that cleared up right now.'

Kelsey shrugged, hoping to convey indifference.

'Back to Cole and Delphina,' Declan said. 'First, Delphina started putting on weight she couldn't lose. Then she had some health problems – nothing serious, but she was violently allergic to one of her medications. Her face swelled and blistered. The blisters healed but they left noticeable pits and her face stayed slightly puffy. Her career took a dive and her self-confidence hit bottom. People weren't kind to her, and there she was with a young, very good-looking celebrity husband who wanted children. Before they got married, Delphina said she did too – but later, when her career slowed down, she thought pregnancy would affect her already fading beauty. Meanwhile, models were coming on to Cole right and left. My brother is outgoing and flirtatious. He enjoyed the attention and returned too much of it. Delphina started making his life miserable. That's the truth, Kelsey. I'm not going on Cole's word. I saw Delphina turn into, frankly, a jealous bitch. I've never been married but I know I couldn't have taken as much as Cole did. Then Lorelei came along.'

'And they had an affair, and Delphina found out about it.'

'Yes. Cole was extremely attracted to Lorelei, and I don't mean just physically. He never talked to me about other women but he did talk about Lorelei. A lot. He even introduced me to her.'

Kelsey blinked, remembering. 'The night she was killed, she told me she knew a private investigator. She must have meant you.'

'Maybe. Cole, Lorelei and I had drinks together one evening.'

'Oh. Cole wanted his half-brother and his girlfriend to socialize? Really?'

'Yes, really. We met in a bar called Black and White. Ever been there?'

'No.'

Declan smiled. 'Delphina never went there, either. It was a safe choice. Anyway, Cole wanted me to meet Lorelei. We spent at least an hour over drinks, and it was obvious that in Cole's eyes she wasn't just a fling. She was unbelievably beautiful,

which I already knew, and even though she was only twenty-one
she seemed even younger. She was intelligent but she seemed
innocent. She wasn't like other twenty-one-year-olds I'd met
who'd been a big name in the fashion business for a couple
of years. I liked her.' He paused. 'I liked her a lot, Kelsey, and
Cole . . .' He jiggled his unlit cigarette. 'I could tell Cole was
crazy about her.'

Kelsey was shocked but didn't want to show it. 'Cole
Harrington, a married professional ladies' man, and my innocent
sister had a meeting of minds?'

Declan's expression changed. 'You don't need to sound so
sarcastic, Kelsey. That is unless you think your sister wasn't
capable of attracting a man with anything except her looks.'

Kelsey felt as if he'd slapped her. That's exactly how she'd
sounded, and her intelligent, sweet, kind sister deserved better.
'I didn't mean to malign Lori,' she said softly. 'I just hate to
think of her being seduced by a serial womanizer.'

'And now it's my turn to defend *my* sibling.' His eyes locked
on hers. 'Cole isn't a serial womanizer. He was serious about
your sister. He kept their relationship extremely low-key. He's
always known Delphina kept a close eye on him. I was surprised
to learn that he'd given Lorelei a necklace. She showed it to me.
It was a heart locket—'

'With *CGH* engraved inside. We found it in her bedroom at
home. I thought maybe she'd bought it for herself.'

'No. Cole said he'd given it to her that day.'

'Giving her a necklace would be one thing. Giving her a
necklace with his initials engraved inside doesn't sound like he
was keeping the relationship low-key.'

'Lorelei said it was a secret gift. He told me later he'd asked
Delphina for a divorce.'

'Divorce?' Kelsey repeated. 'Are you sure?'

'I could always tell when Cole was being sincere. He said he
couldn't stand life with Delphina anymore. He was in love with
someone.'

'But he didn't say this someone was Lorelei.'

'Not when he told me he'd begun talking divorce with
Delphina. After I met Lorelei, he didn't need to say it. He
said Delphina had begged him to wait, to think about things, not

get carried away. He'd expected her to lose it and have a fit like she usually does when things don't go her way. She has the temper of a cobra. But he said she just asked for time. He was suspicious, though. He wondered if she had an ace in the hole, if she was planning something. Then, like every year when neither of them was working, they came to her parents' home in Louisville to see the Kentucky Derby.'

'And Lorelei had come home to Louisville, too.'

Declan nodded. 'Cole knows Delphina better than anyone does. He knows she's crafty and scheming, and that she doesn't intend to let him go without a fight. She also insisted on going back to New York less than eight hours after your sister's death. She didn't want anyone questioning Cole about Lorelei. The day after they got back to New York, Delphina flew to their house in Caracas by herself – Grant had a vacation home there and left it to Cole.' He paused. 'Delphina's never liked it there . . . I don't know if it suddenly occurred to her that Venezuela doesn't have an extradition treaty with the United States.'

Kelsey couldn't speak. Pike had said Declan Adair was extremely smart and very good at his job, and it seemed he was right.

'When Cole heard about Lorelei's death, he was crushed,' Declan went on. 'He called me immediately, and I've never heard him sound so devastated. Aside from his grief, though, he's afraid Delphina may have had her own PI following Lorelei. He wants to know who's behind this.' Declan leaned forward, his expression intense, almost pained. 'Kelsey, Cole is sick with fear that his wife might have hired someone to murder your sister – to shoot Lorelei dead on the street so she would never feel threatened by Lorelei March again.'

TEN

Kelsey applied another coat of mascara, blinked rapidly to dry it, then leaned back to look at her face in her vanity mirror. Was it because she hadn't applied concealer on the dark circles under her eyes, or did she really look at least five years older than she had two weeks ago?

'I do look older, concealer or not,' she said aloud. 'I look more than five years older.' She turned her gaze toward Gatsby, who always lounged on the vanity devotedly watching her apply makeup. 'A month ago, I would've been disturbed that I look older. Now I'm glad. Brad Fairbourne used to tell me I'm cold and unfeeling. He wouldn't look at me now and think I could lose Lori and Grandfather without a shadow on my face.'

Kelsey applied some blush to her unusually pale cheeks. She didn't care about looking pretty. She only wanted to look normal, to act normal, although her sister had lain on top of her bleeding to death from a stranger's bullets; even though she'd watched her grandfather running from the inferno of a barn he'd loved and fall ablaze with fire writhing in front her. No, she knew she would never feel normal again, but she could at least give the appearance of being normal. *That* she could do until they discovered who had caused the deaths of beautiful Lorelei and darling Grandfather Vaden.

Half an hour later, she entered the office of MG Interiors with a smile and said an overly loud 'Good morning!' to Giles Miller, with his lean porcelain-skinned face and blonde wavy hair falling halfway over his forehead. He looked at her with surprise.

'How's your mother doing, Giles?'

'Not at all well,' he said despondently. 'If you remember, she has another operation scheduled for next week. Wednesday.'

'Oh, yes, you did tell me.' At the moment, Kelsey couldn't remember Mrs Miller's health problems – only that she seemed to have a new one every few weeks. 'You'll take Wednesday and the rest of the week off. She'll need you. Of course I'm hoping

for the best!' Giles's pale blue gaze went cold and Kelsey realized she sounded exuberant and insincere. 'Wish her well from
me. From all of us.'

'Thank you,' Giles said stiffly.

He stared at her and she decided to abandon the subject. 'What
are you working on?'

'The Barrett lap pool and fire pit. You assigned that to me.'

'Oh! I guess I did. If you'd rather not do it . . .'

'I'm happy to do it. I've already made a lot of progress.'

'OK. I'm a little absent-minded, Giles. Please forgive me.'

His genteel face softened and he smiled. 'It's understandable,
Kelsey. We all sympathize with what you've gone through lately.
I hope you got my flowers for the . . . well, services.' He flushed.
'I couldn't attend. Mother needed me. But I felt so bad for you.'

Kelsey suddenly felt like she was going to cry. 'We got the
flowers. They were beautiful. Thank you, Giles.'

She wanted to say more but tears were already rising in her
eyes. She turned away from him and hurried into her office, shutting the door behind her. I cannot cry in front of everyone who
works here, she thought. I want their respect. I *need* their respect.

Kelsey wiped away the tears that had spilled down her face and
put a pot of coffee on. This time she chose Irish Crème, which
promised to produce a holiday spirit. While the coffee brewed, she
looked at her African violets in their cream-and-gold glazed ceramic
self-watering pot. Her grandmother had loved violets. Every Easter
Sunday, Pieter used to order an old-fashioned wrist corsage of
violets and lace for her to wear to church. The memory made
Kelsey's stomach clench painfully and tears pressed behind her
eyes. 'I will *not* cry, especially here,' she said aloud. 'Pull yourself
together, Kelsey.'

After a few shaky moments, she decided to talk to Stuart.
Normally, they discussed MG Interiors every Monday morning.
Kelsey wanted to be apprised of how ongoing jobs were
progressing and if they had any new projects. More importantly,
she wanted to show Stuart she wouldn't expect him to shoulder
the responsibility for MG Interiors indefinitely while she spent
another two weeks recovering from grief. She wanted to be the
same competent, focused partner she'd been before Lorelei's
murder.

Stuart hadn't completely closed his office door and it opened nearly a foot when Kelsey tapped on it. Although she didn't go in, she saw that Stuart was standing, his gray, slim-fit jacketed back turned away from her.

'This hasn't been the best time to argue with her,' he said.

Kelsey realized he was talking into his cell phone and started backing away when he exploded, 'I am *not* going to threaten her! That's not the way I operate.'

Stuart turned around sharply, a dark red blush spreading across his prominent cheekbones. Surprisingly, he motioned Kelsey in, his voice almost returning to its usual smooth tones as he said, 'I'm afraid I can't talk any more. My boss just walked in.' He smiled weakly as Kelsey made a face at him. 'We'll speak later.'

'That sounded heated,' Kelsey said as he clicked off his phone and put it in his pocket. She'd never heard Stuart raise his voice before. What had got into him?

'Certain people bring out the worst in me.'

'Well, I've never seen that side of you so that means I'm not one of them, although your conversation seemed to have something to do with me.'

'It was Teddy Blakemore.'

'From prison?'

'He has cell phones smuggled in.'

'What did he want?'

'Something I don't intend to do.' Stuart smiled crookedly. 'He's old and demanding.'

'And a criminal. We don't want to be involved with him!' Kelsey frowned. 'Agree?'

'I don't like Teddy Blakemore.'

Something in Stuart's eyes prompted her to say, 'You didn't answer my question.'

Stuart paused, then smiled. 'You're the boss.'

'I'm *not* the boss. We're partners.'

'Yes. We are. And we both think Blakemore's a sonofabitch.'

'That settles it.' Kelsey grinned. 'But, Stuart, you mustn't think of me as being in charge of MG Interiors.'

'You have more shares than I do,' Stuart said flatly.

'Stuart . . .'

'I don't want to talk about business today.' He smiled, then asked sincerely, 'How are you doing, Kelsey? And I mean *really*. Don't give me the party line.'

'Well, I'm OK. Not great. Not sleeping well. Not able to concentrate. Not on fire with design ideas for the Sanderson project—'

'Not eating.'

'I eat. The calories just don't seem to stick.'

'Can you manage a long lunch today? Because I'd love to take you someplace special.'

'I wasn't hinting—'

'I know.'

'Shouldn't you take out Eve instead?'

'I have a hot date with Eve Saturday night. Dinner, drinking, dancing, howling at the moon – the usual.'

'What's gotten into you today, Stuart?' Kelsey laughed.

'I'm aware that I'm known as a workaholic with no sense of humor. I'm trying to revamp my image. Help me, Kelsey. Even if you don't *really* want to go to lunch with me, think of the speculation it will cause in the office. Nina and Giles will believe you're trying to steal me from Eve. Or that Eve has cut me loose and I'm trying to make her jealous or . . . well, the possibilities are endless.'

'All right. It would be my pleasure.' Kelsey paused. 'Where are we going?'

'Not Conway's Tavern,' Stuart said firmly as if reading her mind. 'I said I want to take you someplace special. How about letting me surprise you?'

'That would be lovely.'

Two hours later, Kelsey swept out of MG Interiors in a white flared dress as Stuart held the door open. Both Nina Evans and Giles Miller gaped at them. As usual, Isaac Baum was in his own world, so caught up in budgets and cost analyses that he never noticed the activities of his co-workers. Eve waved at them and called 'Have fun, you two!', letting Kelsey know Stuart had already alerted her to their lunch plans.

Outside, under the canary yellow sun with a gently warm spring breeze lifting her hair as they headed toward Stuart's car,

Kelsey giggled. 'I feel like we're playing a game.' Then she sobered. 'But I also feel a little guilty.'

'We're not spontaneous, Kelsey. This is a heady if guilt-inducing experience for us.'

'Lori was spontaneous.' Kelsey's voice softened with her memories. 'Even when she was a little girl, she didn't have routines like I did. She was always impetuous, impulsive, passionate, a free spirit – so much fun.'

After a beat, Stuart said quietly, 'Being free-spirited and impulsive *can* be fun. But you can't conduct your whole life that way. It's reckless and leaves you open for trouble because you don't think about the dangers of how you're living.' He linked his arm through hers. 'I know you always thought Lorelei was more fun and loveable than you because she was fancy-free. And I'm certainly not saying she wasn't fun and loveable. She was like some wild, vivid bird soaring above the rest of us!' He pulled Kelsey a couple of inches closer to him. 'But we also need deep, steady streams flowing calmly and smoothly. We need them for balance, for maturity, for peace.'

Stuart's words rang in Kelsey's mind and heart, but she couldn't bear to talk more about her feelings right now. Instead, as he opened his car door for her, she said lightly, 'My, my, you *are* philosophical today, Mr Girard.'

'It happens when I'm hungry,' he returned with equal lightness. 'And I'm starving.'

Stuart did surprise her by taking her to the Captain's Quarters Riverside Grille, one of her favorite restaurants. 'I love this place but I haven't been here for at least a year!' she said in delight as she and Stuart walked through the cabin-style interior. Then they stepped out on to the large outdoor patio overlooking the Ohio River. 'You can't get a table out here without a reservation,' she said.

'We have a reservation. I took a chance that you'd accept my lunch invitation.' Stuart pulled out her chair. 'I thought you'd enjoy eating outside and watching the boats on the river.'

'I love watching the boats.' She looked out at the restaurant's yacht, the three-deck *CQ Princess*. 'My parents chartered the *Princess* for my college graduation party. We went up and down the river. There was a great band and the yacht has a wonderful dance floor. The party lasted until one o'clock in the morning and I was exhausted but *so* happy.' She looked at Stuart, who was sitting down. 'Have you ever been on the *Princess*?'

'No, I haven't.'

'Oh. Well, it would be a fabulous venue for an engagement party.'

Stuart quirked an eyebrow. 'That was subtle.'

'Sorry.'

'Quite all right. Do you think Eve would like a party on the yacht?'

'I *know* she would. Got anything in mind?'

Stuart grinned. 'That's a secret.'

The waitress arrived and asked if they wanted drinks. 'I'll have a white Sangria,' Kelsey said.

'I'll have one, too.' Stuart looked at Kelsey. 'Unless you'll report me to the boss for drinking on the job.'

'You're *not* on the job. Besides, this is a special occasion.'

When the Sangrias came, Kelsey immediately took a sip. 'Ummm. This is *so* good. It feels like I haven't had one of these for a year, but I think it's only been a month.' She closed her eyes. 'Though it's been a hell of a month.'

'I don't know how you've handled it all. And you're already back at work. We didn't expect that to happen for at least two more weeks.'

'I need to work, Stuart. I'll lose my mind if I sit in my apartment and do nothing except think. I suppose I could have stayed longer at Dad's house, but he needs to go back to work too. I called yesterday evening and Helen said he's spending hours on the phone with March Vaden executives, but I know he won't get back to normal until he's actually at the headquarters downtown overseeing everything himself.' Kelsey paused. 'Helen also said Olivia told her she should leave our house. Apparently, Olivia has decided that Helen and Dad sharing a home is *unseemly*.'

Stuart's eyes widened. 'Who says *unseemly* anymore? But I saw for myself how determined Olivia is to get your father down the aisle. Though she's wasting her time, he's not in love with her. Everyone except Olivia can see it.' He took another drink of his Sangria. 'Besides, what's your father supposed to do without Helen?'

'According to Olivia, hire a male housekeeper.'

'Of course! Get rid of the woman who's been with you forever, who's really one of the family, and bring in someone new. A man.'

The waitress returned and gave them their menus. 'I want you to eat a good meal, Kelsey,' Stuart said. 'No picking around at an appetizer.'

'I wouldn't dream of it. I want the smoked beef brisket.'

'Me, too.'

When their food arrived, Kelsey surprised herself by diving into it. She'd lived on sandwiches and snacks for days. She was truly hungry and the beef brisket was delicious. Halfway through her meal, she looked up to see a three-deck yacht sailing by. On the top deck, four young women in colorful tops and denim cut-offs stood beside the railing, waving to people on the restaurant patio. Kelsey joined other restaurant patrons waving back and calling, 'Hi!'

'They look like they're having so much fun!' Kelsey exclaimed. 'I'd like to get on that yacht with them and sail downriver. Or anywhere, for that matter.'

'You want to escape for a while?' Stuart said.

Kelsey nodded.

'Why don't you? You certainly deserve it.'

'Maybe I'll take a trip in a couple of months. Right now I need to focus on the business, particularly the Sanderson house. Aaron and Josie are good friends of mine.' She laughed. 'I won't rest until the place is perfect, even if those two will be ready to get a divorce by the time it's done!'

'Are they that bad?'

'They're no worse than a lot of couples. You've worked on enough house designs to know. I'm just not used to seeing them argue. I've never even seen Josie mad. They've always seemed so mellow – the ideal couple.'

'It's easy to be mellow when you have a ton of money like they do.'

Stuart's voice sounded flat and hard. Kelsey looked at him sharply. 'Do you have a problem with people who have money?' she asked bluntly.

'A lot of them.'

'But Stuart, the Girards have money. Lots of it.'

Stuart stopped eating and stared at his plate. He finished his Sangria in three gulps, then looked at Kelsey and asked quietly, 'Did your father ever tell you anything about my childhood?'

'Not really, except that he's known you all your life. He trusts you and he thought my going into business with you was a good idea.'

Stuart nodded. 'Yes, he knew me. Not well, though. Your grandfather Quinton March was only about ten or twelve years older than my father. He was close to my grandfather and knew my parents well.' He smiled without humor. 'My parents. Now they were a pair!'

'You don't sound like they were a happy pair,' Kelsey said carefully. 'Was their marriage . . . well, rocky?'

'That's a polite word for it. My mother left my father when I was nine. She took me with her.'

'I didn't know that! Where did she take you?'

'New Orleans. She was in love with a guy who owned a bar there. That romance lasted a year.'

'What did your father do when she ran off with his only child?'

Stuart moved food around on his plate. 'My father didn't hunt her down, or set the law on her and force her to give me back to him. Maybe the split was mutual. Neither parent filed for divorce, but they didn't stay in touch. After the bar owner left her, my mother saw other men. I don't know what my father did where other women were concerned. Then, when I was thirteen, Mother decided to come home. I'd really loved my father. I'd idolized him. I was miserable during those years away from him. I was so excited to see him.' Stuart looked up, his gray eyes going cold. 'And when I finally saw him, he said I was not his son.'

'*Not* his son?' Kelsey asked faintly. 'You mean he was mad at you for what your mother had done and said no son of his would have stayed with her?'

'No. He said he was not my biological father. He said Mother was trying to pass off another boy as me so I'd inherit his money. Yes, I'd changed at puberty but, except for being four inches taller and my hair turning dark brown, my appearance wasn't too different from when Mother took me away. Nevertheless, he barely looked at me and wouldn't talk to me.'

Kelsey was aghast. 'Stuart, I can't imagine what that must have been like for you!' He was silent. 'Did they do a DNA test to prove your paternity?'

'Yes. Father wouldn't allow anyone to take a swab from his mouth, so Mother collected some hairs from his brush. Of course the results proved that I *was* his son. But he said he didn't believe in DNA testing. He didn't trust it. He wouldn't budge on the issue. I was crushed. That's when I got to know Teddy Blakemore.'

Kelsey frowned. 'Wasn't he supposed to be involved in business with your father? And rumored to have Mafia ties?'

'Yes on both counts, Kelsey. I barely remember him from before my mother took me away, but after Mother came back and Father rejected me Teddy made an effort to be friends with me. My mother was never involved with him, but he took a great interest in me and spent time with me. He took me to professional ball games. In fact, he was a father figure to me for a few years.'

'Didn't Grandfather say something about him being in prison?'

Stuart's expression was pained. 'Yes. He went to prison, but that wasn't until I was twenty. When I was younger, Teddy pleaded my case with my father. So did Quinton March.'

'My Grandfather March got involved?'

'He certainly did. Quinton talked to me one day. He told me Father had always had psychological problems when it came to the Girard money. My Girard grandfather was extremely tight-fisted. He planted the seeds in Father. He lectured my father, slapped him frequently, berated him constantly about his stupidity concerning money. Quinton told me Father was already predisposed to be suspicious and close with his money but got worse as he got older. He was obsessed with building a fortune, no matter what it took. That's how he got involved with Teddy Blakemore and his not-so-legal money-making schemes. But the more money Father made, the more miserly he grew.

'I don't know who was more influential when it came to getting my father to acknowledge me,' Stuart went on. 'Maybe Quinton threatened him with social ruin. Father was obsessed with what society thought. That's probably why he didn't divorce Mother – it would have looked bad. Then there was Teddy, whom I think threatened to pull out of some financial arrangements with Father

if he didn't publicly accept me. Anyway, Father finally acknowledged me, although he was never affectionate. He was barely
polite. And when he died, he didn't leave Mother a dime. Most
of his fortune went to charity. I think he believed that would win
him divine forgiveness.'

'And he became known as a philanthropist and let me guess
. . . you received almost nothing.'

'Exactly.'

'Oh, Stuart, that's awful.'

'At least, partly because of your grandfather and partly because
of Teddy, I was publicly recognized as my father's legitimate
son.'

'But you never knew the kind of love that my father did, or
that Lori and I did. That had to sting.'

Stuart shrugged.

'It's what you deserved, Stuart.'

'Oh, well, we don't always get what we deserve in life.' Stuart
tried for a jaunty tone, but Kelsey saw the ghost of that crippling
rejection haunting his eyes and lurking around his smile. Stuart
had been wounded. He was still wounded, she realized.

She wondered why he was telling her this, then remembered
her grandfather's outburst. 'Stuart, didn't Grandfather say it was
he and my Grandfather March and Dad that got Teddy Blakemore
thrown into prison?'

'Well, that's a bit dramatic. They certainly helped.'

After a pause, Kelsey asked carefully, 'Didn't that make you
resent them? After all, you cared about Teddy Blakemore.'

Stuart shrugged. 'It was bound to happen sometime. He'd
begun to feel he was invincible and got careless.'

Stuart sounded fatalistic about Blakemore's imprisonment, but
Kelsey wasn't certain he was as OK with it as he seemed. She
didn't want to dig further, though, and perhaps offend him with
her nosiness, so settled for a non-confrontational comment. 'I
can't believe I've never heard any of this before, Stuart.'

'I'm sure your parents didn't talk about it around you.' He
sighed. 'I wish I hadn't brought it up today. I never usually talk
about it. I don't know what came over me . . . Maybe that phone
call this morning. From Teddy. He wants me to do some things
for him.'

'Business things?' Alarm bells started ringing in Kelsey's head. Stuart nodded.

'On the phone you said, "I'm not going to threaten her." Would that *her* have been me?'

Stuart stiffened slightly. 'Did I say *her*? I don't remember.' He smiled at her. 'What would I want from you?'

'A controlling interest in MG Interiors?'

'Why would I want that?'

'Because you deserve it.'

'I don't.'

'Yes, you do. You're more experienced than I am, and you've stepped in time after time when I've been stumped.' Kelsey grinned. 'I try to make up for it by working more hours, but you outrun me on that front too. It's not fair that I own fifty-five percent of the company and you own forty-five. You *should* have a controlling interest.'

Stuart shook his head. 'That doesn't bother me at all.'

But if he had got the inheritance he deserved, Kelsey thought, by now he would have been the sole owner of a business. He wouldn't have needed a partner at all, particularly one who was younger and less experienced and owned a larger share of the business. 'Stuart . . .'

His mood changed as quickly as if a switch had been flipped. 'I wanted to show you a good time, Kelsey, and all I've done is go on about my own embarrassing life. Let's have some more Sangria.'

Kelsey felt as if she should say something else about the experience that had scarred him, but he obviously didn't want to talk about it anymore. She wouldn't make him regret what he'd revealed or think he'd ruined her lunch.

She smiled radiantly at him. 'I'm having a great time, Stuart. That's why I've ordered the Ultimate Brownie Sundae!'

For the next fifteen minutes, while Stuart drank his Sangria and Kelsey dived into her sliced brownie and ice cream drizzled with chocolate and caramel, they talked only about where Stuart would be taking Eve for dinner on Friday and whether or not Giles Miller's ailing mother gave him time to pursue a love life. Another large cabin cruiser passed by, the passengers waving. When Stuart raised his arm to wave, the cuff of his shirt pulled up and Kelsey saw a large bandage just above his wrist.

'Stuart, what happened?' she asked, staring at the bandage.

'My car overheated the other day. I foolishly lifted the hood and the radiator spewed steaming water on my arm.' He grimaced. 'That steam hurt like hell – I had to go to the emergency room. The doctor acted completely annoyed with me, told me I'm definitely not a mechanic and not to tinker under the hood of a car again. I learned my lesson.'

'Oh, I'm sorry!' Kelsey exclaimed, although she thought Stuart's explanation sounded rehearsed. She couldn't stop her mind from flashing back to the barn fire. 'When did you burn your arm?'

'Uh, Saturday.' He quickly pulled down his cuff. 'It was before your grandfather's funeral. I asked Eve not to mention it to you.' He gave her a bright, not-quite-sincere smile. 'It's fine, really Kelsey.'

'Good.'

He smiled again. 'We've been gone nearly two hours. We'd better get back to MG Interiors before there's a mutiny.'

As they walked through the restaurant on their way out, Kelsey spotted the distinctive perfect profile of a man with blonde hair and a golden tan. Although he kept his gaze firmly on his food, Kelsey didn't need a second look to recognize Declan Adair.

Eve sighed as the credits rolled on *Pride and Prejudice*. 'I never get tired of this movie.'

'I don't, either,' Kelsey said, getting up to remove the DVD from the player. 'I wonder how many movie versions have been made from the book?'

'We could look it up on the Internet.'

'I don't want to waste time on research.' Kelsey looked at Eve, who sat in the white leather recliner. 'It's so nice of you to sit here with me all evening watching movies.'

'We've always watched movies I love. Like you, I could see them over and over.'

'That's good because I thought we could see *Julie and Julia* after this.'

'Great. I never get tired of seeing Meryl Streep as Julia Child.'

Kelsey looked away from the case where she stored her DVD collection. 'I should be brave enough to forget about someone who just stood in my alley smoking a cigarette.'

'You are brave enough! *I* asked *you* if we could have a movie night. We haven't had one for almost three months.'

'Still, I'm sure Stuart would like you to be with him tonight – and you'd probably rather be with him.'

After a beat, Eve said, 'Oh, I'm not too sure about that.'

Kelsey turned to face Eve, whose smile couldn't hide a trace of worry. 'Did you two have a fight?'

'Not a fight.'

'An argument.'

'Not that, either.'

'Oh. Well, I should stop guessing. It's none of my business. I'm sorry for being nosy.'

'I set you up to be nosy by saying I wasn't too sure I wanted to be with Stuart tonight.'

Kelsey sat down on the floor beside the DVD case and faced her friend. 'Then there's something you want to tell me.'

'It's probably nothing.'

'Then it won't hurt to tell me what it is. Come on, Eve. I know when you need to talk.'

Eve sighed. 'Stuart's acting different. When I asked about how he got the burn on his arm, he nearly bit my head off. And someone keeps calling him. He usually goes into another room to talk and afterward he seems tense and troubled. Last night I didn't know he was on the house phone in the bedroom when I picked up the living-room extension to call you. I heard Stuart saying, "Ted, I don't know how—" Then an older man interrupted with, "You *owe* this to me! If you don't go along, you know there will be consequences . . ." Suddenly Stuart said, "Eve, get off the phone! Right now!" A few minutes later, he came into the room furious and demanded to know how much I'd heard. I've never seen him like that, Kelsey, and I left. We've barely spoken since then and I'm not going to spend another night at his place until this is settled.' She looked at Kelsey beseechingly. 'If you have any idea what this is about, will you please tell me?'

Ted, Kelsey thought. Teddy Blakemore, the man Grandfather mistook Stuart for the morning of Lori's funeral. The man who was in prison, who Stuart used to be close to. 'I don't know anyone named Ted,' she said, realizing that Eve didn't remember the name. And she wasn't lying – she didn't *know* anyone named Ted. But Stuart had talked about Teddy Blakemore when they had lunch. The man was on Stuart's mind enough for him to open up to her about his past. Why? And why was he threatening Stuart?

'Stuart has been under a lot of strain the last few weeks. He's had to take over responsibility for MG Interiors. And he did care about Grandfather. They'd known each other a long time.'

Eve stared at her. 'Why do I feel like there's something you're not telling me?'

'Eve, I *swear* I don't know what's going on with Stuart. I'm just guessing. Did you tell him you're going to stay at your apartment for a while?'

'Yes. He apologized for getting mad at me but he didn't ask me to stay.'

Kelsey got up, went to Eve and hugged her. 'I'm sure he's *very* sorry. And I know he loves you. He probably didn't ask you to stay because he's going through something and he's afraid of blowing up at you again.' She pulled back and looked into Eve's eyes. 'All relationships have their rocky times. It will pass. I'm sure of it.'

Eve looked on the verge of tears. 'I hope so. I really do love him, Kelsey. I hadn't even admitted to myself how much I loved him until this happened.'

'I wish I had some wise words to give you. All I can advise is to be patient. I think you're doing the right thing by going back to your apartment. Stuart's a private person . . .' She grinned. 'Just like you. He needs to work out whatever is bothering him on his own, and then he'll be the Stuart you love again. Don't worry.'

'Is that an order?'

'Absolutely. Here's what you *should* be worrying about – we've eaten all our treats for the evening and I forgot to go to the store today.'

'That's all right,' Eve said. 'We don't need snacks.'

'We don't *need* them, but we *want* them. It's a tradition. Let's go to a convenience store and stock up. It'll take less than half an hour.'

Minutes later, they settled into Eve's white Kia Optima. 'You haven't been going out alone at night, have you?' Eve asked.

'Not after that guy stood under my window smoking and singing.'

'You did tell Pike about it, didn't you?'

'Yes. I'll admit that he didn't react too badly when I mentioned "Gimme Shelter." I don't think he believed I imagined the serenade with that particular song, but then he's good at hiding his emotions. At least he didn't blow me off by saying he'd check into it. After all, how *could* he check into it? But he advised me to stay tucked away in my apartment with the door locked after sundown. Now all I can think of is places I want to go after dark.'

Eve laughed. 'Just tell someone they *can't* do something—'

'And that's exactly what they want to do.' Kelsey looked around the street, which was aglow with lights, and pointed. 'Right up there on the right is a convenience store. They'll have what we want.'

'And more,' Eve said.

They prowled up and down the brightly lit aisles, carrying a plastic shopping basket and picking up bags of pretzels and potato chips. Eve grabbed a can of cashew nuts. 'I *love* these. I haven't had any for months!'

'Then by all means add them to the basket. Do we need anything else?'

'Coke. Soft drinks are at the end of the aisle.'

As they stood perusing the array of soft drinks, Kelsey sensed someone watching her. She looked up to see Megan Reid standing a few feet away, staring at her. The girl was wearing tight jeans and her long black hair hung loose and shiny. She looked beautiful, fresh-faced and very young. 'Hi, Kelsey,' she said almost timidly.

'Megan. How nice to see you.'

Almost immediately Brad walked toward Megan, although he was looking at the label on a jar of cheese sauce. 'Hey, babe, do you like cheese dip with jalapeño peppers? It goes great with—' He broke off, his gaze meeting Kelsey's. 'Oh. Hi, Kelsey. Uh, small world, isn't it?' He looked at Eve, who'd come up behind Kelsey. 'Hi, Eve.'

'Hello, Brad.' Kelsey saw Eve's glance flick to Megan then

back to Brad. 'I guess everyone's hungry tonight.'

Brad and Megan laughed heartily as if Eve had said something hilarious. Kelsey saw Megan's hand reach slowly for Brad's before she self-consciously jerked it back. Brad clutched his jar of cheese. They were both nervous. 'Are you two off to a bar next?' he asked.

'No. We wouldn't be taking all of this food to a bar,' Kelsey said dryly, and he flushed. 'It's movie night at my apartment.'

'Oh! Oh, yeah! I remember how you like to watch movies at home!' Brad boomed. He nudged Megan. 'She watches them over and *over.*'

Megan's pale complexion colored and she looked like she wanted to kick him. Kelsey would have laughed if she hadn't been so uncomfortable. 'I'm a good-time girl, Megan,' she said lightly. 'Give me an old movie and a bag of potato chips and I'm happy.'

Megan smiled with polite embarrassment. Eve took Kelsey's arm and pulled her gently toward the front of the store. 'I think we have everything we need. It was nice seeing both of you.'

Outside in the car, Kelsey and Eve broke into laughter. 'Could that have been any more awkward?' Eve asked.

'Only if I'd told Megan to say hello to her father for me. At least we now know for certain that Brad and Megan are a *thing*. Her father would have a fit if he knew.'

Then Kelsey's laughter died. 'Brad likes to be a bad boy – to get away with things – but this time he's taking a *huge* risk. If it got out that he was dating Megan Reid, it could end his career.'

ELEVEN

'Hi, Dad,' Kelsey said, still looking at the diagram of a master bedroom on her laptop. 'To what do I owe the honor of a morning call?'

'Morning? It's ten-thirty.'

'At MG Interiors we consider any time before noon as morning.' She paused, tensing. 'Is something wrong?'

'Not with *our* family. I wanted to talk to you about the pictures you sent me last night.'

'The pictures?'

'From your phone.'

'Dad, I don't know what you're talking about. I didn't send you any pictures. Pictures of what?'

'You didn't . . . Oh.'

'Dad, you're scaring me. What pictures?'

'Honey, around ten o'clock last night on my phone I got three pictures of Brad Fairbourne and Megan Reid. In one, Brad and Megan are standing on a porch. A bracket light was turned on and apparently a dusk-to-dawn light in the yard, so I could tell it was Brad's house. In the second picture, they were standing in front of the picture window of the living room. They had their arms around each other and she was looking up at him. In the third picture, they were kissing. Passionately.

'Megan is supposed to be staying with a girlfriend this week. But when Elaine calls Megan, she doesn't answer, and she doesn't return the calls,' Truman said. 'I talked to John yesterday and he was worried. Elaine was planning to go to the friend's house today. Then last night I got these pictures and knew she was with Brad. John suspected they were seeing each other, but Megan has always laughed and told him he was being silly. Megan's been acting strange for weeks. I wondered if you sent the pictures to me rather than directly to John because you didn't know if he should see them. I thought you were leaving the decision to me. I could have just called him and told him Megan's whereabouts

– but I wanted them to have proof so that Megan couldn't lie her way out again, so I called John first and then sent him the pictures.'

'What did John say?'

'He was livid. He was going to Brad's last night and was prepared to drag Megan out if she wouldn't come voluntarily. As for Brad's place at the law firm . . .'

'He'll be fired?'

'John will have to talk to the other two senior partners, but you know Brad was on thin ice because of his poor work anyway. I'm sure he'll get his walking papers today.'

'Oh, lord. Getting involved with Megan was so stupid of Brad. She's beautiful, of course, but she's barely eighteen and John is *so* protective of her.'

'Considering the way Brad has acted since you broke up with him, he certainly wouldn't be a good choice for anyone, no matter what their age. He's really unstable, Kelsey. I dread to think what he might be capable of right now. He needs counseling. I've told Olivia several times, but she nearly takes off my head.'

'I'm surprised you mentioned it to her.'

'Why wouldn't I?'

'For fear of offending her.'

'I don't worry about offending Olivia Fairbourne. If she gets mad at me, she just does. Milton was a close friend of mine. Olivia was his wife and your mother's friend so I've bent over backward to be nice to her. I know Lori thought we were having a love affair, but that was absurd. I hope Olivia makes a happy life for herself, but I certainly don't care if she's angry with me for telling the truth about her son.'

Kelsey felt as if her heart did a joyful little flip at that information.

'But I wonder where the pictures came from if you didn't send them?'

'It's hard to tell,' Kelsey said vaguely, not wanting to discuss her and Eve meeting Brad and Megan in the convenience store. She didn't want to drag Eve into the situation. 'Someone did John and Elaine a favor, but it's a little unsettling that someone was spying on Brad.'

'Even if he's spied on you?'

'I don't think he's done that for a while. I'm not defending him. I don't ever want to see him again, but still . . .'

'You have your mother's kind and forgiving heart,' Truman said affectionately. 'John gave me a quick call this morning. At least Megan is home now, although she's furious. But John is even more furious. I wouldn't want to be in Bradley Fairbourne's position right now.'

Kelsey and Eve decided to have lunch delivered to the business. They both had busy days and neither was in the mood to eat in a restaurant. Two hours after Kelsey spoke to her father, she and Eve were unwrapping chicken gyros at Kelsey's desk.

'Oh, I forgot to order mine without onions,' Eve said after her first bite. 'I'm glad I don't have any meetings with clients this afternoon.'

'Oh, don't worry about the onions.' She paused, taking a sip of 7UP. 'Eve, Dad called me a while ago,' Kelsey began. 'He said that last night around ten o'clock he got pictures on his smartphone of Brad and Megan. There were three – one on Brad's front porch and two inside the house in front of a window. They were kissing. Apparently Megan has been telling her parents she's staying with a girlfriend.'

Eve looked at her blankly. 'Pictures of Brad and Megan? Who sent them?'

'I don't know.'

'Well, it wasn't me. I didn't leave your apartment until almost eleven. Besides, I'm not stalking Brad Fairbourne, much less sending pictures of him and his girlfriend to your father!'

'I know you didn't take the pictures,' Kelsey said calmly. 'I just wanted to tell you what's happened.'

'But how strange!' Eve mused. 'We'd seen them in the convenience store not long before someone took the pictures of them.'

'It's odd all right. I didn't tell Dad about us seeing them. Anyway, last night he called John and sent the pictures to him. John blew up. He was going after Megan last night.'

Eve cringed slightly. 'Oh, God. I don't know John Reid well but I've always gotten the feeling that he has one hell of a temper under that dignified exterior.'

'He does. Though I have to say Megan needs a dose of it.

I know that John can be overprotective, but she turned eighteen a couple of months ago and she's always had a wild streak. She's been leaving home for days at a time, not answering her parents' phone calls and not letting them know where she is or if she's all right. You saw her drunk in The Silver Dollar. John and Elaine are great people. They don't deserve the anxiety she's causing them.'

'What effect do you think this will have on Brad's job?'

Kelsey shook her head. 'I think he's brought on his own downfall.'

Someone rapped on Kelsey's office door then quickly opened it. Nina stuck her head in. She looked excited. 'Kelsey, Declan Adair's here! Do you want me to send him right in? Or wait until you've straightened your desk?'

'Keep him in the reception area. I'll be out in a minute.'

'The reception area?' Nina looked disappointed that Kelsey wasn't jumping into action. 'OK. If you're sure.'

Kelsey wiped her hands, popped in a breath mint and whisked on pink lipstick. She left Eve sitting at the desk and walked quickly into the pale green and ivory reception area awash with sunlight pouring through the large windows. Declan Adair sat on a chair with chrome arms as he idly flipped through a magazine. He'd propped one jean-clad leg over the other. He wore shining black loafers and a light blue long-sleeved shirt with the sleeves rolled up to his elbows, exposing his Rolex watch. For a moment, Kelsey thought that with his thick blonde-streaked hair, golden tan skin and casual grace, he could be a celebrity posing in a high-end fashion campaign.

'Mr Adair?'

He looked up, his sapphire blue eyes sparking, and smiled. 'It's Declan. Hello.' He stood and came toward her. 'I hope I'm not interrupting anything important. Mrs Evans said you weren't with a client.'

'I'm not. I was eating a sandwich at my desk.'

He frowned. 'Oh no! I was going to ask you to lunch.'

'Lunch? *Why?*' Kelsey realized how shocked she sounded and tried to regain her poise. 'I mean . . . why?'

Declan grinned. 'Because it's lunchtime and I'd enjoy your company. I'd also like to make up for barging into your home under false pretenses.'

'Nice of you but you don't have to make up for anything. You've explained yourself.' Kelsey was aware of Nina, Giles and Isaac all pretending to work while listening intently. She was annoyed with herself for being flustered. 'Maybe if you'd called I could have gone. But as I said—'

'You were having a sandwich at your desk.'

'Yes.'

'I should have called.' His brilliant blue eyes seemed to twinkle at her. 'It was nervy of me to arrive without notice, especially if you were already having lunch.'

'Just a sandwich with Eve. I don't think you've met her.'

'I know who she is but I haven't formally met her.'

'Oh.' For some reason Kelsey felt like she was twelve years old and talking to the boy she'd had a crush on. Her face was getting hot and she didn't know what to do with her hands. *You can't trust him,* she told herself. 'Eve's my close friend. She works here.'

Declan nodded, smiling slightly. 'I know.'

'Well, about lunch—'

At that moment, the front door of MG Interiors swung open and a teenage boy with spiky orange hair strode in carrying a long, slender white box. 'Delivery from Aline Flowers!'

'You don't have to shout,' Nina said reprovingly. 'Who are they for?'

'No idea. The card's inside,' the guy said, laying down the box. 'I was told just to deliver this. No peeking allowed!' He giggled at his own humor.

Kelsey walked toward Nina. 'Do we have some money in petty cash for a tip?'

'Sure thing.'

'Never mind.' Declan approached the teenager holding a couple of dollar bills in his hand. 'Thank you.'

'No, thank *you*, Mister!' The guy closed his hand over the dollar bills. 'I love making deliveries. Gets me away from the store.' He beamed at everyone. 'Have a fantastic day!'

The box lay on a mirror-topped console table. A wide gold ribbon with a simple white and gold bow encircled it. By this time, Eve had ambled into the reception room. She glanced at the box. 'Did someone get flowers?'

'Apparently, but we don't know who,' Kelsey said. 'There's a card inside.'

Declan cleared his throat. 'Maybe you should open the box and solve the mystery.'

'Of course. How silly of me.' Kelsey felt embarrassed again, deciding Declan Adair must think the MG Interiors staff unusually slow-witted. Everyone watched as she slid the bow off and lifted the lid of the box. Inside lay a dozen long-stemmed red roses.

'Oh, how beautiful!' Eve said.

Nina rushed to the table and gazed down at the lush blooms. 'Gorgeous! Absolutely gorgeous! Who sent them, Kelsey?'

Kelsey lifted a blank white envelope and pulled out a piece of paper. The sender had used a computer to write the message. She glanced at the words, gasped, then dropped the paper.

Everyone stared at her but only Declan moved, bending down to pick up the slip of paper. He stood and read aloud:

> To Kelsey and Eve,
> Red for all the loves you've lost,
> Red for all the loves to follow.
> Are you happy now?
> You won't be for long.

He looked at Kelsey. 'Do you have any idea who sent the flowers?'

Kelsey felt a chill wash over her as she looked at the lush flowers accompanied by such an ominous message. 'I'm afraid they're from Bradley Fairbourne,' she said slowly. 'I believe he thinks Eve or I – maybe both of us – took pictures of him with Megan Reid and sent them to Megan's father, who's a senior partner of the law firm where Brad works.'

Kelsey glanced at Eve, who had gone pale. 'You know what this means. He's lost his job and he's holding us responsible.'

Declan held the message paper by the edges. 'It's worse than that.' He looked into Kelsey's eyes. 'It's a *threat*. To you *and* Eve.'

TWELVE

Kelsey rolled on to her side and pulled a fluffy down pillow over her head, but it did no good. For the first time in over two weeks she'd slept soundly, peacefully and seemingly dreamlessly. Now noise hammered at her sleep and dragged her to consciousness, forcing her to open her eyes slightly and peep from under the pillow to look at the bedside clock.

It was 9:45 a.m. and someone was nearly battering down her front door.

Drowsiness fled as panic shot through her. Lori had been killed. Grandfather had been killed. Who had been killed now? Who had been ripped from her life?

Kelsey scrambled out of bed and from habit pulled a long robe over her silk sleep shirt. She pushed her hair behind her ears as she dashed through the living room. Gatsby outran her and flung himself against the door, his back humped, his tail forming a curlicue, his green eyes looking twice as large as usual.

'Get out of the way!' Kelsey snapped at him as she flipped the lock and the deadbolt. She swung open the sturdy door to see Olivia Fairbourne standing on the small porch, her fist raised, her silver hair hanging limp almost to her shoulders, and her eyes red-rimmed in her pale face.

'Finally!' Olivia shouted. 'Do you sleep all day? Don't you have a store to run?'

'It's not even ten o'clock and it's Sunday morning! MG Interiors is closed. What the hell is wrong with you?' Kelsey yelled back.

Olivia's voice grated. 'May I at least come in?'

'All right.' Kelsey stood back. Olivia didn't move, throwing a nasty look at Gatsby hovering near the doorway. 'Don't you dare say a word about my cat, Olivia! This is *his* home, not yours!' Kelsey knew how ridiculous she sounded but she was angry. And worse, she was scared. 'What's wrong?' she demanded. 'Is Dad all right?'

'Truman?'

'Yes, Olivia, my dad. Truman.'

'As far as I know your father is fine, but you'd have to ask Helen Norris for a definitive answer. She seems to be in charge of the March family these days. At least that's what your father told me on Wednesday when I was trying to be helpful!'

'By telling him that Helen should leave.'

'Oh. So she called and tattled to you.'

'No, *I* called *her*.' Kelsey glared at Olivia. 'Are you coming inside or not? If I stand here with the door open, Gatsby might run away.'

'God, what a loss that would be!' Olivia stepped into the loft and looked around. 'Not very feminine.'

'No ruffles, no lace, no crocheted doilies, if that's what you mean.' Kelsey drew a deep breath. 'You certainly didn't come to pass judgment on my new loft. What do you want?'

'Is Bradley here?'

Kelsey blinked at her. 'Brad? Why would he be *here*?'

'Because he was your fiancé.' Olivia passed by her and headed toward the bedroom area. 'I thought maybe you'd reconciled.'

'We were *never* engaged and we certainly haven't reconciled! Don't you dare go into my bedroom, Olivia!' The woman ignored her and peered into the dim room, then turned on the overhead light. 'Olivia!' Kelsey stomped barefooted after her as Olivia made her way to the adjoining bathroom and turned on the light there, too.

'Are you satisfied? Brad isn't here.'

'He's not the only man in the world.'

'So you expected to find a different one in my bed?'

'Maybe that handsome blonde man at Lorelei's funeral who no one knew except you. It was obvious you knew him *very* well! Everyone was talking about the two of you.'

'Oh, they were not, Olivia.'

'Bradley certainly noticed. He was embarrassed.'

'Embarrassed about what?'

'About you being so flirtatious. At your sister's funeral, no less. Who is that man? Did you invite him to the funeral? Are you involved with him?'

'I barely know him. He was a friend of Lori's,' Kelsey lied blithely, determined not to give Olivia one bit of information.

'Why are you here, Olivia? Did you want to see if I have a love interest who spends the night?'

'No. Besides, you'll never find anyone like Brad.'

'I hope I won't!' Suddenly the air seemed to drain out of Kelsey. At the same time, Olivia tottered to the long navy-blue suede sofa and sank down, burying her face in her hands, and sobbed. Kelsey looked at her coldly for a few seconds, then sighed with frustration as relief mixed with a twinge of pity weakened her outrage. She walked over and sat beside Olivia. 'Let's stop insulting each other and talk like two civilized women. At least, semi-civilized.'

Remarkably, Olivia made a sound close to laughter and then hiccupped. 'I hate it when I act so weak.'

'That's a refreshing change. I'm sure Brad isn't at his house or you wouldn't be here. I suppose he's not answering his phone either. Why are you scouring the city for him?'

'I'm afraid for him, Kelsey,' Olivia said reluctantly. 'He's been unhappy for a year. After you broke up with him things got worse. He doesn't even act like my little boy anymore.'

'That's because he's thirty-two.'

'Don't be a smart aleck!' Olivia wiped at her face with her hands and sniffed mightily. 'Do you have a tissue?'

Kelsey reached to the glass end table beside the sofa and pulled a tissue from a vintage gold holder. 'Here . . .'

Olivia snuffled from behind her tissue. 'I might need another one.'

Kelsey put the tissue holder on Olivia's lap. 'You can have them all.' Olivia dabbed at fresh tears. 'Would you like some coffee?'

Olivia looked at her in surprise. 'OK . . . I didn't fix any this morning. I was too nervous.'

Kelsey went into the kitchen and took her time measuring coffee and carefully pouring spring water into the coffee brewer. She fixed a tray with coffee, cream and sugar and reached for the china cups, then chose thermal mugs instead. Olivia hated drinking coffee from a mug, and Kelsey wasn't going to take this gracious hostess act too far. When she returned to the living room, she saw Olivia tucked into a corner of the sofa as Gatsby sat across the room, his gaze fixed on her.

Kelsey set the tray on the coffee table in front of the sofa. Olivia immediately leaned forward and poured cream and coffee into her mug without complaint before glancing at Gatsby. 'Does he glower at everyone?' she asked.

'No,' Kelsey said as she fixed her own coffee. 'You aren't one of his favorite people, Olivia.'

'As if I ever wanted to be!' Suddenly, Olivia looked at her with watery green eyes. 'I miss Milton. No one will ever love me like he did. No one ever has.'

Kelsey was so surprised she took a quick gulp of coffee and burned the inside of her mouth. 'That's why I never drink out of those thermal mugs you favor. The coffee stays too hot,' Olivia said. 'I don't blame you for being shocked . . . Everyone thinks I only married Milton for his money, but I loved him.'

Kelsey didn't believe her. For years she'd been wary of her mother's best friend, and since Lori's death her distrust had grown. It would take more than a trembling voice and a few touching words to destroy her skepticism. 'You wanted Milton's money *and* you forced him to adopt Brad.'

'I didn't force him!'

'Brad tells a different story.'

Kelsey saw a flash of alarm in Olivia's eyes before she asked, 'What did Bradley tell you?'

Brad hadn't told Kelsey much of anything, but she didn't want to dig for the truth now. Instead, she changed the subject.

'Why are you so upset about Brad today?'

Olivia hesitated. 'He's been let go at the law firm.'

'Oh.'

Olivia pounced. 'You don't sound surprised! You already knew?'

Kelsey decided to speak carefully. 'He's been on edge about his job for months. Besides, Brad doesn't enjoy practicing law, Olivia. Maybe it's for the best.'

'For the best! I can't *believe* you said that, Kelsey! Oh, he didn't live and breathe law but he definitely had a talent for it. They just didn't give him anything interesting to do. I blame John Reid. I don't think he ever liked Brad. He's held Bradley back – kept him from showing everyone what he can do if given the chance, prevented him realizing his potential!'

'You can't blame the senior partners of the law firm for being disappointed if Brad wasn't giving the job his all. As for John . . .'

Olivia's eyes narrowed with curiosity, and suddenly Kelsey realized Brad hadn't told his mother about the pictures of him and Megan Reid. He probably hadn't told her much of anything.

'Give me a few details. When was Brad let go from the firm?' Kelsey asked innocently.

'Friday morning. Just like *that*!' Olivia snapped her fingers in front of Kelsey's face.

'Did he let you know immediately?'

'Before noon on Friday. He was *so* angry, *so* hurt. He only talked for a few minutes. Later I called him.'

'What did he say? How did he sound?'

Olivia frowned in thought. 'He sounded . . . different. Vague. Rambling. Not at all well.' *Drunk and stoned,* Kelsey translated mentally. 'He mentioned you.'

'What about me?'

'He said you'd be happy now.' Kelsey thought about the message that had come with the red roses: *Are you happy now*?

'Why would he say that?' Olivia demanded. 'Did you *want* him to be fired?'

'No, Olivia. I hoped things would work out for him.'

'Well, they didn't. I told him to come home and we'd go talk to Truman. John Reid is his closest friend. Surely as a favor to Truman—'

'John would reinstate Brad?' Olivia nodded. Kelsey hesitated for a moment, then decided to be totally open with Olivia. 'Has Brad said anything to you about Megan Reid?'

'Megan Reid? John's daughter?'

Kelsey nodded.

'Why would he?'

'Because he's dating her.'

'He isn't!'

'Brad was seen at a bar with a girl who looks just like Megan Reid.'

'*Looks like* being the key words. Megan Reid is only sixteen!'

'She's eighteen, Olivia.'

'Still, she's just a teenager. What would Brad be doing with *her*?'

'Drinking for one thing. They were on a date in the bar. She was drunk. And she was with him Thursday night. They're involved, Olivia.'

'Says who?'

'Me. And Eve Daley.'

'Oh, *Eve*! I should have known! She's been trying to worm her way into the March family for years and now that Sofie is dead, she'd like to marry Truman! She *hates* Brad because he sees right through her. He's warned me about her. She'd do or say *anything*—'

'Olivia, that's enough! Eve's in love with Stuart Girard.'

'He's just a smoke screen. Have you seen the way that scheming gold-digger looks at Truman?'

'People called *you* a gold-digger when you started dating Milton. I think you're projecting your own personality on to Eve.' Olivia opened her mouth but Kelsey cut her off. 'I don't want to hear one more word about Eve pursuing my father. I mean it, Olivia,' Kelsey said in a low, threatening voice. 'You should concentrate on your son and Megan Reid.'

'Why? Brad is *not* dating Megan Reid. What a preposterous thing for Eve to claim!'

'He *is*, Olivia. I've seen them together.'

'You're lying because you want to hurt Brad.'

'I am not lying, Olivia.' She'd told Pike about the pictures an anonymous watcher had taken of Brad and Megan and sent to her father, as well as the flowers and the message she'd received at work on Friday. Now she wanted to tell Olivia about the pictures and the flowers she'd received only hours after Brad had been fired, but she knew Olivia would deny that there had been pictures, no matter what evidence proved the contrary. If she accepted that there had been photographs, she'd probably insist that someone – probably Eve – had sent the flowers, even though the florist who'd supplied the roses identified Brad as the sender. Olivia would have none of it, and Kelsey realized she had to speak in generalities. 'Considering Brad's erratic behavior lately, I don't believe he's thinking of the consequences of his actions. John knows about Brad seeing Megan – drinking in bars with her when she's under twenty-one, probably spending nights with her. And he didn't like it. He's very protective of Megan.'

'So John fired Bradley because of his little tramp of a daughter?'

'I'm just saying that if Brad was stupid enough to date Megan—'

'My son is not stupid!'

'OK. If Brad was *unwise* enough to date John's teenage daughter, it could have been the straw that broke the camel's back.'

Olivia seemed flabbergasted. 'But . . . but John couldn't be so petty as to fire Bradley for *that*. He'd have to know that terminating Brad's place at the firm would leave a permanent black mark on Brad's career!'

'Have you forgotten that the firm has *three* senior partners? John Reid, Roger Alpern and Kenneth Patel. All three must have been in agreement or Brad wouldn't have been dismissed. I don't think the other two would have let John's outrage over Brad's dating situation influence their judgment, although I'm certain it didn't help matters. Brad was already on thin ice.'

'John Reid's father started that firm!'

'He's been dead for over ten years so that has nothing to do with the decisions made by the three present partners. You know that, Olivia, even if you're pretending not to believe it.'

Kelsey was so angry with Olivia she wanted to throw her out and tell her to never come back. Then she looked at the woman's blanched face and red-rimmed eyes filled with genuine panic. She sighed, took Olivia's coffee mug from her trembling hand and refilled it. 'What has Brad said since he called you?'

'Nothing! I haven't talked to him. I've called his landline, his cell phone, the law firm. I've even texted, and I hate to text.' Olivia made texting sound like an act of hard labor. 'Kelsey, will you call John Reid and tell him Bradley hasn't been seeing Megan?'

Kelsey gave her a long, hard look.

'All right, I guess not. Maybe it wouldn't be such a good idea anyway.'

'It certainly would *not* be a good idea, and you're too smart to think that could help matters.'

'I'm frightened.' Olivia set down her coffee mug, stood, and started pacing around the loft. 'Brad's garage door is down. He has an automatic garage door opener but I don't have the thinga-majig that opens and shuts the door, so I don't know if his car is there or he's left town. I've tried the doors of his house but they're locked, and I couldn't see much through the windows. He doesn't answer his phone. He might be hurt, Kelsey. He might have . . . done something to himself. If he's lying in his house injured or . . . near death . . . and I didn't do anything . . .' Her voice was desperate, her gaze pleading. 'Bradley would never give me keys to his house. I guess he thought I'd search the place while he was at work.' *And you would have*, Kelsey thought.

'Kelsey, I know he gave you keys—'

'Keys I didn't want.'

'Nevertheless. Did you give them back to him when you broke up?'

'I meant to, but he got so angry with me that frankly I didn't want to go near him for a while. And then I forgot about the keys,' Kelsey said reluctantly. 'I haven't thought about them for months.'

Olivia walked toward her and sank to her knees. 'I need to get into Bradley's house, Kelsey. I have to see if he's all right. *Please.*'

A tear ran down Olivia's pale cheek. 'All right,' Kelsey said slowly. 'I don't blame you for being worried. Frankly, in spite of all the bad feelings between Brad and me, I'm concerned, too.'

'Then come with me.' Olivia reached out and took Kelsey's right hand in hers. 'I know you don't like me, but your mother did. I think she'd want you to come. If I walk into that house and—' She gulped back a sob. 'If I find—'

'OK, I'll go with you, Olivia,' Kelsey interrupted, unable to let Olivia even think of what could have happened to Brad. 'I'll get dressed and we'll go immediately.'

More tears spilled down Olivia's face. 'Thank you, Kelsey. Thank you *so* much.'

Kelsey tried to give Olivia a reassuring smile, but she couldn't say everything would be fine because she wasn't at all certain a shattered Bradley Fairbourne really was alive and well.

Olivia turned her Mercedes into the driveway of Brad's small gray-shingled single-story house. 'Oh, that dismal color,' Olivia moaned. 'I've asked Bradley to have the place painted.'

'He likes gray.'

'*I* don't and I gave him the down payment for the house. Did I ever mention that?'

About twenty times, Kelsey thought but said nothing. She knew that at the moment, Olivia was just chattering because of nerves and wouldn't have heard an answer if she had given one.

'You have both the front and back door keys, don't you?' Olivia asked as she switched off the car's engine and reached for her sand-colored designer purse.

'Yes, Olivia. I brought all the keys I have to Brad's house.' She'd reassured Olivia of this twice before they left the loft.

'Do you have a garage door opener thingamajig?'

'It's called a transmitter. And no, I don't have one for Brad's garage. We won't need it if we get into the house, though.'

'What do you mean by *if* we get into the house?' Olivia burst out.

'He might have had the locks changed after our breakup. Maybe that's why he never asked for his keys, but we'll find a way to get inside.'

Kelsey got out of the car and looked at the bright yellow daffodils she'd planted in front of the house last spring when Brad was still being nice. He'd been delighted with what he'd thought was an act of love, instead of a simple kindness. They were flourishing, which surprised her. She'd thought he might have destroyed them this year.

Kelsey felt as if a lump of ice was sitting in her stomach when she slipped the key into the lock of the front door and heard a click. She turned the knob slowly and opened the door, letting sunshine into the dark hall that bisected the house. 'At least Brad hasn't changed the front door lock,' she breathed.

Olivia, who'd been babbling since they got out of the car, fell silent as they stepped into the house. Suddenly she started yelling. 'Brad! Bradley Allen Fairbourne!' Nothing. 'Bradley, it's your mother! Are you in here? Bradley, if you're here you answer me right now!'

'Stop shouting, Olivia! You're going to deafen me. Besides, shouting isn't helping anything. Either he isn't here or—'

'Or *what*? He's *dead*?'

'Or he's just not answering. He might have passed out.'

'My Bradley does *not* drink until he passes out.'

That's what you think, Kelsey wanted to say but held her tongue. 'Let's just look around.'

Kelsey was glad she'd managed to sound calm, although she felt something was *off*. The house felt wrong. She couldn't have explained the feeling if her life depended on it, but that didn't make it go away. She was determined she would continue to act serene and in control until they'd searched the whole house, though. She wouldn't let Olivia know how alarmed she felt in this cozy little house where for a few months she'd felt comfortable with Brad.

Brad used to have the house cleaned once a week and usually kept it spotless and neat. Today, Kelsey flipped the switch and light shone on the mahogany hall floor, which showed a rim of dust near the baseboards. To the right, sunshine filtered through the blinds, throwing the living room into dim light. The middle cushion on the brown sofa lay on the floor. A green and gold afghan was wadded into a corner of the sofa, and a half-full ashtray sat on the floor beside it.

Without a word, Kelsey and Olivia walked into the living room. Kelsey headed toward Brad's favorite chair, a bulky green recliner. It was sprinkled with lint and ashes. A scratched wooden end table next to the recliner held copies of *TV Guide, Esquire* and *Sports Illustrated* along with several brightly colored fast-food wrappers. Kelsey also saw a drinking glass holding about an inch of brown-tinged water. She picked it up and sniffed. Bourbon. Two empty beer cans lay on the table. Balled up candy bar wrappers circled the rim of another ashtray, where the remains of a joint lay.

'What's this?' Olivia asked, picking up the joint.

'Marijuana.'

'Bradley doesn't smoke marijuana.'

'Yes, Olivia, he does. Quite a bit of it, in fact.'

'I don't believe it.'

'Believe it.'

'Well, I *never* . . .' Olivia uttered again, then turned her gaze away from the messy end table. 'Brad! Bradleeeey!'

Kelsey closed her eyes, counted to five, then said, 'Olivia, if you don't stop bellowing for him I'm going to leave.'

'Fine!' Olivia snapped. 'Then you can walk home! We came in *my* car!'

Kelsey held her temper and asked calmly, 'Do you see his cell phone anywhere?'

'I haven't been looking for it.'

'Then look for it and stop threatening to abandon me.'

Kelsey walked ahead to the kitchen. She stopped when she saw a nearly empty bottle of bourbon sitting next to an open pizza box on the counter. In the sink lay dirty plates, glasses and flatware. The refrigerator held some individually wrapped cheese slices, a stick of butter and eight cans of beer.

'My son does not keep house this way!' Olivia announced. 'He's neat and clean, and he does *not* smoke marijuana!'

'He does smoke marijuana when he's upset, and he drinks too much.' Olivia's eyes flared at Kelsey. 'Olivia, Brad had been fired from the law firm. Look at this place – he was having a meltdown. Can't you understand that?'

Olivia remained silent as Kelsey headed for the back door of the house that led into the garage. It was unlocked and she opened it. 'Olivia!' she called. 'Brad's car is gone.'

She felt the sudden presence of Olivia, leaning out the door and peering into the shadows. Finally she asked in a thin, high voice, 'Maybe he's just gone for a drive?'

Kelsey didn't bother to answer. She went back in the house to the bedroom, Olivia pattering behind her. The sheets on the king-size bed were rumpled and clothes were scattered every-where, as if Brad had simply turned dresser drawers upside down and dumped them on the bed and floor. She looked into the closet. Spaces appeared between shirts he'd always kept immacu-lately neat. On the floor his expensive shoes lay in a heap. She didn't see any athletic shoes or jeans.

'He's gone, Olivia,' she said firmly. 'I think he just threw some clothes together and left on impulse.'

'Where would he go?'

'You'd probably have a better idea than I would. Just *think.*'

Finally, Kelsey went into the bathroom. She stood transfixed in front of a cracked medicine cabinet mirror. Dried brownish-red liquid had splattered on the wall and drained down into the sink. On the other mirror was a message written crudely in the same dried brownish-red:

Kelsey
R.I.P.

THIRTEEN

'Look at all that blood! Bradley's killed himself!' Olivia shrilled right behind her. She clutched her chest with trembling hands. 'It's your fault – all of it! You wrecked his life!'

Kelsey turned slowly, then put her hands on Olivia's shoulders and shook her. The woman's silver hair flapped around her face and her green eyes blazed. 'You're having a panic attack, Olivia. Get hold of yourself! Brad has not killed himself. He would never kill himself. He must have been drunk and high when he wrote that on the mirror.'

'In *blood*! Look at it and tell me the writing isn't in blood!'

'I'm not certain it's blood, but it could be. That doesn't prove anything, though, Olivia. Do you think he slashed his wrists or his neck? There's not enough blood here to indicate a suicide attempt. He just cut himself. Now pull yourself together. You're no help to Brad if you fall apart.'

Olivia's face was alarmingly pale. She looked at Kelsey in fury then burst into wracking sobs. 'Oh, my baby. My poor, poor baby.'

'He's not a baby but he *is* a troubled young man. He needs you, Olivia. In spite of how much the two of you argue, you are the most important person in his world. I should know – I dated him for five months and I've known him for almost twenty years! He loves you and I think you're the only person in the world who can help him. I mean that, Olivia. You two have always been a team, even when you were married to Milton.'

Olivia gasped, fighting for breath through her sobs. 'Maybe if I hadn't married Milton, things would have been different for Brad. I thought that Milton could give us – especially Bradley – a wonderful life. Instead, Milton was envious of Brad – his looks, his intelligence, his youth, but especially my love for Brad. Milton Fairbourne always had to be number one.'

'At least he adopted Brad and gave him the Fairbourne name.'

To Kelsey's surprise, Olivia started laughing. The laughter grew until it was almost hysterical. 'You might as well know the truth since Brad is probably dead. Everyone thought Milton was being so generous adopting a fatherless kid. But Bradley always did have a father in his life – Milton Fairbourne. Milton was Brad's biological father!'

Kelsey's jaw dropped in surprise. She stared blankly at this tearful, laughing Olivia she'd never seen before now. Finally she managed, 'You didn't meet Milton when Brad was twelve?'

'God, no! I've been in the picture since Milton's wife was still acting like the queen of Louisville society. He didn't love her, you know. Milton *never* loved her! But after they'd been married about ten years, he met me and he fell in love. I thought he'd leave his wife when I got pregnant or after Bradley was born, but he wouldn't. He cared too much about what people would think. So I was patient. Year after year, I waited. I thought I'd lose my mind. I was on the verge of a breakdown when finally my tenacity paid off – literally. After his wife died, Milton married me and I had access to Milton's world and all of that glorious money. It should have been wonderful, but Milton was always jealous of Brad because he knew Bradley was the love of my life. Milton, the bastard, couldn't get past his egotism and possessiveness to love his own son and he let Brad know it every single day.'

Swallowing her shock, Kelsey asked, 'Did Brad know Milton was his real father?'

Olivia closed her eyes. 'He guessed when he was about ten, even before Milton's wife died. Brad's so intelligent, so perceptive. But knowing Milton was his real father made his attitude even harder for Brad to bear, especially after I married Milton and Brad was around him every day. Maybe that made me overprotective, smothering. Maybe Milton's competitiveness and coldness toward Bradley made him feel inferior. After all, when you can't win your own parent's love . . .' Olivia shook her head. 'My poor boy.'

Kelsey could hardly believe it but she felt her arms encircle Olivia and pull her close, patting her back as she sobbed from what felt like the depths of her soul. She'd disliked Olivia, she'd mistrusted Olivia, but at this moment she felt nothing except sympathy for the woman whose confession seemed to have drained her of all strength and left her with only raw grief and regret.

Suddenly, Kelsey heard footsteps. Someone else was in Brad's house. Kelsey froze, panic rising inside her. They were trapped. 'Brad?'

Kelsey looked up to see Declan Adair standing in the doorway.

Kelsey felt as if every breath of air went out of her and the room seemed to tilt. She couldn't make a sound. She simply stared, suddenly frightened, at the man watching her holding a sobbing Olivia Fairbourne. He looked calm and unaffected, his piercing blue eyes steady, his arms folded across his chest.

Finally, Kelsey managed, 'You!'

'Yes,' he said smoothly. 'Me.'

Olivia jerked free of Kelsey and whirled around to face him. 'What are you doing here?' Her taut voice screeched. 'How did you get in? Are you following Kelsey? Do you know my son? Where is he?'

Declan held up his right hand. 'Whoa, Mrs Fairbourne! I got in easily because you left the front door open. I'm not a friend of Brad's. I don't know where your son is. I don't mean you any harm.'

'And I'm supposed to believe you?'

'If you aren't going to believe what I say, why did you ask those questions?'

Declan had managed to shut down Olivia with simple reason. She took deep breaths, shuddering, grabbing Kelsey's arm as if she needed to be physically steadied.

'This is Declan Adair,' Kelsey said. 'He's the man I was speaking to at Lori's funeral reception right before Brad started talking about his horse being put down by Milton when he was at college.'

'Did you have to bring up Brad's horse?' Olivia demanded of Kelsey, then peered at Declan. 'I thought your name was Barrington.'

'Harrington,' he said. 'Kelsey introduced me as Cole Harrington. I didn't correct her at the time but my name is Declan Adair. I'm a private investigator. I live in New York City.'

Olivia looked appalled. 'I don't understand. Are you investigating my son? Did John Reid send you?'

'Can we discuss all of this someplace besides the bathroom?' Kelsey asked. 'I'm getting claustrophobic and Olivia definitely needs to sit down.'

'I want to know who he is before I go *anywhere* with him!' Olivia stormed. 'He could be a killer!'

'He's not a killer.' At least I hope not, Kelsey thought. 'Let's go into the living room. Declan, lead the way.'

He smiled. 'You want to keep me in front of you. Good strategy, Kelsey.'

Five minutes later, all three of them sat around Brad's messy living room. Olivia huddled next to Kelsey on the sofa. Declan had taken an oak Windsor armchair near the television. 'I glanced around before I came to the bathroom,' he said. 'It looks like Brad hasn't been here for at least a couple of days.'

'I talked to him early Friday afternoon,' Olivia volunteered almost triumphantly before narrowing her eyes at Declan.

'Did he call you from a cell phone?' he asked.

'I . . . I don't know. He didn't seem to feel well. Kelsey and I can't find his cell phone. He must have it with him.' Olivia lifted her chin. 'I'm not answering any more of your questions until you tell me who exactly are you and what you're doing here.'

'I've been in Louisville since two days after Lorelei March's death. Today I was following Kelsey.'

'Lorelei March's killer is dead,' Olivia stated. 'Why are you following Kelsey? Do you think she's responsible for Lori's murder? What do you have to do with my son? And why in God's name are you here, all the way from New York City? I want an answer!'

Declan looked at Olivia with faint amusement. 'You asked several questions, Mrs Fairbourne. Which one do you want me to answer?'

Olivia turned on Kelsey furiously. 'Who *is* he?'

Before Kelsey could answer, Declan said, 'You went to Kelsey's loft this morning looking for your son, didn't you, Mrs Fairbourne?' He didn't give her a chance to answer. 'When I said I was a private investigator, you asked if I was investigating your son for John Reid.'

'John Reid wants you to find Brad?'

'I spoke with Mr Reid at the reception after Lorelei's funeral,' Declan said calmly. 'Your son was showing signs of stress that day. You can't deny it. I know his performance at the law firm was subpar and also that he's been seen with Megan Reid, who's only eighteen. Surely you can put two and two together?'

'You got him fired from the firm!'

'Brad did that all by himself.'

'Oh, my . . .' Olivia seemed to sink deeper into the sofa. 'Why are you still looking for him?'

'John Reid isn't heartless. I understand that he's known your son for a long time.' Declan paused. 'And there's Megan.'

'So you've been hired to follow my poor boy to see if he's with Megan?'

Declan said nothing.

'Why isn't she away in college?'

'She will be in September, Mrs Fairbourne. This is May.'

'She's not at home with John and Elaine?'

'Not at this moment. I thought she might be here.'

'Well, obviously she isn't, the little slut.'

'Is she a slut because she's dating your son?'

'She's a slut because she's probably been pursuing him and gotten him into all of this trouble with John. My son hasn't done *anything*.'

Declan looked at Kelsey. She knew he was considering telling Olivia about the roses with the threatening message Brad had sent to her and Eve. Kelsey shook her head slightly – if Olivia believed him, she'd do anything to shield Brad from trouble and they'd never find him.

Declan turned to Olivia. 'Do you have any idea where he is?'

'No. When I talked to him early Friday afternoon, he didn't say he was going anywhere. Now he doesn't answer his cell phone. It's usually glued to his ear but he hasn't taken five minutes to call his mother.' She ran her hands through her silver hair. 'Maybe we should call the police.' Her voice rose. 'Bradley could have been kidnapped!'

'Who would want to kidnap him?' Declan asked calmly. 'Besides, you haven't received a ransom request. And do you want the police searching your son's house with all of this marijuana around?' Olivia blanched and seemed to fold in on herself. 'I think you should give Brad at least two more days to contact you or turn up of his own accord before you go to the police. In the meantime, I'll look for him, Mrs Fairbourne. I'm very good at what I do. I wish you'd trust me.' He waited a beat and said with feeling, 'Kelsey does.'

Kelsey shot him a withering glance. She wanted to snap that she barely knew him, but Olivia seemed to be relaxing. Slightly. Her breathing was slowing to a normal rate. The woman was still upset, but not on the verge of hysteria like she was before Declan arrived.

'But what about all the blood in the bathroom?' she asked meekly.

'There wasn't a lot of blood. And the message on the mirror just means that Brad is mad at Kelsey.'

'*Why?*'

'He could be jealous, or it could have been a threat.'

'My son doesn't threaten people!'

'I think your son has been both drunk and stoned most of the last few days. He's had a shock and he's not himself, but the police wouldn't care about his feelings – only his actions or what they think he might do. So, Mrs Fairbourne, do you really want them to see those words written in what is probably blood on Brad's mirror?'

'No. No, of course not,' Olivia said anxiously. Then she sighed. 'I haven't slept for over twenty-four hours. I'm exhausted. I need to go home to rest and think.'

'That's a good idea,' Kelsey said. 'We came in your car, so if you'll drop me at my loft you can go home.'

Olivia huffed in exasperation. 'Oh, Kelsey, *really*? I'm a nervous wreck. I don't feel like driving all around town. Do you always think only of yourself?'

'All I ask is that you take me back to my loft—'

'I'll take Kelsey home,' Declan said in a helpful voice.

'Oh, *thank you*! That sounds fine,' Olivia said immediately. 'Is that all right, Kelsey?' Her voice was tight and high-pitched. Her hands shook. Kelsey knew the woman was on the verge of another panic attack and suddenly decided she was actually afraid to ride with Olivia.

'Yes, that'll be all right,' Kelsey said, not making eye contact with Declan but feeling his smile. 'We'll just close up here. Do you want Brad's keys?'

'Oh, certainly!' Kelsey handed them to Olivia. 'Maybe I'll come back tomorrow and check the house again. I'm sure Brad will be back by then or will at least have called me. None of this is like him,' she said as she headed for the front door. 'He knows how I worry. This is very bad of him – *very* bad – and it's not like him at all.'

As soon as Olivia left, Kelsey turned to Declan. 'I'll take a cab home.'

'If you like, but I have a car right outside. I promise not to abduct you.'

'Of course you won't,' Kelsey returned acidly. 'You just want to follow me like a stalker. I saw you at the Riverside Grille when I was having lunch with Stuart.'

'I know you saw me. I wasn't hiding. Was your Brownie Sundae good?'

Kelsey glared at him, her breath coming hard in annoyance. 'Very.' Declan looked like he was going to laugh. 'We might as well go. Unless you want to search the house.'

'I already glanced around while Olivia was pouring out Brad's tragic history to you in the bathroom. So Milton Fairbourne is Brad's biological father. How interesting! And our boy Brad is very dramatic. First red roses with a threat buried in a rhyme and then a broken mirror with a message written in blood.'

'I think he's falling apart and someone should help him.'

'I agree, but you're not the one to do it. You shouldn't be here, Kelsey. He's dangerous.'

'I wouldn't be here if Olivia hadn't dragged me into this mess.'

'Olivia couldn't have dragged you into anything if you'd just said no.'

'She didn't have keys to this house.'

'You could have given them to her. That would have been the smart thing to do.'

'As you saw, she was in no shape to walk into this place alone.'

'So now you're Olivia Fairbourne's guardian angel?'

'I don't think I like you, Mr Adair,' Kelsey spat, but not with as much venom as she'd have liked.

'Don't you? My feelings are hurt.' Declan gave her a cool stare. 'Ready to go, Miss March? My humble carriage awaits you.'

As they headed back to Kelsey's loft, she stared straight ahead and said nothing until she couldn't stand it any longer. 'You didn't tell Olivia the real reason why you were at Brad's house – because of him and me.'

'I didn't need to lie,' Declan said. 'She kept coming up with her own explanations. She thought I'd been sent by John Reid because of his daughter. I just didn't set her straight.'

She looked at him. 'And you wouldn't have lied even if she'd asked you a direct question? Because you don't lie.'

Declan cocked his head and gave her a disarming smile. 'That sounded dangerously close to a compliment.'

'Don't flatter yourself. I'm just repeating what you told me.' Kelsey shifted her gaze. 'Where do you think Brad is?'

'I have no idea. I don't like his disappearance, though.'

'Why have you been following me? I thought Cole wanted you to find out who hired Vernon Nott. You know *I* didn't.'

'But Nott could have been hired to kill you too. By whom, I don't know. However, it's not a secret that Brad Fairbourne isn't your biggest fan these days. You think I've been stalking you, but he's done his fair share of stalking. Several people know about it. Also, I'm not certain he didn't have something to do with your sister's death. His mother wants to marry your father and Lorelei was violently opposed.' He glanced at Kelsey. 'Lorelei told Cole about it and he told me. Maybe Brad thought that with your sister out of the way Olivia would have a better chance with your father. That's why I've tried to keep an eye on him.' He shrugged. 'Cole won't be happy that I've lost him.'

Kelsey didn't want to admit that she'd thought the same of Brad. 'Cole Harrington, my sister's secret lover. Does he still also think his wife might have masterminded Lori's murder?'

'I'm still on the job, aren't I?'

'You're dodging the question.'

He shrugged.

'Do you know where Megan Reid is?'

'I haven't spoken to John Reid. I don't work for him. His problems with his daughter aren't my concern.'

'Why did you follow me to lunch with Stuart Girard? Do you think *he* might have had Lori murdered?'

'His motive would be more obscure than Brad's. However, you're the major stockholder of MG Interiors, and according to Lorelei you wouldn't consider selling any stock.'

'What does that have to do with Cole?'

'Cole says Delphina thinks she might move back to Louisville someday, especially if he divorces her. Her ego couldn't stand facing her celebrity friends in New York.'

'What does that have to do with my stock in MG Interiors?'

'Are you aware that Stuart knows Delphina? When they were much younger, they used to date. She's always liked younger men. And they've kept in touch. Hasn't Stuart mentioned her to you?'

'Well . . . no.' Kelsey was surprised but not stunned. Stuart was a handsome man from a prominent family. 'Why would he talk about Delphina to me?'

'I thought you two had been close friends for years.'

'I met him four years ago. We've always gotten along well and he's a great business partner, but I wouldn't say he's a close friend. He certainly hasn't discussed his dating history with me.'

'Maybe not. Besides, it would have been a sensitive subject, especially lately with your sister being involved with Delphina's husband.'

'I knew nothing about that until the night Lori was killed.'

'Then neither Stuart nor Delphina could have known when you found out about the affair?'

Kelsey realized she was getting defensive. 'I still don't know what any of this has to do with my stock in the business.'

'Cole has met Stuart. Delphina's told Cole a lot about Stuart's past – about his father denying Stuart was his son and not leaving him any money. Stuart hates him for it. He's also humiliated. Girard wants to *be* someone besides a junior partner in a business of which the major stockholder is a twenty-seven-year-old woman.'

'Stuart and I talked about this over lunch. He doesn't care that I own more stock than he does.'

Declan looked at her impatiently. 'Do you think a man as

sophisticated and polished as Stuart Girard can't act? He has you convinced that he's able to overlook the dirty deal his father gave him. That it's all just water under the bridge, etc. Like hell it is. He wants *all* of the business, Kelsey, not just forty-five percent. Delphina said so.'

'Stuart doesn't have enough money to buy fifty-five percent of MG Interiors. If he did, he would have built his own business.'

Declan hesitated. 'If you repeat what I'm going to tell you, you could end up in danger. But you *should* know. Stuart's father did business with a man named Teddy Blakemore. Blakemore has underworld connections.'

'I already know about Teddy Blakemore. Stuart told me about him and how good Blakemore was to him during the years when Stuart's father was denying that Stuart was his son. I also know that Blakemore is in prison.'

'Not anymore – he's out on compassionate grounds because he has pancreatic cancer. He doesn't have long to live, and he doesn't have children. What he *does* have is access to money he kept hidden when he was in prison. He also has Stuart Girard, a man he thinks of as a son.'

'So you believe Blakemore's grooming Stuart to be his successor? I don't believe it. And even if I did, I don't see what that has to do with MG Interiors.'

'Blakemore wants all of MG Interiors as a stepping stone for Stuart.'

'So you think that, instead of having Stuart offer to buy me out, Blakemore masterminded a plan to kill me? Even if I were dead, Stuart wouldn't own MG Interiors.'

'He could if your father sold it to him. Why would Truman March want the business? He has enough going on with March Vaden.'

'Is this all speculation? Do you really know anything for certain?'

'I've learned some things. Unfortunately, not enough to go to the Feds about yet.'

'You mean the FBI? I think your imagination is running wild!'

'Enzo Pike thinks my speculation, as you call it, is worth considering.'

'Pike?' Kelsey looked at Declan's clean-cut profile. 'You've been talking to Detective Pike?'

'I introduced myself to him after your sister's funeral. At the reception, he thought I was Cole Harrington. I didn't want to get off on the wrong foot with him, if possible. The police generally don't like having a PI working on their cases. The best way to overcome some of their dislike and distrust is to meet them and be as open as possible.'

'You told him Cole wanted to find out if his wife had put out a hit on his mistress?'

'Well, I wasn't *that* open. I told Pike that Cole knew Lorelei. Pike got the subtext – that maybe there was more to Cole's and Lorelei's relationship than friendliness, that Cole cared for her, and that he wanted to know for certain what had happened.'

'So he knew about Lori's affair—'

'I didn't say anything to him about an affair.'

'You didn't have to. He's not a fool.'

'He sure isn't,' Declan said dryly. 'Before I met him, I did some research. He's beyond smart. He's resourceful and sharp and canny. The Bangor police department was sorry to lose him.'

'Why did he leave?'

'About ten months ago his wife and four-year-old daughter were killed in a car wreck. Pike was seriously injured. The other driver was drunk.'

'Oh, my God!' Pity rushed through Kelsey and she pictured the tall, very thin man with his hawk-like features and his depthless dark eyes – eyes behind which always hovered the images of his wife and daughter. As hard as he tried to hide his sorrow, she'd heard it in his voice on the day he came to the March home and mentioned that his wife *had* loved flowers. 'He must still be in so much pain.'

'I was told not to express sympathy. He can't even talk about what happened.'

'So you told Pike you're a private investigator,' Kelsey said slowly, forcing her mind back to the present matter. 'What did he say?'

'He heard me out. He was polite. A lot of cops aren't polite to private investigators.'

'I have a feeling he's usually polite.'

'Me, too. Anyway, he gave me the party line of hoping that I wouldn't interfere with the police investigation, that he'd appreciate me touching base with him from time to time, and couldn't share information discovered by Louisville Metro.' Declan frowned. 'But I felt he wasn't just getting rid of me, and wouldn't forget about me as soon as I left his office. I thought he might actually work with me in a minor way. And I wasn't wrong. I saw him a second time and told him what I think about Stuart Girard.'

'What was his reaction?'

'He was careful with his wording and his demeanor, but I could tell I wasn't giving him new information. He told me the same thing I told you – that there's not enough information to take to the FBI – and gave me the obligatory warning about keeping the information to myself.' Declan smiled. 'And then he thanked me. I've been in this business for almost eight years and no cop has *ever* thanked me for giving information.'

'He does have beautiful manners,' Kelsey said.

'I'll say! When he tried to shake hands with me, I just gaped at him for a few seconds. He didn't take his hand away. I finally pulled myself together and shook it.'

'Well, I'm glad you talked to him, but I still can't believe that Stuart would do anything illegal. Stuart's father – maybe. Stuart – no.'

'Kelsey, you've already said you aren't close friends with Stuart. How well do you really know him? I'm sure you aren't aware of how deep his friendship with Teddy Blakemore goes. And don't forget – Blakemore was responsible for industrial espionage in March Vaden. Both of your grandfathers and your father gathered the evidence that landed him in prison. This man that Stuart Girard thinks he owes so much to was in prison for *years* because of your family, and he's only been released so he can die outside of prison walls. He is a complete invalid.'

'Now *you* sound sorry for him,' Kelsey said faintly.

'I'm not. Not one bit. Teddy Blakemore has ruined a lot of people financially, and his goons have physically hurt quite a few.'

'*Goons?*'

'That's what they call Mafia enforcers on television. I thought you'd be familiar with the word.'

'Thank you for simplifying your vocabulary to suit my limited intellectual level!'

'Don't be so touchy.'

Kelsey didn't answer, her mind flashing back to Eve telling her about the phone calls Stuart had been receiving that left him tense and troubled. Then there was the one Eve had over-heard when Stuart had been speaking to a man named Ted who was telling him he *owed* something to him and if he didn't go along there would be *consequences*. Eve said Stuart had been furious that she'd accidentally heard part of the phone call and wanted to know exactly how much she'd heard.

'Have I hurt your feelings? Or have you decided not to speak to me?'

Kelsey jerked back to the present. 'I was thinking.'

'About . . .'

'How good Stuart has always been to me.'

'That doesn't really mean anything, Kelsey. It certainly doesn't change Stuart Girard's psychology. Blakemore could have a hold over him and want revenge. I think he's a danger to you. So does Cole.'

'Why would Cole give a damn about me?'

'Cole's a pretty good guy, Kelsey, no matter what you think of him. He cared about your sister and she adored you. That means a lot to him.'

Kelsey couldn't answer. She breathed hard, stared straight ahead and set her jaw stubbornly.

'OK. I understand that you don't want to talk about Lorelei's relationship with my brother, so I won't talk about her. But Cole thinks that Girard wants Delphina, probably because her family owns the Arienne bourbon distillery. They're a big deal in the local social scene and they have a lot of money.'

'Yes, they do,' Kelsey said, 'but Stuart seems devoted to Eve Daley.'

'*Seems*, Kelsey.'

Kelsey closed her eyes in frustration. 'You keep saying that! Why are you convinced Stuart's a danger to me? If I don't want to sell my stock to him, he can't make me.'

'Based on things Lorelei told him, Cole agrees that if Stuart had the capital your father would sell him your stock in MG

Interiors if you were to die. Also, you *and* Lorelei are the daughters of one of the men who put Teddy Blakemore in prison. How do you think Stuart feels about that?'

'So he knows Blakemore was trying to get a foothold in March Vaden, but surely he'd understand it was vital to stop him?'

'Oh, so Stuart Girard is a saint?' Declan paused, then said harshly, 'Wake up, Kelsey! Vernon Nott shot your sister twice, and if Rick Conway hadn't come after him with a gun Nott would have shot *you* in the head! That could have been payback.'

Kelsey gasped, feeling as if someone had punched her. She could hardly get her breath.

Declan reached out to touch her, but she dodged his hand. 'I'm sorry I sounded so brutal. I really am, Kelsey.'

She wouldn't look at him. 'I don't believe any of your paranoid theories, and I don't believe you're sorry you made such *awful* accusations,' she said shakily as a lump formed in her throat.

'That was unforgivable of me. I just blurt out things—'

'You certainly do. Horrible things!'

'I'm *sorry*.'

'So you said.' At last, Kelsey was able to draw a deep breath. 'I wish I'd called a cab. I wish I'd *walked* home from Brad's rather than ride with you!'

'No wonder.' He glanced at her. 'Do you want a cigarette?'

'I don't smoke!'

'I do.'

'Well, at least be polite enough not to smoke with me in the car!'

'OK.' After a pause, he asked miserably, 'Want to go to a bar, get really stinking drunk and forget all this?'

A combination of nerves, anxiety and Declan Adair's ridiculous suggestion were too much for her. Kelsey drew in her breath to verbally cut him to shreds. Then, to her surprise, she started laughing. Loudly. She couldn't stop, even when she saw Declan looking at her in a mixture of astonishment and genuine concern. 'I do this when I've reached my limit,' she told him through gasps and giggles and guffaws. 'Just . . . ignore . . . me.'

'I can't. Are you getting hysterical? Do we need to go to an emergency room?'

'No! Don't you *dare*—'

'All right! I'm sorry!'

'Stop saying you're sorry!' She wiped at the tears of laughter on her cheeks. 'Oh, my God, what a morning!'

'I guess it hasn't been great for you.' Declan kept his gaze on the road. Then he asked suddenly, 'Have you had breakfast?'

She managed a normal breath. 'I fixed coffee when Olivia came banging on my door this morning.'

'You need something to eat.'

'No, I don't.'

'You do. Believe me.'

'You think food will make me feel better?'

'It'll help.'

'You just *can't* be inviting me to breakfast, Mr Adair.'

'I can. I *am*. My mother always said breakfast was the most important meal of the day. Besides, I'm starving and I don't want to eat alone. And my name is Declan. Will you do me the honor of joining me, Kelsey?'

'Oh, whatever!' Kelsey said, her laughing fit draining to a raw, undignified halt. 'I'm too tired to put up a fight. Besides, even if Brad Fairbourne has gone crazy and vanished into the netherworld, I'm starving.'

Declan laughed – a deep, joyous sound that made the lump of ice in Kelsey's stomach melt for the first time since she'd entered Brad's house.

Kelsey speared her last piece of strawberry pancake and ran it around the remnants of strawberry syrup and thick whipped cream mixed with powdered sugar, then popped it into her mouth. She closed her eyes and swallowed. 'Oh my gosh, that was good!' she burst out. 'If I keep eating sweets like I have the last few days, I won't fit into any of my clothes.'

Declan looked at her seriously for a moment, then grinned. 'I always take my mother out for strawberry pancakes on Mother's Day. She's as slender as a ballerina but she eats every bite and doesn't worry about it.'

'Then she's . . .'

'Alive? Definitely. Beautiful, alive, and madly in love with a wealthy man who adores her. He'll be her third husband. They're getting married in late June.'

'I'm so glad!' Kelsey realized she sounded too exuberant. She barely knew this man, after all, but out came, 'Good for her!'

Declan looked puzzled. 'Why the change in tone?'

Because I feel happy when I look at your finely chiseled face, the dimple in your chin, and the depth of your sapphire blue eyes, she thought in surprise, wondering where all of *that* had come from while she tried for a merely polite smile. 'I get loud when I'm on a sugar high,' she said unconvincingly. 'My parents always wanted me to sound like a lady.'

'Really?' Declan looked into her eyes and she felt color crawling up her cheeks. 'I think they always wanted you to sound happy, ladylike or not.'

Which was exactly the truth. 'Well, they did want me to be happy. Lori, too, of course. But I always felt they made a special effort with me.'

'Because you're adopted.'

Kelsey nodded. 'They tried so hard to make us feel that they didn't love one of us more than the other. Sometimes I think they went overboard with me. I wondered if Lori was jealous of me because I was allowed to do things she wasn't or I was given things before she was . . . A car, for instance.'

She looked up to find Declan's blue gaze searching her face. 'I don't know you well enough to express an opinion – but I'm brash, so I'll do it anyway. Kelsey, you're taking on guilt you don't deserve. Of course your parents gave you things before they gave them to Lorelei – you were older. It's as simple as that. She was six years younger than you.' He cocked an eyebrow. 'What would a ten-year-old have done with a car?'

Kelsey glanced at him in surprise for a moment before she giggled. 'I meant I got a car when I was sixteen but she didn't get one at sixteen. She was a terrible driver at sixteen. And seventeen. Then when she was eighteen, she went to New York City and didn't want a car. I did sound dumb, though!'

'You're not dumb. Just the opposite. You're extremely intelligent – maybe more than Lorelei.'

Kelsey suddenly bristled. 'What do you mean by that?'

'Nothing. Just a suggestion. You need to remember that lying isn't my strong point. I didn't know your sister, but I know *you* wouldn't have gotten involved with Cole.'

'So you're admitting it. Cole has a history of seducing young models.'

'He doesn't always confide in me but he's not the man you seem to think he is. I know there have been affairs in the past, but he's always been discreet. He didn't stay with Delphina because she was successful. Her supermodel title ended at least five years ago and she hasn't taken it well, to say the least. In spite of her perpetually foul mood, he stayed, even though they led the life Delphina wanted instead of having the children he wanted.' Declan paused. 'Cole really wanted me to meet Lorelei. We were supposed to spend half an hour or so over a drink. Two hours later, we were still laughing and talking. She was a delight. Cole cared about her, Kelsey. Cole loved her.'

'And Delphina knew about her,' Kelsey said flatly.

'I think she did. Cole thinks she did. But Lorelei didn't destroy his marriage. I think he'd had enough of Delphina and wanted out when along came Lori and gave him the impetus he needed. I'm sure he would have left Delphina within a year or two even if he hadn't met Lorelei. But New York City can be a very small town. The people who are personalities seem to know everything about each other. There were rumors. There had been rumors about Cole and various models before, but if the rumors were true the entanglements weren't serious. Never. Lorelei was different.' He paused uncomfortably. 'And Delphina was different. I don't know if her problem is too many meds for her various real or imagined health problems, too much alcohol, or maybe drugs – but *something* has been really off with her this last year. She's always been possessive of Cole, even though she's had her own flings – but suddenly last year she got out of control. When she couldn't go places with him, she had him followed. She called him constantly. She wasn't happy with him, but she wasn't going to let go of him without a desperate fight.' He shook his head slowly. 'I'm not certain how far she'd go to hold on to him and Cole's not certain, either.'

'But he still got involved with Lorelei,' Kelsey said bitterly. 'Why would he do that if he loved her?'

Declan was silent for a moment. Then he asked, 'Do you know the phrase "the heart wants what it wants"?'

'Would that be from the poet Emily Dickinson or the singer Selena Gomez?'

'I'll ignore your sarcasm. You know I meant from Emily Dickinson. My mother said it a lot. "The heart wants what it wants – or else it does not care." Cole isn't a perfect man, Kelsey. He can be selfish. I think he was being selfish when it came to Lorelei. Even though I'm sure he was serious about her, he shouldn't have dragged her into the mess of his marriage. But he did.'

'And what happens if you find out Delphina hired a hitman to kill Lori?'

Declan stared at her steadily, although Kelsey noticed his hands clench and his jaw tighten. 'If I or the Louisville police find that's the truth, Kelsey, she won't get away with it. I swear to God – if she's guilty, she'll be pay for what she's done.'

FOURTEEN

'Dad, I can't believe I got you! I've been calling since Saturday!' Kelsey stood in her kitchen nibbling a piece of dry toast for breakfast. Her mood immediately lifted when she heard her father's voice.

'I'm sorry, honey.' Truman March sounded slightly distracted. 'I've been so busy with March Vaden that I've ignored my daughter. Well, I didn't purposely ignore you—'

'You just forgot to call me back. That's OK. Helen has been keeping me apprised of your busy schedule. She said that today you're going into your office for the first time since . . . well, since Grandfather died.'

'Yes and it feels strange. On Monday mornings, he was always rested and full of ideas and energy. I tried to go back last Monday but the place felt worse than empty without him. It was like the heart of the business had stopped beating, and I came home after a couple of hours. Helen and I agreed that if you knew you'd worry about me, so we decided not to tell you. I'm trying again this week.'

'Grandfather was such a force of nature that everyone must feel his absence, but you're a force too, Dad. People will adjust to Grandfather being gone. More important, *you* will adjust.'

'Maybe.' Her father sounded doubtful and Kelsey closed her eyes, wishing she could do something to help. Only time could help, though. Time and her father's strength and devotion to the business her father and grandfather had built. 'To what do I owe this pleasant morning call?' he asked.

'Nothing in particular. I just wanted to hear your voice and catch up a bit.'

'It's great to hear *your* voice, honey. As for catching up . . . Well, you've probably heard that Brad was dismissed from the law firm.'

'Yes. Olivia came to my apartment yesterday morning. She couldn't reach Brad and she thought I might have keys to his house. I did. We went together but he wasn't there. The place was a wreck. Do you know if he's come home yet?'

After a beat of silence, Truman said, 'I haven't talked with Olivia since Friday evening. I don't believe I'll be talking to her again for quite some time.'

'Oh? Did you have an argument?'

'I guess you could call it that. Brad called me on Friday afternoon. He was drunk. He wanted me to go to bat for him with John Reid. I was honest with him, Kelsey. I told him that someone had sent me the photos, that I'd forwarded them to John, and that I wouldn't help him. Well, he blew up, started shouting, and told me something that shocked me to the core. Honestly, Kelsey, I still can't believe it. I'd like to think he was lying, but . . .'

Kelsey heard the pain in his voice. 'Brad told you that Milton Fairbourne was involved with Olivia for well over thirty years and that Milton is his real father?'

'So he told you too?'

'Olivia did yesterday when we went to Brad's house. I was surprised that she told me. Maybe it was because she knew you'd tell me.'

'When I refused to help him with John, he struck back. Brad believed I was in love with Olivia and I'd be hurt because of what she'd done. I was hurt, but not because of Olivia. Milton was my friend and I thought highly of his wife – she wasn't charming but she was a good woman and completely devoted to him. To find out that Milton was cheating on her for years was bad enough. To know that he was having an affair with Olivia, that Olivia had a child with him and that they'd both passed the child off as the son of a man who'd died when Brad was a toddler—'

Truman took a deep breath. 'Milton's gone, so I don't have to confront him – but I could never look at Olivia the same way, although all I ever felt for her was friendship, mainly because she was so close to your mother. At least, Sofie *thought* they were close. That relationship was built on Olivia's lies, too. Sofie always felt sorry for poor Olivia, who'd been widowed with a small boy. Ha! Widowed, hell! But she milked that story for all it was worth.

'On Friday evening, Olivia came here all to pieces about Brad,' her father went on. 'She expected me to intervene with John. I told her Brad was not only a lousy employee, he was fool enough to seduce the boss's teenage daughter. I showed her the pictures I'd received of Megan and Brad at his house and told her I'd forwarded them to John. Then I let her know everything Brad had told me about her relationship with Milton.' Truman paused, then said in a harsh voice, 'She went berserk. When I told her I never wanted to see her again, she flung herself at me, crying and clutching and flailing like a madwoman! She left a good-sized scratch on my face.'

'My God! I'm sorry, Dad.'

'It was a terrible shock.' Surprisingly, he started laughing. 'Helen came to my rescue. Normally she's always polite to Olivia, but that evening she nearly dragged her out of here. I've never seen anything like it!'

'Well, Helen is full of surprises, Dad! She's the one who's always had our interests at heart – not Olivia Fairbourne. And Helen is remarkably strong.' She giggled. 'I thought she was just strong emotionally, but I guess she can handle herself physically, as well!'

'Olivia won't forget Helen tossing her out the front door! What a sight! The venom that poured out of Olivia's mouth shocked me. She told me to be happy with Eve, whatever that meant.'

'She told me that Eve has been pursuing you since Mom died.'

'Oh, good lord! I think of Eve as a daughter and I believe she thinks of me as a father!'

'She does.'

'Anyway, you're right. Helen is remarkable. I think I've always known that about Helen, and so did your mother.' Truman paused then said lightly, 'Enough about me. What's on the agenda for my beautiful, brilliant daughter this week?'

'Most important, before work today I'm taking Gatsby in for his yearly shots and a check-up.' She glanced at the cat lying on his pad in the bookcase. 'He knows something's up and he's watchful and expecting the worst – I can tell. I have a busy day, so I can't pick him up until just before the veterinary clinic closes. He'll be there all day.'

'Oh, poor guy. Tell the staff to be gentle with him.'

'They already know to be gentle, Dad. He's been there before and they've learned the hard way that Gatsby doesn't put up with much. Also, you know that I'm renovating Aaron and Josie

Sanderson's house. Yesterday the contractor began work on one of the major stumbling blocks in the project – skylights. Honestly, Dad, I thought Aaron and Josie would end up in divorce court over the damned skylights!'

Truman laughed again. 'The things couples waste their time arguing about always surprises me. I assume they came to an understanding.'

'Yes. Josie got her way, and I'm glad because *she* had the best ideas.'

'Which I'm sure you let Aaron know in a diplomatic way.'

'I tried. I'm not known for my diplomacy. I usually depend on Stuart for that side of the business.' She thought of what Declan Adair had told her about Stuart and wanted to ask her father a dozen questions, but it was time he left for work. 'I'm glad you're feeling better, Dad. I can hear it in your voice.'

'Thanks, honey. Tell Gatsby he has my sympathy but to be a tough guy. Also, I'm sure the Sandersons will be happy with their skylights. After all, they're dealing with the best interior design firm in the state. You're coming home this weekend, aren't you?'

Her father always referred to the March house as 'home.' 'Yes, Dad. I'm looking forward to it.'

'Good. I love you, Kelsey. See you this weekend.'

Half an hour later, Kelsey pulled out of the veterinary clinic's parking lot. Gatsby had yowled loudly and continuously as she pulled the carrier from her back seat and trudged toward the clinic. 'You feel like you weigh fifty pounds,' she'd muttered. His yowling raised in volume once they were inside, until an assistant quickly took him to the back because he was upsetting a lively yapping beagle in the waiting room.

'He'll settle down in a few minutes,' the sweet-faced girl at the reception desk told her.

'Don't count on it,' Kelsey said gloomily.

As soon as she entered MG Interiors, Nina Evans rushed up to her. 'Giles's mother was scheduled for surgery tomorrow, but she took a turn for the worse and they decided to operate this morning. He called about ten minutes ago. I told Stuart and he talked to Giles. He won't be in today.'

'Of course not,' Kelsey said. 'We'll send flowers. I hope she'll be all right.'

'Giles would fall apart if she dies, but I don't think she's as sick as he thinks.' Nina was intelligent and creative but always blunt, which was why Kelsey rarely let her interact with clients. 'I don't think he has any friends besides us and we're not really friends. I mean, we're not close. He doesn't have anyone else except for a crazy old great-aunt. I've met her. God she was awful! If Giles was left alone in the world with only *her*—'

'We'll *all* hope that his mother pulls through,' Kelsey said patiently. 'If not, Giles will manage to make more friends. He's young, smart, personable and good-looking.'

'He is but he's so *shy*. I don't think I've ever met a grown man as bashful as Giles Miller! Why, just last week—'

'I know he's shy. He'll get over it. Thanks for telling me, Nina.'

Kelsey fled to her office and shut the door. She glanced at the coffee pot and immediately nixed the idea of making coffee. The last thing she needed was caffeine. Instead, she settled behind her desk, opened her laptop computer, and began working on a pink and white luxury closet with scores of shelves, a chandelier suspended from a high ceiling dotted with round flush LED lights, and a matching French country sofa and chair and antique French glass-topped tables, all of which would be reflected in a dizzying array of mirrors. The closet was far too ornate for the house, which Kelsey had pointed out to the haughty young new trophy wife, who was determined to have a closet like ones she'd seen on television. Her husband was still so enchanted with her that he didn't balk at the cost or the clash of designs between the bedroom and the closet. Kelsey wasn't enjoying the project, but the design needed to be completed by early next week so remodeling could begin immediately afterward. She would be happy to finish this job and decided if this particular young woman ever sought the services of MG Interiors again, she'd turn the work over to Nina.

At eleven-thirty, Kelsey stood up and stretched. She was slightly hungry but decided she didn't want to go out for lunch. She'd order a sandwich and a drink. Maybe Eve would like the same. She hadn't seen Eve all morning and hadn't talked to her over the weekend. Eve didn't even know about Olivia coming to her door on Sunday in search of her errant son.

Kelsey knocked on Eve's closed office door. She heard a soft 'Come in' and opened the door. Eve sat behind her desk, her face pale and wet with tears. Without a word, Kelsey walked toward the desk and stood waiting for Eve to speak. Finally, Eve held up a piece of plain white paper with blue handwriting on it. 'This letter from my mother came in the morning mail. My brother is dead,' she said raggedly. 'David. I loved him so much and now I'll never see him again.'

'Oh, my God,' Kelsey gasped. 'Eve, I'm *so* sorry. Of course you need to go home. You must leave right away.'

Eve looked at Kelsey bleakly. 'David died four months ago.'

Kelsey stared at her, stunned. 'Four *months* ago?' Eve nodded. 'And your mother has just let you know?'

'She says my father didn't want me told at all – he doesn't consider me part of the family – but she felt a *little bit* guilty about not letting me know. Although if I hadn't left home, I could have been a comfort to David when he was dying of pneumonia and a help to his wife and children! That's a cross I have to bear, she says. However, I'm not to come home even now. In fact, if I do, I won't be welcomed by her or Papa or David's wife, and I won't be allowed near my niece and nephew. I made my bed years ago and now I must lie in it.' Eve looked down at the letter and then crumpled it in her shaking hand. 'I don't even know the names of my brother's children!'

Kelsey went to Eve's chair, knelt, and put her arms around her friend. 'I can't imagine how you must be feeling. It's hard to believe that your family can be so cruel. I'm so, *so* sorry, Evie.'

'You've never called me "Evie" before. Only Stuart does.' She drew a deep breath, then sobbed against Kelsey's shoulder. 'David was only thirty. He was so smart, so kind, so selfless. He shouldn't have died, Kelsey. He shouldn't have died!'

'I know, honey,' Kelsey crooned, holding Eve and beginning to rock her gently. 'Life isn't fair sometimes.'

'No . . . no it *isn't*! To take David away—'

Suddenly Eve pulled away from Kelsey, her eyes widening. 'Lorelei! Oh, Kelsey, I'm sorry. You know how I feel. I shouldn't be going on and on . . .'

'It's all right. I *do* know how you feel! But that doesn't change anything. You need to go home for the day.'

Eve seemed to think about it for a moment. 'No, I don't. Being alone at home would only make things worse. I'd rather stay here.'

'Do you want me to get Stuart?'

'*No.*' Eve's voice was sharp and her face reddened.

'Is everything all right between you two?' Kelsey asked hesitantly.

'He's preparing for a one o'clock lunch meeting with Mr Albrecht. After lunch, they're going to look at the store – or rather, the shell of the store. The interior is almost completely empty.'

'Well, yes, but—'

'Really. There's plenty of time for me to tell Stuart later. This store is important, Kelsey.'

Against advice that a retail store was not a wise investment at this time, Edmund Albrecht remained determined to build the best luxury men's store in the city. Kelsey had been elated when he chose MG Interiors to design the large, tastefully lavish two-story interior, and Stuart had immediately won Albrecht's confidence. They'd been working closely for three months and now that the exterior of the store was finished, the real work would begin for Stuart. He seemed devoted to the project and Kelsey had complete confidence in his ability to both please Edmund Albrecht and create a jewel in the crown of MG Interiors.

Even in the midst of her shock and grief, Eve was concerned about Stuart's needs. It was obvious how deeply Eve loved Stuart. Once again Kelsey's thoughts flew to the accusations Declan Adair had made about Stuart, and she fiercely hoped he was wrong. Kelsey didn't want either danger or more hurt to touch Eve, but she wasn't entirely unselfish. She realized that if Declan's conjectures about Stuart and his 'connections' and his relationship with Delphina Harrington were right, then she could be facing a threat not only to MG Interiors but to her own life. *No!* She pushed the thought aside.

'I was going to order some sandwiches and drinks to be delivered at noon,' Kelsey told her. 'Do you want something?'

Eve shook her head. 'I can't eat. Maybe I'll get something later. Right now I just need to be alone.' She smiled. 'Do you understand?'

'Sure, but if there's anything I can do for you, let me know.'

Kelsey leaned forward and kissed Eve on the forehead. 'I love you like a sister.'

'Oh, thank you, Kelsey,' Eve quavered, her eyes filling with tears again. 'I love you, too. I don't know what I'd do without you.'

The afternoon dragged for Kelsey. She tried to do more work on the opulent closet, but thought she'd added just about every embellishment the over-decorated room could handle. She'd call her customer and make arrangements to show her plan by the end of the week. Around two o'clock, someone tapped on her office door. When she called 'Come in,' Nina opened the door and stood beaming at Kelsey, her gray eyes even livelier than usual.

'Let me guess. Declan Adair is here?' Kelsey said. Nina nodded vigorously like an excited little girl. Kelsey decided pregnancy hormones were getting to her. 'Please show him in.'

Nina pointed at her eyes then at Kelsey, who got the hint and took off her reading glasses. In a moment, Declan strode into Kelsey's office carrying a paper bag that he set on her desk. 'Chocolate chip cookies fresh from Nord's Bakery!'

Kelsey laughed. 'Why do men keep trying to feed me? First Stuart and now you!'

'Because you're not one of those women who claims to have a dainty appetite.'

'Is that a compliment?'

'Absolutely.'

'I just made a fresh pot of coffee. Why don't we both indulge in coffee and cookies?'

'Sounds great. I skipped lunch.'

As Kelsey poured coffee, she realized how happy she was to see Declan. Some of the darkness that had hovered over the day lifted when she looked at his smile. Stop being a fool, she told herself sternly. You don't even know him. Wordlessly, she gave him a mug and sat down behind her desk.

'What's wrong?' Declan asked.

'Why do you think something's wrong?'

'I have ESP,' he answered lightly. 'I can see the sadness behind the smile.'

Kelsey pulled a cookie from the bag and took a small bite. 'It's good.'

'What's wrong?'

She swallowed. 'Oh, OK. This morning Eve found out her brother died. Her mother wrote a letter. His name was David, he was thirty, he had two children, and he died four months ago. Four *months* ago. Eve is estranged from her family. They're—'

'I know all about them.'

'You do?' Kelsey looked at him levelly. 'Of course you do. You know everything about everyone who works here, don't you?'

'Just about everything. It's my business to know who works for the sister of the woman Cole loved.'

'The woman who was murdered by a hired killer who almost murdered her sister too.'

Declan nodded, gazing back at Kelsey with no shame in his eyes. 'I don't apologize for being thorough. Unfortunately I don't have any answers yet, although I've gathered a lot of information.' He paused long enough to eat half a cookie. 'Has Eve gone home for the day?'

'No. She didn't tell me about her brother until nearly noon and she didn't want Stuart to know at all. He had a one o'clock lunch meeting with a client and then they were going to look at a building site. She didn't even go out for lunch. I hope she'll be OK.'

'Were she and her brother close?'

'Not after she came to Louisville. He married a woman who sounds to me like Eve's parents' dream – narrow-minded, selfish and cold. Eve just learned that she has a niece and nephew but not their names. Also, she's forbidden to come back to Pennsylvania to see them.'

'That's a damned shame. I think having a close family is one the greatest gifts anyone could ever hope to have. Just throwing one away is unfathomable to me!'

He'd lost his light, often cheeky, tone. He sounded completely sincere and a bit angry. And hurt, Kelsey thought suddenly. He's talking about the life he wishes he'd had instead of the one Grant Harrington provided. He valued family. If he'd had one like hers—

'Did I say something wrong again?' Declan asked.

'What? No, not at all. I was just thinking about . . . uh, Eve's situation.' Which wasn't true, although Eve's tragic loss had been at the back of her mind for hours. 'She's told me how much she loved her brother, although to please his parents and his wife he'd cut off communication with her when she left home. I don't believe he was as strong as she is.'

'I suppose there's nothing you can do for her except be a good friend.' Abruptly Declan's demeanor changed and his brilliant blue eyes sparkled. 'Your other good friend, Bradley Fairbourne, Esquire, has returned home.'

'When?'

'Last night. I drove by his house around nine and it was dark. I took another look at midnight and just about every light in the house had been turned on. I thought it might have been his mother searching for him again, but I'm fairly sure I saw Brad walk past the front window.'

'What do you mean by "fairly sure"?'

'Brad has those translucent blinds like yours. The one at the front window was closed, but there was a light behind it and I could see the silhouette of a man the same build as Brad.'

'Then it might not have been him.'

'If you're so curious about him, why don't you call him?'

'Because my name would show on his Caller ID and he wouldn't answer.'

'Maybe his mother knows whether he's home. You could call her and the two of you could have a nice, long chat.'

Kelsey finally relented, tilted her head and grinned. 'That's a horrible suggestion! I'd rather never talk to her again.' She paused. 'Are you going to keep an eye on Brad?'

'Sure. He's on my list of suspects. Which reminds me that I'd better be going.' He stood. 'It's been a pleasure, Miss March.'

'Do you want to take some of the cookies with you?'

'No. They're all yours.'

'Good! They'll be gone before quitting time!'

Declan Adair was laughing as he left Kelsey's office.

Kelsey had been dimly aware of the light flowing through the light-filtering blind on her office window, but it took a loud clap of thunder to pull her from work. She hadn't checked the weather report today or gone out for lunch. Often, when she went out at lunchtime she found that the weather prediction for the day had been wrong. She glanced at the wall clock. Three-twenty. Damn.

If rain was coming, work would slow on the Sandersons' skylight installations.

By four-thirty, sheets of rain were battering the streets of Louisville. Kelsey went to her window and watched water fall relentlessly, drenching the parking lot and bouncing off the hoods and roofs of employee cars as thunder rolled ominously. The afternoon had turned dark as twilight. She groaned, thinking of having to stop by the veterinary clinic to pick up Gatsby. He feared storms and would no doubt be on his worst behavior, yowling and hissing as if he could scare away the storm.

Twenty minutes later, Kelsey told Isaac Baum and Nina to leave early. Stuart hadn't returned from his one o'clock meeting with Edmund Albrecht, which didn't surprise Kelsey. Albrecht, politely known as an eccentric, talked more than anyone Kelsey had ever met and had probably turned lunch into a two-hour affair followed by a stop at the site where his men's store was being built. A little rain wouldn't deter him. Kelsey had tapped on Eve's door, and when Eve didn't answer glanced into the office to find it empty. She looked out a window and saw that Eve's car was gone. No doubt she'd left without a word, exiting by the back door so she wouldn't have to talk to anyone.

Kelsey locked the front door and put up her red umbrella as soon as she stepped out of the rear door. She hurried across the parking lot, splattering rain on her three-inch-heeled beige leather pumps, glad she hadn't worn her new linen-covered heels, which would have got stained. Closing the umbrella, Kelsey clambered into her blue BMW convertible. She'd kept the top closed since Lori's death. She too had almost been killed, and she didn't want to drive around feeling exposed. Being shut in the sturdy car gave her a sense of safety.

'Oh, Miss March, you're here!' the receptionist at the vet's office exclaimed when Kelsey darted into the waiting room. 'Gatsby's anxious to go home!'

'You mean he's been hell on wheels today,' Kelsey said dryly.

The girl's smile faltered slightly. 'Well, he hasn't been happy.' At that moment, Kelsey heard a familiar caterwaul coming from the back area. 'Not happy at all.'

The girl retrieved notes made by the veterinarian, who was busy doing an emergency surgery on a dog. She assured Kelsey that Gatsby had gotten his yearly vaccinations and passed his check-up with flying colors, with the exception of an extra four pounds he could lose. Kelsey paid the bill and the girl hurried to the back. Kelsey heard her squeal once and say 'Bad cat!' Then she returned with Gatsby in his carrier.

'Did he scratch you?' Kelsey asked.

'Not really. I only got a little nick.' She held up her wrist. 'He's very . . . spirited.'

'That's putting it mildly. When a friend had to collect him for me, she put on a pair of thick oven mitts I have before trying to stuff him into his carrier.'

The girl laughed. 'I'll ask the doctor if we can get some oven mitts. That's a great idea!'

'Shame on you!' Kelsey said as she lugged Gatsby's carrier to the car. 'I don't know why you make such a big deal over a couple of little shots. It's not like you're a scared kitten.' She opened the passenger door and placed the carrier on the front seat. When she got in the other side, she looked at Gatsby through the carrier's aluminum grill door. He glared, indignant. She knew he'd be glaring for at least the next twenty-four hours. Maybe more.

Just as she was putting the key in the ignition, her cell phone rang. Kelsey sighed and fished in her purse for the phone. She was surprised to be getting a call from Eve.

'Hi. I'm at the vet's. Is something wrong?' she asked.

After a moment, Eve said in a tense voice, 'We have a problem at the Sanderson house.'

'The Sanderson house? What are you doing there, Eve?'

'I thought I'd come by and take a look.'

'Today? In the rain?'

'Yeah. I know it sounds crazy, but . . . I've assisted on this house and it means a lot to me and it's raining buckets. I was uneasy about the skylights so I came by and . . . well, there's a problem.'

'What kind of problem? Leaking?'

'Yes. And more. I can't really explain it.' She paused. 'You need to look at it. Maybe you can get the contractor to come back.'

Kelsey would have pressed harder for details but Eve's day had been awful and she sounded upset. Besides, the Sanderson house was an important project and Kelsey knew Eve wouldn't be calling her about something minor even if she couldn't explain what was wrong.

'OK, Eve. I just picked up Gatsby from the vet. I'll come straight to the house instead of dropping him off at home first.'

'I *am* sorry, Kelsey. It's raining and I know you've had a long day but I don't know what else to do . . .'

'It's all right. I'll be there in about fifteen minutes.'

'OK. I've left the back door unlocked for you.'

The phone went dead. Eve hadn't said goodbye, which was odd, but she was clearly distressed, probably more about her brother than the house. Still, Eve wasn't an alarmist. If she said there was a problem with the house, then there was. But why had Eve been so cryptic?

Kelsey drove to the Sandersons' three-story square brick building, which stood on two acres of land. White shutters had been added to all the windows, and the front of the structure softened by the addition of a small portico porch with white pillars. She turned down the side street bordering the Sanderson property until she came to the area behind the house that was being used as a parking lot for trucks. It was empty now except for Eve's car parked near the door.

'I'm going to leave you in the car while I go inside,' Kelsey told Gatsby as she turned off the ignition. She'd fallen into the habit of talking to him as if he was a child who needed to be reassured. 'You'll be fine here. I won't be gone for long.'

Gatsby let loose one of his loud, plaintive meows as she stepped from the car. The rain had slackened to a dreary drizzle falling from a leaden sky, so she hurried through the back door and as she crossed the concrete floor that would later be covered with hardwood she called, 'Eve? I'm here! Where are you?'

Kelsey had half-expected Eve to be standing or sitting near the door waiting for her, but she didn't answer. Kelsey called again. Nothing. Suddenly she had the feeling she was alone in the big house – the house she had designed with every ounce of her talent, mixed with care for the new inhabitants who had declared the design perfect and far beyond their expectations. Now it seemed cold and lonely and somehow sinister.

'Oh, for God's sake, Kelsey!' she said aloud. 'Why don't you let your imagination run completely wild?' Exasperated with herself, she reached for a wall switch and flipped it. Glorious light bloomed all around her, completely transforming gloom into what would be a dazzling white and navy blue kitchen. 'At least the electric is on,' she muttered. The way her luck was going today, she'd fully expected it to be shut off because of the rain.

'Eve?' she called again. 'Eve, where are you?'

Still no answer. Eve wouldn't be outside in the rain. So where was she? Kelsey walked through the kitchen and the large dining room area. She glanced at the rectangular skylight located three stories above on the flat roof. She tried to imagine sunlight streaming through it on to the exposed-brick wall and pale wood floor when the room was finished. It would be beautiful. And best of all, it wasn't leaking, which was often a problem with skylights – particularly those on a flat roof, if the box frame wasn't secure. So far, the contractors that MG Interiors used had had a perfect success record with skylight installations.

Across from the kitchen was the large space designated as a family room. 'In other words, it will have a gigantic television and a hundred video games,' Josie had told Kelsey and Eve. 'Aaron and the boys will live in that room. Angela is twelve and I want her to have her own space where she can practice her piano and her ballet and listen to music.' Josie had grinned. 'It should be the kind of place I wanted when I was her age.'

The family room was empty. Kelsey glanced into what would be Aaron's office and next to it, Josie's office. Then she walked into Angela's special room – the one that had been Eve's project since she and Angela had met and immediately seemed *simpatico*. No Eve, and none of the rooms had as much trash as usually found on building sites. So far, Kelsey hadn't the slightest idea what Eve had found wrong with the Sanderson house.

'Eve!' Kelsey was tired and getting frustrated. She wanted to go home, let Gatsby out of his carrier, fix something simple for dinner and watch television. Even reality television would be OK.

Then a frightening thought seared through her brain. What if Eve was hurt? What if something had fallen on her or, more likely, she'd tumbled down the three-story floating staircase? Kelsey ran to the location of the staircase then felt like a fool.

There was no staircase. It wouldn't be built until all the skylights had been installed and the roof finished. She stood where the staircase would end its gentle, magical curve and, looking upward, imagined the beautiful octagonal pyramid skylight that would grace the roof above the stairs. Only there was no skylight just yet. Instead, she saw a large hole and hazy translucent plastic sheeting. Apparently the hole for the skylight had already been cut when the rain began earlier than expected. The workers had covered the hole with polythene and secured it in order to keep out the water. So far it was working. Kelsey heard water beating on the plastic but didn't see one drop fall to the floor at her feet. Was this what had concerned Eve? Had she been afraid the plastic cover wouldn't hold firm?

No. On the phone Eve hadn't sounded worried about something that *might* happen. In fact, she hadn't sounded worried at all – she'd sounded scared. Dammit, Kelsey thought abruptly, she'd been so sure Eve was wretched over her brother she hadn't realized Eve sounded on the edge of terrified.

'Eve, I can't find anything wrong with the house,' Kelsey yelled at the top of her voice, trying to keep her own sudden fear in check. 'I don't know where you are, but I'm tired and I'm leaving. Do you hear me, Eve? I'm *leaving!*'

Kelsey felt rather than heard movement overhead. She went motionless, barely breathing, as she stared at the plastic-covered hole three stories above her. Almost immediately, the plastic ripped away. Kelsey briefly saw the gray sky before something black flashed across the hole. Bare legs in high-heeled pumps dangled above, then a shrill scream ripped through the quiet rain. In what seemed merely a heartbeat, a body burst through the hole and crashed downward in a broken, bleeding huddle at Kelsey's feet.

FIFTEEN

Kelsey was too shocked to scream. She stood rigid, listening to the small, constant, pathetic mewling coming from the body on the floor. She looked at the tan and dark brown dress, the silver and turquoise bangle on an out-flung arm, the ash brown hair. The head was turned face-down and blood pooled around it, the circle growing larger and larger. When it almost touched her shoes, Kelsey stepped back and gasped in horror. This was *Eve*! She'd been slinking away from Eve who was so terribly, unspeakably injured. Kelsey moved closer, kneeled, and pushed Eve's hair away from the bloody ruin that was her face. Her stomach clutching in pain, her body almost frigid, Kelsey let the wet hair fall back into place and gently stroked it, remembering how Eve had brushed her dry, tangled hair after Grandfather died in the fire.

'Eve, I'm here.' She managed to keep her voice steady. 'I'm here, honey. Don't be afraid.' Kelsey jumped when Eve whimpered. Had she heard her? Kelsey longed to turn Eve's head so she could look into her eyes, but didn't dare move her. 'I'm going to call for help. Just hang on.' Eve whimpered again and again. Kelsey leaned away, reached for her handbag, and dug out her cell phone. 'The ambulance will be here in a jiffy. Do you hear me, sweetie?' She tapped the numbers 911. 'Everything's going to be all right. Everything will be all right now.'

But the whimpering slowed, then stopped even before the 911 operator answered. Kelsey put her hand on Eve's back. She was so quiet and still that Kelsey knew she was gone. As she managed to give the information to the operator, Kelsey lovingly stroked her friend's back, even though she knew Eve was beyond the help of anyone on earth.

After a couple of minutes, Kelsey looked up at the circular hole in the roof. All she saw was gray sky. No evil face grinned back at her. She didn't see a flash of black like she had before Eve was pushed through the skylight hole. And she *was* pushed, Kelsey thought. If she'd merely tripped, her body wouldn't have attained the immediate momentum Kelsey had witnessed. Someone had deliberately sent Eve plummeting to her death. That person could still be on the roof, Kelsey thought with a shudder. Why? To watch the gruesome aftermath of the destruction of a life? Or to kill her, too?

Rain sprinkled down on to Eve's body. Kelsey thought of running out to her car to see if she had anything in the trunk she could use as a cover for Eve, but she didn't trust herself not to let fear force her to lock herself in the car. People would say that was the safest thing she could do in case the murderer still lurked around the building, but Kelsey knew she would never forgive herself for leaving Eve, even though she was dead. Besides, that might be exactly what the killer was waiting for her to do – run into the open where she would be even more vulnerable than in the house.

Instead, Kelsey hovered over Eve, touching her limp hand while listening for any whisper of motion, any stirring of air, or exhalation of breath from someone who still lived. Finally she heard sirens, and dashed to the front door, flung it open, and ran on to the front walk, waving her arms although the ambulance driver would know the address. People rushed past her, one asking if she was all right, the others heading into the house and toward Eve's twisted body. She heard more sirens – the police. After that, she slipped into a nightmare similar to that she'd lived through the night of Lorelei's murder. The world filled with flashing lights, shrieking sirens, people shouting, and she sank to her knees on the sidewalk.

Kelsey refused to ride in the ambulance with Eve so the paramedics could check her out. She brushed them aside. 'I'm all right!' she shouted. 'I'm *always* all right! It's Lori . . . and Eve.' She drew a deep breath. 'My car's here. I'll drive myself to the hospital!'

They insisted she was not in a fit state to drive, but Kelsey gave them no choice short of dragging her to the ambulance or picking her up, kicking and screaming, and carrying her. When the paramedics gave up, Kelsey talked briefly to the police officers who had come in response to her 911 call. She went back into the house and showed them the circular hole in the ceiling. 'It was cut for a skylight,' she said. 'The contractors probably had to stop installation because of the rain. The hole was covered with plastic. The killer pulled it back and shoved Eve through.'

Kelsey felt as if something heavy lay on her chest and she fought for breath. 'You'll have to talk to the contractors and ask what time they left. I don't know why Eve came here. She called me a little after five o'clock and said there was a problem. She sounded odd but she wouldn't tell me what was wrong. That's all I know.' She grabbed her handbag, still lying on the floor next to the shockingly large bloodstain. 'I'm not answering any more questions now. I can't. I'm going to the hospital.'

Kelsey almost ran around the house to the parking space in back. Eve's car still sat next to Kelsey's BMW. It seemed like a silent witness. What was Eve thinking when she pulled up to the Sanderson house? Had she come to check on the progress of the skylights? If so, who had been waiting for her? Someone she expected to see? Someone she knew? Someone who turned out to be a murderer.

Kelsey opened her car door and slid on to the seat. She was fishing in her bag for the keys when she suddenly thought of Gatsby. All this time he'd been in the car . . .

Except that he wasn't. She'd left the carrier on the front seat. When she didn't see it, she looked in frightened disbelief at the back seat. No carrier. 'Gatsby? Gatsby!' Kelsey knew calling for him was useless. He hadn't escaped from his carrier.

The carrier was gone. Gatsby was gone.

Kelsey wasn't certain how much time had passed before Detective Pike approached her in the hospital. Bloodstained and shaking, she'd refused to sit in the Emergency Room waiting area. Instead, she sat on the floor opposite the room where Eve's body lay. She leaned against the wall. A nurse had taken pity on her and wrapped a thin white blanket around Kelsey's trembling body. 'You really should scrub the bloodstains off your hands, have a cup of coffee, and get a chair in the waiting room instead of sitting on this cold floor, dear.' Kelsey had shaken her head vigorously. 'Well, OK. Is there anyone you can call?'

'Yes,' Kelsey said, although her mind was blank. 'I'll call . . . someone.'

'Good.' The woman's voice grew tender. 'I'm really *so* sorry about your friend.'

Kelsey nodded. The woman left and Kelsey huddled into the blanket, although it seemed to offer little warmth. Maybe nothing could warm her, she thought. Not coffee, not a down comforter, nothing.

The nurse was right – she should call someone. Normally she would have called a husband or parents but Eve had only Stuart, who wasn't answering his cell phone, and Kelsey had no idea how to get hold of Eve's parents. Would they want to know their daughter was dead, though? After all, they wouldn't even let her come home.

'Are you all right, Kelsey?'

She looked up at Enzo Pike's pale, slender face and depthless dark eyes. 'Oh, you're here!' A mixture of relief and hopelessness rushed through her – relief because Pike knew what to do, hopelessness because his knowledge related to what to do when someone had been murdered.

'A nurse told me I should go to the waiting room, but I'm all right.' Her throat tightened. 'I'm all right, but Eve is . . .'

'I know.' Dressed in one of his usual loose dark suits, Pike sat down on the floor beside her. 'You can move in a few minutes but I understand you wanting to stay here, needing to be near someone you loved. When my wife and daughter—' He broke off sharply. 'I understand.'

'I was right there. I saw her die just like I saw Lori die. I didn't help either one of them.'

'You *couldn't* help either one of them.'

'You don't even know what happened to Eve.'

'I know the basics. There was nothing you could do, Kelsey. Nothing.'

'I should have known something was wrong. Eve had gotten the most awful news that morning. Her brother died months ago but her mother only just got around to telling her. She stayed in her office all afternoon before leaving without a word. Then came her phone call. She said there was a problem at the Sanderson house. She wanted me to come. She was so vague. I don't know why she didn't tell me she was in trouble!'

'Probably because whoever killed her already had her. She was forced to make the call to you, to say just enough to get you to the house.'

'*Why?*' Kelsey demanded. 'Why did someone want me to see Eve die? Why did someone *want* her to die?'

'I don't know. But I'll find out. I promise you that I'll find out who did this.'

Kelsey squeezed her eyes tight. Almost as if Eve stood beside her, Kelsey could hear her saying, 'Someone keeps calling Stuart . . . I picked up the living-room extension . . . He came into the room furious and demanding to know how much I'd heard.' And an image flashed in front of her – red roses and a threatening note.

She turned to Pike and said fiercely, 'I want you to make me a promise, all right? I want you to promise to find out where Stuart Girard and Bradley Fairbourne were at the time of Eve's death.' Her voice rose. 'Do you *promise*?'

Pike put his hands on her shoulders. 'I promise, Kelsey. As God is my witness, I promise.'

Two hours later, after Pike had driven her home, assured her he was posting an officer outside for the night, and made an appointment to take her statement tomorrow, Kelsey swept the cool, damp cloth off her closed eyes and raised up from the sofa. Although the only light in the room came from the floor lamp with the opal shade, it might as well have been a spotlight. Her eyes felt full of sand. Tears refused to come. Her head pounded. She hadn't fallen asleep and was glad. A nap might have kept her from sleeping when night came. The thought of sitting up all night filled her with dread.

Before lying down, she'd called her father to tell him about Eve. His voice had gone completely flat, almost robotic. He'd asked only a few questions, then told her he would call Stuart and deliver the news. 'I can call him,' Kelsey had said. 'No, darling, you sound *slutkörd.*' Truman used the Swedish word for *exhausted* that Grandfather had always used, but her father's Swedish accent was even worse than hers. 'I hear the pain in your voice, Kelsey. You can't talk about this anymore tonight.' And he was right, Kelsey thought. 'In fact, I forbid you to talk about it anymore. Is that clear?' 'Yes, sir,' she'd answered with love. 'Whatever you say, Daddy.' So for the first time she could remember, she unplugged her landline phone and turned off her cell phone. Unless someone came banging on her door, she would be incommunicado.

But she had to do *something*, she told herself. She felt too dazed to watch television or read, yet she wouldn't let herself simply sit feeling stony and remote as if the events at the Sanderson house hadn't touched her. Deep inside her something ached and niggled, begging for release, but her body was stiff and resistant.

Kelsey glanced at the open kitchen and saw three glasses, a couple of plates and some flatware lying by the sink – not enough for a dishwasher load. She'd wash them by hand, she decided, and walked purposefully to the sink, where she squeezed out too much detergent and flipped on the hot water full blast. Suds foamed wildly as she slipped the plates into the water. She forced herself to hum as she washed and rinsed. Then she opened a kitchen drawer and looked for a dishtowel.

And there they were – the big, thick, ugly alligator oven mitts that beautiful, gentle Eve had donned before trying to stuff a grouchy, defiant Gatsby into his carrier. Both had been strong and determined and devoted . . .

Suddenly, all the lost faces flashed through her mind: Lorelei, Grandfather, Eve, Gatsby. She shuddered as she realized she would never see any of them again.

At last tears came and Kelsey sank to the floor, her body doubled up by deep, wrenching sobs that hurt so badly they took her breath away and felt as if they would never end.

SIXTEEN

Kelsey had planned to close MG Interiors for the rest of the week, but early Tuesday morning Nina Evans called and begged her not to shut the business. 'I'll come in even if it's just to keep the door open,' she told Kelsey. Last night Stuart had called Nina and told her about Eve's death. Nina's voice was still nasal from crying.

'If I stay home, I'll just cry all day and eat. I'm dehydrated from crying and I already weigh more than Giles and Isaac combined. Please, Kelsey, we can't just communicate with clients by telephone. Several of them expect the personal touch. You and Stuart won't be there. Giles's mother had her surgery yesterday and he's with her. By the way, I called him and she came through with flying colors. Giles is thrilled and said thanks for the flowers we sent. Anyway, we can't seem rudderless and shake our clients' confidence. I can talk to the people who call or stop by and assure them we're still in control and it will be business as usual after Eve's funeral. Stuart couldn't tell me anything about funeral arrangements. He sounded absolutely shattered and I didn't press for information. But about the funeral . . . well, where do her parents live?'

'Pennsylvania, but I don't think they'll be handling Eve's funeral. They won't want to,' Kelsey said flatly.

'They won't? Well . . . I know there's a sad story. I mean, Eve never confided in me. I just thought she wasn't close to her parents and once she said something that made me believe they didn't approve of her. But she's their *daughter*! I'd have thought they'd want some say about her burial.'

'I'm sure they won't want to be involved,' Kelsey snapped, thinking of the letter Eve had received just yesterday from her mother coldly informing her of her brother's death four months ago. And telling her not to come home, and that she would not be welcome. Then Kelsey realized how bitter she sounded. 'I'll let you know just as soon as arrangements have been made, OK?

Please do hold down the fort at the business, if you don't mind. I would really appreciate it, Nina. Is Isaac coming in?'

'He will if I tell him that I expect it,' Nina said firmly. 'Don't worry – I'll get Isaac to come into MG Interiors today and tomorrow too. He's our business manager, after all. It's where he belongs, like that bookkeeper in *A Christmas Carol*. You know – the one with all the kids.'

'Bob Cratchit?' Kelsey asked, smiling in spite of her sadness.

'Exactly.'

'I guess that would make me Scrooge.'

'Nonsense. You're the nicest boss in the world. Anyway, Isaac needs to be here today at noon because I'm going to Conway's Tavern for lunch. I'm craving one of their barbecue sandwiches and potato salad.'

'Nina, did you see Eve leave yesterday afternoon?' Kelsey asked abruptly.

'Well, no. Come to think of it, I didn't. She must have gone out the rear door. I'm sorry I wasn't more observant.'

'Don't be, Nina. You had no reason to be keeping track of Eve.'

'But if it's important . . .'

'It probably isn't.' Kelsey drew a deep breath. 'Thanks for keeping things afloat at MG Interiors. You're an angel. I don't tell you often enough how valuable you are to the business.'

'Oh, Kelsey, I'm not as talented as you and Stuart and . . . well, as Eve was. But thank you. If I don't see you, please let me know about Eve's funeral.' Nina's voice thickened. 'I want to come. I liked her so much.' She sniffled. 'Oh, here I go again with the tears. And you don't sound well today. You must have had such an awful shock last evening. I promised Stuart I wouldn't ask you to describe anything and I won't, but I just can't imagine . . . You poor thing. What you've been through lately! Anyway, take care of yourself. Let me know if you need anything. I'll talk to you soon.'

Later, Kelsey wasn't certain if either she or Nina had said goodbye. And Nina had sounded as if Kelsey would be far away, not just upstairs from the business. Oh well, she'd drop in later today or maybe tomorrow to see how Nina and Isaac were doing. And she would never forget Nina's loyalty or affection for Eve.

*   *   *

Kelsey had a ten o'clock appointment with Enzo Pike and, after talking to Nina, she went to her closet and stared tiredly at her clothes. She'd dozed for three nightmare-haunted hours last night but wouldn't take a sleeping pill because she wanted her mind to be clear when she gave her statement to Pike. Having the events at the Sanderson house remain laser-sharp this morning was a mixed blessing, though. She would be able to tell Pike everything, but nothing else seemed quite real to her. Certainly not her loft, which felt big and empty and somber without Gatsby padding after her meowing and purring, seemingly fascinated by every mundane thing she did. She closed her eyes. 'Just get through this morning,' she said aloud. 'You have to do this for Eve. You will do *everything* in your power for Eve.'

Forty-five minutes later, a freshly showered and shampooed Kelsey looked at herself in the full-length mirror on her bedroom door. Navy blue trouser pants, a white long-sleeved shirt with navy blue trim, pumps with three-inch heels, her hair pulled back into a low, loose bun, and just enough makeup to camouflage eyes puffy from tears and lack of sleep. She decided she looked professional and controlled. If only she felt as professional and controlled on the inside as she looked on the outside. But she would be talking to Pike. He wouldn't be threatening. He would be thorough, keen, intuitive, and considerate.

Half an hour later, he greeted her with quiet warmth. Kelsey noted the dark circles under his eyes. He looked as if he'd gotten little sleep.

'Are you all right?' he asked.

'I guess I am. None of it seems real.'

'I can imagine. Frankly, it doesn't seem real to me, either. I probably shouldn't say that to you. I'm supposed to be the unflappable detective, but what happened to Miss Daley . . . well, I'll tell you truthfully that I was shaken. And *so* sorry. She seemed to be a lovely woman – lovely in all ways.'

'She was.' Kelsey swallowed hard. 'Before I give you a detailed account of yesterday, will you tell me what you found out about the whereabouts of Brad Fairbourne and Stuart Girard?'

'Certainly.' He motioned to a chair and Kelsey sat down. 'I went to Fairbourne's house yesterday evening. No one answered the door, and an evening newspaper lay on the porch. I went back at nine and again at around eleven-thirty last night. The house was completely dark and still.'

'So he's disappeared again?'

'Maybe.'

Kelsey frowned. 'Did you check on Megan Reid?'

'As a matter of fact, yes. She was home with her parents. Her father seemed anxious – he wanted to know if Brad was in trouble. I said no, that I just wanted to check something with him. Mr Reid had more questions, but I got off the phone quickly.'

'What about Edmund Albrecht?'

'You saw Eve die a little before five-thirty. Stuart says he was with Albrecht until six. Mr Albrecht said he'd met with Girard during the afternoon and taken him to his store. He couldn't remember if he and Girard had parted company at four or six. He seemed extremely annoyed that I was bothering him with questions.'

'He gets extremely annoyed about anything that doesn't concern his interest at any moment,' Kelsey said. 'I think he's a complete pain, not to mention strange as hell, but Stuart has more patience with him than I do. Also, Albrecht is wealthy and has plans for a pricey store. We're lucky to get his business.' She sighed. 'Couldn't he be any more precise about when Stuart left him?'

'He left Stuart at the store site. He said it was raining. He didn't mind the rain. In fact, he *loves* rain, but Stuart seemed *antsy*. His word. Albrecht thought the rain was distracting Stuart, so he cut the meeting short.'

'At four o'clock or six.'

'Precisely. He had on a very expensive Rolex watch. But apparently he doesn't look at it often.'

Kelsey sighed. 'Well, you certainly tried. Thank you, Pike.'

'I did promise.'

'And you kept your promise. Now it's my turn to tell you everything I know about Eve's movements yesterday.'

'I'm afraid so. It's procedure but a necessary one.'

'I understand.'

For the next twenty minutes, Kelsey replayed every moment of the evening from the time she was leaving the vet's and got the phone call from Eve to the horrible moment when Eve crashed through the hole for the skylight to the concrete floor three stories below. Then her memory became frustratingly blurred.

'Did you see anyone looking down from the skylight?' Pike prompted.

'No,' Kelsey said. 'But I didn't look up for maybe a minute. No, it must have been longer than that. I stared at her – she was making an awful, mewling noise, and blood was spreading around her head. So much blood!' She shuddered. 'You would have thought a fall like that would have killed her immediately.'

'Whoever did this wasn't taking any chances on her living through that fall. The right side of her neck was slashed, opening the external carotid artery and the external jugular vein. He didn't cut her throat. Her vocal cords were intact, which is why she could make those mewling sounds you described.'

'The sounds I'll hear until I die,' Kelsey moaned.

'I just learned those details about the slashing in a preliminary report from the medical examiner's office. They're still running tests.'

'What kind of tests?'

'Tissue and, of course, blood. Eve could have been drugged. She also suffered a blow to the left side of her skull that could have caused unconsciousness. Maybe that's how the perpetrator got her up on to the roof without a fight. If she was drugged or unconscious from a concussion, she might not have felt the pain of having her neck slashed.'

'I hope so,' Kelsey said fervently. 'I hope she was so doped up she didn't feel a thing!'

Pike's somber dark eyes shifted away from her and she knew he thought Eve hadn't been unconscious when she hit the floor at Kelsey's feet. The sounds she'd made said she'd felt *something*.

'He must have taken her up the metal fire escape stairs on the north side of the building because he couldn't have reached any of the skylights without a ladder and the only ladders found were folded, dry, and covered with plastic. Also, we found what looks like a leather tip from the high heel of a woman's shoe on the fire escape. One of the tips was missing from Eve's right shoe, and the tip we retrieved matched the one on her left shoe.'

'Well, that sounds conclusive,' Kelsey said faintly, remembering the lovely beige and blue linen-covered high heels Eve had worn yesterday. 'But if he took her up the outside stairs, why was the back door leading into the kitchen open?'

'The lock on that door had been jimmied. He must have done it so you'd walk inside. Kelsey, he wanted you to be under that skylight before he pushed Eve through it.'

'Oh.' Kelsey felt sick. 'How could he have jimmied the lock and also held on to Eve? She would have been struggling.'

'Not if she was unconscious.'

'Oh, yes, of course . . . Didn't anybody see him taking Eve to the roof?'

'We've canvassed the area. No one saw them. There aren't any close neighbors and it was raining. People weren't walking outside. Also, there's an eight-inch-high brick parapet around the roof. That would also have partially obstructed the view of the roof's floor.' Pike paused before asking, 'Was Eve supposed to go to that house?' Pike asked.

'No. She'd had a rough day.' Kelsey told him about Eve receiving the letter about her brother's death. 'I'm not sure what time she left MG Interiors, but she was gone when I left a little before five. Giles Miller was away that day because his mother had an operation. Stuart had been gone all afternoon because he had the meeting with Albrecht, who talks so much that any meeting with him always turns into a marathon. Anyway, Eve must have gone out the rear door, because no one saw her leave. I went to the vet's to pick up my cat. I'd just gotten back into the car when Eve called. She sounded strange. I was a little bit worried because of her state of mind, but I didn't think something was really wrong.'

'You didn't see anyone leaving the scene after Eve's death?'

'No, I was trying to call nine-one-one.' She paused. 'But whoever it was took my cat out of the car.'

Pike's eyebrows shot up. 'You didn't tell me that yesterday!'

'To most people it would sound trivial after what happened to Eve.'

'Not to me. His name was . . . is . . . Gatsby, right?'

Kelsey nodded.

'Are you sure whoever killed Eve took him?'

'Gatsby was in his carrier in the car when I parked behind the house. I walked through the house to the front – that's where Eve was thrown from the roof – and stayed there until the police arrived. When I went back to my car, he was gone. I don't know who except Eve's killer would have taken him.'

'Were your car doors locked?'

'No, dammit. I wasn't thinking about anything except Eve, why she wanted me to come to the house instead of calling the construction foreman. Gatsby's carrier was sitting on the passenger's seat. I found the car door slightly open. Whoever took him didn't want to slam the door shut.' She paused. 'Maybe there are fingerprints on one of my car's door handles.'

'Maybe. We'll check if you'll give us your car today.'

'OK. I don't really need it. I'll take a cab home.'

Pike frowned. 'Why would anyone want your cat?'

Kelsey struggled for a moment, then told him the truth. 'It may sound paranoid, but I think someone wanted to torture me just a little bit more.' She looked at Pike in despair. 'I know the murders have something to do with me – my sister, my grandfather, my closest friend. It can't be a coincidence. Someone is trying to make me suffer.'

'Why?'

'I don't know. I didn't think I had any enemies. Well, Brad Fairbourne certainly doesn't like me. He was fired from his law firm on Friday morning and he blames me. And Eve. And probably my father, now.' She'd already told him about the photographs sent to her father and the roses sent to MG Interiors, but now she filled him in on what her father had said to Brad. 'You know that Declan Adair has been sporadically watching Brad's house and he's almost certain he saw Brad there Sunday night. At least he saw a silhouette through the blinds that looked like Brad's. He doesn't know when Brad came home.' She shook her head. 'I know Brad has emotional problems, but I can't imagine him *murdering* people!'

'Because he has a moral code?'

'Because he's weak. Maybe he could hire a killer but I can't imagine him messing with kerosene to set a barn – and an old man – on fire. I certainly can't imagine him slashing a woman's neck and pushing her through a skylight.' Kelsey drew a deep breath. 'But maybe I never knew him. Not *really*.'

'I've been a cop for years and I've learned how often people think they know someone else when they don't. People can wear masks.'

'You mean like Stuart Girard? Declan Adair says that Stuart has Mafia connections.'

Pike looked at her steadily. 'Girard knows some questionable people. His father knew a lot of questionable people and did business with them. After he died, they latched on to Stuart – or have tried to latch on to him.' He paused. 'I've said more than I should. Please don't repeat it.'

'I won't, but Declan already told me that Teddy Blakemore is out of prison on compassionate leave because he's dying. I also know he's been hounding Stuart. I just don't know what he wants Stuart to do or if Stuart is willing to do it.'

'And that's not good. Not good at all.' Pike looked distracted for a moment, then gave her a half-smile. 'Now, I have to ask you to write down everything that happened from the time Eve called you. It's—'

'Procedure. I know.' Bitterness edged Kelsey's voice. 'Every detail is scorched into my brain. I won't have any trouble writing it all down.'

Kelsey took a cab home and quickly changed into a U2 Joshua Tree T-shirt, jeans and sandals. After wandering aimlessly around her apartment for a while, her gaze continually straying to the empty cushion on the bookshelf, she lay down on her bed and promptly fell asleep. She dreamed of rain falling in the gloom, of blood spreading and pooling, of a slashed neck, of a rag doll falling down and mewling, mewling, mewling . . .

A sound tore at her sleep, a regular, relentless mechanical ringing that wouldn't stop until it had drawn her up from deep sleep to half-wakefulness. In a minute, she realized it was the phone.

Kelsey rolled toward her nightstand, picked up the receiver of her old-fashioned white Princess phone, and mumbled, 'Hello.'

'Were you taking a nap?' her father asked.

'Yes, Dad, but I was having a nightmare. I'm glad you woke me.'

'Did you see Detective Pike this morning?'

'Yeah. I told him everything about yesterday evening and then wrote it all down. It doesn't sound like much, but I felt drained when I got home.'

'No wonder.' Truman paused. 'Honey, I want to run an idea by you.'

'Something to do with March Vaden?'

'I can't think about March Vaden now. No, this is something about Eve. Last night police officers in her parents' county let them know what had happened. They thought that when her body was released, the Daleys would want it returned to them as they're her next of kin.' Truman swallowed hard. 'They didn't want to claim the body.'

'I knew they wouldn't,' Kelsey said dully.

'I can't even imagine people like that, but it doesn't mean she doesn't have any family. *We* are her family, and I'd like for her to be buried with us.'

The Marches and the Vadens had adjoining cemetery plots. Her mother, her sister and her maternal and paternal grandparents all rested beside each other in the beautiful cemetery not far from the March home. Kelsey felt tears rise in her eyes. 'Dad, that's so sweet of you! Are you sure it would be OK with everyone else?'

'We can't ask the current residents, honey.' Kelsey immediately felt silly. 'But if your March grandparents had known Eve, I'm certain it would have been fine with them. It certainly would be with the Vadens and your mother. They would have said Eve belonged with her Kentucky family, not those people in Pennsylvania. And Lorelei loved her. So did you and I.' Tears rolled down Kelsey's face. 'I'll handle all expenses, of course. You can choose the kind of service she would have wanted.'

'Oh, thank you, Dad. I've been upset about this all day. Even if her parents would have allowed her to be buried in their cemetery, I know she wouldn't have wanted that.' She took a deep breath. 'When will the police release her body?'

'I'm sure Pike will let me know within the next couple of days. In the meantime, I'll let a few people know that Eve will be buried here.'

A sob escaped Kelsey. 'Oh, Daddy, I never dreamed I'd be saying something like that about Eve and I can't help feeling responsible for her death. I know if she hadn't been my friend, she wouldn't be dead.'

'You don't know that, Kelsey and *you* did not murder her. You are in no way responsible for her death.'

Kelsey didn't answer. She knew her father was only trying to bolster her spirits, to make her stop blaming herself, but she did and she always would. Eve had been a victim of the dark, malignant presence that had boldly entered Kelsey's life the night Vernon Nott killed Lori.

At four o'clock Kelsey went into MG Interiors. Isaac was sitting behind his desk frowning at his computer screen. Kelsey couldn't help thinking that the Dickens character Bob Cratchit must have looked the same way when studying his ledger. Nina had firmly planted the image in her mind.

Nina rushed to Kelsey and hugged her. 'How are you doing?' she asked, drawing away and frowning at Kelsey's face. 'You're so pale and you look tired.'

'I didn't get much sleep last night. I took a nap when I got back from police headquarters, but my sleep wasn't restful. I'm OK, Nina.'

'I'm not convinced that you're OK, but I don't have any suggestions about how to make yourself feel better besides drinking lots of liquor.'

'And getting a hangover. No thanks. How has today gone?'

'The Sandersons have called twice wanting to talk to you,' Nina said. 'They said they're not certain they want to continue with the house. Their treasured project is now a crime scene. I told them that they don't want to make a decision when they're so shocked about what happened. I said that you understand and you'll be glad to talk to them in a few days when you've straightened out the situation. I don't know how you'd straighten out a murder, but I made it sound as if you're in control of everything. I think I managed to settle them down, Kelsey, and I don't believe they'll be pursuing you again until next week.'

'You're a miracle worker, Nina.' Nina beamed at the praise. 'It's so kind of you – and Isaac – to come in and handle everything for me.'

'It's our job,' Nina said stoutly. 'We're happy to do it, aren't we, Isaac?'

Isaac's small brown eyes appeared over the top of his computer monitor. 'Yes, we are. Nina's fielded all of the phone calls and the two people who've come in. I'm not good at those things. She's very articulate and persuasive.'

'He means I can talk people into a stupor,' Nina said. 'They back off in self-defense.'

Isaac grinned before lowering his gaze. He didn't smile often, and Kelsey was relieved to see that he and Nina were meshing even at this strange time.

Kelsey told them that her father wanted to have Eve buried with the March and Vaden families. Nina abruptly burst into tears, declaring how very generous and thoughtful he was, how touched Stuart would be. And last, and most awkwardly, how appreciative Eve would have been. From the corner of her eye, Kelsey saw Isaac wince. 'I don't know what day the funeral will be, but I would like for the two of you to come,' Kelsey ended.

Nina turned to Isaac. 'Of course we'll be there, won't we, Isaac?' He nodded. Nina looked down at her large, pregnant belly. 'I might bring my husband. I don't like being so reliant on him, but given my condition . . . I'm now thirty-two weeks along. I know some women enjoy looking like this, but I don't. My feet are so swollen I had to buy two pairs of shoes a size larger than normal.'

'Nina, if you're not feeling well—'

'I'm perfectly fine. Well, I'll be fine for at least a couple of weeks. Then I'm afraid I'll have to admit defeat and stay home.'

'You probably should begin your maternity leave next week, not in two weeks' time.'

'Maybe,' Nina said vaguely, then she burst out, 'Oh, guess what, Kelsey? I ate lunch at Conway's and the sweet little waitress, Janet, told me she's leaving!'

'Just leaving her job or leaving Louisville, too?'

'She said she's going to Atlanta with her husband. He has a new job there. Wednesday will be her last day at Conway's. I asked if she'd miss Louisville and she said yes, but maybe she needed a change. Rick Conway came up and said he didn't know how Conway's Tavern would get along without her. She blushed

and looked really uncomfortable. That beautiful milky skin of
hers was even whiter than usual – her freckles stood out like ink
spots – and she seemed nervous. She was trembling and she had
on a sweater although it's nearly eighty degrees.' Nina lowered
her voice, although Isaac didn't seem to be listening. 'When the
sweater sleeves pulled up, I knew why she was wearing it. She
had a big bruise on her right arm near her wrist and a smaller
one on her left forearm.'

'Oh, no,' Kelsey said slowly. 'Rick told me that her husband
is abusive.'

Nina's eyes widened. 'Physically? He must have given her the
bruises. She probably has more. Maybe she doesn't want to go
to Atlanta with her husband.'

'Rick said she's afraid of him. He must be insisting she go
with him and she can't say no without getting some hard slaps
and maybe a few punches. I wish I could help her, but I'm not
close to her. I think Rick is like a big brother to her, but even
he can't help if she won't let him.' Kelsey sighed, thinking of
the lovely petite girl with the big hazel eyes who'd been starstruck
when she met Lori and seemed broken-hearted when Lori died.
'I'll miss Janet,' Kelsey said softly. 'I'll miss her very much.'

Later that day, Kelsey cleaned her apartment until it was spotless,
reorganized her closet, and dusted all of her books on the shelves,
trying to ignore Gatsby's cushion on the fifth shelf, between
Moby Dick and *Anna Karenina*. By evening, she was exhausted
and lay down on the sofa, uninterested in watching television or
reading. Instead she closed her eyes and let her mind wander
over happy times in the past. Her sixteenth birthday party; her
first visit to Lori in New York, Lori having already become a
successful model at nineteen; the last Christmas before
Grandmother Vaden's death, when the entire family had gathered
in the March's lavishly decorated living room and basked in the
glow of countless colorful lights while singing carols, both
English and Swedish; outings to the Kentucky Derby at Churchill
Downs with Grandmother Vaden and the March ladies wearing
splendid hats as they watched the powerful horses run with sleek
beauty . . . Now it was all gone. She could never have those
experiences again. She had to be content with memories.

Kelsey felt the tears coming and jumped up from the sofa, determined not to cry again. She paced the room that suddenly seemed hot and stale in spite of the air conditioning. She opened the window near the bookcase – the window overlooking the alley, which was shrouded in shadows. At least the air, once again threatening rain, smelled fresh. She took a deep breath, wandered back to the sofa, and picked up her beautifully bound copy of *Brideshead Revisited*, her mother's favorite book.

She was on the fifth page when she heard what sounded like singing. Her skin tingled. She stopped breathing, listening with all the acuity she possessed. Then she crept to the open window and ducked down, crouching on the floor as the singing continued.

'War . . . it's just a shot away . . .'

It was the Rolling Stones song 'Gimme Shelter' – the song sung by the man who'd lingered beneath her open window and slowly smoked a cigarette. And the voice was the same.

'Death . . . it's just a breath away . . . Death, sister, it's just a breath away . . . Just a breath away . . .'

Abruptly the singing stopped. Then came a long, loud, plaintive meow – a meow that sounded like Gatsby's. It came again and again, lonely and desperate as it floated up to the open window. Very slowly, Kelsey rose to her knees, peered down, and saw a cat carrier sitting in the middle of the alley. Nothing else. Only a cat carrier, left on the asphalt. The cat within wailed its melancholy panic.

Gatsby! Someone had brought Gatsby back. But why? To lure her into the alley?

Kelsey scooted away from the window. The man who'd sung 'Gimme Shelter' had brought her cat – the cat he took after killing Eve. And now, she mused darkly, he's brought the cat back to me.

I can't go down there, Kelsey thought. I *can't*. He wants me to come down. He thinks he can force me to abandon the light and safety of my apartment to fetch the cat I love.

The cat wailed again, the meow sharp and frightened. Kelsey squeezed her eyes shut. She had to ignore the fearful cries. But what if Gatsby was hurt? What if she didn't retrieve him and whoever had left him in the alley took him back and killed him because he'd been useless? She knew most people would say she was insane for even considering going after him.

But Kelsey knew she wasn't most people.

She ran into her bedroom and pulled her fingerprint safety box from the second drawer of her bedside table. She placed her finger on the biometric sensor, opened the steel box, and looked at her Glock 26 handgun. Beside it lay a box of bullets. With shaking hands, she loaded the Glock's magazine, pushed it into the gun, and rushed from her bedroom trying not to think of what she held – a weapon of death.

As she passed near the window, she heard Gatsby emitting slow, rhythmic cries. She'd never heard him meow time after time without a break. He'd never been a bothersome cat given to annoying unrelenting vocal outbursts. Usually a couple of loud, sharp meows had got him what he wanted. He'd been lovingly spoiled ever since he was six weeks old.

Kelsey unlocked and opened her apartment door and stepped out, taking a deep breath. Her gaze swept the alley twice. She saw only the cat carrier sitting beneath one of the alley's few dim lights. Slowly she descended the steps, continually searching for a movement in the shadows as she firmly held the gun with both hands, keeping it pointed downward. When she reached the bottom of the metal stairway, her heart was pounding and sweat had popped out on her forehead.

Something to her right rattled and she whipped around, gun raised, to see a cardboard fast-food cup skittering down the alley as the breeze carried it toward the main street – the main street that was unusually empty for this time of evening. Or was it always this way? MG Interiors faced the street, but she was rarely in the office past seven o'clock unless she was working on a rush job. She was certain Nina and Isaac had left promptly at five so now the business – her second home – was dark and empty. Suddenly she felt alone in the world, alone and scared.

Gatsby let out another piercing meow. Kelsey turned back toward him, looking at the cat carrier sitting in the middle of the alley. 'Gatsby?' she called although she knew it was him. 'Gatsby, I'm here.'

His meows grew louder and more urgent. Come and get me, he seemed to be saying. Don't leave me here!

She took a few measured steps toward the carrier then stopped and did a slow 360-degree turn, her gaze probing every shadow-protected nook and corner. Gatsby wailed again. 'Coming, boy,' she called. 'I'm coming and I have a gun! *I have a gun.*' If someone was hiding in the alley, they couldn't help hearing her. She went forward five more steps then turned again. She was within two feet of the carrier. She was certain someone was watching her. She could feel a gaze lazily traveling up and down her body, and chills overtook her.

Finally the carrier was within her reach. She took two more hurried steps, leaned down, grabbed the handle and lifted the carrier, which as usual felt as if it weighed fifty pounds. She took a deep, shuddering breath. Gatsby wailed.

'It's all right, Gats. Four minutes and we'll be safe.' Her left arm felt strained from the weight of the carrier, and her right hand had begun to tremble. Her grip on the gun handle wasn't as steady as it had been when she started down the alley. She *knew* someone was watching her, waiting for her to slow down or drop the gun or—

A high-pitched squeak made her shriek and almost drop both the carrier and the gun. She whirled to see a disgustingly fat rat running along the side of the building directly across from her. A calm part of her mind asked what she'd done to scare a rat from cover. Nothing. She wasn't alone in the alley. Someone was close.

Her breath grew shallow and fast. Sweat trickled down her back. She whirled around in a circle, pointing her gun at shadows as Gatsby yowled. Her vision seemed to narrow when she saw a form at the opening of the alley – the form of a man.

As she opened her mouth to scream, he ran toward her. Slowly, her sight dimmed and she began sinking to her knees in the shadow-haunted alley.

SEVENTEEN

Strong arms closed around her. She let go of the carrier and tried to fight, but only managed to flail with arms and legs that felt as if they'd turned to liquid. Now he has me, she thought. And now I'll die.

'Kelsey, hold still!' She heard a voice that seemed to come from far away. 'My God, what are you doing out here?' He held her tightly. Gatsby let out a shrill meow.

'Go on, kill me!' she cried. 'Just get it over with!'

'*Kill you?* Kelsey, it's Declan!'

'This was a trap,' Kelsey sobbed wildly. 'A trap! A trap! A—'

Declan shook her hard. He clenched her shoulders and his blue gaze blazed into hers. 'It's me! Declan! I came to see if you were all right. What the hell are you doing out here with a cat . . .' He looked down at her limp right hand. '. . . And a *gun*?'

She went mute for a few moments, unable to draw enough breath to speak. Then, slowly, she realized that if he was going to kill her, he'd had plenty of time. Her panic ebbed slightly. 'He stole Gatsby yesterday after . . . after he killed Eve,' she said jerkily. 'He . . . he brought him back and left him . . . just left him in the alley. I *had* to get my cat, Declan.' To Kelsey's surprise, she began to cry weakly. 'I couldn't let that person take someone else I loved from me! I *couldn't*!'

Declan looked at her as if stunned. Then his jaw hardened. 'I'm getting you inside. Give me the gun and lean on me.'

'I have to hold the gun—'

'Your hand is shaking. Give me the gun, Kelsey. *Now*.' His hand closed over hers and she released her hold on the Glock. 'I'll take you upstairs and come back for the cat—'

'*No!* I won't leave him. You can't make me! I *won't*!'

'OK, you damned stubborn woman!' he shouted. 'You have to carry the cat thing. I can't hold it and the gun *and* support you.' She stooped and picked up the cat carrier. Then she let

Declan lead her to the outside stairs. 'One step at a time. *Slowly.* I'm holding you – you won't trip. Just a few steps, Kelsey. You can do it.'

'Yeah, yeah, OK,' she said as she lifted one leaden foot and then the other. If Declan hadn't been holding her, she would have fallen backward. Finally they reached the platform at the top of the stairs and Declan opened the door. Kelsey stumbled in, feeling as if she'd never been so happy to see familiar surroundings in her life.

'Oh, God,' she moaned in relief as she set down the carrier. 'We made it.' She peered in at Gatsby. 'Are you all right, sweetie?'

'*Sweetie!* My ass!' Declan exploded before he slammed the door shut, locked it, unloaded the Glock, and laid both the gun and the magazine on a table beside the door. Then he turned on her. 'You went out into a *dark alley*, carrying a *gun*, to rescue your *cat*? After what happened to Eve Daley yesterday? What in God's name is wrong with you?'

'Don't you yell at me!' Kelsey stood, nearly choking on her own enraged breath. 'He's not your cat. He doesn't mean anything to you. How dare you challenge what I did! You don't know *anything* about love, but then how could you since you had Grant Harrington for a father and Cole Harrington for a brother—'

'Stop it, stop it, *stop* it!' Gatsby let out a protesting meow as Declan shouted at her. She glared at him, breathing hard. He glared back. 'I do know about love, Kelsey. I also know about taking foolish risks that could easily get you killed and that's exactly what you did tonight. I know about Eve's murder and how she was found – by *you*. Someone drew you into that sick, bloodcurdling scenario. You're shocked. You're *beyond* shocked. I get it. But does that cat mean more to you than your life? If it does, then think about your father. Do you want him to lose *another* daughter? Don't you care about him enough to save him that grief?'

Kelsey's eyes blazed at him. Her hands curled into fists. Her legs tensed as she almost sprung at him. Then, without warning, she burst into long, broken sobs. She bent her head, blinded by tears, unable to speak. Finally Declan pulled her against him. He stroked her hair. 'Don't cry, darling girl. Don't cry. You're safe.' He paused and said grudgingly, 'And Gatsby's safe too.'

She couldn't stop crying, burying her head against his soft T-shirt, even as he stooped and released Gatsby from the carrier. Kelsey was dimly aware of the cat dashing to his safe place on the bookshelf. 'It's all right. *Shhhh*. You're all right,' Declan crooned to her.

'I'm a f-fool.'

'You did something foolish. That's different from being a fool.'

'Oh yeah?'

'Yeah.' Declan gently tilted back her head. 'You have tears all over your face. I don't suppose you're carrying a lace-edged handkerchief, are you?'

'I'm afraid not.'

'What a shame. I don't know what ladies' manners are coming to these days.' Kelsey laughed slightly giddily. 'Why don't you find some tissues? And may I stay for a few minutes? Or do you want me to get out as soon as possible?'

'I'd like you to stay. If you want to, that is.'

'I want to.'

Kelsey went to the bathroom and washed her face. Her eyes were still huge with fright and her skin looked blanched, but only time could repair her appearance. She crept back to the living room, fearing Declan would start yelling at her again. Instead, he was casually perusing her bookshelves.

'You have eight books about Amelia Earhart,' he said calmly.

'Well, ummm, yes. I told you I was fascinated by her.'

'Also that you wanted to be a pilot.' He turned, smiling easily at her. 'Only unlike Amelia, you'd hope to make it home after every flight.'

'Which is why I never took flying lessons.' She heard the slight tremor lingering in her voice. 'I didn't have enough confidence that I *would* make it home after every flight. I didn't think I'd be a good pilot.'

'You could never have known unless you'd tried.'

'That's true. I let doubt stand in my way.' She tried to smile but her lips trembled. 'I really want a drink. How about you?' He nodded. 'Beer, wine or rum?'

'I could use a very strong rum and Coke.'

'Me, too.'

While Kelsey dropped ice cubes into two glasses, she tried to gain control of her unsteady hands. Her armed rescue mission into the alley still didn't seem quite real, but the presence of Gatsby and Declan in her apartment told her it truly had happened. Thank goodness it had been successful. Dangerously reckless but successful.

As she carried the drinks into the living room, Declan stood near Gatsby, watching the cat methodically washing himself. 'I would have expected him to be hiding after his experience.'

'Oh, not Gatsby.' Kelsey set the glasses on the coffee table and sank on to her sofa. 'After he's had a fright, he wants to be on his own special cushion. Then he has a long, leisurely wash and lies quietly, sometimes for hours. He won't eat until no one is around. Maybe he feels vulnerable when he's eating. I don't know all the workings of his complicated mind, but if he was hurt he'd be yowling his head off. He's not stoic.' Kelsey took a deep breath. 'I'm so lucky that he's all right. Hell, I'm so lucky that he's even here! I never thought I'd see him again . . .'

Kelsey's voice deepened and shook. Declan sat down beside her and took her hand. 'It's all over now. He's home and he's OK.'

'And I'm happy, but that makes me feel guilty.'

'Why?'

'How can I feel happy when Eve was murdered *so* brutally, so needlessly—'

'Stop!' Declan picked up her glass and held it to her lips. 'Drink!' She took a gulp of the strong rum and Coke, almost choked, then recovered. 'Do you feel up to telling me about your evening and how you found Gatsby in the alley?'

'I guess,' she said reluctantly. Within a minute, though, she was describing the night when she'd first seen the man smoking a cigarette in the alley, his hood pulled up, and singing 'Gimme Shelter' as he walked away. Then she told him about tonight when she'd heard the singing again, then looked from the window to see the carrier in the middle of the alley and heard Gatsby's loud, frightened meowing.

After she'd finished, Declan looked at her and asked carefully, 'Are you sure it was "Gimme Shelter" the man was singing?'

'Don't look at me that way!' she flared. 'I know it sounds ludicrous, but I'm absolutely sure.'

'Did you tell Pike about the first time you saw the guy?'

'Yes, I did. Eve convinced me to do it, although I was afraid he'd think I was imagining the singing. If he did, he didn't act like it.'

'Does the song have a special meaning to you?'

'No, except that I like it. But a lot of people like it. It's still popular even though it's been around for decades.'

'Was the voice singing it at all familiar?'

'No.'

'Was the voice tonight the same as the voice the first time?'

'Yes,' Kelsey said definitely. 'Only tonight he sang, "Death is just a breath away . . . Sister, death is just a breath away." I don't think that's a line from the song.'

'Someone was improvising?'

'Maybe. Or he just got the lyrics wrong.'

'Why do you think Gatsby was taken?'

'To torture me.' Kelsey took another gulp of her drink and said, 'It sounds paranoid and narcissistic, but I think I've been at the root of everything that's happened – Lori's death, Grandfather's death, and Eve's death.'

'You?' Declan said softly. 'Why you?'

'I have no idea, but I know one person is behind all the terrible things that have happened and they're meant to be a prelude to *my* death. Gatsby was taken as a reminder of that to me.'

Kelsey was aware of Declan going completely still. She felt blood creeping to her cheeks and she couldn't look at him. 'I know I sound crazy.'

'Not crazy. Stricken. Overwhelmed. Responsible. But Kelsey, you are *not* responsible for someone else's actions. You're only responsible for your own, and you didn't murder Lorelei and Eve. We don't know that anyone planned to murder your grandfather. We only know someone set fire to the barn.'

'In order to burn three horses to death – three horses my family loved. And they then threw kerosene over Grandfather.'

Declan sighed. 'Kelsey, maybe these tragedies have nothing to do with you specifically. Maybe they have something to do with your father. Have you ever thought of that?'

'My father? What has he done to anyone?'

'He's the head of a huge corporation. People in positions of power like him make enemies, no matter how sterling their morals, how high-minded their intent.'

Kelsey looked away from Declan and sipped her drink, thinking. 'Lori's murder, Grandfather's death . . . When they happened, it never occurred to me that the two were connected. It wasn't until Eve's murder and someone taking Gatsby that I saw a thread linking everything. But tracing it back to something Dad did concerning March Vaden – well, I still don't see it. I know you do, though. You think someone is striking back at Dad and Grandfather because they were responsible for sending Teddy Blakemore to prison.'

'Blakemore was a fool for trying to get a foothold in March Vaden. Delusions of grandeur. *Pride goeth before destruction, and an haughty spirit before a fall.*'

'You're quoting the Bible now?'

'Teddy should have read Proverbs.'

'What about Stuart?'

'I haven't made my mind up about him yet.' Declan looked at his empty glass. 'May I have a refill, just as strong?' He grinned, the shallow lines appearing around his dazzling blue eyes. 'I didn't realize I was drinking so fast.'

'My glass is empty, too. Don't be embarrassed.'

As she walked toward the kitchen, Declan said, 'I noticed you're wearing a U2 Joshua Tree T-shirt. Would you happen to have the CD?'

'Of course. I love U2. I guess that dates me to my parents' generation.'

'It shows that you have good taste. It's a classic.'

After Kelsey placed the fresh drinks on the coffee table, she slipped the *Joshua Tree* CD into her stereo. In a moment, 'The Streets Have No Name' filled the room. Gatsby stopped washing himself and stared at Declan, who began lustily singing along with Bono. Kelsey giggled and, slightly woozy from the rum, loudly joined in. When the song ended, she laughed. 'I'm glad I don't have neighbors or they would have called the police by now!'

'I thought we were great. We should form a band.'

'I don't play an instrument. Do you?'

'The guitar. A little.'

'I should have known. You're a surfer, guitarist and private detective. Was your father proud of you?'

'He liked the surfing and the guitar playing.' Declan paused. 'I became a cop when I was twenty-one. He did *not* like that. He saw law enforcement as mundane grunt work, not the career for a son of the creative genius Grant Harrington.'

'Why did you leave the force to become a private investigator?'

Slowly Declan's expression changed from nonchalant to serious. 'I don't like to talk about it.'

'Then don't. I'm sorry for asking. It's none of my business.'

Declan took another sip of his drink and looked into her eyes. 'Maybe it would do me good to talk about it – with you, that is.' His gaze shifted. 'I went to California when I was eighteen and joined the police force in Los Angeles when I was twenty-one. I came back to New York City when I was twenty-three and later joined the NYPD. Four years after that, I had a young partner named Juan. He was very green but he had so much drive, such dedication. He wanted to be the very best. One January we had the evening shift, and I had a bitch of a cold. The sleet was so heavy the windshield wipers could barely keep up with it. I was coughing and sneezing and shivering. It seemed like every joint ached. Juan insisted on stopping to get me some coffee. I didn't argue too much. I could have done without the coffee, but I *really* wanted it.

'When we stopped, he went into a bodega. I should have gone in, cold or no cold. Anyway, he walked right into a robbery in progress. He killed one of the guys and saved the clerk, but the second guy got Juan in the chest. He made it through a serious operation, and his wife was ecstatic. They had two little boys – one was two and the other one, my godson, was nine months. Then Juan developed blood clots that went to his brain – one after another until finally he was on life support. His poor young wife had to give the order to pull the plug.' Declan looked at Kelsey, tears brimming in his beautiful eyes. 'Juan was dead, his wife widowed and emotionally scarred beyond belief, and two little boys orphaned, all because I wanted a cup of coffee. I quit the force the next week.'

Kelsey barely remembered wrapping him in her arms and pulling him to her. As they kissed slowly, she felt as if she were melting into his strength, his warmth, his gentleness. When she woke up the next morning, she was still holding him as they lay tangled on the sofa. Soft morning light filtered through the blinds and fell on his face, which looked handsome and strong yet younger and vulnerable in sleep. Gently she kissed his cheek then cuddled against him, realizing that for the first time in weeks she didn't feel bereft anymore. Death seemed far, far away at that moment.

Kelsey hadn't been embarrassed or uncomfortable wrapped around Declan. He just smiled lazily and asked, 'Did I snore?'

'No,' she answered. 'Do you usually?'

'I don't think so. I just talk.'

'If you talked, I didn't hear it.' Kelsey had smiled and kissed his forehead. 'That's the best night's sleep I've had for ages. Thank you.'

They'd gone out for breakfast and spent the rest of the day together. Declan had even gone to the veterinarian's with her when she took Gatsby in to make certain he hadn't suffered any physical trauma from his abduction. Later they ate dinner at Ruby's Steakhouse and talked about music, movies and their childhoods – anything except the murders.

The next morning, they slept late then lay in bed, their bodies close together. Kelsey reached down and touched a scar on Declan's abdomen. 'What happened here?'

'When I was seven, Mom and I visited her brother one winter. I have three cousins – all male, all show-offs, all older than I was, and all scathing about my "city boy" upbringing. When eight inches of snow fell within twenty-four hours, they dragged out their sled. Each one sailed down a hill, laughing and triumphant. They bullied me into trying it. I went down terrified, flipped the sled, and one of the blades cut me.'

'Ouch!' Kelsey yelped.

'It would have been worse if I hadn't been wearing so many clothes. I managed not to cry. My uncle rushed Mom and me to the hospital. I only needed six stitches but I thought my mother was going to have a nervous breakdown. We never visited them again.'

'No wonder!' She leaned down and gently kissed the scar.

Then her gaze traveled over his long, lean muscled body with its golden tan. She ran her finger over a slender scar on his chest. 'And this?'

'I was in a bar one evening having what I thought was a friendly disagreement with a guy about politics. All at once he picked up his glass, broke it, and slashed me. He was a lot drunker than he seemed.' Declan paused, grinning. 'And I was a cop.'

'Oh, bad news for him!'

'You bet.'

She kissed that scar. Her hand drifted over what looked like a bite mark beneath his left nipple. 'And this? Or should I not ask?'

'It's a bite mark, all right. I got it from one very bad-tempered Chihuahua that belonged to Grant.'

'Your father had a *Chihuahua*?'

'Yeah. I know it seems like an intrepid photographer of big game should have had a Doberman or Pit Bull, but he was partial to Chihuahuas.' Kelsey's cell phone rang. 'Oh, damn, I have about ten other war wounds I was going to show you!'

'I don't think my heart could take it.' She laughed, picking up the phone. 'Hello?'

'Hello, Kelsey. Feeling well this morning? Or are you tired from your night with Declan Adair?'

'Brad.' Kelsey went cold. She felt Declan raise up on an elbow beside her. 'To what do I owe the honor of this call?'

'I'm just checking on you. Friends can do that, can't they? Make sure all's well?'

'Where have you been? Not at home.'

'No, not at home. I know Adair has been looking for me. Pike, too. I'm a popular guy, especially when you're telling them I'm a murderer.'

'I didn't say you were a murderer.'

'But you let them know you suspect me of killing Eve. Have you told them I killed Lori and your grandfather, too? There is a law against slandering someone's good name, Kelsey. I ought to know. I'm a lawyer. An unemployed lawyer, thanks to you and your father, but a lawyer nevertheless.'

By now Declan was sitting up in bed, his head close to hers as she held the phone slightly away from her ear. 'Where have you been? In hiding?'

'In hiding?' Brad laughed. 'My, you are a flatterer, Kelsey.' She didn't answer. 'I wasn't *hiding*. I just needed solitude so I could think.'

'Oh. Solitude. That *does* sound better than hiding. So what were you thinking about?'

'About all the damage you've done to my life. I know you've hated me since I was a teenager. You dated me to set me up for a terrible fall. Mother told me, although I'd already figured it out for myself. You're going to pay for what you've done, Kelsey.'

'Your mother doesn't know *anything*, Brad. If someone has damaged your life, it's her.'

'I guess we'll have to agree to disagree about that. Anyway, I just wanted to let you – and Adair and Pike – know that I've moved back into my house again. They don't need to drive past every hour. The fugitive has been run to ground and I have no intention of going anywhere for a few days with one exception. I'll see you at Eve's funeral, Kelsey. I certainly wouldn't want to miss it.'

EIGHTEEN

The day Lori was buried the day had been unbelievably beautiful. Saturday, the day of Eve's funeral, dawned low, gray and flat. Even at eleven o'clock, the air was thin and close. Standing by the graveside, Kelsey felt as if she'd been shut in a metal box.

She and her father had chosen a rose-granite headstone with the engraving EVE SARAH DALEY, CHERISHED FRIEND along with her birth and death dates. The stone would not be ready for three weeks, so for now Eve's grave bore only flowers from her few friends. Knowing she wouldn't have the plethora of floral tributes that had been sent when Lorelei was buried, Truman and Kelsey had ordered extra flowers, which were dwarfed by a blanket of pink roses, carnations, orchids and lilies from Stuart. She'd spent the night before the funeral with her father, who seemed even more shaken than when Lori had been murdered.

As the minister delivered the service, Kelsey glanced around at the mourners, whose number was pitiful compared with how many had come to Lori's funeral. Nina, wearing a dress as gray as the day, cried into a handkerchief as her husky, red-haired husband kept his arm tightly around her as if she might fall. Isaac Baum had come alone looking decorous in a dark suit, his rim of black hair slicked down, his expression mournful. Kelsey had been surprised to see Giles Miller. She'd thought he'd stay home with his mother, but he'd arrived looking pale and almost ethereal in a light blue suit that matched his large eyes and nearly platinum-blonde hair – so like the color of Lori's – cut short above his ears but long with silky curls on top. Stuart seemed to have lost ten pounds since Monday. His cheekbones were more prominent than ever and his gray eyes lightless. His movements were slow and vague, as if he were in a dream. Finally, Kelsey glanced at Rick Conway, taller than anyone present, his face somber beneath the glossy brown hair. She knew he'd come to pay tribute to a frequent customer he'd liked. Kelsey remembered him laughing and joking when she'd come to Conway's in the evenings with Stuart and Eve. Seeing him without Janet by his side seemed strange. In her mind, they'd become a team, although they hadn't been married or even dating. Today, Janet was probably in Atlanta with the abusive husband she seemed unable to leave.

Kelsey was surprised to see Declan and Pike arrive together. Pike had barely known Eve and she knew Declan had only spoken to Eve at the reception after Lori's funeral. Since this morning, Kelsey's eyes had remained stubbornly dry when crying would have been a release. Now, looking at the two men who'd come to pay their respects to a woman who'd been a friend to her family and especially to her, Kelsey's throat tightened. She drew a long, shuddering breath, and Helen Norris reached over and clutched her hand. Dear Helen, Kelsey thought. She'd loved Eve, too. She'd loved everybody who'd been lost in just a few weeks.

And, finally, there was Bradley Fairbourne, dressed impeccably, his face stony, his eyes cold. He stared at Kelsey almost constantly and she pretended not to notice. But no one else was pretending, especially Pike and Declan. Pike rarely took his dark gaze from Brad, and Declan's intense blue eyes blazed at him.

When the service ended, the mourners – all of them, including Brad – went back to the March home for a short reception. Helen had baked two pies, a cake, cookies and muffins. Hot coffee and tea were waiting for everyone, and she began serving quickly as if satisfying everyone's hunger and thirst was the only activity that could hold her together.

People ate and drank self-consciously in the uncomfortably quiet March living room. Kelsey finally asked Giles how his mother was doing after her surgery. He immediately beamed and began giving details about her operation. Then he caught Nina's disapproving eye and abruptly stopped talking. Helen asked Nina when her baby was due. Nina smiled beatifically and announced, 'Two weeks and I'm going to name him Declan. I love that name.' Her husband Harry's face turned bright red and he nodded. Now he's obligated, Kelsey thought. Clever Nina.

They struggled on for twenty minutes until Isaac announced he was needed at home to help his wife with the youngest of their four children, who'd picked up a bad cold from a neighbor's

child. Kelsey could almost hear the sighs of relief as everyone
set down their refreshments and came up with reasons why they
must leave as soon as possible. Brad, with a long, malignant look
at Kelsey, was the last to go.

Kelsey was helping Helen clean up when her cell phone
rang. 'Oh, I hope this isn't business!' she complained. The Caller
ID read 'UNASSIGNED.'

'If it's one of the Sandersons, I swear I'll—'

She clicked the phone on and said sweetly, 'Hello?'

'Kelsey? Miss March?'

'Yes.' The voice sounded familiar.

'This is Janet. Janet O'Rourke from Conway's Tavern.'

'Oh. Hello, Janet. Are you in Atlanta?'

'No. I didn't go to Atlanta.' Janet paused, and then asked
breathlessly, 'Are you alone?'

A tingle of fear crawled up Kelsey's spine. 'How did you get
my cell phone number?'

'You gave me your business card a couple of months ago. I
never throw away business cards. I know it's almost time for
Miss Daley's funeral, but I wanted to talk to you.'

'The funeral is over, Janet. It was originally scheduled for
three o'clock but we're supposed to have thunderstorms, so we
moved it up until eleven and told people who we knew would
be attending about the change in time.' With the exception of
Brad, she thought, who'd obviously called the cemetery to check
the time of the burial.

'Oh. It was a good idea to miss the storms. Are you alone?'
she asked again.

Kelsey walked out of the kitchen, through the dining room
and out on to the terrace. 'Now I'm alone. Go ahead.'

'Oh, gosh, Miss March, I've got some *real* important things
to tell you.'

Kelsey could hear the tension in Janet's voice. The young
woman wouldn't be calling to talk about her abusive husband.
She'd barely mentioned him in the past. Something else was
going on and Kelsey knew that, whatever it was, it couldn't be
good.

'Janet, please call me Kelsey,' she began, keeping her voice
even and calm. 'Take a deep breath and tell me what's wrong.'

'OK. Well, this all started about three months ago. You see, I knew Vernon Nott. I've known him for years.'

Kelsey stiffened. 'I see,' she said tonelessly.

'No, you don't see. I can tell by your voice. I'll try to explain it right. My full name was Janet June Nevins. O'Rourke is my married name.'

Janet June Nevins! Kelsey remembered the photograph of Nott that Pike had shown her. The inscription had said, 'Here's my favorite guy, J. J. N.'

'I grew up outside of Lawrenceburg,' Janet went on. 'My family was really poor, and Daddy died when I was little. Mama had a lot of boyfriends, some not very nice. Vern – Vernon Nott – lived next to us. His family was bad, too, especially his step-father. He was *so* mean to Vern. He beat Vern and burned his face with cigarettes, and his mother didn't even care. Vern had a lot of anger in him, but he could be sweet. He was eight years older than me and for some reason he liked me. He treated me like a little sister and protected me from Mama's boyfriends. I know he got arrested later on for assaulting women, so it really doesn't make sense that he was so nice to me – but I think the women he hurt reminded him of his mother or something psycho-logical like that. Anyway, even after Vern went to prison the last time he was arrested, we stayed in touch. I'd married Joey O'Rourke to get away from home. I hardly knew him and right off realized I'd made a mistake, but I figured I'd made my bed so had to sleep in it. Joey knew about Vern and said I couldn't see him or talk to him, so I kept my letters to Vern a secret. Then Joey and I moved to Louisville and I got the job at Conway's. I wrote all about it to Vern, and after he got out of prison he moved to Louisville, got a job, and started coming to Conway's regularly. His mama was dead, he didn't have any brothers or sisters, and he didn't have anyone else but me. He said I was his family. He was always *so* nice to me, Miss March . . . Kelsey.

'When Rick started asking me about him because he came to Conway's so regularly, I told him the truth,' Janet continued. 'Even though he knew how good Vern had been to me when I was little, I could tell that at first Rick didn't like him coming to the bar. But when he saw how well-behaved Vern was, he calmed down – especially when I told him that if my husband knew about Vern, Joey wouldn't let me see him. The bar was the only place we had to meet that was safe, and Rick knew that Vern meant a lot to me. Without Vern, I don't know what would've happened to me when I was just a little girl. Rick said that he had great parents and felt bad for people like Vern and me who'd had bad home lives when we were young.'

Kelsey heard tears in Janet's voice. She sympathized with Janet's position, but she couldn't imagine Vernon Nott as anything but a monster who'd assaulted women and killed Lori. She barely managed to say, 'Go on, Janet.'

'So Vern came in twice a week. I knew he didn't come so often just to see me. He really liked the place. He said it felt warm and happy. He also liked it when someone played the piano and people sang along. Then one evening I saw Rick talking to him. Later I asked Vern what Rick had said and Vern told me Rick was just being friendly, asking a few questions about his life and if he had kids. Rick didn't say a word about Vern to me. Vern coming twice a week didn't seem to bother him. And Joey never came to the bar after my first couple of weeks there, so I thought everything was fine. But then things changed . . .'

Kelsey's anxiety level ratcheted up a notch. 'How did they change, Janet?'

'I wish I'd paid more attention and given the situation more thought, but hindsight is twenty-twenty. Rick says that.'

As she listened, Kelsey wandered around the terrace and looked at the cypress birdhouses. No bluebirds darted and soared today. It was almost as if they too mourned for Eve.

'Anyway, I noticed Rick talking to Vern several times. When I went to Vern's table for another order, they'd just be shooting the breeze and laughing. Then Rick changed my station. I didn't work in Vern's section anymore, but Rick still sat and talked to him and I could tell they were talking about serious stuff. Then Vern began seeming sort of . . . gosh, I don't know how to describe it. Kind of nervous and excited at the same time. I used to see him look that way when we lived next to each other and he was going to do something he shouldn't.'

Janet sighed. 'Kelsey, I'm not a brain so I shouldn't throw stones, but Vern wasn't real smart. He did awful in school and dropped out. He couldn't read very well. People made fun of him and he hated it. When he was around certain people he'd try to show that, no matter what other people said, he was smart. He'd get a look on his face – I guess I'd call it *eager*. Also, he wanted terribly to please people he admired . . . Does all of this make sense?'

'Yes. I think I understand.' Kelsey sat down on one of the terrace chairs, trying to ignore the increasing pace of her heartbeat and the soft beep on her cell phone that meant the batteries were low. 'When Vernon talked to Rick, did he have that eager look?'

'Yes! I could tell he looked up to Rick, who's handsome and really intelligent and has his own business even though he's just thirty-five. And Rick can charm the birds out of the trees. You know that. Poor Vern would get tongue-tied every time he tried to talk to someone he didn't know.

'So the night Vern . . . oh, God I can hardly say it . . . shot your sister . . . well, I was so surprised and horrified I could barely think. I felt *so* guilty for bringing Vern into your sister's life I thought I'd die too. Then people kept saying Vern was a stalker, but I never knew of him getting crazy over any *real* girl, much less one he just saw in a magazine. The whole thing didn't make sense to me but I didn't say anything. Then Detective Pike talked to Rick. They were in Rick's office and I eavesdropped. Rick said he'd only talked to Vern *once*. He *lied* to a policeman. Why? I got kind of worried, but I thought Rick must have been protecting me because I hadn't told Detective Pike that I'd known Vern for years. That was really bad of me not to tell Detective Pike, but the whole situation was so awful and I was scared.'

Kelsey's cell phone beeped again. 'I can understand you being afraid,' Kelsey said truthfully.

'Well, I just let things drift with Rick,' Janet went on. 'We never talked about what happened to your sister – about Vern shooting her, that is. And Rick was a hero. But when people said his parents must be proud, he said they were dead. Just the week before, he'd told me they were planning a trip! Then when we were at your house after your sister's funeral, your grandfather thought he recognized Rick. It didn't seem bad at all to me and everything was straightened out. At least I thought it was. I'd ridden with Rick in his car, and on the way home he said he couldn't believe your grandfather thought he recognized him. And a few minutes later he brought it up again. Then Rick started

talking about it a third time, and he seemed upset. It didn't seem
natural, Kelsey. Your grandfather had just been confused, but
Rick got really wound up. I started thinking that although Rick
wasn't the person your grandfather thought he was, he *did* recognize Rick. Then that night your barn was burned and your sweet
grandfather got caught in the fire . . .' Janet's voice caught and
she sobbed softly. 'What happened was *horrible*, but Rick didn't
seem upset anymore. Not one little bit!'

'*He didn't?*' Kelsey's voice was raspy. Her hand tightened on
her beeping cell phone. 'Are you sure Rick wasn't just . . . well,
hiding his feelings?'

'If he was hiding his feelings, he's one fine actor,' Janet said
sharply. 'Then this past Monday afternoon he took off around
four o'clock without a word. He usually says where he's going
and when he'll be back, but not on Monday. We get a lot of
business on Mondays, so he always likes to be there when it
starts, a little after five. But he didn't get back until around six-
thirty. He seemed tired and distracted. He had on different clothes
than earlier and I could smell strong soap on him like he'd just
taken a shower. His hair was damp and he was favoring his right
side, like he'd pulled muscles in his arm and side. And Kelsey,
I saw some blood behind his ear. Not a cut or scratch – just a
little *streak* of blood behind his ear lobe and down his neck a
tiny bit – and something made me think "That's not *his* blood."

'The next day, your employee, Nina Evans, came in and told
me about Eve Daley. My gosh, Kelsey, Eve was *so* nice and
pretty and . . . Well, hearing she was dead just about *broke* my
heart – and hearing she'd been murdered just about *stopped* it.
I mean, my heart actually skipped a beat, especially when she
said Eve had been thrown through a skylight three stories high.
Somebody strong would have had to do that and it could still
have caused strained muscles. By that time, Rick had come up
to talk to Mrs Evans. He acted shocked and upset and made a
big deal about what a terrible thing Eve's death was. But his
carrying on just didn't ring true – something about him was
wrong. That's when I knew I had to do something. I'd told Rick
that over the past weekend Joey had said we were moving to
Atlanta, and that I'd said I wasn't going and Joey'd got rough
with me. Which was true.'

'Nina told me she saw bruises on your wrists,' Kelsey said above the annoying beeps of a dying battery.

'I have more bruises than those but I held my ground. So Joey went alone, but he said he'd be back this weekend. When I heard about Eve, I just burst out to Rick that I'd decided to go to Atlanta with Joey. In front of Mrs Evans, I told him that Wednesday would be my last day. Rick didn't like it, but I showed him some of the bruises I'd gotten on Sunday – they hurt but came in handy. I thought that if Rick called up the place where Joey worked to check whether or not he'd really quit to go to Atlanta, at least he'd find out I was telling the truth.'

'Well . . . I don't know what to say.' Kelsey felt as if the wind had been knocked out of her. She could barely hold on to the phone, which was beeping. 'Janet, are you staying in Louisville now?'

'Oh, you bet! I've been staying with a friend, so if Rick goes by my apartment he won't find me. It did occur to me that I should have called Detective Pike about all this – I have his card with his phone number – but I don't *know* anything. From watching television, I realize that the police want evidence. But I don't have any. I didn't even tell that handsome private detective who talked to me. I have his card too, but I didn't know if I could really trust him. He's not the *real* police.'

'You can trust him, Janet. He used to be a police officer in New York City.'

'Every time I've thought about calling either of them and just saying what I think based on what I've seen, I've been worried about getting Rick into trouble if all of this is just my imagination running wild—'

Kelsey's phone beeped maddeningly. 'Janet, you should stay away from Rick!'

'You, too. Did he came to the funeral?'

'Yes, and the reception at the house afterward.'

'But he's gone. Right?'

'I saw him drive away. I don't *think* he came back . . .' Kelsey felt panic rising. 'Janet, get help!'

'I will, Kel—'

The phone died.

NINETEEN

Kelsey closed her eyes, a cloying sense of dread descending over her. Janet had been trying to warn her of imminent danger, but she was too late. Kelsey had a ghastly feeling that danger had already arrived. But how did you fight danger? By thinking clearly. By maintaining calm. By being smart.

Kelsey walked into the kitchen, expecting to see Helen, but the room was empty. She slipped out of her shoes and crept back to Helen's suite to find no one in the small sitting room or bedroom. She picked up the receiver of Helen's landline phone beside her recliner. Dead. She glanced around both rooms for Helen's cell phone but she couldn't find it.

As she left Helen's suite, she stopped herself from calling Helen's name. If her intuition was right, someone was in the house – someone who didn't belong – and she didn't want to betray her knowledge. Silently, she padded through the dining room and living room and lifted the receiver of the landline phone. Like Helen's phone, it was dead. She hung up quietly and picked up her handbag lying beside the phone. Her spirits sank even lower when she felt how light it was. In spite of Declan warning her not to carry her gun, she'd ignored him. And now the gun was missing – someone had taken the Glock, which she'd carried since the night Gatsby had been left in the alley. Her only protection was gone.

'Don't panic,' she whispered to herself. 'Think.' What could she use as a weapon? The silver candle holder sitting beside her handbag? It was better than nothing, she thought, grasping it in a sweating hand. She could swing hard with her right arm.

Kelsey wondered if her father had retreated to his study after everyone had left. She crossed the wide hall that divided the house, moved to the door of his paneled study and peeked through the doorway. He wasn't sitting behind his large desk, or on the leather chair near the bay window.

As she stood by the doorway, she heard a noise upstairs.

Someone tapped on a door and dishes rattled. Kelsey heard her father call 'Come in.' A moment later she heard Helen say, 'I've made some ginger tea for your headache. It always helps.'

Oh God, Kelsey thought. Her father had felt one of his migraines coming on and gone to his bedroom. She rushed up the curving staircase and started across the landing leading to her father's room.

'I took a pill for my migraine,' Truman was saying.

'But Sofie always made ginger tea for you.'

'I *hate* ginger tea, Helen. I only drank it so I wouldn't hurt Sofie's feelings!' After a moment, Truman said kindly, 'I didn't mean to snap at you, Helen. It's been a hard day. I really don't want ginger tea on top of everything else.'

'Well, if you're sure—'

At that moment Kelsey rushed into the room, which was dimmed by cellular shades. 'We have to leave the house!' Helen and her father looked at her with wide, startled eyes. 'I don't have time to explain. Just come with me!'

'What on earth is wrong with you, honey?' Truman asked anxiously.

'Yes, what on earth is wrong with you, honey?' Rick Conway stepped through the doorway of the adjoining bedroom that used to be the nursery. 'What on *earth* is wrong with you, Kelsey? Or should I say *sister*?' He pointed a large handgun at Kelsey, then at Helen, who dropped the silver tray she was carrying. A china teapot hit the floor, splattering hot water on her shoes. She yelped then cowered backwards. 'Isn't everyone glad to see me? After all, I am the master's son. Or hasn't he ever told you about me?'

'Rick?' Truman asked in bewilderment. His gray eyes narrowed and he frowned. '*You?*' He started to rise from a white club chair. 'You can't be—'

'Truman Edmund March, Jr? Well, yes I am, Father. Hard to believe you don't recognize me, but I guess we only see what we want to see.' Rick looked at Kelsey and Helen. 'What a surprise, eh? I'm his son.'

'You are *not* my son and your surname isn't March,' Truman said crushingly.

Rick's brown gaze hardened. He raised the gun and pointed it at Truman. Helen gasped and cried, 'No! Oh, *please,* no!'

'What? Oh, I get it!' Rick looked at Helen pityingly. 'You're in love with him, too, aren't you? What a shame. Nothing good comes to women who fall in love with this man.'

'Why are you here?' Kelsey ground out.

Rick's dark eyes burned in skin that looked unnaturally pale, although color blazed high on his cheekbones and sweat sheened across his forehead. His usually beautiful brown curly hair stood up in knots and spikes, as if he'd run damp hands through it several times. He held on to his gun so tightly his knuckles were white.

'First of all, stop hovering in the doorway. Step into the room.'

Kelsey hesitated, then looked at his ferocious expression. This isn't the time to defy him, she thought, as she entered the room. He smiled crookedly and nodded. 'Very good. Now I'll answer your question. I'm here, Sister, because I want to claim my birthright.'

'She's not your sister,' Truman growled.

'You're right, Father. She's not. She's adopted. We don't share the same blood – *your* blood. She's nothing to me except the kid you took into your home and loved and spoiled, while you let me make it through life any damned way I could. And that's just what I did. I made it in spite of you, Truman March!' Rick's gaze shot to Kelsey. 'Stop holding that stupid candlestick. What do you plan to do? Beat me to death with it?'

'You took my gun out of my handbag.'

'So I did. That pitiful little Glock.' He held up his gun. 'This is a Desert Eagle .44 Magnum.'

'You don't mess around, do you? Is this a case of a big gun masking giant insecurity?'

'You shut up!' Rick's eyes narrowed. 'Sit down on the bed and stop trying to act brave, Kelsey. I know what you really are – just a rich man's spoiled daughter trying to act tough.'

Kelsey edged toward the bed and sat beside Helen, who'd sunk down on it as soon as Rick announced he was Truman's son. Now she seemed on the verge of sliding off the side in a faint.

'We're all in place, Rick. We're all at your mercy. Happy now?'

'Stop baiting him, Kelsey,' Truman said evenly.

'I only want to know why he says he's your son.'

'Because I *am!*' Rick shouted. 'My mother was Anna Akers. Do you even remember what she looked like, Truman?' His gaze shifted to Kelsey. 'When she was twenty-one, she and this fine specimen of a man had a love affair. I'm the result. Then your mother from the good, *wealthy* family – the family that formed March Vaden with your father – appeared on the scene and Truman kicked both of us out of his life. I was his *son* and he turned his back on me!'

Kelsey had put her arm around Helen, who was trembling. Suddenly Truman looked small and old in his large white chair, while Rick seemed to grow taller, stronger, and more menacing every minute. Kelsey suddenly felt some of her earlier courage deserting her. 'Dad, what is he talking about?' she asked. 'Who is Anna Akers?'

'A young woman I met at my very wild twenty-fourth birthday party. Anna was pretty and I was drunk. That night we started what I guess you'd call a fling. It lasted a week before I broke off with her. She called me countless times. She cried. She screamed. She sent me threatening letters – in those days we actually sent letters on paper. And a year after our brief affair ended, she turned up with a baby that she said was mine.'

'But you'd met Mom by then?'

'Just a couple of months before Anna came to see me, bringing a baby.'

'Not *a* baby,' Rick snarled. ''Me!'

'All right,' Truman said tiredly. 'You.'

Kelsey looked at her father. 'But you were falling in love with Mom, so you hid what this woman was saying about her baby?'

'I did at first. For less than three months. By then I knew I wanted to marry Sofie. So I told her and her father about Anna and about the baby. It was a hard thing to tell them, but especially hard to tell Sofie. I said I didn't see how Anna could have gotten pregnant with *my* child. I'd always used protection, but I know accidents can happen.'

Rick said furiously, 'So I'm to be dismissed as an *accident*? I'm your *son*, dammit!'

Truman looked at him steadily. 'I am going to say this one more time. I am *not* your father. Your mother claimed I was, but I'm not.'

'She had proof!'

'At first she provided falsified blood-test results.'

'Of course you'd say they were fake.'

'I had experts look at the test results—'

'*Experts* you paid to claim they were false!'

'I didn't pay off anyone. I asked that Anna let my doctor run blood tests – she refused. I asked that a respected doctor with loyalty to neither of us run a test – she refused again. When you were five, she turned up with DNA test results. DNA testing was fairly new then. She thought she was being smart, but once again the documents your mother presented were proved false. So *I* had DNA tests run.' Rick couldn't hide his surprise. 'Anna always brought you to me back then and thrust you at me and told you to hug me. You'd rub your head against me. You had a lot of hair even then and you left a few strands with roots on my jacket. I had them tested against my own hair – twice. Each time, the results did *not* match.'

'I've been with the March family for twenty-eight years and I never saw a woman come here with a little curly-haired boy.' Helen suddenly quavered. 'And you don't look a thing like Mr March! I would have noticed when you came here after Lorelei's funeral.'

'I look like my mother. And I'd never been in this house until Lorelei's funeral reception. When I was a little boy, my father set up meetings with my mother in his office.'

'I didn't set up meetings with Anna anywhere,' Truman snapped. 'She followed me to work because she knew she couldn't get near the house. I hired security for the house after I married Sofie. I didn't want Anna coming here confronting and threatening my wife!'

'And your wife, that kind and wonderful woman everyone has heard so much about, didn't want to see *me*. She didn't want anything to do with *me*!'

Truman's back stiffened and he leaned forward. 'When you were about two years old, Sofie suggested that we adopt you! She said that even if you weren't mine, you needed a home, a place away from your mother, who was clearly unstable. But Anna wouldn't just let go of you. She told me she wanted me either to divorce Sofie and marry her or for me to let you stay in her care and pay her. The amount she demanded was enormous. I knew she'd spend a bare minimum on you and spend the rest on herself. She would have retained full custody of you *and* would have always wanted more – more money, more attention. By the time you were three, she was making veiled threats against Sofie.' Truman looked at Rick closely. 'You know she was crazy, don't you? You knew it when you were a kid. I used to see it in your eyes when she brought you along for one of her confrontations with me.' Truman paused then asked softly, 'How old were you before you got away from her? And how *did* you get away from her?'

Rick looked like he'd been punched in the abdomen. The air seemed to go out of him and he sagged slightly. Finally, he took a deep, labored breath. 'She was bringing me to see you again,' he said in a flat, detached voice. 'There was a storm. She was *so* mad. She wouldn't stop – she wouldn't pull off the road even though it was raining so hard she couldn't see. My favorite song came on the radio – "Gimme Shelter" by the Rolling Stones. I even made up a line that should have been in the song. "Death is just a breath away, a breath away." Mick Jagger didn't write that line, *I* did and it was good. I sang along with the radio so I wouldn't be so scared, but she yelled at me and turned off my song.' His breath came faster. 'She turned off my song! She wouldn't even let me have *that*! Then the car slid off the road. I survived the crash . . . she didn't.' His gaze sharpened. 'I was thirteen.'

'So that's why she stopped harassing me so abruptly,' Truman said faintly. 'Are you sure she was dead after the wreck? Did you call for help?'

'What's it to you?' Rick demanded. 'That was your lucky day.'

'So you didn't try to get help even though you weren't sure she was dead?'

'Oh, she was dead, all right. She was *dead*.'

'Where did you go after the wreck?' Truman asked. 'You were only thirteen and you didn't come to me.'

'Why the hell would I come to you? Would you have taken me in?'

Truman drew a deep breath. 'Maybe.'

Rick strode toward him. 'You hadn't even seen me since I was a scrawny ten-year-old. You refused to see me after that!'

'I didn't refuse to see you. Your mother wouldn't *let* me see you unless I agreed to her terms. In other words, unless I signed papers saying I'd pay her.'

'I don't believe you! You hated me!'

'I didn't hate you,' Truman said evenly. 'I never hated you.'

'Easy to say now. Much *safer* to say now when I'm standing over you with a gun.'

Kelsey noticed that the air in the room was growing close, almost smothering. Everyone was shocked, angry and frightened, and their emotions radiated like auras. She closed her eyes, thinking of Janet. Janet had said she'd get help, and she didn't doubt that Janet would make every effort possible to save them. She just wasn't certain whether Janet's efforts would be enough. They were trapped, Rick was in charge, and Kelsey knew time was running out.

'Where did you come up with the name Rick?' she asked, trying to keep him distracted. 'Richard Conway. Did you just invent it?'

'Do you think I'm a fool?' Rick asked scathingly. 'I knew someone named Richard Simon Conway. After my lunatic of a mother died, I made my living on the streets.' He looked at Truman. '*Your* son made himself available to men, any time, any place! I wasn't really streetwise at first. It was luck that I met Richard "Richie" Conway. He was fifteen although he looked older. Street life will do that to you – add years to your appearance. I realized almost as soon as I met him that he could be my savior. He'd been on his own since he was my age. His parents had never even reported him missing, much less searched for him.

'I hung out with Richie for almost two years until he found what he thought was a real lover. The big love affair lasted about six months. Richie's benefactor found someone prettier and more trustworthy, but by the time the guy cut him loose Richie had acquired some money, an ID card, a Social Security Card and a driver's license. He said he'd made out fairly well in spite of being kicked out of the castle.' Rick paused, smiling. 'He shouldn't have bragged, especially after deserting me. I killed him and took everything he had. One day I was Tru Akers, fifteen years old with no money and no ID, the next I was seventeen-year-old Richard Conway with two thousand bucks and all the identification I needed. Even his driver's license photo could pass for me if you didn't look too close. After that, I started side careers. I was a popular hustler – and robbed quite a few of my clients, and blackmailed a few prosperous ones. Finally, after *years*, I made enough money to buy a building and create Conway's Tavern.'

'Which just happened to be a couple of blocks from MG Interiors?' Kelsey asked.

'It didn't *just happen*. As soon as I knew your daddy had bought the building for you to start your business, I bought my own.'

'So you'd been watching me for years?'

'Yes, Kelsey, I had,' Rick said witheringly. 'Why the hell wouldn't I? Truman abandoned me and left me in the hands of that vile woman, but he adopted you. You weren't even his natural child, but he gave you the life I should have had. You robbed me. You *robbed* me, you bitch!'

Kelsey could feel his rage growing. She knew he was reliving the years he'd spent with Anna Akers and the later years he'd spent on the streets selling himself to anyone who'd have him. At fifteen, he'd become a murderer. Maybe even before that. There was no proof that his mother had been dead after the wreck. Maybe he'd escaped from the car and simply left her to die. *And maybe by then that was the only way he thought he could survive*, Kelsey thought, a treacherous vein of compassion springing up in her. Immediately, she strangled it. She couldn't let herself feel sorry for this man. Any conscience he might have had had died long ago. Now he was only a vicious killer.

She had to do something. If she didn't, Rick was going to kill all three of them. She could lower her head and lunge at him, throw him off balance if not knock him down. Maybe he'd drop the gun. But what if he didn't, and it went off? If that canon of a gun went off in the direction of her father or Helen? It *won't*, she told herself as she tensed. Rick was turned at a forty-five degree angle from her. If she could charge and hit him beneath his ribcage—

As Kelsey began to tense for a lunge at Rick, her father asked coolly, 'Why did you murder Lori, Pieter, and Eve?' Rick turned

to face Truman, his right hand holding the gun, his left arm
hanging at his side. At this angle, the best Kelsey could do would
be to knock his arm away. Her chance was gone.

'Isn't it obvious? I wanted to hurt you like you hurt me. When
I got to know Vernon Nott, I realized he wasn't any different
from me except he was stupid. At first, he was only supposed
to shoot Kelsey. Then that woman who works for Kelsey – Nina
something – got excited that Lorelei was coming to visit, and
she was certain Kelsey would bring Lorelei to Conway's. I saw
the chance to get both of them. I offered Nott ten thousand dollars
for the job – half before, half after. The night Kelsey came in
with Lorelei, Nott got nervous and started drinking too much. I
knew he was going to botch the job. I'd always intended to kill
him immediately after he shot the women, but because he was
so drunk I didn't wait for him to try to get Kelsey. Someone
could have stopped him and he'd have started talking about *me*.
So Kelsey escaped with her life that night.' Rick smiled. 'But it
wasn't a botched job after all – Lorelei March was dead and her
sister and your whole family were traumatized. And it had only
cost me five thousand dollars.'

Kelsey's heart seemed to squeeze as Truman's eyes closed
briefly. Then he looked back at Rick. 'And Pieter?'

'After Lorelei was murdered, I realized it was better to inflict
as much pain as possible on your family before I destroyed you.
I planned to kill Vaden, but not the way I did. How could I have
known he prowled around at night and went to the barn? I'd
come only to burn down the barn with your horses inside. You
were so proud of those damned horses! It made me sick. But the
old man tottered in to save the day. He got the stall doors open
. . . and then I doused him with kerosene and set him on fire for
his trouble.'

Kelsey's stomach clenched as the image of her grandfather
writhing in flames blinded her. She felt Helen shaking with silent
sobs.

'But it worked out for the best. After he seemed to recognize
me at Lorelei's funeral reception, he had to die,' Rick said conver-
sationally. 'It really shook me up when he boomed "I remember
you." I sure as hell remembered him!'

'You met Grandfather? When?' Kelsey asked, hoping to

buy more time while her mind worked frantically on how she could get the three of them out of what seemed like a hopeless situation.

'I was fifteen and in bad shape.' Rick's gaze seemed to cloud slightly as he dredged up a memory. 'Richie had always sort of looked after me since I was thirteen. Then he thought he'd hit a mother lode when he met his wealthy boyfriend, and he deserted me. Just left me alone with my coke habit. I ran out of money and couldn't make enough to take care of myself. Plus I got beaten to a pulp one night. I was hurt and in withdrawal. I had to get help. I kept an eye on the March Vaden building but, although I hadn't seen my loving father for a couple of weeks, Old Man Vaden was around. So I waited for him by the March Vaden building, in the underground garage.

'He finally showed up and I told him I was Truman March's son. I gave him details about his wife, his daughter, his grand-daughters. You should have seen his face! He believed me. I said I was addicted to cocaine and badly off. I was skin and bones, shaking and sweating and dirty. He said he'd take care of me and to get into the car. I was too strung out to ask any questions. I just remember ending up at the office of some big-shot doctor who said he'd get me admitted into a rehab facility that afternoon. Like hell, I said, and ran. In spite of the shape I was in, neither Old Man Vaden nor the doctor could catch me.'

'He told me what happened,' Truman said. 'He was trying to help you.'

'All he was trying to do was get me locked up somewhere to keep his darling daughter's family safe from scandal!' Rick shouted bitterly, then drew a deep breath. 'I've changed a lot since I was fifteen but Vaden still recognized me at the reception after Lorelei's funeral, the wily old fox. He just got me mixed up with some guy who'd dated his wife a hundred years ago. I couldn't take a chance on his head clearing enough to remember me, though.' He grinned at Truman, and then at Kelsey. 'Besides, I knew the two of you were crazy about him. I had luck on my side and was able to finish him that very night.' He laughed. 'I sent him out of this world in a blaze of glory!'

'And you enjoyed it,' Kelsey said without emotion.

'Yes! Oh, yes I did!'

'Even though Grandfather had never done anything except try to help you?'

'I told you that I saw through him,' Rick spat. 'I know he wanted me to disappear, for me to die rather than tarnish his family.'

Kelsey forced herself to hold his gaze. 'That's not why you killed him. You destroyed Lori and Grandfather because you knew Dad loved them. And I guess you murdered Eve for the same reason.'

'Yes. She was really just another orphan the Marches took in and treated like a princess.'

'I see.'

Rick frowned. 'What are you thinking about, Kelsey? Tell me!'

'I was wondering how you lured Eve to the Sanderson house.'

'I didn't. I went to her apartment complex and waited in the parking lot until she came home. I wore a black poncho with the hood pulled up. Before she could open her door, I jerked open the passenger door and jumped in the car. I pushed my gun in her side. I forced her to call you and I told her what to say. Then I made her drive to that old factory you're remodeling, half-dragged her up the iron staircase on to the roof and took her to that skylight hole. I held her there until you appeared right beneath it. Then I pushed her. She landed right at your feet!' Rick laughed. 'The pretty girl went *splat*!' Kelsey cringed as Rick's laughter grew loud and wild, as if he was losing control.

In spite of his laughter, Kelsey thought she heard a soft noise downstairs – the sound of the front door opening. *Oh, please*, she thought. *Please let that be someone coming to help us.*

'You took the pictures of Brad Fairbourne and Megan Reid and sent them to Dad, didn't you?'

'Sure. I would have sent them directly to John Reid if I'd had his phone number.' He looked at Truman. 'I knew you'd send them, though. After all, Megan Reid is another pretty, spoiled girl. I had to ruin her fun. And Brad is yet one more orphan that hit the jackpot! God, what is it with you people? Oh, well, I got him fired from his fancy law firm so he probably hates the Marches as much as I do.'

'Why did you take Gatsby?' Kelsey demanded loudly, hoping to mask any more noises coming from downstairs.

Rick almost choked as he struggled to stop laughing. 'Because you love him.' He paused, then said scathingly, 'A *cat!*' He smirked. 'When I brought him back and left him in the alley, you should have seen yourself shaking and shuddering, holding your little gun with a trembling hand as you tried to save your *cat!*'

'I did save my cat.'

'It wasn't in any danger.' Rick's expression shifted into one of disgust. '*I* don't torture dogs and cats to death. Those pathetic serial killers in the making, like Jeffrey Dahmer, do that stuff. I'm nothing like those people, and don't you *ever* compare me to *them!*'

Kelsey marveled in horror at Rick's distinctions. Murdering the real Richard Conway and Lori, Grandfather and Eve meant nothing to him, but he abhorred killers who began their savage lethal career by torturing dogs and cats. He wanted everyone in the room to know that he was different. He believes he's different, Kelsey thought. It would be sad if it weren't so frightening.

There was a nearly inaudible creak on the stairs. Helen tensed, and Kelsey knew she'd heard it. Had Rick? 'What are you going to do after you kill the three of us?' she asked loudly. 'You can't get away with these murders.'

'I can do things you wouldn't imagine.' Rick glared at her. 'I've gotten away with murders since I was fifteen. I got away with murders – the murders of your family and friend – while hiding in plain sight. I'm smart, Kelsey.' His fierce gaze turned to Truman. 'I'm brilliant, Dad. You have a handsome, *brilliant* son and you turned your back on him. How does that make you feel? Stupid? Are you *stupid* as well as cruel?' Truman sat rigidly in his chair, sweat running down his face. Rick raised his gun and pointed it at Truman. 'How does that make you *feel?*' he roared.

Although Kelsey's attention was focused on Rick, she glimpsed movement in the doorway to the landing and saw a shadow that was tall and very thin. She knew instantly that Enzo Pike had arrived. In spite of her intense relief, she kept her eyes on Rick.

'Drop your gun, Conway,' Enzo said in a hard, toneless voice. Surprise flashed across Rick's face. He stood rigid for a moment, then turned to face Pike. 'Drop the gun!'

Rick stared at him for a moment. Then he dropped his gun on the thick carpet. 'It's all yours, Detective. Come and get it.'

'First, step away from it.'

Rick sighed and took a step backwards. 'Is that good enough?'

'One more.'

Holding a gun, Declan appeared in the doorway that led to the adjoining bedroom. Rick glanced at him before his gaze moved back to Kelsey. As he stared at her, a chill ran down her spine. She saw amusement in his brown eyes. He didn't look frightened or defeated. He looked smug, she thought. How could he—

Rick's right hand moved stealthily to his side. 'He has my gun!' she screamed just before she saw him slide the gun out of his pocket and aim it at her.

Kelsey heard a blast and Helen shriek as pain seared through her. Blinding, bludgeoning pain. She heard another shot. Helen was still screaming as Kelsey's world swirled and she slid from the bed into a crumpled, unconscious heap on the floor.

EPILOGUE

One week later

'Are you warm enough?'

'Helen, if you put one more blanket on me I'll burst into flames!' Kelsey laughed. 'It's almost eighty degrees today!'

'Well, you can't be too careful, that's what I always say. It's the first time you've spent all afternoon outside. You don't want to overdo it.'

Kelsey lay on a chaise longue on the terrace of the March home. Before Enzo Pike shot Richard Conway in the head, killing him almost instantly, Rick had fired at Kelsey and the bullet had torn into her shoulder. Janet had already called 911, and an ambulance arrived only minutes later, but not before Kelsey had lost a lot of blood. After surgery, the doctors at the hospital told her how lucky she was that the bullet had passed through her body, leaving an open wound that had not injured her shoulder joint or the long bone of her arm. She'd suffered no serious arterial or nerve injury – only damage to soft tissue and cartilage. Within months she would probably need further surgery to correct minor injuries, but for now she just needed to take antibiotics and keep her bandaged shoulder in a shoulder stabilizer.

Also, because of the shock and the need for rest, she was 'home' with her father and Helen hovering over her. Today, while Kelsey lay on the chaise longue, Gatsby had been installed in a large steel cat enclosure complete with a colorful awning and matching hammock, although for the last fifteen minutes he'd been positioned on a padded ledge, watching the bluebirds dart and swoop around the birdhouses on the spacious back lawn.

'He's the most spoiled cat I've ever seen,' Truman commented as he took a sip of Helen's iced tea with mint.

'Gatsby has been through a rough time, Dad,' Kelsey said. 'After all, he was *catnapped*.' Truman laughed. 'Also, we've been separated three nights in the last three weeks. He's four years old and we've never spent a night apart. He has emotional scars from separation anxiety.'

'The poor thing. I guess he's bearing up fairly well considering the damage to his psyche.'

'How's everyone?' Kelsey looked up to see Declan Adair striding across the terrace toward her. 'Are you sure you're up to this today?'

'Since *this* entails me lying here sipping iced tea, I don't think I'm overdoing it. Would you like some tea?'

'Sure,' he said, pouring a glass then smiling at Truman. 'And how are you today, sir?'

'I'll be fine if you'll stop calling me *sir*. It's Truman. That's a courtesy I extend to men who've saved my daughter's life, and mine.'

'Truman it will be from now on, although I didn't save anyone. Actually, Janet O'Rourke did. Thank God she anticipated trouble. Hell, the woman even had Kelsey's, Pike's and my business cards with our cell phone numbers on them! She's a wonder! She called Pike and me before we'd gotten halfway home from the funeral. Then she called 911 because she feared the worst. But I'm not saying anything you don't already know.' Declan smiled and shook his head. 'I'm amazed at what a plucky little thing she is.'

'That's an understatement. Janet is wonderful,' Kelsey said. 'I don't think I mentioned this, Declan, but while Nina is on maternity leave Janet's working at MG Interiors. She doesn't have any interior design experience but her people skills are beyond compare. Dad has hired a very good divorce lawyer to end her marriage with as little friction as possible. Her husband isn't a nice guy to put it mildly. She can work at the business until she either finds another job or else decides to study interior design. Stuart says she shows talent. If she wants, she can work for MG Interiors and go to design school part-time.' Kelsey grinned. 'I know that would suit Giles Miller. I think he might have a crush on her.'

Declan's vivid blue eyes widened. 'Really?'

'Yes. He met her when he went to Conway's Tavern to pick up lunch for all of us, and unbeknownst to me he went there several times by himself for lunch. It seems they began hitting it off at least a month ago. Now if Giles's mother would just give him a little room to breathe . . .'

'I know her type,' Declan said. 'She'll want *all* of his attention. She's not likely to accept an interloper.'

'I believe Giles might not be as self-sacrificing as she assumes. He's talented, handsome, and on his way to becoming a successful twenty-six-year-old. I've seen his confidence in himself growing for months.'

'You're turning into a matchmaker, like Nina,' Declan teased.

'She likes to see the people around her happy. And she likes you. That's why her new baby is named Declan Harry Evans.'

Declan shrugged. 'She likes the name.'

'She likes you. She likes *you* for *me*.'

'Then I love her.'

'That was quick.'

'I'm impulsive.' He smiled. 'Speaking of falling in love quickly, Truman, what do you think of Bradley Fairbourne marrying Megan Reid? We thought he'd gone missing after killing Eve. Actually, he'd taken Megan away for a surprise wedding.'

'A surreptitious wedding! John is furious. He thinks Brad might have talked her into marriage because he'd been fired from the law firm.'

'John thinks Brad married Megan to spite him?' Kelsey asked.

'Maybe. Or else Brad thought if he was married to John's daughter, he'd be taken back at the firm. John told me that will *not* happen, even though Olivia is certain it will. I think she's forgiven Brad for disappearing for days. In her mind, an elopement with Megan Reid was worth causing her some distress.'

'*Distress?* When I saw her at Brad's house, she was nearly hysterical,' Declan said.

'My wife used to say Olivia was mercurial. I think she's unstable. I always did. I don't know why everyone thought I might marry her. Aside from not loving her, I believe being married to her would be like being married to a tornado!'

Declan threw back his head and laughed, startling Gatsby away from his intense scrutiny of the bluebirds fluttering around their cypress houses. 'I didn't know Olivia's husband, but he must have been a patient man.'

'He wasn't, actually,' Truman said thoughtfully. 'But he fell in love with Olivia when she was very young. Maybe she wasn't such a whirling dervish back then. Anyway, John told me Brad says if he can't come back to the firm he intends to open his own law practice. I don't think it will be successful, but I could be wrong. I do know that if he doesn't earn a decent living quickly Megan will leave him. She's used to the best.' Truman drained his iced tea. 'I think I'll go inside and watch CNN for a while. I need to catch up on what's going on in the world.'

Kelsey knew he really wanted to give her and Declan some time together. They hadn't been alone for over a week. Declan refilled their glasses and smiled at her. 'So what's new these days, kid?'

'I found out yesterday that the Sandersons are going to keep their new home. According to Stuart, they said Eve had put in so much work on it, selling it would feel as if they were rejecting her.' Kelsey smiled. 'And that's not all. Josie Sanderson has a superstitious side. She told Stuart that they'd walked Amber, their golden retriever, through the house. Animals, especially dogs, are supposed to be more sensitive to bad energy than humans are. Amber seemed relaxed and happy in the house, and that clinched it. Also, their twelve-year-old daughter Angela especially liked Eve. Josie and Aaron have bought a six-month-old golden-retriever puppy as a companion for Amber, and Angela has named her Eve. Stuart said Angela wanted me to know that. I'm sure Eve would have been pleased.'

'I'm glad. I'd like to see the place when it's finished. I know it will be beautiful.' He stared out at the birds. 'That brings up the subject of Stuart. Has he made an offer to buy you out of MG Interiors?'

'No. But Stuart told me more about Teddy Blakemore, and how the man had seemed like a father when he was a teenager. He cared for Teddy, but didn't realize that he never gave something for nothing. He expected Stuart to be his guy, to do as he was told. Teddy wanted him to start by getting control of MG Interiors, whatever it took. Stuart had no intention of doing so, but Teddy had been driving him crazy after being released from prison.

'Teddy had lost most of his "goons" as you called them, but he still had three. One of them burned Stuart's wrist with the lighted end of a cigar as a threat. Stuart lied to all of us about how he got the burn, but he went to Pike and told him everything. The guy was arrested and the other ones warned. Teddy slipped into a coma three days ago. He'll probably die within the week. There's no threat to me or the business.'

'Says Stuart. He lied to you at least once and you believe him now?'

'I understand why he lied about his wound. And yes, I believe him now, at least until something happens that lets me know I can't. He's been a good friend for four years, Declan. And he's heartbroken that his tension about Teddy drove him apart from Eve before her death but he thought she was safer away from him. He truly loved her.'

'I want to believe in him because you do, but I'll have to see how he acts when Delphina Harrington comes back to town,' Declan said morosely. 'Cole is definitely divorcing her. She'll arrive in Louisville a single woman with lots of money, and a soft spot for Stuart.'

'Are you sure she's still interested in Stuart?'

'According to Cole she is. Delphina doesn't do well without the constant admiration and companionship of a man. I think she's already counting on Stuart adoring her and showing her off at all the social events around Louisville as soon as she gets here.'

'I think it will take Stuart a long time to recover from Eve.' Kelsey watched a bluebird couple teaming up to scare a flying squirrel away from their house. 'I just hope he doesn't get involved with Delphina. She sounds awful.'

'She is.'

'How are things with Cole?'

'He's going to Africa to do the *Vogue* shoot. Then he plans to stay in Africa to become the next Grant Harrington.' Declan shook his head. 'I give him a year of dealing with the heat and bugs and sleeping in a tent. But at least he's going to try to make it work. He's also trying to get over Lorelei.'

After a moment, Kelsey said quietly, 'I guess I misjudged him when Lori told me about him.'

'Who wouldn't have under the circumstances? He wouldn't hold it against you.'

'We'll probably never meet.'

'Says who?'

'I don't know. I just assumed he wouldn't have any desire to visit Louisville again, unless he wants to attend the Kentucky Derby next year.'

'He might. He always enjoyed it.' Declan looked in the direction of the debris from the horrendous fire that had claimed Pieter Vaden's life. 'Any plans to rebuild the barn?'

'Dad wants another one – something much smaller, of course. We have no intention of selling our horses. And when they return home, I'm going to spend time improving my equestrian skills. It's just disgraceful that I'm not a better rider.'

'I thought you might take flying lessons.'

Kelsey grinned and lowered her voice conspiratorially. 'I intend to but I don't want Dad to know. He'd be a nervous wreck at the thought of me flying a plane. I intend to surprise him after I get my license.'

'Good.' Declan's smile faded. 'How's he doing after what happened last week?'

'You mean after he, Helen and I were almost killed by the man we believed had saved my life but who turned out to be someone who thought he was Dad's son? As well as can be expected. I didn't see him at first because I was in surgery, but Helen said she'd never seen him look so devastated.'

'Being trapped in the bedroom with that lunatic must have been horrible.'

Kelsey nodded. 'It wasn't just the threat to our lives. It was also hearing the vitriol that poured out of Rick. He seemed hardly human, yet there was something tragic about him.'

'You have a big heart if you thought he was tragic.'

'There was a lot of blood on the carpet after Pike shot Rick, and Dad had another DNA test run.' Declan looked surprised. 'Of course it showed that Dad's DNA and Rick's weren't a match. Dad definitely wasn't Rick's father.'

'No one believed he was! Your father had tests done when Rick was a baby, and they didn't match. I'm surprised he had another set of tests run.'

'I think he wanted *us* to be absolutely certain that he didn't turn his back on his own son.'

'He didn't turn his back on the guy we knew as Richard Conway, even though he knew Rick *wasn't* his son. He tried to help him and Rick's mother wouldn't let him. Your grandfather also tried to help him, but that time it was Rick who wouldn't take the help. I don't know what else anyone could have done.'

'I don't, either, but Dad has always had a strong conscience and set high standards for himself. I think he feels that he failed. And if he hadn't, then Lori, Grandfather and Eve would still be alive.'

'I suppose you've told him he's bearing too much guilt.'

'Yes, but it'll take time for him to reason it all out and see clearly.' Kelsey looked at Declan. 'He will, though. Dad usually manages to find a balance.'

Declan abruptly abandoned his lawn chair and kneeled beside her, taking her right hand in his. 'And what about our situation?' he asked. 'What about you and me?'

Kelsey lowered her eyes. 'I don't have an answer.'

'You mean that you don't want to have a relationship with me?'

She looked up. 'I don't mean that at all. I feel different about you than I've ever felt about another man. I suppose I should be more coy . . .'

'I hate coy.'

'OK. Then I care about you very much. I don't want to say goodbye to you. But you live in New York City and I live in Louisville. They're over seven hundred and fifty miles apart.'

'So you've done the math.'

'Well, yes. And I know long-distance relationships rarely work.'

'Rarely – but you can't say they *never* work.'

'I don't have the statistics, if that's what you're asking.' Kelsey smiled into Declan's brilliant blue eyes. 'But long-distance relationships are hard.'

'No one ever said life is easy.'

She tilted her head. 'You have an answer for everything, don't you?'

'I was on the debate team in high school.'

'Oh!' Kelsey laughed. 'Just my luck!'

Declan turned over her hand lightly and slowly ran a finger up her arm, then lifted her hand to his lips and kissed it tenderly. Kelsey closed her eyes, temporarily forgetting the sadness of the past few weeks and her worries about a future with Declan. All she thought of was the feel of his warm lips on her palm.

'You're not really playing fair,' she murmured.

'All's fair in love and war.'

'I swear, Declan Adair, if you spout one more cliché . . .'

'Then what?' She opened her eyes and gazed into his – those intensely blue eyes that seemed lit by an inner fire, those eyes looking at her with such affection, such promise, such passion. 'If I spout one more cliché, darling girl, what will happen?'

Kelsey sighed. 'Then I'll have to admit it's true that the heart wants what it wants. And mine wants yours,' she murmured as her lips met his.